Raymond-jean François

PRAISES
&
DISPRAISES

◆

Also by Terrence Des Pres

The Survivor

TERRENCE DES PRES

PRAISES
&
DISPRAISES

Poetry and Politics,
the 20th Century

VIKING

VIKING
Published by the Penguin Group
Viking Penguin Inc., 40 West 23rd Street,
New York, New York 10010, U.S.A.
Penguin Books Ltd, 27 Wrights Lane,
London W8 5TZ, England
Penguin Books Australia Ltd, Ringwood,
Victoria, Australia
Penguin Books Canada Ltd, 2801 John Street,
Markham, Ontario, Canada L3R 1B4
Penguin Books (N.Z.) Ltd, 182–190 Wairau Road,
Auckland 10, New Zealand

Penguin Books Ltd, Registered Offices:
Harmondsworth, Middlesex, England

First published in 1988 by Viking Penguin Inc.
Published simultaneously in Canada

1 3 5 7 9 10 8 6 4 2

Pages 245–246 constitute an extension of this copyright page

LIBRARY OF CONGRESS CATALOGING IN PUBLICATON DATA
Des Pres, Terrence.
Praises & dispraises.
Bibliography: p.
1. Poetry—20th century—History and criticism.
2. Poetry—Political aspects.   3. Politics and
literature.   I. Title.   II. Title: Praises &
dispraises.
PN1081.D47   1988   809.1′9358   87–40540
ISBN 0–670–80406–1

Printed in the United States of America by Arcata Graphics, Fairfield, Pennsylvania
Set in Galliard
Designed by Victoria Hartman

For Liz

What looks the strongest has outlived its term.
The future lies with what's affirmed from under.

—Seamus Heaney, "The Haw Lantern"

Acknowledgments

These acknowledgments are based on notes and comments made by Terrence Des Pres prior to his death.

The following individuals provided aid and encouragement during the writing of *Praises & Dispraises:* Carolyn Forché, Paul Mariani, Reg Gibbons, Peter Balakian, and especially Morton Bloomfield. For assistance with individual chapters the author acknowledges: Howard Iger (Brecht); Patricia Hampl and the writers at the Loft in Minneapolis (McGrath); the feminist reading group at Colgate University (Rich). Special thanks to George Hudson for help in moments of computer crisis and to Helen Kebabian for proofreading. For the care he gave this manuscript the author is grateful to Dan Frank at Viking.

Contents

Prolog

This book has been written for men and women who care about poetry and read it first of all for personal reasons. Such readers, I would like to think, know well enough the violent spirit of our century, and exactly for *this* reason expect at least one kind of language to hold its own against the grim disquiet. If they value it further as a means to poise and self-possession, they do not ask too much of a serious art. Poetry helps us seize our being-in-the-world, the better to enjoy, the better to endure. In this book, accordingly, poetry is prized and spoken of, in Kenneth Burke's fine phrase, as "equipment for living."[1]

About the violence of our century, its lethal strife and endless misery, there seems little doubt that politics has played a central, and too often a ruinous, part. Less clear is the impact of political havoc on poetry, an affliction put this way by Czeslaw Milosz: [2]

> The first movement is singing,
> A free voice, filling mountains and valleys.
> The first movement is joy,
> But it is taken away.

The poetic impulse—hope's proof and finest messenger—arises to fulfill itself in praises and in blessings. Now it finds more exercise in cursing, and Milosz goes on, in another poem, with dispraise of his own:[3]

> We learned so much, this you know well:
> how, gradually, what could not be taken away
> is taken. People, countrysides.

And the heart does not die when one thinks it should,
we smile, there is tea and bread on the table.

That Milosz speaks from a time and place as strange to us as Baltic
woodlands or the streets of occupied Warsaw, that he writes as a witness
to some of the century's worst occasions, makes him not the less but
rather the *more* familiar to us—an unusual circumstance, to say the least.
Yet Milosz is not alone in this oddity. The great Russians, Akhmatova,
Mandelshtam, Tsvetayeva, and Pasternak, lived and wrote amid terrible
upheavals; now they are regarded by us as the patron saints of poetry
in dark times. Others—Neruda and Vallejo, for example—have been
with us some time already, and more recently Milosz's peer in Poland,
Zbigniew Herbert, has been taken up with high esteem, along with
many another poet from traditions not our own—Vasko Popa and Miroslav Holub in Slavic, for example, or Seferis and Ritsos in Greek; nor
do we forget the example of Nazim Hikmet, who from his Turkish cell
wrote prison poems that are among the finest of that twentieth-century
genre. These poets come from places burdened by political torment but
blessed with zealous care for poetry; and now they have gained an
important hearing among us despite the uncertain dignity of translation.
If we should wonder why their voices are valued so highly, it's that they
are acquainted with the night, the nightmare spectacle of politics especially. The sense of familiarity got from their poems resides in an
undervoice, an emerging consciousness in common that we, too, are
beginning to share.

Not that most of us in North America (unless black or female or
native American) find ourselves caught in history's path; not, at least,
in directly damaging ways. The point is rather that now a wretchedness
of global extent has come into view; the spectacle of man-created suffering is *known*, observed with such constancy that a new shape of
knowing invades the mind. From South Africa, here is André Brink's
sense of it:[4]

> One may ask: is there anything new in this condition? Has
> there not always been suffering and injustice and oppression?
> Of course. But until recently the condition of the world was
> not wholly intolerable—because the full measure of the truth
> was not known. . . . Mass communications have propagated
> these events around the world; and "no man can claim that he

has not personally SEEN the intolerable condition of the world."

The miracles of modern communications—the instant replay of events on TV, the surfeit of images provided by photojournalists, the detailed accounts of inhumanity given by survivors of all kinds, and then too the documentation from organizations like Amnesty International and Americas Watch, every page of it open to those who would know what can be known—all these sources combine with the cold-war order of things to make a uniquely twentieth-century sense of reality, a consciousness that began in the wake of World War Two with the film footage, miles of it, that gave us our first window on "the world." That shock of recognition, that climate of atrocity, is now our daily fare.

"The real," said Henry James, is that which "we cannot not know."[5] With his imagination of disaster, James was on the right track but could hardly guess the enormity of things to come. Thanks to the technological expansion of consciousness, we cannot not know the extent of political torment; and in truth it may be said that what others suffer, we behold. If the mechanical reproduction of art diminishes art's aura, as Walter Benjamin argued, he might have said further that the media's reproduction of politics demystifies the exercise of power and makes it into a spectacle that is immediate, encompassing, supercharged with shame and disgust and also, of course, with dread inspired by the tyranny of the Bomb. It's at this point and in this way that the world is too much with us.

The press of the real is problematic for all of us but especially for poets because their art requires attention to humanity's sad still music that now, amid the awful nonstop roar of things, is hard to make out. There is the need for a diction that won't be outflanked by events, and the further need to support, through the stamina of language, the trials of spirit in adversity—a struggle that is often appalling, painful merely to observe. Among poets alert to these conditions, Charles Simic is exactly on target in his "Notes on Poetry and History," written in 1984:[6]

If not for the invention of photography and motion pictures, one could perhaps still think of history in the manner of nineteenth-century painting and Soviet Revolutionary posters. There you meet the idealized masses and their heroic leaders leading them with chests bared and sleeves rolled up. They are marching with radiant faces and flags unfurled through the carnage of the battlefield. The dying young man in the arms of his steadfast comrades has the half-veiled gaze of the visionary. We know that he has glimpsed the future of humanity, and that it looks good. Unfortunately for all concerned, people started taking pictures. I remember, for example, a black-and-white photograph of a small child running toward the camera on a street of collapsing buildings in a city being fire-bombed. The smoke and the flames are about to overtake her. She's wearing a party dress, perhaps a birthday party dress. One is also told that it is not known where and when the picture had been taken.

With a shift in the means of representation, a radical change occurs in the way the world is known. Epic fantasy gives way to stark realism. And now politics is everywhere and hopeless. The photo of the luckless girl is an image of ubiquitous suffering; and in the gaze of the dying hero we behold the end of faith in the future. The myth of Progress has run its course and failed; now no political agenda, East or West, can appeal to the old triumphalism. No glory at some future date, or plan of greatest happiness to come, can dismiss the actualities of power taking its toll. The agony of third-world peoples is with us; terrorism is with us, death squads and torture; and an arms trade boldly supplying the whole of the world with weapons, that too is with us. None of it is going to go away tomorrow, and when this recognition arrives, as indeed it has, politics begins to be seen less as a means than as an end in itself—a condition, in fact, that the human spirit and therefore poetry must take into account.

Politics, then, as the play of impersonal force disrupting personal life; and politics, therefore, as a primary ground of misfortune. Taken to its tragic extreme, this kind of experience is the matter of *Antigone*, a drama of selfhood beset by the state, perhaps also of poetry hemmed in by political power. I therefore take Sophocles as my starting point; and here, too, I align politics with "world" and poetry with the powers of "earth." Moreover, if political experience is felt as a pressure, an intrusion of "the real" for those who absorb its impact, Wallace Stevens' notion of "a violence from within that protects us from a violence without" needs remarking. Then we can go directly to Yeats, whose revival of bardic practice illustrates "the scene of poetry" as I observe it in these pages—namely, as the poet in tribal relation to his or her audience through the force of the poem's occasion.

I shall not argue that all poets embrace a bardic protocol, but only that those studied here—Yeats, Thomas McGrath, and Adrienne Rich especially, but Brecht and Breyten Breytenbach as well—take up, and put to unique use, an ancient institution most accessible in its Irish example, an example long famous, or rather infamous, in the eyes of its English antagonists:[7]

> There is amongst the Irishe a certen kind of people Called Bardes which are to them in stead of Poets whose profession is to sett fourthe the praises and dispraises of menne in their Poems and Rhymes . . .

That was Edmund Spenser's view in 1596, as the British took bloody measures to colonize Ireland and met, thanks to bardic incitements, with a resistance that simply would not die. What this tradition meant in Spenser's time, and what it might entail for poets today, is directly the matter of this book, habits of voice that reach from antiquity into the present and embrace a political scale from Yeats's reactionary bitterness to the radical feminism of Rich. I am after rites of poetic address that emerge when poets and their tribes become embattled. Of course, the poet must have a tribe, an audience; on this condition, by no means common in our time, depends the poet's will to speak *for* and *against*.

In the late years of a discouraging century, the problems poets face are multiple, deeply troubling, and not to be solved by a single idea of the poet's office. The notion of bardic practice, however, helps make sense of relations between poetry and politics more generally. Also to be gained is an outside vantage on the situation of poetry in America, much of it still Emersonian in spirit, still enamored of self, nature, and escape to worlds elsewhere. Insofar as poets stay shut in those imperatives, the results are less than sufficient to hard times. Poetry that evades our being-in-the-world affords no happy fortitude, no language to live by, gifts that have always been the poet's job. At very least, then, the poets studied in this book provide a variety of hopeful examples, not only of an art taking place in the world, but also of the ways in which politics becomes a challenge to, and an occasion for, renewal in American poetics.

Finally, a few words about the role of critics. There has been, recently, a remarkable surge in critical theory, and along with it solid studies—Jameson's *The Political Unconscious*, for example—of politics in the case of fiction. For poetry, on the other hand, there is as yet, in America, no poetics equal to the import of politics in language or in life. All the more reason, therefore, to be glad for Kenneth Burke, whose work is as instructive now as it was when, during my student days, I first encountered his *Attitudes Toward History*, his *Philosophy of Literary Form*, and the *Grammars*. For I thought then, and still do, that in Burke's notion of language as symbolic language is room for politics and as well as for poetry's role in the world. I find useful his way of melding Marx and Freud no less than his alignment of tragedy with social order generally. In particular, I have relied on Burke's notions that "poetic forms are symbolic structures designed to equip us for confronting given historical or personal situations";[8] that formal functions include the poem's occasion; and that the "dramatistic" approach, which takes ritual drama as the model for poetic form in action, best suits the problems of poetry in relation to political experience.

In my own prose I have kept to a style that is aware of, but that declines to employ, the vocabularies of various criticisms now in ascendance. Ordinary language, open to the formalities of bardic tradition, has been my mainstay. I have, however, kept in view the feminist approach to poetry. Feminism's way of connecting the personal and the political is useful. So is its alertness to power and its claim that patriarchal order has perjured institutions generally, not least the study of literature. Insofar as bardic practice has begun to be active again in poetry, its foremost exercise—the poet summoning his or her tribe—is likely to be with embattled groups, women first of all. That Antigone is our sister must now, I think, be conceded.

· ONE ·

POLITICAL INTRUSION

·I·

Creon's Decree

Terror is the feeling which arrests the mind in the presence of whatsoever is grave and constant in human sufferings and unites it with the secret cause.
—Stephen Dedalus[1]

In the beginning, what can be further from politics than Antigone's grief? Her pain is hers alone. She tries to share it with her sister, but Ismene is afraid. Creon, after all, has issued a decree. Guards have been posted and the dead man can't be touched. Even so, a brother must be buried and Antigone is determined to do it; nothing else matters, not the decree, not the fact that Polynices died attacking the city. This is a family affair, an obligation to the dead, but certainly it's not a public issue. Challenging Creon is not part of Antigone's plan. There is no plan, but only a passion compounded of reverence and love. Therefore she goes out to bury her brother. Birds must not pick his eyes. Some gesture of blessing there must be. That a king has ruled otherwise is nothing to her.

It becomes something, however, and reasons of state preempt the heart's purpose. From the moment Creon puts forth his decree, Antigone's behavior becomes a public issue, with consequences not intrinsic to her life but that follow nonetheless. For her the springs of action are interior, while for him they are public and expedient. Creon imposes his will upon others, but believes that he acts for the good of the *polis*. Thebes has weathered an attack and order needs restoring. Heroes must be praised, betrayers cursed. Above all, leadership must demonstrate control. Creon has only just become king—"the new man for the new day"—and his authority needs sealing with a sign of his power. Thus Creon orders a funeral with honor for Eteocles, who died defending

· 3

the city, and proclaims that Polynices, who led the attack, shall be left unburied:

> carrion for the birds and dogs to tear,
> an obscenity for the citizens to behold![2]

That is the decree. It is an arbitrary act; but as a law backed up by force it carries the weight of necessity. To the city it's an insult, and to the gods as well. But the stakes are treason and defense, issues anyone in power might exploit, and Creon is no exception. Therefore the dead man rots in public view.

In confrontation, the protagonists in *Antigone* are slowly pushed to extremes by a situation overwhelming them both. Under pressure Creon becomes more and more the tyrant. Antigone grows heroic but also fanatical. Thus does character reveal itself in adversity. But something larger than a contest of wills is at work. At the outset power is exercised, then challenged; and as the drama gains momentum the increasingly irrational logic of power begins to determine much, perhaps all, that happens thereafter. In political tragedy, terror's "secret cause" is the power—the mystery—of politics itself. Notions of hubris or a tragic flaw become irrelevant in drama of this kind. No error in judgment or fault of character accounts for disaster erupting from such depths. Things turn out as they do because a power greater than human will or understanding moves the action to its end.

In the *Poetics*, Aristotle is concerned with the special connection between action and character in tragic situations. More than once he insists that tragedy represents not men but the actions of men. Tragic action is whole—with beginning, middle, and end—and must therefore include, or be prior to, the character of its participants. Aristotle calls this executive aspect of action the "plot," and goes on to say that plot is the "soul" of tragedy—not the foibles of men and women thus caught up, but action in its unstoppable unfolding. Tragedy, therefore, is the literary form that dramatizes human conflicts for which, in the end, fate governs.

Most of the time we (the lucky ones) stay inside the boundaries of a realm where character counts, where options abound, a world where self-determination is effective. Now and then, however, hard circumstances arise and force us to difficult choices. We may then go the way of Ismene or Antigone, and if the latter, freedom gives way to necessity and the world of desire vanishes. Some of our best plays in the tragic mode—*Hamlet* or *King Lear*, for example—include the struggle for and with power. All of them have a political dimension. But not all strike us as, in the first degree, dramas of politics. Political tragedy in the formal sense is rare and involves a contradiction that can be put, to begin with, as a question: If, on the one hand, fatality is the soul of tragedy, and if, on the other hand, politics is the art of the possible, by what coincidence can such contrary realms be brought to occupy each other?

Oedipus meets his fate at a crossroads, a moment of junction in which choice is overtaken by necessity. Political situations, on the other hand, are political to the degree that possibilities stay open. Among power's options, however, is the choice to close things down and turn into a path from which there is no going back. It's here that violence arises; and it's here, in the freedom to resort to force, that the fatality of politics resides.

In *Antigone* the action is best described as the closing down of possibility, very fast in Antigone's case, much more gradually for Creon. Disaster occurs when options are exhausted. The oddity is that while we watch "the art of the possible" destroying itself, the spectacle before us has an aura of anxiety unusual in tragic art. What remains disturbing about *Antigone* is that at any point before the hero's death, we feel the course of action *could* be changed. The plot might take a different turn and violence be averted. Or so we feel. But that is the feeling of any political crisis—the waiting to see, the unnerving hope that maybe the worst won't happen. Even so, the strangeness of tragic action in *Antigone* is that it does not look iron-clad, not even in hindsight. In *Oedipus*, the hero's fate is sealed by the gods before his birth. Nothing so relentless appears to govern *Antigone*. How, then, does fatality enter?

At the beginning of the play we glimpse a pivotal moment of freedom. When the action begins, the attack on Thebes is over, nor is the fact of Polynices' death an issue in itself. True, that is the one circumstance beyond change, but the action is put on its fatal course by, first, the public decree, and then by Antigone's reaction. This initial moment recalls Act One of *King Lear*, the other towering instance of political tragedy. In both cases, a fluid situation becomes fixed after an arbitrary decree is proclaimed and met with unexpected resistance. Creon's reasons of state are less flimsy than Lear's, but both men act officially, both wield the power invested in them, and both are undone by the reluctance—Cordelia's, Antigone's—of the heart to betray itself.

In political tragedy the misuse or squandering of freedom as a political resource is the immediate, although not the ultimate, cause of misfortune. The protagonists refuse or do not see their options. In *Antigone*, tragic necessity reveals itself little by little as choices arise only to be cancelled. Denial of freedom is, in fact, the play's central gesture. Creon did not have to forbid the burial of Polynices. Had he fixed upon some other show of power, Antigone would have been free to fulfill her private need. But once the decree intervenes, she cannot act without destroying herself. Or can she?

There is, in fact, a gap of possibility to be tried—but that Antigone refuses to consider. Hearing the decree, she might go first to Creon and make an appeal, privately or in public, for her brother's burial. She might invoke royal blood or special favor, as well as tradition and the city's honor. She might also ask Haemon, to whom she is betrothed, for help; and if broader support were useful, she might appeal to the chorus of elders. Finally, she might approach Tiresias and enlist an authority backed by the gods themselves. Antigone is not without resources. But to use them would be to descend to political methods— enroll in the game and play politics—and this Antigone will not do. Although she is open to attack, she refuses the defense that is hers. To become "political" and try the art of the possible is not, for Antigone, a possibility.

Her alternatives do indeed look petty compared to the stand she takes and the solemnity of her death. Greatness of soul does not stoop to tactics, and Antigone holds to her heroic course. This nobility of spirit, however, should not obscure the fact that it fails. When Antigone dies, her brother still rots in the sun. All that is certain, when weighing her plight, is that her intensely private perspective denies the public world. Even the decree is seen in personal terms. Speaking to Ismene, Antigone refers to "the martial law our good Creon / lays down for you and me— yes, me, I tell you." She has no point of reference outside of self and family, nor would she seek one. She goes, then, directly to her task.

After her arrest, the initiative passes to Creon, and Creon, of course, is king. His freedom is commensurate with his power, which is nearly absolute and, in time of peace, capable of indulgence. If Antigone will not bend, Creon can turn the occasion to political advantage. He might simply forgive her, either magnanimously or in such a way as to shame her. He can say her case is special, or declare her action the outcome of madness brought on by grief. For these same reasons, he might display his mercy by assigning a lesser punishment—house arrest, for example. Or with loud faith in their judgment, he can turn things over to the elders. Creon has choices. Ways exist to impress the citizens of Thebes with their new king's sagacity. His job is to be tough, but also wise, and negotiation is the natural resource of his office. Yet he too acts as if no alternative were possible. Having issued his decree, Creon becomes as singleminded as Antigone—as blind, and as bent on the absolute course.

For both protagonists the stakes are larger than self-interest. In the moment of confrontation Creon feels responsible to the polis, while Antigone honors the deeper grounds—ancestral, poetic, religious—of selfhood. Her manner is consistently inward, passionate, lyrical. Hers is in fact the poet's way of taking the world. And like most poets of lyrical bent, Antigone becomes more, rather than less, solipsistic as the pressure of politics builds. Her loyalty is to inner vision; in the emergency she falls back upon an inwardness of self that puts her in touch with the whisper of the gods. These interior powers are the ground of her strength, and to three in particular she and the elders of the chorus appeal. First is Eros, fountainhead of desire and builder of life. The most insistent is Hades, guardian of the ancestral dead. Beyond these, vague but the greater for his mystery, is Dionysus, festive giver of dance and poetry, godhead of daemonic commingling and tragedy itself, the presiding power of orphic earth.

It's with these primal energies that Antigone aligns herself; thus empowered she can neither bargain with the king, nor calculate support, nor, by calling on Tiresias, set one authority against another. To enter the public arena would be to forfeit the strength that selfhood derives from at-oneness with its own deepest sources. Integrity is all, or so it must seem to Antigone. Herself she will not compromise. She will not play the game and never sees that politics is anything more than a phantom spectacle, as if Creon were nothing but the "fool" she takes him for. Were her vision dramatic rather than lyrical, she might appreciate, or at least recognize, worldly power's danger. But then she would be a hero of knowledge rather than, as she is, a hero of passionate will. The dead, for whom she speaks, have their powers at one with the earth, but like Eros or the tragic god himself, they are blind to the world. This blindness is Antigone's strength and the cause of her downfall.

But Creon too is blind, and to understand *his* tragedy we need not dwell on his despotic temper, but look to the office he holds as ruler of Thebes. He is not guided by self-interest but by the compulsions of his high position. Within the boundaries of the city-state his power is absolute; but possessing such power is, more than a little, to be possessed in turn. On the one hand, great power confers assurance of omnipotence; on the other hand, it provokes paranoia to an endless degree. These delusions are the price of Creon's position; and when it comes to small mistakes at vast cost, he is neither better nor worse than our own kings and chieftains.

Creon feels almighty, and thinks he does *not need* to negotiate. At the same time, he is beset by chronic suspicion and feels he does *not dare* negotiate. He is faced with a challenge far beneath his majesty and will not, as he says, be swayed by the whim of a girl. However, he also imagines that invisible enemies are working to unseat him, bribing his soldiers, suborning his son. And so, to a king, it must seem. Creon thinks he has enough strength to handle Antigone no matter what happens. But he also thinks negotiation would threaten his authority. And he is misled still further by the sense of commitment that power breeds, the thrust of urgency and mission with which great power invests its agents. Might *feels* right, and for these reasons: because it seems invincible, and because it seems besieged; because its every action carries the weight of necessity, and because the deep excitement of power is godlike and blinding.

Creon does at last relent. This change of heart comes too late, of course, and if we ask why Creon does not reverse himself sooner, the answer is again a function of power. He acts belatedly, as Hegel would say, because the Owl of Minerva flies only at dusk; because power understands itself only in its aftermath. What this means is that the cost of wisdom is excessive, often tragic, always sacrificial. Tiresias is wise, but he comes to speak with Creon only after the king's decree has infested the land. When the altars are polluted and the sacred birds defiled, then the prophet arrives. Tiresias appears in time of need, but the need comes after its cause.

And even then, Creon must first reject the advice he receives. The truth Tiresias offers—that Creon's own decree plagues the land—comes at him as a challenge, and the reaction of power to challenge is entrenchment. Once the king and the seer no longer stand face to face, Creon can drop his guard and consider that Tiresias has always given true counsel. This also accounts, in part, for Creon's inflexible stand toward Antigone. She is a threat that, in the moment of face-to-face encounter, requires quelling. She is not seen as a niece or a grieving sister but as a "criminal." She is not the bride of his son but a force to be met with force. Once Antigone has been condemned and led away, the challenge is over and Creon can take time to reconsider. But by then his time has run out.

Creon wields a power that in turn wields him, and in the encounter with Antigone he is as much the victim as she is. Both of them have been trapped by the decree from the moment it was declared. To make an issue of Polynices' burial, as I suggested earlier, is in itself arbitrary. But once the law exists the king acts in accord with his policy and the decree becomes sovereign. Antigone breaks the law but the law came first. The decree determines everything, Antigone's rebellion and Creon's tyranny no less than the end to which the conflict leads.

The fact that Creon did not have to choose *this* decree must make us wonder why this one was his choice. Here we approach the mainspring of tragedy in political form. Here, in what looks to be an arbitrary sign, we meet the "secret cause." For if we agree that Creon's decree is a political act, meant to show forth a new king's might, we must suppose a symmetry (in this most symmetrical of dramas) between the nature of the decree and the nature of power at its tragic extreme. On this equivalence everything hinges. The decree is one option among many; but in the tragedy of politics, as we shall see, Creon's choice is inevitable.

Vico was among the first to observe that societies "all have some religion, all contract solemn marriages, all bury their dead."[3] These "human customs," as he calls them—religion, kinship systems, and funeral rites— are institutions necessary to social order and they are also, as it happens, at the center of *Antigone*. Creon manages to offend all three, but most pointedly he violates the imperative of ritual burial, our communal rites (and rights) as creatures of earth that Vico (citing Classical sources) calls "compacts of the human race" and "fellowships of humanity."[4]

To bury the dead and dignify death's occasion seems profoundly needful and even, as Vico implies, a constitutive act for human community. Ceremony makes death meaningful; it formalizes our griefs and our fears, and certifies human continuity by binding the past to the present, and the living to the dead. Certainly we feel better for the disburdening that ritual allows. Grief and fear are not, however, the whole of it. Anthropologists use the site of the grave to distinguish human from anthropoid forms of life. There will *be* a grave, and also signs of identity—weapons, jewelry, household utensils, perhaps a death mask—to signal that these bones once lived like you or I, and were returned to earth in a communal ceremony involving the living as much as the dead. Symbolic procedures of this kind are anchored in death, but they are meant for the living, for religious reasons no doubt, but principally because through ritual disposition of the body we certify its human worth despite death's terribly visible negation.

Hegel agreed with Vico that burial rites establish humanness. In the *Phenomenology of Mind* Hegel retraces Antigone's story and calls burial the "ultimate ethical act" in fulfillment of "divine law."[5] The nothingness of death is cancelled through symbolic confirmation of personal significance. Even more important, ritual burial becomes the act that separates human beings from mere nature and, beyond that, mediates individual existence with universal being. Against death, burial is the one thing we can do. By treating the body as a person, we assert that the person was never merely a body, never nature's abstract object. The ceremony performed for a loved one, as Hegel goes on, "weds the relative to the bosom of the earth, the elemental individuality that passes not away."[6] In this special case, the earth is part of the ritual and is not to be confused with mere nature. For Hegel as for Antigone, earth is the concrete substance of eternity. It is the fundament of birth and becoming, the dwelling of creation's nether powers and the place, finally, to which the individual returns "as a member of a community"—a community that is not political but rather human and ancestral.[7]

Opposing blank nature, burial rites affirm at-oneness with the indwelling powers of earth. The distinction is crucial because at the level of the physical body, nature is an amoral field of force and necessity; and insofar as politics rests on force, as it does in Creon's exercise, nature's nothingness is power's real foundation. Insofar as we are creatures of nature and subject to political order, any of us can be reduced, like Polynices, from "thou" to "it." Creon favors, Antigone opposes, this emptying out of human significance. The body of Polynices is the field of their struggle, a vivid reminder that we are the object of politics to the extent that we are things of nature. The function of burial is to keep these two spheres separate, the political (grounded in nature) on the one hand, and the human (sustained by earth) on the other.

And therefore the central place of last rites in *Antigone*. Alive, Polynices was a traitor; but in death he resumes his essential humanity, at one with the earth, free of any social role or political identity. As Hegel puts it, the act of burial "does not concern the citizen . . . [but] takes him as a universal being."[8] For this reason, when Sophocles speaks of "the dead" he sometimes refers to the individual, whereas at other times he refers to all human beings who through death have returned to earth's ancestral realm. But this much is certain: having entered the community of the dead, Polynices is no longer to be judged by worldly power.

In *Antigone*, therefore, the body of Polynices is the drama's central emblem. As we behold Antigone and Creon face to face we cannot forget the man-become-thing in the dust dividing them. It is the mirror of Antigone's wound and the image of Creon's misrule. While one of them strives to sanctify the dead man's humanity, the other insists on reducing it to carrion. At the start a dead man is left unburied; at the end a living person is buried alive. This monstrous symmetry suggests a perversity at the heart of power's exercise, a horrid disorder imposed upon the cosmos of earth and humankind together. In the extremity that results in tragedy it is politics that brings on disaster. The "secret cause" is power itself and its sign is mutilation of the human image.

In *Oedipus* the hero's fate is terrible but at least it is his. If the gods seem hostile, no other agency comes between the oracular dark and what happens. With Antigone the case is otherwise. Her death is not the working out of private destiny (even though she acts for interior reasons) nor does she die in fulfillment of divine design (even though she and the gods are in perfect accord). She is robbed of both by politics, and the immediate and final causes of her fall are therefore one—the public pronouncement of a man who proceeds in good faith, but for whom piety, kinship, human worth, and finally (for so it will turn out) the polis itself are expendable loss in the service of power. Under pressure Creon is deaf to counsel and blind to human need, the perfect slave of politics. Antigone stands up to him; she resists her situation and takes her life to escape the decree, but the decree destroys her nonetheless. Her fate is therefore divided; it is hers but not her own.

There are many ways to read *Antigone*, but no recent reading ignores its political spirit. And increasingly, dramatic revisions of the play have put politics at the center. I think in particular of the stage versions by Jean Anouilh (France, 1944) and Bertolt Brecht (Germany, 1948), and also Athol Fugard's *The Island* (South Africa, 1973). In *Antigones*, his recent study of the play's cultural destiny, George Steiner points to a sudden increase of interest in Antigone's story at the beginning of the nineteenth century, an exaltation of her fate that passed through the whole of that century into our own. The ground of this obsession, in Steiner's estimate, was the impact of the French Revolution. For it was then that historical consciousness began to crystalize; then that men and women began to feel "the new immersion of the private individual in historical extremity," as if after the Terror, after the march from Corunna to Moscow and back, no one could be entirely free from "the burn of history in his or her bones." In *Antigone* we behold "the meshing of intimate and public, of private and historical existence," a drama of consequence because, as Steiner concludes, "after 1789 the individual knows no armistice with political history."[9]

After the Revolution, as was often said at the time, life—and, even more, the *sense* of life—was different. History began to *move*, and the basic metaphor of politics shifted from "the body politic" to "the ship of state." The speed of events increased, and large-scale change became pervasive. Eternity, as William Blake put it, fell in love with the productions of time. It was a love-hate courtship, with more of agitation than of bliss, and poets like Blake and Yeats have given us names— "fearful symmetry," "terrible beauty"—to account for the spectacle, sometimes awesome, sometimes hateful, of the political sublime. In *Mimesis*, Eric Auerbach traces the rise of what he calls "tragic modern realism," and in his chapter on Stendhal he observes of *The Red and the Black* that "contemporary political and social conditions are woven into the action in a manner more detailed and more real than had been exhibited in any earlier novel."[10] In the wake of the Revolution came a general consciousness of participation in history, a process Auerbach sums up as follows:[11]

> for the progress then achieved in transportation and communication, together with the spread of elementary education resulting from the trends of the Revolution itself, made it possible to mobilize the people far more rapidly and in a far more unified direction; everyone was reached by the same ideas and events far more quickly, more consciously, and more uniformly. For Europe there began that process of temporal concentration, both of historical events themselves and of everyone's knowledge of them. . . . Such a development ab-

rogates or renders powerless the entire social structure of orders and categories previously held valid. . . . He who would account to himself for his real life and his place in human society is obliged to do so upon a far wider practical foundation and in a far larger context than before, and to be continually conscious that the social base upon which he lives is not constant for a moment but is perpetually changing through convulsions of the most various kinds.

Since then political turmoil has become an expected part of the environment. To understand even local affairs, we now require a space-time map that covers the whole of the globe. More recently, Milan Kundera has observed the political compression of life as the "world" hems us in:[12]

That life is a trap—well, that we've always known. We are born without having asked to be, locked in a body we never chose, and destined to die. On the other hand, the wideness of the world used to provide a constant possibility of escape. A soldier could desert from the army and start another life in a neighboring country. Suddenly, in our century, the world is closing around us. The decisive event in that transformation of the world into a trap was surely the 1914 war, called (and for the first time in history) a world war. Wrongly, "world." It involved only Europe, and not *all* of Europe at that. But the adjective "world" expresses all the more eloquently the sense of horror before the fact that henceforward, nothing that occurs on the planet will be a merely local matter, that all catastrophes concern the entire world, and that consequently, we are more and more determined by external conditions, by situations no one can escape, and which, more and more, make us resemble one another.

The "Great War" of 1914–18 was not called a "world war" until after World War Two, but Kundera's sense of political reality is accurate, and with good cause. He saw the Russians invade Prague in 1968, saw the Czech spirit founder, and ended up in Paris knowing the slap of history firsthand. The percentage of important writers uprooted by politics has been, in this century, very high. *Mimesis*, for example, was written in

Istanbul during the second of our "world" wars. Auerbach was a scholar trained in the German philological tradition, but also a Jew in flight from the Third Reich. Had there been no earlier world war, no economic collapse, no social unrest to intensify the prior defeat, Hitler might not have happened. Great thinkers like Heidegger and Jaspers and Arendt would not have been faced with such difficult choices. Hitler was their Creon, and his decree—the Nuremberg Laws, for example—entered the world of art and the universities to alter in a single sweep the European mind. Auerbach might otherwise have pursued his career with the usual prospects, advancing quietly in a quiet profession to the eminence that would have easily been his. When he began, the realms of literature and politics seemed comfortably separate. But they did not stay that way, and in a series of dislocations that drove Auerbach to the Bosphorus— that pushed Walter Benjamin to suicide at the Spanish border and Paul Celan to the bridge in Paris—politics intrude to mock the happy notion that we can be in the world but not of it.

Who among us has not known men and women broken or destroyed for refusing to follow their government's will? Ordinary people, burdened with the ordinary problems of birth and love and death, suddenly find private responsibility blocked by public decree. In the era of Cold War, with terrorism on the one hand and nuclear threat on the other, Antigone's fate can be anyone's or everyone's at once. Innocence counts for nothing, if only because terrorism and police-states both require random victims. That is the terrorist's terror, the state's proof of power— and the real threat in nuclear deterrence. One is amazed, and perhaps also instructed, by the way Americans protest their "innocence" when planes are hijacked and hostages taken.

In fact and in spirit, Antigone's drama is the heart of our time. How, then, shall it go unremarked that the hero is a woman? And what's to be said for the fact that she draws her strength from the gods of the earth, in opposition to Creon's worldly authority? This much we know directly from the play: that a patriarchal order is challenged by a woman; that when political power intervenes, it asserts the primacy of world over earth; and finally, that conflict of this kind is kept in motion by the logic of power and can lead to terrible ends. George Steiner has pointed out the "martial" element in Creon's diction, recalling the ruthless world of the *Iliad*, and Creon's remarks, we see from the text, attack Antigone's status as a woman. The struggle of the individual against the state is thus compounded by a premodern, or in fact a perpetual degradation of women to noncitizens, deprived of dignity and public space. That Antigone should challenge this arrangement is not, for Creon, an option. These ancient inequities are now being tested. The coopting of personal being by public force has given rise to the notion that the personal is political. And feminism, even in its milder forms, confounds established order in the same way Antigone stands up to Creon.

But what, finally, of the conflict between world and earth? Greek literature of the Classical period contains a general tension between the *polis*, dedicated to war and public order, and the *oikos*, the zone of immediate life, dedicated to hearth, home, the generative powers of earth. With his high regard for Greek thinking, Heidegger took the poetic notion of an earth-world antagonism and gave it conceptual form in "The Origin of the Work of Art." Here is the heart of his argument:[13]

> The world is the self-disclosing openness of the broad paths of the simple and the essential decisions in the destiny of an historical people. The earth is the spontaneous forthcoming of that which is continually self-secluding and to that extent sheltering and concealing. World and earth are essentially different from one another and yet never separated. The world grounds itself on the earth, and the earth juts through world. . . . The world, in resting upon the earth, strives to surmount it. As self-opening it cannot endure anything closed. The earth, however, as sheltering and concealing, tends always to draw the world into itself and keep it there.

With earth as fundament, humankind builds up and sets forth a world, and in the process attempts to subdue and then negate the primal forces on which it depends. Earth, meanwhile, pushes to displace and shut down world's opened spaces. Each, in this contest, needs the other; earth only comes into view when world provides a perspective, and world, as Heidegger puts it, "cannot soar out of the earth's sight if, as the governing breadth and path of all essential destiny, it is to ground itself on a resolute foundation."[14] But in fact the human world does presume to "soar," a capacity granted us by our genius of artifice and the colossal powers of technology, a kind of illusory flight that men, less often women, have always praised ecstatically. And here the logic of apocalypse asserts itself; here, in our dreams, we would do away with our condition as earth-bound creatures altogether.[15]

In a technological world, the wisdom that allowed premodern peoples to live at one with the blessings of their environment is no longer effective. At some point, as world transgresses its boundaries, we must expect that earth will "jut" back and reclaim its injured dignity. This is, of course, the logic at work in *Antigone*. If, today, world seems to conquer earth's limits, the victory is only apparent. Each time our spacecraft lift off, the terrible pull of earth ascends also, as the tragedy of *Challenger* made clear. At the same time, only by world's utmost exertion—from a precarious station in space—does earth reveal herself whole. In broadest terms, what this imagery suggests is that poetry defends and draws authority from the powers of earth, while politics is authorized by any world it happens to uphold.

In *Antigone* the conflict between earth and world cannot be overlooked so long as Polynices lies in the sun unburied. His decaying body serves the public good, or so Creon decrees; but as Antigone asserts through action and Tiresias backs up with prophecy, failure to bury the dead upsets an order of things that is sacred. Against Creon's authority Antigone's sole resource is her dependence on the powers of earth. It's these powers Creon aims to override, insisting that the polis comes first. And he does override them, only to be undone by forces he thought he had vanquished. The political world exploits the earth and presumes to cancel earthly claims; but in the end no order or regime can sustain itself without respect for, and support from, the finite energies of earth.

At present we are served by a military world-order that holds the planet hostage. We are sustained by an economy that destroys creation's plenitude. These are not sane ways to care for life on earth. They have about them the blindness of a Creon doing what's expedient. How strange it is, how out of joint our time, that hope for the world now depends on the odds of the earth. Poetic justice, we might suppose, were it less disturbing. For as things now stand, the planet is alive and vulnerable and, like Antigone, a sister to us all.

·II·

The Press of the Real

Far in the woods they sang their unreal songs,
Secure. It was difficult to sing in face
Of the object. The singers had to avert themselves
Or else avert the object.
                                        —Wallace Stevens[1]

Thinking of poetry and politics together does not, ordinarily, bring
to mind the likes of Wallace Stevens, who is among the grandest
of our modernist masters but not a poet of the kind to whom politics
mattered, neither in his life nor in his work. But in fact, he was alert to
the damage politics can do, not only to life in the world, but to imagination and the spirit's interior life. To say, as he did, that poets must
"resist or evade" political reality is to acknowledge quite starkly the loss
of earlier freedoms. If Stevens was the last of the great evaders—a strat-
egist whose mainstay tactic was "the intricate evasions of as"—if Stevens
managed his feints supremely well, he was also intelligent about the
forces he aimed to outfox.

His most pointed statement about politics and poetry is "The Noble
Rider and the Sound of Words,"[2] a lecture delivered at Princeton and
first published in 1942, at a time when grim messages from Europe
were vexing the American dream of detachment. Looking for the difference between the Victorian era and our own, Stevens points to the
First World War as a turning point and sums up the spirit of the time
this way: "Reality then became violent and so remains." He goes on to
say that in a century rife with war and unrest we have been increasingly
crowded and diminished by events. It's in this overtly political context
that Stevens formulates "the pressure of reality":

... in speaking of the pressure of reality, I am thinking of life in a state of violence, not physically violent, as yet, for us in America, but physically violent for millions of our friends and for still more millions of our enemies and spiritually violent, it may be said, for everyone alive.

Stevens takes for granted that the increase in havoc, with its spiritual repercussions, is political in character. "Reality," he goes on, "has ceased to be indifferent." Malignity has found its motive and the victims, on any given day, are those the crossfire catches. Given this state of affairs, Stevens offers his prescription for poets to come:

A possible poet must be a poet capable of resisting or evading the pressure of reality of this last degree [spiritually violent for everyone alive], with the knowledge that the degree of today may become a deadlier degree tomorrow.

The notion of "the pressure of reality" is an entrance to the heart of the problem. For as soon as we ask what happens when poetry and politics collide, we are speaking of forces external to language, but which impinge so severely upon imagination's freedom that the poetry, in order to suffice, must resort to resistance or evasion. To speak of "reality," as Stevens speaks of it, is to designate a condition in some sense universal—political intrusion, that is, as the general case arising from countless special cases. One way to test Stevens' formulation is to ask the following question: What happens when communal misfortune disrupts the life of the poet who might otherwise feel free to pursue less noble, more indulgent matters in his or her art?

By way of answer I shall go to one of C. P. Cavafy's historical parables, one of the several Hellenistic anecdotes that he invented, or adumbrated upon, in his poetry. The circumstances of Cavafy's life—that he wrote in Greek, that he was born and lived most of his life in Alexandria, a city fabulous with the past—are not coincidental to his ironic grasp of events, his view of personal stories as marginalia to history's dense and endless text. That Cavafy was homosexual is also, I think, important to his work; boundary positions alert us to the limits of the self, to the loneliness of vision, and also to the flux and hazard that history throws up along its fault lines. Cavafy made his living as a minor bureaucrat, and in any political way his life was invisible, a circumstance he seems to have relished. At the same time, however, and especially when we consider Cavafy's detached, almost exquisite awareness of historical bad luck, it can't be ignored that the span of his life (1863–1933) was one with the arrival of the political moment that, in Stevens' words, "became violent and remains so."

A poet with Cavafy's Old World sensibility would not assume that poetry automatically transcends time, or history's imprint, or the predictable down-slide of empire. He wrote, anyway, a number of famous poems that challenge such assumptions. The best of these are unpretentious portraits from the distant (usually Hellenic) past, in part historical and in part imagined, snapshots that throw their momentary light upon the condition in which men and women find themselves when overtaken by events. One such poem, entitled "Dareios" and written in 1920, is an apt parable for poetry in dark times. The poem's persona, Phernazis, is imagined, but his situation rests in historical fact. Among the ancient Persian kings, Darius was the grandest, and his dynasty, along with his late successor referred to in the poem, eventually fell to the Romans. Here, then, is Cavafy's "Dareios":[3]

Phernazis the poet is at work
on the crucial part of his epic:
how Dareios, son of Hystaspis,
took over the Persian kingdom.
(It's from him, Dareios, that our glorious king,
Mithridatis, Dionysos and Evpator, descends.)
But this calls for serious thought; Phernazis has to analyse
the feelings Dareios must have had:
arrogance, maybe, and intoxication? No—more likely
a certain insight into the vanities of greatness.

But his servant, rushing in,
cuts him short to announce very important news:
the war with the Romans has begun;
most of our army has crossed the borders.

The poet is dumbfounded. What a disaster!
How can our glorious king,
Mithridatis, Dionysos and Evpator,

bother about Greek poems now?
In the middle of a war—just think, Greek poems!

We are, at this point, midway through the poem. The bad news arrives and in an instant all is changed. The situation, so "crucial" a moment ago, now tilts toward real disaster. In what becomes a rush of insight, Phernazis starts to see the folly of his project. The alarm puts an end to inflated ambitions and at the same time raises serious questions. With war under way, what will become of this or any work of art? The poetic enterprise—how valid, how worthy of respect can it be when life and the security of nations are directly at stake? Who bothers, in an emergency, about poems?

Pressured by the turn of events, Phernazis begins to ask hard questions—exactly the kind we who care for poetry have been asking, with increasing bewilderment, since roughly the end of World War Two. How, in bad times, shall the poet be honored? Is poetry equal to the news? And *Greek* stuff to boot—poetry modelled on past glories? In the middle of nuclear buildup, terrorism gone berserk, just think, *poems*?

As the rest of Cavafy's poem make clear, Phernazis has been forced to confront his poem's "crucial" moment in more ways than one. We can see, for example, that in searching after the dynastic motive—the feeling that Darius "must have had"—our poet is divining his own motives. The reference to "our glorious king" in the first stanza is more than parenthetical; it breaks up the call to serious thought and alerts us to the fact that, if the question of empire is pivotal, our poet's scheme for preferment is equally demanding. Before the bad news arrives, fame and the fruits of recognition urge him on at least as much as loyalty to "the poetic idea." As the rest of the poem will make clear, Phernazis begins by seeking critical acclaim and its benefits—equivalents to the grant, the prize, the university slot. Aiming to please, our poet would write a poem irrelevant to life but still of service to a fine career.

Cavafy's Persian poet, by producing a flattering work in an outdated style, aims to win attention from the powers that be, in this case the small king whose preposterous triple name, especially when repeated, suggests his ballooning idea of himself, in particular the arrogance and intoxication he reveals by his decision to take on the Romans. And in this minor despot's example we see something of Phernazis as well. He is arrogant toward his task and exalted by his prospects. He forfeits poetic integrity and turns the "poetic idea" against itself. By opting for the false theme, he attributes nobility of purpose to brute conquest, and would obscure the stupidity of power extending, and then overextending, its reach. Darius, we recall, met his match at Marathon in 490 B.C. Mithridatis VI Evpator went down in similar style. History tells us that he ended against Pompey in 66 B.C., a suicide, betrayed by his own son.

These contextual details give the poem its irony; and as a method this is one of Cavafy's triumphs, the way he uses history to compel prophetic inspection. Any leader's strength, we might agree, is the firmer for its grasp of tragic irony—"a certain insight," as Phernazis puts it, "into the vanities of greatness." But this is an unlikely wisdom, given what we know about leaders then or now. We can suppose, moreover, that until he hears the unfortunate news, our poet has little understanding of greatness, and none at all of vanity, although vanity is what he serves. And thus the "disaster"—the fact that with history on the move and events deflating illusions, the poet's pretensions collapse: "In the middle of a war—just think, Greek poems!"

His pretensions collapse, but what of the poet himself? He turns out to have more character than we—or he himself—might have guessed. Once his careerist schemes are defeated, he begins to see that his personal misfortune is in fact a minute part of full-scale catastrophe. The war, with its dumbfounding impact, jars him into an integrity that, earlier, he thought he could dismiss. A darker, more accurate awareness begins to develop, and the real poem—a kind of poetry equal to its occasion—begins to be possible. The rest of Cavafy's poem traces the stages of this turn:

> Phernazis gets all worked up. What a bad break!
> Just when he was sure to distinguish himself
> with his *Dareios*, sure to make
> his envious critics shut up once and for all.
> What a setback, terrible setback to his plans.
>
> And if it's only a setback, that wouldn't be too bad.
> But can we really consider ourselves safe in Amisos?
> The town isn't very well fortified,
> and the Romans are the most awful enemies.
> Are we, Cappadocians, really a match for them?
> Is it conceivable?

Are we to compete with the legions?
Great gods, protectors of Asia, help us.

But through all his nervousness, all the turmoil,
the poetic idea comes and goes insistently:
arrogance and intoxication—that's the most likely, of course:
arrogance and intoxication are what Dareios must have felt.

As the "setback" becomes more than personal bad luck, and as the
meaning of the historical moment begins to open upon him, Phernazis
looks beyond himself, sees the disaster thus set in motion, and turns
back to his tribe. He loses sight of himself in the fate of his people ("we,
Cappadocians"), is astonished that the king, for all his self-deluding
grandeur, could have gone so far as to provoke the Roman war machine
("Is it conceivable?"), and turns with humility to the gods that his people
might be spared their king's folly. Released from his self-serving plans,
Phernazis the poet can assume his true office. He can allow "the poetic
idea" its hegemony and write the real thing, a poem alive with its time
and the true concerns of its audience. Most interesting is the way "the
poetic idea" persists, awaits the coming of its incarnation. When it asserts
itself it lifts the poet beyond his fear, beyond his pettiness and mere
ambition. Earlier the poetic idea was in his service, but now he serves
it—which is what makes poetry possible. Having faced history and abandoned heroic pretense to "the vanities of greatness," Phernazis escapes
his own delusions and does in fact gain insight into the vanity—its pride
and awful cost—of political "greatness."

Counting his options, Phernazis might have given up altogether, once
the "setback" occurred; or he might have gone vainly on with his initial
plans; or, he might turn as in fact he does turn. He adjusts his art to
the pressure of reality. Now, and perhaps for the first time, he can take
up "the poetic idea," can thrive on its power, can be directed onward
by the interior force of a vision that presses back "insistently," through
personal confusion, through historical trauma, against external forces.
He is no longer troubled by the question of caring for poems in the
middle of a war. The answer is as it always is, a matter of poetic integrity,
an openness to the press of the real. We see, then, that the man's bad
luck becomes the artist's gift of grace. Facing up to politics, he becomes
the poet that earlier he only pretended to be; and in so doing he gains
what had seemed, just seconds ago, to have been lost—the opportunity

to write important poetry. We might even suppose that his audience, waiting for the Romans to arrive, will appreciate and find a fortitude worth having, in poetry "condemned [as Seferis said to Cavafy] to truth."[4]

Cavafy and Stevens both conceive of the poet as an *outside* observer distressed by the march of events but not—not yet—an *inside* participant overwhelmed and mute in the face of events themselves. The poet, here, occupies the same situation most readers of this book are likely to be in—the position of someone apart from political havoc but well within reach of its shock waves. The press of the real, in this situation, is less from politics itself (brute forces that mangle and destroy) than from the impact of politics (more subtle forces that unnerve and undermine) on those of us at a crucial remove. Poetry—anything more than raw cursing—is always language at a crucial remove. For Stevens, however, the question of distance becomes the heart of the matter. With enough space between self and world, the press of the real is diffuse and can be evaded. When this space cramps and shuts down, the real is unavoidable and must be resisted.

Stevens points out, to begin with, that there are "degrees of imagination," differences in poetic language at different times in history, and that "a variation between the sound of words in one age and the sound of words in another age is an instance of the pressure of reality." We know, of course, that the sound of words depends in part upon their sense but also upon the degree of their referential commitment. Words in their sounding register the degree of relation, or its lack, between poetry and the world. This peculiar circumstance leads Stevens to question the notions of his day: "If it is the pressure of reality that controls poetry, then the immediacy of various theories of poetry is not what it was." He cites critical ideas that seem to him discredited, among them the poet's older claim to a "highly complex and unified content of consciousness," which, as he says, cannot compete with the kind of consciousness that "every newspaper reader experiences today." And to Croce's notion of the poet as "the whole man," or of poetry as "the triumph of contemplation," Stevens replies: "Croce cannot have been thinking of a world in which all normal life is at least in suspense, or, if you like, under blockage." Imagination is crowded and cowed by the press of the world, until finally the collapse of distance has "cast us out on reality":

It is not only that there are more of us and that we are actually
close together. We are close together in every way. We lie in
bed and listen to a broadcast from Cairo, and so on. There is
no distance. We are intimate with people we have never seen
and, unhappily, they are intimate with us.

These things "constitute," says Stevens, "the drift of incidents, to
which we accustom ourselves as to the weather," and the weather, we
know, can make itself felt in our bones. Stevens is trying, as he says,
"to think of a whole generation and of a world at war, and trying at
the same time to see what is happening to the imagination." This leads
him to the first of his big definitions:

> By the pressure of reality, I mean the pressure of an external
> event or events on the consciousness to the exclusion of any
> power of contemplation.

Among the causes of this intrusiveness there is, to begin with, "an
extraordinary pressure of news." This is a phenomenon that Stevens
insists upon—"news incomparably more pretentious than any description of it, news, or firm, of the collapse of our system, or, call it, of life;
then of news of a new world, but of a new world so uncertain that one
did not know anything whatever of its nature, and does not know now."
He is correct, even prophetic, to dwell on the impact of "news." Through
the media the world comes at us every day nonstop, and in ways that
undermine the distance imagination needs to make sense of what we
behold. Gradually what we see informs the limit of what we know until,
as Stevens puts it, "the war is only a part of a war-like whole." And it's
here, in this degree of intrusion, that the pressure of news and events
cannot be ignored or further put off by ordinary means:

> Rightly or wrongly, we feel that the fate of a society is involved
> in the orderly disorders of the present time. We are confront-
> ing, therefore, a set of events, not only beyond our power to
> tranquillize them in the mind, beyond our power to reduce
> them and metamorphose them, but events that stir the emo-
> tions to violence, that engage us in what is direct and immediate
> and real, and events that involve the concepts and sanctions
> that are the order of our lives and may involve our very lives;

and these events are occurring persistently with increasing
omen, in what may be called our presence. These are the things
that I had in mind when I spoke of the pressure of reality, a
pressure great enough and prolonged enough to bring about
the end of one era in the history of imagination and, if so,
then great enough to bring about the beginning of another.

When this point is reached the press of the real is severe enough to
instigate a change in imagination's stance toward the world. Stevens
notes that imagination "is always attaching itself to a new reality, and
adhering to it," but he adds: "It is not that there is a new imagination
but that there is a new reality." In Stevens' time and in ours, the cause
of reality's change is time's acceleration and the collapse of space, the
increasing reach and beat of political clamor—events "that stir the emo-
tions to violence," events beyond the capacity of mind to tranquillize,
reduce, or transform them; events, finally, that threaten "the concepts
and sanctions that are the order of our lives and may involve our very
lives." At this point Stevens is ready to generalize the impact of history
upon art:

> To sum it up, the pressure of reality is, I think, the determining
> factor in the artistic character of an era and, as well, the de-
> termining factor in the artistic character of an individual. The
> resistance to this pressure or its evasion in the case of individ-
> uals of extraordinary imagination cancels the pressure so far as
> those individuals are concerned.

The world is always with us; the question is whether it can be evaded
or whether, when it intrudes too far, it must be resisted. If the latter,
then how shall the "possible poet" carry on? It's at this point that Stevens
makes his remarks (quoted earlier) about "life in a state of violence,"
and says that "a possible poet must be a poet capable of resisting or
evading the pressure of reality of this last degree." This position raises
a question about "the social, that is to say sociological or political,
obligation of the poet," a question that Stevens answers bluntly: "he
has none." Stevens concedes that "if a social movement moved one
deeply enough, its moving poems would follow," but at the same time
and emphatically: "no politician can command the imagination." Coer-
cion of this directly political kind is itself "a phase of the pressure of

reality" that any poet today "is bound to resist or evade." The poet is not absolved of community. On the contrary, Stevens has a definite sense of the poet's role in times of political torment:

> What is his function? Certainly it is not to lead people out of the confusion in which they find themselves. Nor is it, I think, to comfort them while they follow their readers [leaders?] to and fro. I think that his function is to make his imagination theirs and that he fulfills himself only as he sees his imagination become the light in the minds of others. His role, in short, is to help people live their lives.

Poetry can help people live their lives, not by instruction but by creating potent figures that anyone's imagination might kindle to and take hold of—language that takes a place in the mind, allowing us to anchor ourselves and reclaim our self-possession—even amid the grim confusions of politics in dark time. Then especially, works like *Antigone* and *King Lear* serve us as *As You Like It* or even *The Tempest* cannot. Prokofiev's *Romeo and Juliet* rallies the spirit as Tschaikovsky's no longer can. And many a poem not otherwise strong will help restore presence of mind if uttered in a voice to match—or oppose—its occasion. The point, in this last instance, is that the poem is spoken aloud and not merely read. Thinking of the ways language resists the shove of the world, Stevens concentrates on "the sounds of words," and in terms of a force he calls "nobility." This strength of language is the key to Stevens' argument; by way of approaching it he goes on with these questions. "And what," he asks, "about the sound of words? What about nobility, of which the fortunes were to be a kind of test of the value of the poet?"

If we ask how poetry equips us for living, the further answer has something to do with the sounds of words and the character of imagination (here called "nobility") inherent in words and the music of their endless mixing. "Poetry," says Stevens, "is a revelation in words by means of the words." Or again: "A poet's words are things that do not exist without the words." Things, then; but things whose dwelling is sound and the soundings of lyric combination, words as they exist in their audible saying. About this Stevens is adamant; he says "that above everything else, poetry is words; and that words, above everything else, are, in poetry, sounds." He is stressing the importance of art's concreteness, the oracular action of words taking place. He is also endorsing

Heidegger's notion that language, in poetry, is the earth that imaginative worlds are set into.

The odd carnality of words is that they arise *ex nihilo,* become incarnate in their saying, then instantly depart while at the same time they leave an imprint that resounds. Poetry activates memory through its soundings—through rhyme, alliteration, etc., but also tone, inflection, and finally the entire ensemble of "voice," which is the earthly shape of sound in motion. Language of this memorable kind is capable of persisting through a void or, on the other hand, through the dense chaos of language in the world. Poetry—any set of lines we prize—sorts itself out from the infinitude of babble and allows us moments of coherence, of lucidity and self-possession as close to unity of being as most of us shall come:

> The deepening need for words to express our thoughts and feelings which, we are sure, are all the truth that we shall ever experience, having no illusions, makes us listen to words when we hear them, loving them and feeling them, makes us search the sound of them, for a finality, a perfection, an unalterable vibration, which it is only within the power of the acutest poet to give them.

That formal language empowers is a point on which poets and politicians agree. Stevens reserves this executive power for poetry by saying that "the peculiarity of the imagination is nobility," and further that "nobility" of this kind resides in "the sound of words." Language and imagination together constitute a system of grace and a *force,* and by way of analogy Stevens gives an example worth quoting in full, ellipses included:

> Late last year Epstein exhibited some of his flower paintings at the Leicester Galleries in London. A commentator in *Apollo* said: "How with this rage can beauty hold a plea. . . . The quotation from Shakespeare's 65th sonnet prefaces the catalogue. . . . It would be apropos to any other flower paintings than Mr. Epstein's. His make no pretense to fragility. They shout, explode all over the picture space and generally oppose the rage of the world with such a rage of form and colour as no flower in nature or pigment has done since Van Gogh."

"How with this rage shall beauty hold a plea, / Whose action is no stronger than a flower"? That is the whole of Shakespeare's conceit. Stevens cites the catalogue description to suggest how the challenge might be answered. These flowers explode, they rage and oppose, and urge him to conclude; "What ferocious beauty the line from Shakespeare puts on when used under such circumstances! While it has its modulation of despair, it holds its plea and its plea is noble." He has in mind a kind of strength or power generated by imagination in vigorous contest with reality. That his poetic action is elusive, hard to pin down, he does not deny. What he insists upon is that "nobility is a force," an agency that opposes the rage of the world with a rage of its own. Imagination and reality meet as equals, and the former draws its character and strength from the latter. In this way art sustains itself *in* the world, surviving rushes of negative force that to innocent eyes might seem overwhelming. And the way poetry sets itself in relation to the world is summed up in these lines:[5]

The poem is the cry of its occasion,
Part of the res itself and not about it.

Without being afraid or self-serving, art of this kind faces its own negation; it meets the pressure of reality and uses the world's force to call forth a counterpoise of its own. That is its nobility. In this view the poet can claim to be a realist, while the realist will always be a poet *manqué*. It's on this ground that Stevens stands when he says, as he often did, "that the structure of poetry and the structure of reality are one." The poem is "part of the res" and draws its force from its occasion.

In the concluding paragraph of "The Noble Rider and the Sound of Words," Stevens tells us that his "description of it as a force" is the best he can do toward explaining what "nobility" means. He then adds: "It is not an artifice that the mind has added to human nature. The mind has added nothing to human nature." At first this remark seems out of place, there having been no mention of "human nature" until this late moment. But Stevens is moving, at this point, from "nobility" as an attribute of poetry to "nobility" as an element of our humanity. He is arguing that *nobility as a force* is a kind of action or behavior needful to our being-in-the-world. It is the human way of keeping dignity alive in violent or demeaning situations, with the added sense that poetry and the arts play a key role in spiritual well-being. With these ideas in mind, here are the last sentences of Stevens' essay:

> It is a violence from within that protects us from a violence without. It is the imagination pressing back against the pressure of reality. It seems, in the last analysis, to have something to do with our self-preservation; and that, no doubt, is why the expression of it, the sound of its words, helps us live our lives.

The formula is famous and often cited, although not always as Stevens intended. Coming at the end of the essay, it sums up the whole of his argument and reveals what hadn't been visible before, namely that the poet as a "noble rider" is a *martial* figure. The way Stevens constructs the poet's situation—imagination contending with reality, powers within against powers without—suggests an art that is embattled, and Stevens speaks not only of violence and pressure, but of help and survival. These are substantial ideas, the more interesting for coming from a poet in whose work the martial element has seldom been recognized. We might all agree on the urbane Stevens, the ornate and carnivalesque Stevens. But Stevens as a noble rider? Stevens embattled?

But of course he was, and not only with old themes like loss and mutability. His deployment of metaphor in sequence—one image or phrase overtaking another to keep poetic consciousness diverging and imagination impossible to pin down—holds him at a distance, yet on occasion also allows him to move in close. Stevens takes his subject by degrees, but he gives "reality" its due, from the early *firecat,* bristling in the way no matter which way the bucks go swerving, to the late gray *rock* that is "the habitation of the whole." His art thrives on "the spirit that goes roundabout," but at the same time Stevens is ever mindful that "a blank underlies the trials of device, / The dominant blank, the unapproachable," against which summer's crickets sing in vain. His deepest strategy, the *basso continuo* of all his airy flights, is to outflank the world's avid uproar by stationing himself upon the bleak and empty backdrop of existence. At the heart of darkness is grim nothing, and the violence of confronting this is, for Stevens, strength. He never loses sight of life's essential poverty, "the nothing that is not there and the nothing that is." Reading him with care, there is a "misery in the sound of the wind." The real nobility, for this poet, is that despite the strain of pushing back he stays so poised. Preferring to bless rather than to blame, he leavens reserve with humor and braids his cursing into larger fabrics of praise.

With language that confronts and resists we mobilize "a violence from within that protects us from a violence without." For poetry to help us live our lives, the force of its diction must be equal to the world in which the poem itself takes place. And these strengths, it seems to me, are of especial value for the late years of this century. The world founders in political torment; it is ours yet not ours, the same world Stevens faced when he says: "I am thinking of life in a state of violence, not physically violent, as yet, for us in America, but physically violent for millions of our friends and for still more millions of our enemies and spiritually violent, it may be said, for everyone alive." That is our predicament but not, in Stevens' view, without resources to help us endure.

TWO

BARDIC PRACTICE, THE IRISH EXAMPLE

·III·

Yeats and the Rat-Rhymers

Theare is amongst the Irishe a certen kind of
people Called Bardes. . . .
—Edmund Spenser, 1596[1]

I write it out in a verse. . . .
—William Butler Yeats, 1916[2]

S hortly after his death in 1939, Yeats was praised by T. S. Eliot as
"one of those few whose history is the history of their own time,
who are a part of the consciousness of an age which cannot be understood without them."[3] As Eliot suggests, Yeats was always alert to
politics. More often than not, he confronted history head-on, eagerly,
sometimes with venom. But often, too, he sought a "ghostly solitude"
apart from the clamor around him. It is not, therefore, his poetry in
total that concerns me, but the part of his work that is like backbone
to body, the part that Yeats spoke up for when (in 1936) he summed
himself up as "a man of my time, through my poetical faculty living its
history."[4]

To take Yeats as a man of his time, living his age through his art, is
to take for granted that politics is central to his work. This does not
mean poetic practice at the cost of political conformity or reductiveness
but, exactly as Yeats says, responding to events *through* poetry. The Irish
Free State came into being under Yeats's watchful eye, and much of his
art responds to affairs of his time, kinds of events that still today set the
character of experience for many countries and peoples—in Yeats's case
a nationalist movement in politics and the arts; a culmination to centuries of colonial strife in war with empire, terrorism right and left
followed by civil war; and at last the setting up of an independent (but
not untroubled) republic.

After *Responsibilities* (1914), the greater number of Yeats's poems address an event or public circumstance, a person or persons involved in political affairs, or otherwise come braced with topical references. He was especially attentive to events that looked like signs of the times, and then to men and women who by lonely acts of will stood out from the fray. One of his heroes was Charles Stewart Parnell, whose downfall Yeats described as the last of "Four Bells, four deep tragic notes" sounding disastrous turning points in Irish history, beginning with the Flight and ending with the hysteria surrounding Parnell's death in 1891.[5] Praised as a savior, reviled as a sinner, Parnell was called "the Chief" and then "the dead King." He had united Ireland in an all-out push for independence, but then he found himself dragged down by private issues (adultery and divorce), with the clergy and much of his Catholic constituency against him. As Joyce later said: "To their eternal credit the Irish never threw Parnell to the wolves. They tore him to pieces themselves.[6] The rage that Joyce observed is Yeats's concern in "Parnell's Funeral," a poem not written until 1934, but a good example of "living" one's time through one's art.

The poem begins by sounding the theme of sacrifice, which is introduced by the fall of a star, and then extended into an arcane mythological reference:

> What shudders run through all that animal blood?
> What is this sacrifice? Can someone there
> Recall the Cretan barb that pierced a star?

Yeats goes on, in the next stanza, with language even more obscure, and the first fourteen lines of "Parnell's Funeral" are the least successful part of the poem. The star pierced by an arrow is equated with the extracted heart in ancient ritual, and the theme of sacrifice is expanded to suggest a way of life so ceremonious and whole that what occurs in the body politic is rendered perfectly in public art. This kind of elaboration—not unusual for Yeats—serves to dignify the theme and keep the poet distant.

But Yeats does not stay at a distance, nor does visionary calm prevail. Having seen—over and over—his own programs for the nation rejected, he embraces a mood of defeat and asks if sacrifice, and the communal regeneration that comes of it, can succeed in his own time and country. As late as 1932 Yeats said of Parnell: "from that sacrificial victim I derive almost all that is living in the imagination of Ireland today."[7] Yeats links Irish art to Irish politics, a connection that becomes explicit in the poem as it goes on, along with dramatic or even startling changes in tone and diction. In his meditation on Parnell's defeat, Yeats is forced out of myth into history; he falls from detachment into vehement reaction—as if he were embracing the progress of an actual fall, in language, syntax, and voice, enacted in the poem's onward plunge:

>   . . . . popular rage,
> *Hysterica passio* dragged this quarry down.
> None shared our guilt; nor did we play a part
> Upon a painted stage when we devoured his heart.
>
> Come, fix upon me that accusing eye.
> I thirst for accusation. All that was sung,
> All that was said in Ireland is a lie
> Bred out of the contagion of the throng,
> Saving the rhyme rats hear before they die.
> Leave nothing but the nothings that belong
> To this bare soul, let all men judge that can
> Whether it be an animal or a man.

The progress of the first four stanzas (Part One) suggests that politics did sometimes provoke Yeats so severely that myth no longer sustained him. His meditation on Parnell's death becomes so troubled that Yeats turns into a different *kind* of poet—not a wise and timeless voice beyond the grave, but the bard in agitated outcry, praising his lost lord while cursing the tribe's perfidy. Stanzas three and four describe the hero's downfall, met by a voice that accuses and blames, that lays down the law ("let all men judge") and then will go on, in Part Two, to praise the hero's good name.

Yeats has taken up the role of the Irish bard, the kind of poet known from Ireland's well-documented tradition of bardic schools and tribal poetry—the kind of poet whose professional calling was to praise, curse, bless, and cast blame. Yeats was a great curser, but also quick to bless and be blessed. Much of his work is based on blame and praise, and these fields of announcement become more insistent as politics becomes more directly the subject of particular poems. Yeats was nothing if not confrontational, and often the role of the Irish bard became his preferred office when he responded to political occasions.

Given the importance Yeats placed on voice,[8] and his love of ceremony, we can appreciate that bardic practice is formulaic, rhetorical, and self-aware, a position rather than a posture. In "Parnell's Funeral" we come upon bardic formulae like "one sentence I unsay" and "but I name no more."

In Part Two Yeats offers a chronicle of Irish politics, using the bardic custom of naming to move from 1891 to 1934:

> The rest I pass, one sentence I unsay.
> Had de Valera eaten Parnell's heart
> No loose-lipped demagogue had won the day,
> No civil rancor torn the land apart.
>
> Had Cosgrave eaten Parnell's heart, the land's
> Imagination had been satisfied,
> Or lacking that, government in such hands,
> O'Higgins its sole statesman had not died.
>
> Had even O'Duffy—but I name no more—
> Their school a crowd, his master solitude;
> Through Jonathan Swift's dark grove he passed, and there
>
> Plucked bitter wisdom that enriched his blood.

Part of the "rest" passed over is the Easter uprising of 1916, an omission important to the poem's dark mood. The sentence that the poet would "unsay" (from stanza two) ends with "when we devoured his heart." Some did not partake of Parnell's heart but should have.

"Parnell's Funeral" is an elegy, a lament, a praise-poem. It is also a curse upon "the crowd" and its captains, including "even O'Duffy." The word *even*, with its suggestion of scorn followed by the gesture of dismissal, counts heavily for any poem about Irish politics in 1934. Cosgrave and then de Valera ran the republic in its early years, with O'Higgins as strong man until he was murdered. Then O'Duffy appeared as leader of the Blue Shirts, the Irish fascist movement that, briefly, drew praise from Yeats and lifted his political spirits one last time. "Politics are growing heroic," he wrote in July 1933—"Our chosen colour is blue."[9] To this ludicrous low point Yeats came in his yearning for an order that could make the world cohere, an outcome his own art contradicted. The Blue Shirts were not defeated but simply fell apart. And with O'Duffy's collapse Yeats recognized overwhelmingly, just as his life was ending, that politics was not heroic and, except for the Easter uprising of 1916, that it had never been so in his lifetime. In 1936 he admitted that "Communist, Fascist, nationalist, clerical, anti-clerical, are all responsible according to the number of their victims."[10]

Yeats's own brand of politics—an aristocratic order embracing a tragic sense of life—had been improbable from the start. In 1934 he would have done better to depend for fortitude on the wisdom of an earlier time, a remark he made during the darkness of the civil war: "There is no longer a virtuous nation and the best of us live by candle light."[11] To come at Yeats correctly we must keep in mind that politically he was always in a position of defeat; but also that his celebration of defeat as an opportunity for heroism served his poetry, if not his politics, wonderfully well. Political despair, strong enough to make the whole of the past seem waste, was the occasion for "Parnell's Funeral." The fascist lunge fell apart in early 1934; later that year came the poem.

Against defeat Yeats summons gaiety or rage. The former sometimes strains, but the blaze of the latter is straight from the heart. In Parnell's funeral poem, rage is compressed into perfect iambics. If the Chief's downfall calls for a curse, this is its saying:

> All that was sung,
> All that was said in Ireland is a lie
> Bred out of the contagion of the throng,
> Saving the rhyme rats hear before they die.

Yeats is making strong charges, but also a singular claim. Irish politics has been false, so has Irish poetry, everything said or sung except this— "the rhyme rats hear before they die." But what sort of rhyming is that? The usual gloss is from As You Like It (III, ii) where Rosalind mocks: "I was never so berhymed since Pythagoras' time, that I was an Irish rat." For Shakespeare the allusion is no more than a stitch in a patchwork of humor. For Yeats it would be something more, as it was for Ben Jonson, who had his pretentious peers in mind when he threatened to

Rime 'hem to death, as they doe *Irish* rats,
In drumming tunes.

Doubtless they existed, the "rat-rhymers," and perhaps exactly as the
loose ends of legend record—wandering poets trading off the status of
their bardic betters, going about the countryside chanting poems in
front of infested hovels and barns, working charms and incantations,
earning a living by cursing. The notion of rat-rhyming is remarkably
apt for what Yeats has in mind; it is also, I think, an accurate emblem
for poetry confronting politics. In English literature there are a few
further allusions to poetry's business with rats. Sir William Temple connected runic incantation (the kind "to cause Terror in . . . Enemies")
with "the proverb of rhyming rats to death." Alexander Pope had it that
"Songs no longer move, / Nor Rat is rhym'd to death, nor Maid to
love," mocking the notion that once they might have. And at the conclusion of his *Apologie for Poetrie*, Sidney bids his reader a wry farewell:
"I would not wish unto you . . . to be rimed to death, as is said to be
done in *Ireland*." Sir Philip ought to know, as one whose father had
been Lord Deputy in Ireland during the period of Tudor campaigns to
savage the Irish.

These allusions to rat-rhyming suggest a tradition or field of practice
specific to earlier Irish ages, centering on "the supposed potency of the
verses pronounced by the professional rhymers,"[12] a power sometimes
reputed to reach further than rats. As late as the 1820's it was said
among Ireland's peasantry that "many a man, who would kindle into
rage at the sight of an armed foe, will be found to tremble at the thought
of offending a rhymer."[13] Irish bards were often more famous for their
cursing than for their more constructive powers, their duties and privileges as ministers to the tribe. In 1912 Osborn Bergin, an Irish scholar
and translator of Gaelic manuscripts, sketched the following picture of
the bard as he existed in Ireland from prehistoric times until the end of
the sixteenth century, a portrait that with minor retouching would fit
and, I do not doubt, have flattered Yeats:[14]

He was, in fact, a professor of literature and a man of letters,
highly trained in the use of a polished literary medium, belonging to a hereditary caste in an aristocratic society, holding
an official position therein by virtue of his training, his learning,
his knowledge of the history and traditions of his country and

his clan. . . . He was often a public official, a chronicler, a political essayist, a keen and satirical observer of his fellow-countrymen. At an earlier period he had been regarded as a dealer in magic, a weaver of spells and incantations, who could blast his enemies by the venom of his verse, and there are traces down to the most recent times of a lingering belief, which was not, of course, confined to Ireland, in the efficacy of a well-tuned malediction.

In common discourse the bardic notion of the poet is honored for its antiquity. But at the same time, we have reasoned away the magical properties of language, and nowadays to talk of "bards" seems frivolous or old-fashioned. In current criticism it no longer occurs to us that a keeper of bardic powers is what a poet—any poet—is. But Yeats did not think as we do. He avowed that magic and the supernatural were real, and saw himself as the receptacle of tribal wisdom, a mystical lore he called the *anima mundi*. His relation to bardic practice is thus of more than passing interest. Most poets are atavistic in degree, but in Yeats the tendency was nearly total, so much that his politics as well as his poetics could be summed up in this once-and-future way: What Ireland had been it should be.

The rat-rhymers were a minor but colorful part of a tradition that, among the Irish, goes back very far indeed. Ireland has been the home of distinctive peoples since at least 6000 B.C. A grand civilization—its jewelled brooches, its golden torques and war gear are on view in Dublin's National Museum—flourished between 3700 and 1800 B.C. Irish mythology contains numerous references to occupation of Ireland before the coming of the Celts themselves, who began arriving around 1200 B.C. in successive waves from the continent. Ireland's heroic sagas grew out of the exploits of these early Celtic tribes, a period that lasted into the fourth century A.D. Among these are the stories of the "Ulster" or "Red Branch" cycle, the best-known of which is *The Cattle Raid of Cooley*, a battle saga dominated by the figure of Cuchulain. In this epic poem, moreover, bards appear as characters in the plot, and their power to curse is a serious part of the action.

The magical-religious functions of the bards went unquestioned until Patrick began the Christianization of Ireland in 432. With the new breed of Irish saints—themselves renowned for cursing—the bards found their authority challenged and sometimes usurped. But also, it was during this early Christian period that clerical scribes began to record, in bulk and pell-mell, the countless stories of the earlier oral tradition. (*The Cattle Raid of Cooley*, for example, began to be recorded in the seventh and eighth centuries but was fully written down only around 1150 in the *Book of Leinster*.) The bards added the Christian art of writing to their repertoire of skills, and went on to regroup themselves into a literary caste with specific duties, schools, and ranks. The bardic schools were a great success and flourished from about 1200 into the 1600's—until the British were able to destroy the old Gaelic order supporting the bardic system. During the time of the schools, Irish verse reached its highest level of perfection and stands today as the oldest, most finely wrought vernacular of medieval Europe. By the end of the seventeenth century, however, the complicated craft of the schools was dying. The bards found themselves adrift, lacking patronage and courtly function. Now came the turning point, the great divide in bardic practice. Accentual meter replaced syllabics, and vowel rhyme gave way to consonantal chiming as the base of Irish poetry. Bards turned from court to countryside, and this "stepping down," as it was called, meant that poets had to take up the popular and usually penniless ways of the wandering rhymer.[15]

With rebellion crushed and England in control, poets sang of local events and the trials of neighborhood peasantry at the hands of alien overlords. In the bardic poetry of dispossession, lament and rage combined, and now the *aisling* appeared, the vision poem that catches a glimpse of Ireland's once and future glory in the form of a grieving young woman. The development of bardic craft was thus toward democratic forms. For the first time the figure of the bard emerges as the voice of "the Irishry." The paradox is that while Ireland's misery—its failed rebellions, its poverty and cultural deprivations enforced by the English—all but annihilated the earlier bardic order, there remained a distinct spirit of "bardic ambition," as I would call it, ready to serve the nation's need. Imagination had been transformed by political circumstance into a nationalistic force with enormous potential. The bardic past, with its capacity to empower, lay repressed but alive.

The ruin of Gaelic society was complete with Cromwell's invasion (1649–50) and the Williamite wars at the close of the seventeenth century. Even then, bards were remembered with respect. Writing in 1760, Oliver Goldsmith praised Thurlough O'Carolan, who died in 1738, as the last famous bard. Goldsmith also mentions, however, that among the Irish of his own day "their bards, in particular, are still held in great veneration."[16] For Yeats, writing in 1906, the last bard was "blind Raftery," who died in 1835 and whose grave, in 1900, Lady Gregory and Yeats honored with a headstone. Yeats gives Raftery an honored place in two poems, and makes him the example of oral artistry in his important essay "Literature and the Living Voice." Lady Gregory wrote twice about Raftery's life and art, essays that T. R. Henn edited with the following comment: "He [Raftery] was a remarkable man, and perhaps the last of the satirists of power, whose verses and epigrams were feared and admired by all. We may remember that satirists were regular members of the battle staff of ancient Irish kings, their business being to make poems against the enemy that might 'rot the flesh from their bones,' or, in lighter moments, destroy rats."[17]

When Yeats refers to "the rhyme rats hear before they die," he calls up an old and potent tradition, a fabric of practice and belief that can be recognized on decent evidence and pointed to concretely. As far back as documents reach (and not in Ireland alone), poets are famed and feared for their power to curse. The universal name for verse of this kind is *satire*, and the target—the person satirized—could expect terrible things to result: one might "lose face," or break out in a blistering rash, or die outright. Whether or not these effects stemmed from the force of a poet's words, whether they occurred at all, is not the point. The remarkable fact is that such anxious beliefs were so widespread and ingrained. Remarkable, too, is that neither in ancient times nor more recently has the Irish tradition admitted a distinction between the primitive *magical curse* and more sophiscated notions of *literary satire*. Fred Norris Robinson has taken up this point in detail; "Satirists and Enchanters in Early Irish Literature," his 1912 essay, remains the classic study of Irish bards at their malefic best:[18]

> It seems like an unjustifiable looseness in language to use the same word [satire] for such dissimilar things. But as soon as one begins to examine the so-called satirical material in Irish literature, one finds difficulties in dispensing with the name. In the first place, the Irish language itself employs the same words (most commonly *aer* and its derivatives) for the rat-spells of Senchan and for the stricter satire of a later age. Furthermore, the persons described as pronouncing satires, even of the old destructive sort, were by no means always

merely enchanters, but in many cases poets of high station, either in history or in sage. And finally, the subjects of their maleficent verse—often, for example, the inhospitality or other vices of chieftains—are such as might form suitable themes of genuine satire; and the purpose of the poets is frequently described as being to produce ridicule and shame. In short, it seems impossible in old Celtic literature to draw a line between what is strictly satire and what is not; and one ends by realizing that, for the ancient Celts themselves, the distinction did not exist. Just as their poets were not clearly separable from druids and medicine-men, but often combined in one person the functions of all three, so they freely mingled natural and supernatural processes in the practices of their arts. Destructive spells and poems of slander or abuse were all thought of together as the work, and it sometimes seems almost the chief work, of the tribal man of letters.

Robinson observes that "the association of mockery, invective, and magical injury" was "usual" in Gaelic practice. Ireland's ancient Brehon laws list many kinds of satiric abuse, with gradations as fine as these—"the blemish of a nickname, satirizing a man after his death, and satire of exceptional power [?]." This last kind isn't described; quite possibly it was connected with the dangerous skills of "hard attackers," as one class of bards was called. But with such powers assigned, we see why abuses of bardic privilege were classified as "crimes of the tongue."[19] As late as the seventeenth century a famous bard (Teig, son of Daire) challenged his own patrons (the O'Briens) by threatening to "nail a name" on them with his "blister-raising ranns."[20] The power implied here draws its force from values that anthropologists ascribe to "shame" cultures, although "fame" or "prestige" might better describe a culture of this kind. To "nail a name on a man" could ruin his tribal standing, destroy his reputation and the honor on which his personal worth depended. Pride, we recall, was chief among virtues for Yeats. Also interesting is that in Gaelic the same word stands for "face" and for "honor." In tribal Ireland, one's good name was one's pride and source of power. We get some idea of this from Frayes Moryson, an Elizabethan traveller who saw Irish chieftains "assume their old barbarous names whensoever they will have the power to lead the people to any rebellious action. For in those barbarous names and nicknames, the Irish are proud to have the rebellious acts of their forefathers sung by their bards and poets at their feasts and public meetings."[21]

For many centuries bardic practice was indigenous to the whole of the Indo-European world. In one regard, however, Ireland is special; its bardic tradition is more abundantly documented, and its practices survived a great deal longer than elsewhere in Europe. Because Ireland was never invaded by the Romans, the vernacular remained the language of learning and power. The spirit of the Renaissance, moreover, never crossed the Irish Sea; while other nations were pursuing the disenchantment of the world, Ireland was fighting for *its* world against the Tudors. The Normans had arrived in 1169, but made no attempt to stamp out native customs. But with the Reformation, and the decision of Henry VIII to centralize England's empire, Ireland found itself in a renegade posture, a defensiveness that was cultural as well as military.

Thanks to the hazards of history, the Irish held to a system of practice and belief that was common to the Indo-European past but that had vanished or been demoted to folklore and superstition on the continent. In *The Power of Satire*, Robert C. Elliott broadens this view by suggesting that the archaic reputation of poetry owed its prestige not only to the centrality of memorialization in oral cultures, but likewise to the authority of the curse as a formal or legal device—"Cursed be he who does (or does not do) this or that"—a patriarchal echo, perhaps, of "the father's curse." Elliott speculates, and I would agree, that cursing's magical rites are the spring from which bardic forms derive, and that the hegemony of poetry in antiquity had as much to do with fear—in other words, with power—as with the more obvious services that Plato had in mind when he advised poets to hymn the gods and praise famous men.[22] To suggest that Ireland's bardic tradition empowered Yeats to write as he did is not so wild a claim. If his confrontation with politics derives authority from bardic practice, this is only to say that an Irish poet took to heart an Irish option, a native and highly developed disposition that has often played its part in Irish art.

Sir John Davies called Ireland "the land of Ire." Edmund Campion, another Englishman observing the Irish, said in 1571 that "greedy of praise they be, and fearful of dishonor."[23] The English conviction that poets were responsible for Ireland's outlaw spirit provides the perspective from which to view Edmund Spenser's famous hostile remarks against Ireland's poets. Spenser was fascinated but also alarmed, and felt he should censure bardic behavior as he observed it from his castle in Cork. In *A view of the present state of Irelande*, written in 1596, he reports that the Irish "feare to runne into [bardic] reproach" because to be satirized is to "be made infamous in the mouthes of all men"—infamy of a sort that, to an Englishman, might be amusing. Not so the honor got from praise; in this case, Spenser judged, the rhymers were dangerous:[24]

> But these Irishe Bardes are for the moste parte of another minde and so farre from instructinge yonge men in morrall discipline that they themselues doe more deserue to be sharpe-lye discipled for they seldome vse to Chose out themselues the doinges of good men for the argumentes of theire poems but whom soeuer they finde to be moste Licentious of life moste bolde and lawles in his doinges most daungerous and desperate in all partes of disobedience and rebellious disposicion him they set vp and glorifye in theire Rymes him the praise to the people and to yonge men make an example to follow.

Spenser, of course, wrote the longest praise-poem in English. He would know that one policy dignified by *The Faerie Queene* was the Tudor attempt to quell the Irish by killing them off. What is interesting in Spenser's critique is how perfectly, by observing the Irish rhymers of his day, the Elizabethan poet foresaw Yeatsian preferences. In poem after poem Yeats celebrates figures who in orthodox terms can only be called "moste bolde and lawles" as well as "desperate in all partes of disobedience and rebellious disposicion." Maude Gonne is a capital instance, she who would

> Have taught to ignorant men most violent ways,
> Or hurled the little streets upon the great,
> Had they but courage equal to desire.

To praise is to recommend, to present an image for respect and emulation. It is also to endorse communal identity by lifting heroes into everyone's sight. This Yeats does, be it with Parnell and early martyrs like Robert Emmet and Wolfe Tone or, in "Beautiful Lofty Things," his father's "mischievous head thrown back" in answer to Abbey rioters. There is no question but that Yeatsian heroes are politically licentious;

no question but that Yeats was attentive to violence and embattled situations. But his delight in contention has the backing of bardic tradition. Irish bards have always cursed and called to battle. That has been their job, and in "Parnell's Funeral" the call to fight is direct:

> Come, fix upon me that accusing eye.
> I thirst for accusation.

It has been suggested that Yeats is calling Parnell's spirit to come and accuse him, but these lines are in the imperative mood and can be read as a command as much as a challenge. Of course there *is* a challenge here, but further on in stanza four we come to another command, this time overtly imperative: "Leave nothing but the nothings that belong / To this bare soul," and then yet another: "let all men judge that can." These charges summon a tribe and at the same time indict a collective antagonist. Those who destroyed Parnell, or made his kind of leadership impossible, are called by the poet to confront him face to face. When he says, "Come, fix upon me that accusing eye," Yeats spurns the *evil eye* of his opponents. Against their power he has powers of his own. He *thirsts* for confrontation, knowing Parnell and Swift will be with him. In this small but superlative instance Yeats sets himself up for a fight. He enacts the stance of the bard upon a field of war, then proceeds to do that which, in time of battle, bards do: hex and chant down the enemy.

That Yeats knew bardic tradition is certain. In an early letter he remarks that he has "found a wonderful account of the old bardic colleges" in *Memoirs of the Marquis of Clanricarde* (1722), a standard description of an actual bardic school (Yeats particularly liked the fact that fledgling poets were required to compose in the dark).[25] In his polemics of the 1890's he makes repeated use of the words *bard* and *bardic*, sometimes to designate a general type, at other times with meanings more historically exact. From early on, he took delight in "the power of the bards," as he calls it, including their satiric prowess:[26]

> The bards were the most powerful influence in the land and all manner of superstitious reverence environed them round. . . . Their rule was one of fear as much as love. A poem and an incantation were the same. A satire could fill a whole country-side with famine. Something of the same feeling still

survives, perhaps, in the extreme dread of being "rhymed up" by some local maker of unkind verses.

For Yeats and his generation, the recovery of Ireland's heroic literature, and therefore of bardic tradition, began with Standish O'Grady's *History of Ireland*, published in two volumes in 1878–80, along with his *Early Bardic Literature*, published in 1879. His aim was to inspire the Irish with their own heritage, and this, for Yeats, was "the start of us all."[27] O'Grady argues in a fanciful but vigorous way that the heroes of bardic literature owe their origin to historical figures, and that thanks to the bards this important past has not been lost. He leaves the impression that the early bards were as grand, as large, as crucial to the nation as the legendary heroes themselves.

If O'Grady was the catalyst and prophet to bardic recovery, Douglas Hyde was its conduit and active oracle. Even today Hyde's books on Celtic literature are worth reading. His *A Literary History of Ireland* appeared in 1899 and is a work of real sweep and inspiration. A smaller study, *The Story of Early Gaelic Literature*, came out in 1895, in which the kernel of Hyde's larger argument first appeared. Perhaps the best summary of his *History*, especially about bardic practices, is his *Irish Poetry*, an essay in Gaelic with English translation for the little volume of 1902. Finally, the whole of this tradition was wedged into an entry called "Bards (Irish)" that Hyde wrote for Hastings' *Encyclopaedia of Religion and Ethics*, including the following passage:[28]

> We know, in the first place, that the poet was regarded as possessed of powers sufficiently supernatural to make even princes tremble; for with a well-aimed satire he could raise boils and disfiguring blotches upon the countenance of his opponents, or even do them to death by it. This belief continued until the later Middle Ages; and, even down to the days of Dean Swift, the Irish poet was credited with the power of being able to rhyme at least rats and vermin to death. Again, the early Irish poet was, by virtue of his office, a judge in all cases of tribal disputes and in other matters. He was also, if not a Druid himself, probably closely allied with the Druidic order.

Hyde was an open advocate of Irish culture as it encouraged national identity. In his work there is a steady mix of research and excited speculation. These ideas were available to Yeats at the peak of his own concern for literary nationalism, and at a time when Hyde's scholarship was (as we would now say) state of the art. That Yeats and Hyde were often together is clear from Yeats's early letters. They also ran into each other at Coole Park as frequent guests of Lady Gregory. When later Hyde allowed political programs to use him as a figurehead, Yeats took a dim view. But in the beginning he had nothing but respect; in his *Memoirs* he calls Hyde "the man most important to the future."[29] He went so far as to have one of his *Hanrahan* stories translated into Gaelic by Hyde, hoping that in this way it "might pass into legend as though he [Hanrahan] were an historical character."[30]

The "Stories of Red Hanrahan" were written in 1897 and revised, with Lady Gregory's help, in 1907. There is little doubt that Yeats put into his creation of Hanrahan much of the bardic lore that he and Lady Gregory gathered on their excursions among the peasantry in Ireland's western counties. Hanrahan begins as "the hedge schoolmaster," and spends most of his time wandering "among the villages," the village of Ballylee included, "finding a welcome in every place for the sake of the old times and of his poetry and his learning." During his lifetime Hanrahan has visions, encounters the Sidhe, and cannot be asked to leave any house he visits because "he is a poet of the Gael, and you know well if you would put a poet of the Gael out of the house, he would put a curse on you." In the story entitled "Red Hanrahan's Curse," the poet blasts the neighborhood's old men and has the children sing it about. The curse makes an interesting poem, but more to the point is that Hanrahan's rite of composition mimics the method practiced in the bardic schools: "he went and lay down on the bed to make a poem or a praise or a curse. And it was not long he was in making it this time, for the power of the curse-making bards was upon him."[31]

The Hanrahan stories show the slant of Yeats's concern, and it seems fair to suppose that he invested some part of himself in these tales. [It has been suggested, in a psychoanalytic sort of way, that the development of the character of Red Hanrahan is the poet's hidden script for his own aspirations, and possibly it is.[32]] I would also guess that the figure of the outcast poet, as it emerged in Irish history from the seventeenth into the nineteenth century, was the historical ground for Yeats's praise

of beggars and visionary fools, "blind Raftery" in particular, the Gaelic
poet famous among the farms and villages of Galway.

Hanrahan and Raftery make their appearance together in "The
Tower," one of Yeats's central poems about his career as a poet. At age
sixty, Yeats laments physical debility and is troubled by how to conduct
himself. Section two opens with the poet pacing "upon the battlements,"
a defensive position in need of support—and thus the motive for the
next twelve stanzas: he will summon, as he often did, powers of assistance. Chief among them are Hanrahan and Raftery. Yeats refers to
Raftery's poem in praise of a young woman's beauty; certain men were
"maddened by those rhymes," and in a later stanza Yeats says that "if I
triumph I must make men mad." Next comes the story of Hanrahan
turning a hand of cards into a pack of hounds. With these fabulous
images in mind, Yeats goes on to ask a question of those he has summoned: Did they "rage / As I do against old age?" But of Hanrahan he
asks a further question—Does imagination dwell most on defeat or
victory?—and it is, finally, the figure of the bard that Yeats wants for
assistance through the "labyrinth" of self-doubt. He bids farewell to the
tribe he has summoned on these terms:

> Go therefore; but leave Hanrahan,
> For I need all his mighty memories.

Possibly these "mighty memories" include the whole of Ireland's past,
the heroes of bardic remembrance among them. At this point Yeats is
ready for the poem's finale, where he wills his "faith and pride" to
Ireland's poetic posterity. There is more to "The Tower" than my attention to symbolic action discloses; but by making the poem's resolution depend on help from Hanrahan and Raftery, consanguinity is
established between Yeats's poetic identity and his notion of Ireland's
bardic heritage.

This is what Yeats knew himself to be, an inheritor of powers very old
and very Irish. In confrontation with politics he relied on bardic practices, centrally on praise and blame, blessing and cursing, and then on
lament and celebration, remembrance and instruction, complaint, consolation, and the keeping of wisdom. All poets make use of bardic
resources in degree, but Yeats deployed them openly, in full force, and
was most effective with these poetic tools—and weapons—in hand. They

justified his calling and grounded his identity. They gave him the authority of a tradition that was undeniably grand and specifically Irish; and this ready tradition, in turn, was the source of his unusual confidence. Thus equipped, he could meet the world and know his audience. He could speak *to* and *for* and *against*. Moreover, as politics and the bardic stance emerge, the oppositional structure of Yeats's verse becomes more apparent: myth versus history; tragedy versus comedy; the crowd versus the lonely hero. He could assume poetry's importance in spite of politics—and then again because of politics.

Bardic practice does not restrict the poet's themes nor limit it to public occasions. Praise and blame are elementary or even elemental dispositions, and under their hegemony much else takes place. The bardic foundation of Yeats's poetry hinders neither the complexity of his art nor the range of private energies—thematic, symbolic—that Yeats sets going in his poems. In "Parnell's Funeral" moments of lament and blame are surpassed, in the end, by praise. These choices anchor the poet in relation to the world he speaks for and against, and also the world he speaks to. Once sure of his points of departure, he goes forward with a liberty the greater for the stability he enjoyed in setting forth. There might be several veins of concern, multiple beds of meaning, and much that transpires will be difficult to fathom.

Why, for example, does Yeats play out the drama of Parnell's downfall at this point in time, so many years after the event? The poem enacts a purgation of political sin, a cleansing that is national and private at once, but still—Why now? Possibly because lament for a dead leader is the occasion Yeats picks to broadcast his own quitting of politics. The poem is an elaborate rite of death and resurrection (Parnell's), a venting of despair (Yeats's), as well as a forum for bardic announcement. What Yeats declares is that from now on he will refuse the hospitality of any tribe—any party or ideological group—involved in Irish politics. Possibly, too, he feels that by identifying with the poem's hero (a symbolic action in any elegy) he partakes of the poem's regenerative blessings. His own "bare soul" having passed through Swift's dark grove is enriched by a bitter wisdom. We might even guess, as Auden once suggested, that in the end it's Yeats who eats of Parnell's heart.

Poetry of this kind is public and private at once. Threads of personal meaning can be traced so far and no further. For public issues, however, the use of bardic practices ought to include clear signals of social function—signs that an audience is part of the poem's occasion. In some final way, of course, the audience is anyone who takes delight and nourishment from what the poet has to say. More immediately, however, we can expect evidence of an auditor or addressee, named or implied. And this is, in fact, how Yeats proceeds. With poems of strict praise, the one spoken *of* is the one spoken *to*—for example, Maude Gonne in "Her Praise," which begins: "She is foremost of those that I would hear praised." The same can be said—speaking *of* as a means of speaking *to* —in poems that strictly blame or curse. "On Those That Hated 'The Playboy of the Western World,' 1907" is a poem aimed at the riotous defamers of Synge's play, and the delight in insult is plain to see:

> Once, when midnight smote the air,
> Eunuchs ran through Hell and met
> On every crowded street to stare
> Upon great Juan riding by:
> Even like these to rail and sweat
> Staring upon his sinewy thigh.

Yeats calls his enemies envious and vulgar, tells them to go to hell, and says they are lacking manly parts. As with much of bardic blaming, the poem attacks unworthy patronage, in this case the Abbey Theatre audience. In these instances the poet speaks to and about members of his own personal-professional world. Overall, Yeats's bardic "court" in-cludes the following: persons he has known (the Gregorys, Maude Gonne); and then people he has known about (Parnell, Raftery); then the heroic figures of the Irish nationalist tradition (Tone, Fitzgerald et al.); then names from literature and legend (Blake or Swift on the one hand, Fergus and Cuchulain on the other); and finally fictional characters (Hanrahan, Crazy Jane) of his own imagining. Oddly interesting are moments when Yeats seems to be speaking *with* those whom he is speaking about. In "All Souls' Night" he praises dead friends as a way of evoking their presence—for thus, one by one, he would "call" them.

About Yeats's bardic ambition there is, however, a pressing question. In the twentieth century, a time of artistic as well as political alienation, how can someone like Yeats set up as a bard? He can choose any persona he likes, of course, and with it an appropriate manner. More to the point, Yeats had the good (if troubled) fortune to live in Ireland, where the century's tumult had been enacted small-scale, amid allegiances still distressingly tribal, with the added excitement of a recently recovered

"Celtic" tradition. And then—like any post-traditional poet—he simply had to rally what he needed to fulfill the requirements of his art. A poem like "The Fisherman," written in 1914, may seem an odd choice to follow "Parnell's Funeral," but in one way they are similar. The process of lifting Parnell into Swift's high company took Yeats many years, and this same process is the theme of "The Fisherman." In both poems the heroic image evolves from its unheroic opposite, and is praised against a background of blame. Here are the first lines:

> Although I can see him still,
> The freckled man who goes
> To a grey place on a hill
> In grey Connemara clothes
> At dawn to cast his flies,
> It's long since I began
> To call up to the eyes
> This wise and simple man.

Yeats might have had someone particular in mind, but the figure here is all archetype, a dawn-light hero to be praised for his solitude and patient skill, virtues that confer (or so Yeats would have it) wisdom and simplicity. These are virtues against the grain of modern personality, elements of an image antithetical to the real, and thus the poem continues:

> All day I'd looked in the face
> What I had hoped 'twould be
> To write for my own race
> And the reality.

What is looked in the face is both the reality and what the poet "hoped 'twould be," the magical word being 'twould with its half-hidden it. Out of this mirror-like gap the fisherman begins to emerge, apart from the blameworthy crowd:

> The living men that I hate,
> The dead man that I loved,
> The craven man in his seat,
> The insolent unreproved,

> And no knave brought to book
> Who has won a drunken cheer.

"In scorn of this audience," Yeats summons an ideal recipient, someone fit to praise, and also someone glad for the gift of a poem:

> A man who does not exist,
> A man who is but a dream.

Yeats's concern for audience is constant, and much of his art depends on a bardic reciprocity whereby the poet summons a tribe even as the tribe has need of its poet. But how can an imaginary auditor suffice? The question of audience is crucial for poets in our century, especially for those who profess or attempt to take up bardic duties. In Yeats's case we should remember that, as a voice allied with the nationalist movement in politics and the arts, he had from early on a large and enthusiastic readership; at the turn of the century Ireland's literary consciousness was higher, more alert, than it would ever be again and Yeats often addressed the public—and expected to have an impact—by publishing his work in newspapers and popular magazines. Then too, he always had his friends; no modern poet has written more often or finely of loved ones and compatriots. Yeats, that is to say, was luckier than most; his tribe was never merely imaginary.

At the same time, however, he had a sort of genius for setting himself against prevailing opinion, especially in politics, and as a member of the Protestant Ascendancy he would always be apart from the Catholic majority in Ireland. These differences were pronounced to the degree that Yeats took seriously his role as bard to the Irishry; and here he did prefer to project an ideal audience, based on his embattled faith in what was possible to Ireland. In this latter sense, the lone figure in "The Fisherman" is the first member of a visionary company. Ten years later, in "The Tower," the poet begins by cursing his life, then goes on to praise his life, and ends by greeting—through naming—his once-and-future tribe:

> It is time that I wrote my will;
> I choose upstanding men
> That climb the streams until
> The fountain leap, and at dawn

> Drop their cast at the side
> Of dripping stone; I declare
> They shall inherit my pride,
> The pride of people that were
> Bound neither to Cause nor to State,
> Neither to slaves that were spat on,
> Nor to the tyrants that spat,
> The people of Burke and of Grattan.

The solitary fisherman has multiplied and formed alliance with a community of intellect beyond the shame of politics. This is Yeats's Anglo-Irish band of heroes that, in "The Seven Sages" especially, he liked to think of as his "tradition." Critics have been skeptical of a lineage so selective, but we might suppose that Yeats also had in mind an imagined court or tribe of the kind that any bard would value. (It's an interesting jolt to recognize that the last stanza of "Sailing to Byzantium," with its golden bird and drowsy Emperor, celebrates bardic practice—the court poet at work—in visionary terms.) Yeats's ideal audience becomes more elite as his political values become more aristocratic. And in this latter sense, Yeats's "tradition" begins with "The Fisherman," gathers head in "The Tower," and comes to resolution in "Under Ben Bulben," where the poet's will is a set of instructions passed on to those the poem evokes:

> Irish poets, learn your trade,
> Sing whatever is well made,
> Scorn the sort now growing up
> All out of shape from toe to top. . . .
> Cast your mind on other days
> That we in coming days may be
> Still the indomitable Irishry.

In sum, Yeats's audience finds itself named, or otherwise signified, in the rhetorical strategies of poem after poem. The poems I have mentioned carry with them their own scenes of reception, and they depend for their success on a rhetoric of address that creates its addressee or receiver. Yeats goes out of his way to let us know that he has an audience in mind, or that he wishes to include us in the tribal court he constructs for himself. And once his audience is right, praise follows.

Very rarely, however, did Yeats have the actual audience he wanted. Only in special circumstances does his embattled voice transcend the call to confrontation and address an audience from which no one is excluded—or at least no person Irish. One audience of this special kind was created by the Easter uprising. To that event Yeats responded with "Easter 1916," a poem often cited for its excellence. This famous example of poetry in the political vein is also a poem in the bardic mode. Much of its power derives from the bardic formalities Yeats used to speak for all of Ireland on this exceptional occasion.

The Easter revolt of 1916 had not been foreseen by Yeats, a circumstance that must have challenged his bardic prowess. He was in England and "fretted somewhat that he had not been consulted, had been left in ignorance of what was afoot."[33] Three years earlier he had thought the extravagances of romantic nationalism were dead, and in "September 1913" announced that the time of heroes was over:

> Romantic Ireland's dead and gone,
> It's with O'Leary in the grave.

Yeats had been expecting less and less from his compatriots at large. But from at large the uprising came; from men and women who had grown up on Yeats's own celebrations of heroic Ireland, especially his early and wildly popular political drama, *Cathleen ni Houlihan*, a play that insinuates the need for sacrificial blood ("They that have red cheeks will have pale cheeks for my sake") in Ireland's cause. A number of the rebellion's members Yeats knew personally, among them Thomas MacDonagh and Padraic Pearse. To Yeats MacDonagh dedicated his first book of poems; he also wrote a "rebel" play that was produced by The Abbey Theatre in 1908. Yeats's association with Pearse was closer and more profound. At St. Edna's School, Pearse taught Gaelic and the legends of heroic Ireland. Over the school's entrance he painted Cu-chulain's motto: "I care not though I were to live but one day and one night, if only my fame and my deeds live after me." Later Yeats would say, in a letter, that "the young men who got themselves [killed] in 1916 had the Irish legendary hero Cuchullain [sic] so much in their minds that the Government has celebrated the event with a bad statue,"[34] the monument now in the Dublin Post Office. Pearse had a play staged at the Abbey and several times Yeats loaned the theater to St. Edna's students for benefit performances. There is no doubt that Pearse revered Yeats; and from Pearse came the call to rebellion. As Yeats put it without quite seeing the point: "There is going to be trouble—Pearse is going through Ireland preaching the blood sacrifice."[35] These men—along with John MacBride, the estranged husband of Maude Gonne, and the labor leader James Connolly—were among the heroes-to-be, the small souls grown magnificent under siege in the Dublin Post Office, and afterward shot by the British.

In stanza one of "Easter 1916" Yeats presents the leaders of the uprising as "them," a group of Dubliners such as the poet knew and moved among daily:

> I have met them at close of day
> Coming with vivid faces
> From counter or desk among grey
> Eighteenth-century houses.

Their lives conspire with the "casual comedy," or seem to; yet from this place "where [only] motley is worn" the uprising came. And it hit Yeats with greater impact than at first he could handle. In a letter to Lady Gregory, he described his initial reaction: "I had no idea that any public event could so deeply move me—and I am very despondent about the future."[36] That was in May 1916, when Yeats feared involving his art in issues directly political. But politics had intruded profoundly; he was unable to forswear his own deep feeling and the poem was finished in September.

In stanza two, the heroes of the uprising are individualized, but only as they appeared *before* the event—Constance Gore-Booth, who in her youth "rode to harriers"; Padraic Pearse, who "kept a school / And rode our winged horse"; Thomas MacDonagh just "coming into his force"; and John McBride, who "had done most bitter wrong." In stanzas one and two Yeats does the bardic work of announcing the heroes he intends to praise, but without naming them, and so far the verse—except for the visionary codas—has been descriptive only. But then an abrupt change occurs. Stanza three is wholly metaphorical, suggesting that the poem's formal movement is from "comic" scenes of desk and street to the "tragic" dais of sacrifice, from historic to prophetic envisionment. The poem likewise moves from blame to highly dignified praise. Much of the matter in stanzas one and two would be, in other poems, solely occasion for blame. To call someone a "drunken, vainglorious lout" is exactly what the bards meant by "nail[ing] a name on a man." In normal times, this kind of blame (and praise) would be enough. But in this poem the point is that normal times are suspended. Something extraordinary has burst upon the scene, transforming everything. Yeats brings up, and then overrides, his job of casting blame and gradually rises to praise purely. The condition of acceptance becomes so thorough that even the English—who "may keep faith"—are given the benefit of doubt. This generous stateliness of mood is possible because on this occasion the poet addresses his perfect audience. For once Yeats isn't counting his enemies. He leaves off bitterness and is reconciled with everyone, seeing instantly that in this the whole of Ireland shares:

> Now and in time to be,
> Wherever green is worn.

A condition of atonement informs "Easter 1916," and perhaps the sudden release from factiousness is reason enough to speak of astonishing change. But of the poem's four stanzas, three end in versions of the famous refrain, and it is clearly the transformation itself that is being praised as well as underscored by prophetic announcement:

> All changed, changed utterly:
> A terrible beauty is born.

Yeats had a habit of using "all" as a quick way to universalize his themes, but here the "all" is strictly meant. Every aspect of Irish life had been altered in the wake of the uprising, for good and for ill; and while critics like to stress the latter, playing on the reservations Yeats voiced in letters, there are no lines or sets of lines that stand up to, or against, the "terrible beauty" of the poem's refrain. What, then, does Yeats mean by this insistent chant? Very possibly, that the heroic dream has been reborn, compounded of honor for blood sacrifice and faith in the power of martyrdom. These energies are terrible (the violence) and beautiful (the poetic idea of heroism Yeats consistently praises). What saves this event, in Yeats's view, is that the resolve of sacrifice remained wholly ideal. The uprising was not undertaken in a spirit of practical politics. Knowing they were outflanked and outgunned, the rebels could not hope for an actual seizing of power. They were there as O'Rahilly was there:

> "Because I helped to wind the clock
> I come to hear it strike."

We might therefore ask, as Yeats does, what else besides death is there to announce? Or in that death, what spirit? What other triumph was at stake in a rebellion where defeat was foreknown? Might was not on their side; but the rebels had, instead, the tradition of romantic nation-alism. They possessed the compelling authority of long-praised examples, the empowerment of figures like Cuchulain first of all. And if so, the uprising was invested with bardic energies. Yeats says as much in one of his last poems:

> When Pearse summoned Cuchulain to his side,
> What stalked through the Post Office?

If we conceive of poetry in postmodernist terms or in the fashion of practical criticism, we shall conclude that it can have no bearing upon life or action's deeper passions. But if we come at poetry from the bardic point of view, and assume a social-political situation in which the poet stands to his audience as the bard once stood to his tribe, then it begins to be possible that a connection exists between poetry and action *on occasion*. Yeats's "Easter 1916" is a praise-poem and its deeper theme is the splendor of the poetic idea as it transforms political action. About the "poetic idea" itself, furthermore, there is no shade of doubt; to look back upon the long torment of Irish history is to know that in Ireland one idea prevails, or so Yeats believed. In "The Literary Movement in Ireland," an important early essay, he wrote: "The popular poetry of England celebrates her victories, but the popular poetry of Ireland re-members only defeats and defeated persons. A ballad that is in every little threepenny and sixpenny ballad book asks if Ireland has no pride in her Lawrences and Wellingtons, and answers that they belong to the Empire and not to Ireland, whose 'heart beats high' for men who died in exile or in prison; and this ballad is the type of all."[37]

It was certainly the "type" for Yeats, the kind of heroism that stirred his imagination most and, during Easter week of 1916, the spirit that inspired not only "Easter 1916," but also "Sixteen Dead Men," "On A

Political Prisoner," and "The Rose Tree." The last of these ends with
the resolve of sacrifice that informed the uprising:

> O plain as plain can be
> There's nothing but our own red blood
> Can make a right Rose Tree.

But actions of armed rebellion—especially those in which the rebels
are at strategic disadvantage—do not reach the stage of no-return without imagination, broadly alive and fiercely focused, to carry them. Such
actions will be bloody and Yeats's principal care, expressed in "Parnell's
Funeral" and lodged at the heart of "Easter 1916," is to have violence
informed by the poetic idea of sacrifice, and by the heroic resolve that
sacrifice entails. This alone makes violence acceptable in Yeats's view.
Quite possibly, therefore, the "terrible beauty" celebrated in this poem
is a highly peculiar union of politics and poetry. It bears repeating,
however, that for Yeats the only case in which a poetic idea informs a
political action without the latter betraying the former is when the
resolve of sacrifice is embraced as its own end. There will be no poems
of praise for the victors but only for those on the losing side—or rather,
the side that in the immediate event goes down.

This attitude toward sacrifice is a part of Yeats too often played down
or denied, as if by going on and on about "heroic death" he could not
mean real blood. But he did; he also believed that defeat is the condition
for heroism and becomes thereby a prophetic force. That this was his
conviction is plain in his praise for Robert Emmet: "Emmet had hoped
to give Ireland the gift of a victorious life, an accomplished purpose.
He failed in that, but he gave her what was almost as good—his heroic
death. . . . And out of his grave his ideal has risen incorruptible. His
martyrdom has changed the whole temper of the Irish nation. England
celebrates her successes. . . . In Ireland we sing the men who fell nobly
and thereby made an idea mighty."[38] In our time good poets won't be
praising winners. Yeats makes this plain in "A Model for the Laureate":

> The Muse is mute when public men
> Applaud a modern throne.

I stress the centrality of defeat because beauty cannot be terrible, nor
can terror call forth an exalted response, unless the beholder stands

against the power that directly does the destroying. And it's exactly here that Yeats develops his notion of the sublime. Power is in every case the ground of exaltation, but there is vast difference between acceptance of external power (identification with the aggressor) and the kind of counterpower arising from within in the moment of terror. This crucial difference suggests that "terrible beauty" is Yeats's version of the *political sublime*, something as fitly Anglo-Irish as Edmund Burke saying "I know of nothing sublime which is not some modification of power,"[39] and as penetrating as Kant's notion of sublimity in which fear and grandeur meet to quiet the will and purge the self of pettiness. Speaking of boundless forces like the ocean in storm (Yeats's "murderous innocence of the sea"), Kant described sublime encounters this way: "we readily call these objects sublime, because they raise the forces of the soul above the height of vulgar commonplace, and discover within us a power of resistance of quite another kind, which gives us courage to be able to measure ourselves against the seeming omnipotence of nature."[40]

This "violence within," pushing back against "violence without," is a victory got from the knowledge of possible ruin, and the feeling that arises is not fear but sudden elevation. If one faces and stands up to terror, one discovers resources of one's own, "a power of resistance of quite another kind"; and it's this interior potency, in Kant's view, that gives us the courage to confront forces capable of extinguishing us. This isn't always possible, of course; but it is, all the same, the crucial point. The sublime moment is the key to human dignity because, in terms Yeats would approve, it provokes a necessary pride. As Kant says, it "saves humanity in our own person from humiliation, even though as mortal men we have to submit to external violence."[41]

In "Easter 1916" Yeats twice announces the advent of "terrible beauty," then turns to praise the agent of transformation. Stanza three is the singular section of the poem, the only sustained metaphorical part, the point where the poetic idea of sacrifice is introduced in its image of the stone and then connected to the power or agency of spirit that during the uprising showed itself equal to the forces of empire. Stanza three begins:

> Hearts with one purpose alone
> Through summer and winter seem
> Enchanted to a stone
> To trouble the living stream.

By the end of the stanza we know that "the stone's in the midst of all," and also that it stands in relation to "hearts with one purpose." Like the stone, this purpose and the hearts that hold it do not change with the seasons or the eroding motions of time. Everything else—horse and rider, cloud, stream, the moorcocks and hens—signifies life going on, ordinary and unheroic, the humdrum stream of Heraclitean flux. But just here, "in the midst of all," stands the stone. In moments of near-miracle it instigates another kind of change, the kind that transforms the human world by altering our sense of destiny. We might conclude that heroic potential always exists, at least in its poetic idea, and that no one knows when next it will break forth. We might also conclude, in Yeats's more metaphysical vein, that beyond the multitudinous surface of daily living the great historical gyres continually turn.

At first glance "Easter 1916" asserts that fundamental changes in our sense of destiny are owed more to events than to ideas; but *political* events are informed by ideas of their own. Yeats might scorn political beliefs in the abstract, but he saw instantly that the idea behind the Easter uprising was the poetic distillation of long experience, and that when it found its occasion, things did in fact change drastically. But if the poetic idea sometimes works wonders, its costly side effect is a hardness of heart in those who embrace it and a depleting impatience in those who love its promise. Thus stanza four begins:

> Too long a sacrifice
> Can make a stone of the heart.
> O when may it suffice?

The poem's last stanza is where critics find evidence to set Yeats at a distance from the violent action and obvious blood the poem commends. But Yeats is not at a distance. The objections usually cited—that sacrifice is "excessive," that "dreaming" can get you killed, that the British might be trustworthy and heroism "needless"—are raised to be transformed. The terms "needless" and "excess," as they appear in the poem, are not liabilities; within the framework of heroic striving they are virtues, and if needless excess allowed the uprising to embrace the poetic idea, then to "know they dreamed and are dead" is redemptive. To quiet doubts that might edge toward blame, Yeats fastens on hard fact ("No, no, not night but death") and makes it the unqualified ground for final praise—

precisely the tactic he used to insure challenged praise in "Sixteen Dead
Men":

> You say that we should still the land
> Till Germany's overcome;
> But who can talk of give and take,
> Now Pearse is deaf and dumb?
> And is their logic to outweigh
> MacDonagh's bony thumb?

"Sixteen Dead Men" is an angry poem as "Easter 1916" is not. There
Yeats addressed an opposition to the action he praised. "Easter 1916"
envisions no opposing element. To everyone on this occasion the poet
says that "our part [is to] murmur name upon name, / As a mother
names her child" in sleep. The heroic names, once the poet gives them
public life, will nourish from the cradle Ireland's dreams. Like the stone
at the center, the poetic idea is everywhere on this occasion, shared by
the dead, by the living, by the living with the dead. In the last lines the
present is projected into the future ("Now and in time to be"); the
implication is that the dream will be known and shared *because* the poet
sets it forth in verse.

In "Easter 1916," Yeats was aware of his own bardic dignity more
than he was in most of his poems. The roles of poet and audience are
assigned; "we" is used twice, the "I" seven times and twice in an overtly
bardic manner. In stanza two the poet says, "I number him in the song."
Then in the great last lines of the poem, he shifts from his reckoning
of communal responsibility ("our part," "We know") to an obligation
solely his own as bard to the Irishry. With these distinctions in place,
the formality of bardic utterance becomes the certification for what is
announced in the poem's last lines. Yeats names the heroes in a way
that celebrates community, and in a mood of muted exaltation offers a
prophecy to the nation:

> I write it out in a verse—
> MacDonagh and MacBride
> And Connolly and Pearse
> Now and in time to be,
> Wherever green is worn,

Are changed, changed utterly:
A terrible beauty is born.

The formal progress of "Easter 1916" makes clear Yeats's strategy to heighten an expectation that shall then be fulfilled. He begins with "them," as if they were unnamed Dubliners merely. Then individual lives are cited, but without names. In stanza three they are elevated and set apart by the emblematic grandeur of the stone, but still unnamed. Finally, in the fourth and last stanza, the audience is told "to murmur name upon name," an instruction that anticipates the public success of the bardic naming in progress. Only *then*, after having foreseen this ceremonial moment through the whole of the poem, does Yeats write "it" out in a verse—as if these names were everything, which in the poem they are; as if a sacred rite were brought to conclusion, which in the poem it is.

Like many poems in response to political events, this one does not indicate or establish in the poem itself what its occasion is. The title sets the scene and sounds the theme of resurrection, but historical context must be found elsewhere—if, that is, the reader is not a member of the poet's tribe. No one ignorant of Ireland's torment could surmise, from the information in the poem, what the poet celebrates, although one might, as I suggested, determine the intended audience. This kind of obliquity is not unusual, not in Yeats nor in political poetry more generally. But here the omission works to enforce the poet's closeness with his tribe—those who know. This rapport accounts for the poem's compromise in response to an event so momentous. And the mood of atonement, in turn, allows for the simplicity of the poem's formal arrangements. The three- and four-beat lines are modest and exact; the rhyming is hushed, hardly noticed—not an easy feat for the shortness of line—and the rhyme scheme quietly stitches a pattern of quatrains into the larger stanzas. These minor traits of line and rhyme call attention to the fact that "Easter 1916" is a political ballad, a joining of praise and lament that, in Ireland, has been the bardic way.

·IV·

Yeats and *Hysterica Passio*

With their vehement reaction against the despotism
of fact, with their sensuous nature, their manifold striving, their adverse destiny, their immense calamities,
the Celts are the prime authors of this vein of piercing
regret and passion. . . .
—Matthew Arnold, 1867

The Easter uprising of 1916 was the only time Yeats saw his notion
of the poetic idea—what I have called the resolve of sacrifice or
the heroism of defeat—enter history directly, and with an integrity
unshaken by circumstance. Soon the memory of that event would merge
with a theology of bloodletting that haunts the Irish even now. Yeats
went on to publish "Easter 1916," along with "The Rose Tree" and
"Sixteen Dead Men," in 1920, in the middle of the Anglo-Irish war—
a bold political maneuver that did not stop short of praising blood. To
revive the mystique of the rebellion and turn it to account against the
British was his aim. But if the poetic idea had worked for colonial
conflict, it was of little use to what came next. Once Ireland's civil war
got under way, Yeats saw his vision of "terrible beauty" become a shame-
less horror. As he said in 1922, "Perhaps there is nothing so dangerous
to a modern state, when politics take [sic] the place of theology, as a
bunch of martyrs. A bunch of martyrs (1916) were the bomb and we
are living in the explosion."[1]

In later years Yeats questioned his role in Ireland's violent rise to
nationhood. He knew "whatever flames upon the night / Man's own
resinous heart has fed," and knew his work had helped inflame that
heart:

> Did that play of mine send out
> Certain men the English shot?
> Did words of mine put too great strain
> On that woman's reeling brain?

From "The Man and the Echo," these are questions a poet sensible to
bardic obligation would ask. They are also examples of Yeats's preference
for rhetorical questioning, a much-used strategy allowing him to put
forth his convictions in suspended form and goad the tribe to agreement.
The rest of the poem suggests that they are night-thoughts as well ("I
lie awake night after night"), the kind of what-ifs at three in the morning
that make the dark seem darker. The power of language is at issue, and
that Yeats troubles himself suggests his care for the ongoing way his
words would be "modified," as Auden put it, "in the guts of the living."

Bardic responsibility is therefore part of it; but when *this* poet ex-
amines his relation to the tribe he has something more in mind, something deeper and more darkly shared. In Yeats's case, despite love of
country and a steady will to bless, there's no doubting that his deepest
disposition was his proneness to rage. Like Thersites among the Greeks
at Troy, Yeats thrived on execration. This might have blighted his art
but did not; one of the foremost things about Yeats is that he is splendid
to the degree he holds his daemon in check. I have already mentioned
the exceptional calm of "Easter 1916," a tranquillity unusual for Yeats
in that so much of his work enacts a drama of opposites, keeping the
poems impassioned and the poet in a fervor. The remarkable thing is
the degree to which Yeats and much of his Irish audience were given
to seizures of political hate:

> popular rage,
> *Hysterico passio* dragged this quarry down.

Public passion of this kind isn't special to Ireland, but is the outcome
of extremity anywhere. Even so, to take Yeats seriously is to come away
with a feeling for the poet and the Ireland of his time that is thick with
political wrath. He suggests that dreaming too often defeated can be
terrible—as the civil war was terrible—in its outcome:

> We had fed the heart on fantasies,
> The heart's grown brutal from the fare;

More substance in our enmities
Than in our love.

Yeats is speaking for the nation and himself, as well he might, knowing his daemon with almost fearsome candor. In "Remorse for Intemperate Speech," dated August 28, 1931, he blames himself in a keen determined sort of way, but the sound is closer to praise than to blame or remorse. I quote all three stanzas, the better to appreciate the way the end-lines speak obsession:

> I ranted to the knave and fool,
> But outgrew that school,
> Would transform the part,
> Fit audience found, but cannot rule
> My fanatic heart.
>
> I sought my betters: though in each
> Fine manners, liberal speech,
> Turned hatred into sport,
> Nothing said or done can reach
> My fanatic heart.
>
> Out of Ireland have we come.
> Great hatred, little room,
> Maimed us at the start.
> I carry from my mother's womb
> A fanatic heart.

The poem is part confession, part curse, its hardness made the harder by the line "my fanatic heart" having (as Yeats says in a page note) only two beats. The poet unburdens himself by placing the onus of his curse on Ireland as a whole, moving from "I" to "we" and from "my" heart to "a" heart. The result seems almost prideful. Or is it despair? If the latter, then it's of the kind that Kierkegaard called "demonic despair," the kind that vaunts in its own damnation as, for example, Satan does in *Paradise Lost*. Is the poem a plaint or a boast—or both together? Nothing, the poet tells us, can rule or reach a core of brazen anger at the heart of him. That, I believe, is the stark unlovely truth about Yeats. But at the same time I take the hint from "mother's womb" to suggest

that although Yeats was a large and inveterate hater, his portion of
"Celtic ferocity" was also his mother-wit, the dark strain in his vision
that was his motive, often, for metaphor.

Perhaps I overstate. In a poet whose capacity to bless was also great,
hatred may be muted or transmuted by the interplay of praise and blame.
And Yeats did often "bless." The word and its variants appears some
fifty times in his poetry. In "A Prayer On Going into My House," for
example, the poem begins:

> God grant a blessing on this tower and cottage
> And on my heirs.

The occasion is a happy one, the Norman tower Yeats purchased in
June 1917 being now, in October 1918, ready to inhabit. The poem
ends with a playful curse:

> . . . and should some limb of the devil
> Destroy the view by cutting down an ash
> That shades the road, or setting up a cottage
> Planned in a government office, shorten his life,
> Manacle his soul upon the Red Sea bottom.

Ten years later, in "Blood and the Moon," the blessing and the curse
are more serious—and harder to sort out:

> Blessed be this place,
> More blessed still this tower;
> A bloody, arrogant power
> Rose out of the race
> Uttering, mastering it,
> Rose like these walls from these
> Storm-beaten cottages—
> In mockery I have set
> A powerful emblem up,
> And sing it rhyme upon rhyme
> In mockery of a time
> Half dead at the top.

What had intervened, amid much else, was the terror of the civil war, and it's in "Meditations in Time of Civil War" (1923) that Yeats makes one of his most extreme curses. Here he does his best to bless his house, his table, his descendants; yet with his visionary sense of "Coming Emptiness" he fears his children may betray the place and tradition his work of a lifetime would give them. Should that come to pass,

> May this laborious stair and this stark tower
> Become a roofless ruin that the owl
> May build in the cracked masonry and cry
> Her desolation to the desolate sky.

Only in "Nineteen Hundred and Nineteen," in the section on mockery, does Yeats elsewhere utter a curse so severe. His daemon was often provoked, sometimes beyond the help of blessing. And then the hard sayings came. To think otherwise is to mistake Yeats and not to know his art, or its kind, or the dark fount from which its famous power sprang.

As critics like to point out, Yeats had at least two views on every issue, the outcome of his attraction to antinomies. His attitude toward hatred was true to that form. Sometimes he praised it, sometimes he condemned it. In "Poetry and Tradition," an early essay, he takes a surprisingly splendid view. Criticizing Maude Gonne for too much engagement in "little" enmities, he goes on to say: "All movements are held together more by what they hate than by what they love, for love separates and individualises and quiets, but the nobler movements, the only movements on which literature can found itself, hate great and lasting things."[2] We get some idea of what Yeats means by "great and lasting things" in "A General Introduction for My Work," one of his later essays, where he argues that the historical conflict between Ireland and England, so replete with misery and failure, is the ground of the hatred he finds in himself: "No people hate as we do in whom that past is always alive; there are moments when hatred poisons my life and I accuse myself of effeminacy because I have not given it adequate expression. . . . I am like the Tibetan monk who dreams at his initiation that he is eaten by a wild beast and learns on waking that he himself is eater and eaten. This is Irish hatred and solitude, the hatred of human life that made

Swift write *Gulliver* and the epitaph upon his tomb, that can still make us wag between extremes and doubt our sanity."[3]

Yeats praises Parnell by saying "through Jonathan Swift's dark grove he passed," and the affiliation of hatred with eating or being devoured might also suggest why the author of "A Modest Proposal" was chief among Yeats's Anglo-Irish heroes. "Swift's Epitaph" is Yeats's homage to a species of rage that in his view is exemplary, a version of political *virtu*:

> Swift has sailed into his rest;
> Savage indignation there
> Cannot lacerate his breast.
> Imitate him if you dare,
> World-besotten traveller; he
> Served human liberty.

If Yeats's capacity for anger is understood in the wider context of Irish history, and if to that is added his horror of impotence in any form, another perspective opens on his readiness to arm his poems with rage. In the "Introduction" to his edition of *The Oxford Book of Modern Verse*, Yeats said he did not include "poems written in the midst of the great war"—work by Wilfred Owen, for example—because these poets felt bound "to plead the suffering of their men [and] passive suffering is not a theme for poetry."[4] There is very little depiction of suffering in Yeats's poetry, although much pain is taken for granted. More to the point, the Christian exhortation to accept suffering and bear it with humility is an abnegation, for Yeats, of necessary pride. Ireland loves its martyrs, but the pagan or tragic sense of life Yeats celebrates permits no cult of the victim. (In this he is very unmodern, and at odds with more recent Irish poets, Seamus Heaney in particular.) The substantial irony is that while Yeats's heroic ethic rejects the pathos of suffering and defeat, his atavistic politics compels him always into no-win situations. His solution, his way out, has everything to do with the active attitude he takes in his art. Rather than be cowed or wear blood on his sleeve, he chooses instead to praise the heroism of defeat on the one hand, and on the other to rail, blame, curse, accuse, and generally thrive on rage. He will *not* be passive, he will *not* feel powerless. Rather, he takes up an honored stance and performs an honored office. He exercises his bardic right, long blessed by Irish example, to savage indignation.

The numerical instance of angry poems, of hate songs plain and simple, is as manifest as other voices in Yeats's work, often within poems that register blame and praise by turns or as one amid several voices in discordant chorus—lines, for example, in "Under Ben Bulben," Yeats's bardic farewell:

> Know that when all words are said
> And a man is fighting mad,
> Something drops from eyes long blind,
> He completes his partial mind,
> For an instant stands at ease,
> Laughs aloud, his heart at peace.

Yeats liked to be "fighting mad." At the same time, however, he was often of a mind to condemn this kind of passion. Perhaps the lines best known, and most often used by critics to defend Yeats from himself, come from "A Prayer for My Daughter." Here he says, "to be choked with hate / May well be of all evil chances chief," and he concludes by affirming that "hatred driven hence, / The soul recovers radical innocence." Certainly Yeats knew the effects of political rancor, but rather than blame himself, his habit was to put the burden on women who had entered politics. Maude Gonne is called "an old bellows full of angry wind." The mind of Constance Gore-Booth becomes "a bitter, an abstract thing." Yeats projects his own opinionated mind upon women whom he would rather see, in the old Pre-Raphaelite way, as icons of mysterious beauty. His constant instruction is to avoid contention. His constant promise is a ceremonious grace to be gained. These are blessings he would like to have, but cannot manage, for himself.

Yeats had plenty of reason to know that political wrath is dangerous energy. What saves him is the responsibility—and even more, the formality—that comes with his bardic obligation to cast blame. When he curses in a fit of rage he condemns abuses worth the curse. When he blames women for indulging in public anger, he produces a critique of habits harmful to himself or anyone. Either way the poetry gains. A hatred so primal, however, argues more than thematic vigor, more than bardic authority. There is also, as Conor Cruise O'Brien has suggested, hatred's sheer prophetic power in Yeats's case.[5] O'Brien argues that Yeats's extraordinary talent for hate put the poet in touch with the monstrous capacity for hatred emerging all across Europe—the national self-hatred of Russia under Stalin, of Germany under Hitler, or the way lesser nations, France, Italy, the Balkans, allowed the "growing murderousness of the world"[6] a stranglehold upon their own abysmal destinies. O'Brien quotes the passage I cited earlier from Yeats's "A General Introduction to My Work," and goes on to quote these further remarks from the same essay:[7]

> When I stand upon O'Connell Bridge in the half-light and notice that discordant architecture, all those electric signs, where modern heterogeneity has taken physical form, a vague hatred comes up out of my own dark and I am certain that wherever in Europe there are minds strong enough to lead others the same vague hatred arises; in four or five or in less generations this hatred will have issued in violence and imposed some kind of rule of kindred. I cannot know the nature of that rule, for its opposite fills the light; all I can do to bring it nearer is to intensify my hatred.

Yeats's view of Dublin in 1937 expresses the despair of national destiny he announced in "Parnell's Funeral"—a revealing, or even damning, moment of horror at the modern world's gross discord. Yet one appreciates these remarks for their honesty. Yeats's candor is the more valuable for the connection he makes between his own political nihilism, born of defeat, and the furious nihilism, born of political vacuum, that would soon flatten Europe and change the world utterly. Yeats, who died in January 1939, was right more deeply than he had the time to know. His great prophetic poem "The Second Coming" is remarkable for the force of its forecast, and also for the precision of Yeats's instinct for political catastrophe: ·

> Things fall apart; the centre cannot hold;
> Mere anarchy is loosed upon the world,
> The blood-dimmed tide is loosed, and everywhere
> The ceremony of innocence is drowned;
> The best lack all conviction, while the worst
> Are full of passionate intensity.

O'Brien concludes that his capacity for rage gave Yeats, more than other poets of the time (except perhaps Brecht, also a hater), the visionary means to grasp the political character of the century he lived in—which is largely, I believe, why the poetry of Yeats continues to strike us as news that stays news. O'Brien sums it up this way:[8]

> The 'fanatic heart', an unusual capacity for hatred and an unusual experience of it, probably made him more sensitive and more responsive to the 'telepathic waves' coming from Europe than other writers in English seem to have been. The forces in him that responded to the hatred, cruelty and violence welling up in Europe produced the prophetic images of 'The Second Coming' and the last part of 'Nineteen Hundred and Nineteen.'

The demonic element in Yeats cannot be ignored, in particular his share in the political passion he named, with mingled fascination and disgust, *hysterica passio*. Yeats took the phrase from *King Lear* (II, iv, 57), where the old king first detects the madness welling up within him. Lear has lost his kingdom and his kingly powers. He has exiled Cordelia and Kent, and now sits open to disasters that are greater than human agency but are still, in no small part, of his own instigation. Foretelling the whole of his mad rage on the heath, Lear says:

> O how this mother swells up toward my heart.
> *Hysterica passio!* Down, thou climbing sorrow!

Shakespeare got his terms from Harsnet's treatise on demonic possession, a source that Yeats might have appreciated. But the surest gloss is the spectacle of *Lear* itself—the crazed wedding of storm and madness on the heath; the ruling metaphors of blindness and monstrosity; the indissoluble mix of personal and political emotion; and not least, in this darkest of tragedies, the ubiquitous rhetoric of cursing. Such are the symptoms of politics gone mad with rage. The peculiar horror of *hysterica passio* is that it engulfs its cause; it consumes everything it embraces and feeds upon itself but, like the world before creation, remains without form and void. To think of historical examples—Robespierre's Terror or the Stalinist purges—is to behold the underside of apocalypse.

Yeats uses this peculiar phrase to deepen the view we take, presuming immunity, toward political fanaticism generally. Rarely have victims of rabid politics survived, or recovered sufficiently to testify to symptoms that arise from hysteria of this collective kind. In his last poem about Maude Gonne, he imagines her eternalized by art, her soul forever facing the "*hysterica passio* of its own emptiness." That Yeats himself was subject to this affliction means that he was daemon-driven but more exactly that a principal problem for his art was how to handle it, how to seize to art's advantage "the uncontrollable mystery on the bestial floor." No poet, after all, can hope for clarity of vision while caught up in frenzy. Possibly this explains why so many poets in our century prefer to believe that political passions cannot matter. To decide otherwise is to risk confronting a *hysterica passio* destructive to art and life both. Yeats, to his credit, did confront it. He took the risk, and through it turned his art into its great maturity.

The commonplace about Yeats is that he started a dreamer in the languid ornate style of Pre-Raphaelite aestheticism, but that he then revised himself—*Responsibilities*, the volume of 1914, is the turning point usually cited—and thereafter became tougher and more direct, as if speaking *to* someone. As he himself put it, his early style was "dream-laden," but by 1902 he was starting to change: "My work has got more masculine. It has more salt in it."[9] Critics who prefer Yeats's occult speculations point to the emergence of an "anti-self" as the circumstance that changed his style. Critics who think poets only respond to the goings-on of other poets attribute the change to Ezra Pound, who, from around 1912 to about 1916, was often in Yeats's company. Doubtless Pound helped; but Yeats had embarked upon a major revision of his earlier poems in 1908, and the mature style of his later poetry is plainly visible in such pre-Poundian work as "The Fascination of What's Difficult," written no later than March 1910:

> My curse on plays
> That have to be set up in fifty ways,
> On the day's war with every knave and dolt,
> Theatre business, management of men.

The endless ordeal of "theatre business" brings us closer to the truth where, to begin with, the writing of plays—the requirements of speech responsive to situation; the need for language alive with the force of its occasion—accounts for part of the change in Yeats's style. He and his friends founded the Irish National Theatre Society in 1902, followed by The Abbey Theatre two years later, and by 1908 Yeats had a dozen plays to his credit. That writing for the stage accounts in part for Yeats's stylistic shift seems certain. But there would also be the social and political "business" of Dublin theater, the "day's war with every knave and dolt." The Irish had never had a theater, and Yeats expected drama to do great things for the nation. The author of *Cathleen ni Houlihan* was pleased, moreover, to produce drama involving politics. But he was besieged by people insisting that a play was not "political" unless its value as propaganda was declared outright, nor would the strident sectors of the Dublin audience—the press and the burgeoning middle class—tolerate portraits of Irish character not cast in saintly light.

The history of Yeats's disillusionment involved more than I can recount here. The point to keep in mind is that once Yeats came into his own as poet and playwright and then director of The Abbey Theatre, he possessed real power but ran into nonstop resistance from every side. And gradually his rage kindled. He saw Maude Gonne hissed off the stage for daring to separate from her husband. He saw Synge's *Playboy of the Western World* answered by riots and Synge dead, in 1909, at the age of forty-five. Other of Yeats's cherished friends, Lady Gregory included, were reviled by the press. The audience Yeats hoped to inspire with heroic ideals was showing instead a penchant for bigotry and spite. During this same period, further cause for bitterness came with Hugh Lane's attempt to build an art gallery and donate his valuable private collection to the nation, an act of largesse defeated by rancor and rebuff in a sequence of shameful events lasting into 1913. About the Lane affair Yeats wrote some of his finest early political verse. In "To a Shade" he calls to Parnell and, ringing praise against blame, curses the "pack" for once more dragging down a benefactor:

> A man
> Of your own passionate serving kind who had brought
> In his full hands what, had they only known,
> Had given their children's children loftier thought,
> Sweeter emotion, working in their veins
> Like gentle blood, has been driven from the place,
> And insult heaped upon him for his pains,
> And for his open-handedness, disgrace. . . .

The poem is dated September 19, 1913, just when the design for Lane's Dublin museum was rejected, causing Yeats to say: "I had not thought I could feel so bitterly over any public event."[10] Decidedly, his dream of a nation insuring its "children's children loftier thought" was foundering. Approaching his fiftieth year, Yeats saw Ireland's heroic tradition abandoned, the public import of his own work cancelled. Now it was he wrote "September 1913," one of the poems of "bitter wisdom" that makes *Responsibilities* his first important book:

> Was it for this the wild geese spread
> The grey wing upon every tide;
> For this that all that blood was shed,
> For this Edward Fitzgerald died,
> And Robert Emmet and Wolfe Tone,
> All that delirium of the brave?

"The wild geese" is Ireland's name for a military elite that held out against the British after the Gaelic chieftains fled in 1607, but that finally departed for courtly service in Europe. Yeats, too, felt forced to abandon home ground. And because he was proud and quick-tempered, because he loved the fight but found himself outflanked, years of anger swelled into a rage that set him contending with attacks of *hysterica passio*. That this was his own especial daemon is not the least in doubt. Here is how he describes it: "The feeling is always the same: a consciousness of energy, of certainty, and of transforming power stopped by a wall, by something one must either submit to or rage against helplessly. It often alarms me; is it the root of madness?"[11] Yeats is describing a profoundly political emotion. When he speaks of *hysterica passio*, he knows what he means. And he knew it would destroy him if the one weapon always his, his great gift for language, did not provide rescue.

Rage controlled is the circumstance of power as we feel it in Yeats's language. He said in his memoirs, "I had to subdue a kind of Jacobin rage. I escaped from it all as a writer through my sense of style."[12] And in a letter to Dorothy Wellesley, speaking of the power in his art, he said: "[it] comes from the fact that the speakers are holding down violence or madness—'down Hysterica passio'. All depends on the completeness of the holding down, on the stirring of the beast underneath."[13] This is the deep and final dynamic of the stylistic change so often remarked as the factor that turned Yeats to greatness. Fundamental to everything else about Yeats is the intimate degree to which political

experience is integral to his genius. His confrontation with politics pre-
cipitated a crisis that, by resorting to his art to save him, saved his art
and brought his bardic powers to full exercise. He always insisted that
heroism is born of self-struggle and self-overcoming. This was his struggle, and in his art we see the overcoming.

Yeats's strengthened art is first evident in the fistful of political poems
in *Responsibilities*. Here he curses the *Playboy* rioters, curses likewise "the
obscure spite / Of our old Paudeen in his shop," and mocks the dolls
that deride the living child. Here, too, he warns Maude Gonne's daughter, Iseult, against "the monstrous crying of the wind" and counsels
Lady Gregory to "be secret and exult" when attacked by the press. And
here, finally, he praises Hugh Lane by comparing him to the figure of
a Renaissance prince "upon Urbino's windy hill." In a fury over Dublin's
refusal to appoint Lane curator of the Municipal Gallery, Yeats wrote
"An Appointment," a poem that may appear slight or merely playful
but that addresses a bitter occasion and is a good example—in fact this
is its theme—of rage reined in and transformed by style:

> Being out of heart with government
> I took a broken root to fling
> Where the proud, wayward squirrel went,
> Taking delight that he could spring;
> And he, with that low whinnying sound
> That is like laughter, sprang again
> And so to the other tree at a bound.
> Nor the tame will, nor timid brain,
> Nor heavy knitting of the brow
> Bred that fierce tooth and cleanly limb
> And threw him up to laugh on the bough;
> No government appointed him.

The poem begins in angry impotence, but then goes on to praise a
style the poet would salvage from his rage, a style neither tame nor
timid, with "fierce tooth and cleanly limb," and with a voice, agile as a
squirrel, that leads its occasion. In this light, the poem reads like a small
manifesto. Right style is equated with the investment of rage in a stance
that is "wayward" and lean. In *Responsibilities* Yeats masters political

hatred. At this point in his work the bardic voice, speaking to and for and against, begins to be his mainstay.

In his later poetry, Yeats confronted the climate of atrocity that prevailed in Ireland as the Irish Free State was coming into being, a terror of the kind that typifies violence in our century, terror blank and unredeemed, with nothing heroic about it and no poetic idea to absorb the blood or dignify the loss of life. As times grew darker, Yeats's sense of political violence hardened as well. In its more disastrous enactments, politics seemed something impersonal, demonic, a force like the "levelling wind." And in its aftermath came bitterness. The word *bitter* carries an aura of political meaning in Yeats's later poems, signalling the spiritual outcome of long wounding that is very like scar tissue—except that to "be bitter" implies an active state, a "holding down" of ruinous passions. And while bitterness is not without its cost, it also has its uses. In 1928 Yeats wrote to Olivia Shakespear: "Re-reading *The Tower* I was astonished at its bitterness, and long to live out of Ireland that I may find some new vintage. Yet that bitterness gave the book its power and it is the best book I have written. Perhaps if I was in better health I should be content to be bitter."[14]

When Parnell passes through "Jonathan Swift's dark grove," he is blessed by "bitter wisdom"; he moves, that is, from fallenness to redemption. The fall is into time and politics, and when it happens, innocence is lost; so is sweetness of soul. Life is inescapably tragic because we take "our greatness with our bitterness"; everyone falls, but few gain understanding. Ireland is a "blind bitter land," and Dublin a "blind bitter town." Wisdom is the highest prize Yeats knows, a bardic gift he labors to conserve and pass on to others of his tribe. But they "turn dull-eyed away" when (in "The Results of Thought") he tries to "summon back" their "wholesome strength":

> The best-endowed, the elect,
> All by their youth undone,
> All, all by that inhuman
> Bitter glory wrecked.

What kind of bitter glory might be anybody's guess—except that this is Ireland and the poet is Yeats. We know, that is, that politics has played its part in the wreckage. We might also guess that these—the elect, the best-endowed—succumbed to the sort of hysterical passion that Yeats most dreaded, having barely survived it himself. The power of politics is "inhuman" in its exercise, but also in the way it possesses mind and soul, and makes of the self "a bitter, an abstract thing." When it takes hold of a nation, it is like the rough beast arriving—or the ruinous brunt of a mainforce wind.

In 1903 came a devastating storm that impressed Yeats for the damage it did to Lady Gregory's woodlands at Coole Park. That was also the year of Maude Gonne's marriage to MacBride, another sort of disaster. And 1903 was when *In the Seven Woods* appeared, the volume that included "Adam's Curse" and "Red Hanrahan's Song About Ireland," to which Yeats added a note about "the big wind of nineteen hundred and three [that] blew down so many trees, & troubled the wild creatures, & changed the look of things."[15] As early as 1899, in *The Wind Among the Reeds*, Yeats imagined the wind in mythical terms. In a note to "The Hosting of the Sidhe" he speaks of transhuman powers, and in a reference to Herodias he anticipated by twenty years the nightmarish ending of "Nineteen Hundred and Nineteen":[16]

> The gods of ancient Ireland . . . still ride the country as of old. Sidhe is also Gaelic for wind, and certainly the Sidhe have much to do with the wind. They journey in whirling wind, the winds that were called the dance of the daughters of Herodias in the Middle Ages, Herodias doubtless taking the place of some old goddess. When old countrypeople see the leaves whirling on the road they bless themselves, because they believe the Sidhe to be passing by.

In Yeats's imagery of wind there is an expanding significance, from early associations with the inhuman Sidhe to later usage in the poems about political terror, where again it signals a calamitous power. Like so much of Yeats's work, this kind of imagery includes vein upon vein of reference, until finally the hope of mapping it becomes impossible. Yeats's usage of what he called "the symbol" or "the poetic image" exploits the fact that figural language carries meaning in excess of that which, in any controlled thematic sense, particular contexts can account for. This is true of words generally, a condition of language that the poets of the Symbolist Movement explored with great excitement in the 1890's. Their lesson was not lost on Yeats. He delighted in ending poems with grandly overdetermined images—the beast of "The Second Coming," the great horse-chestnut in "Among School Children" are proof of his genius for turning doubtful theories (in this case the symbolist mystique) to potent account. A poem like "Easter 1916," with its abrupt shift to the image of "the stone" in stanza three, and the last part of "Nineteen Hundred and Nineteen," with its elaborate image of the wind as cause of demonic compulsion, suggest that the symbolist manner and prophetic announcement work well together in bardic practice, increasing Yeats's capacity to deal with political violence.

At the close of his elegy on the death of Robert Gregory, Yeats says the poem was prompted by "seeing how bitter is that wind / That shakes the shutter." In "To a Child Dancing in the Wind," he worries at a young girl's ignorance, but praises the charm of such intrepid disregard:

> What need have you to dread
> The monstrous crying of the wind?

In "A Prayer for My Daughter" he answers that question. He foresees the worst, then counters his vision of the tree-wracking wind with praise for innocence rooted in the wisdom of the laurel. Yeats dated this bardic invocation June 1919, as the war with England was edging toward horror, when like any parent anywhere he feared for the life and mind of a child born into dark times:

> I have walked and prayed for this young child an hour
> And heard the sea-wind scream upon the tower,
> And under the arches of the bridge, and scream
> In the elms above the flooded stream;
> Imagining in excited reverie
> That the future years had come,
> Dancing to a frenzied drum,
> Out of the murderous innocence of the sea.

Images of howling storm and "roof-levelling wind" announce the disturbance approaching. The storm of 1903 comes to mind, but this one screams like a voice out of the whirlwind. It is a sign of the times, and Yeats is certain he knows what it means. In "excited reverie" he beholds the coming of calamity, disasters already under way. The world begins its "dancing to a frenzied drum," driven by the political distraction of elemental energies.

The sea is innocent, a realm of primal energy; but when the waves are wind-swept, innocence turns murderous. The union of these images suggests that the world's increasing violence is political (the open meshing of human actions), but also metaphysical (necessary cycles in historical time). These contraries mark the ultimate antinomy in Yeats's poetry. When he rails against politics he blames and curses, looking upon the world of action as a mass of events created by men and women acting freely. But when he takes up the bardic office of prophecy, he gains a vantage from which all things are brought to pass by forces at once transhuman and inexorable. In this visionary perspective, the world of action is blameless; no one rails against the wind, and history viewed under the aspect of eternity suggests that the world isn't what it seems. Up close one sees politics as a field of bitterness and rage. But at a distance the design comes into view, and one beholds the great relentless gyres that inspire wise acceptance.

This duality—violence as freedom, violence as necessity—is the heart of politics as tragedy. What Sophocles said in *Antigone*, Yeats repeats in his poem on civil war: we "take our greatness with our violence." In the prayer for his daughter, what therefore can the poet do, once he hears "the sea-wind scream," except bless his child, bless her repeatedly and in the old conventional ways: "May she be granted beauty . . . O may she live like some green laurel." He curses political hatred, makes an example of Maude Gonne, then offers this assurance:

> If there's no hatred in a mind
> Assault and battery of the wind
> Can never tear the linnet from the leaf.

If these lines are not received for what they are—a bardic blessing—an apparent conflict arises between the premonition of violence so convincingly announced in stanzas one and two, and the gracious certitudes Yeats seems to utter thereafter, as if "in custom and in ceremony" his daughter might somehow find real safety. But there is, Yeats knows, no safety. What, then, can be the point of setting the polite laurel against the tree-wracking wind? If this were a poem in the high Romantic manner, wherein poetic imagination is sufficient to transform that which threatens it, we might accept an image of the world in which "ceremony's

a name for the rich horn, / And custom for the spreading laurel tree"—
accept it and take it for a victory. But not here. The poem is replete
with warning and instructs us to take the vision of political violence—
the catastrophic bodings of "excited reverie"—as the poem's occasion.
The most the poet can do for loved ones is bless them. As he tells
us, the poem is a *prayer*, a bulwark of words against misfortune.

In both "A Prayer for My Daughter" and "Easter 1916" the immediate
(political) office of the bard invites the wider (visionary) authority of
the prophet. That this doubleness of vision is proper to Yeats's blessing
seems certain from "A Meditation in Time of War," the brief poem that
follows the prayer for his daughter:

> For one throb of the artery,
> While on that old grey stone I sat
> Under the old wind-broken tree,
> I knew that One is animate,
> Mankind inanimate phantasy.

The One compels the Many; the strife of worldly affairs gives way to
invisible order. In his finest poems Yeats is alert to politics as the field
of action but also, and equally, to history as mankind's transhuman
ground. From this perspective the two sides of bardic inclination—
political scrutiny and prophetic announcement—act to enhance and certify each other.

In "A Prayer for My Daughter" and even more in the later poems of
political violence, the terror Yeats faces is no longer on a human scale.
He is forced to admit that he has no resources—no triumphant powers
to fall back on—except the bardic capacity for naming. But the power
of naming can be a formidable weapon, especially when impelled by
rage, by energetic "hate of what's to come." Without question Yeats is
at the height of his powers when excited by the turbulence of events.
Readers are sometimes troubled by his apparent intimacy with the violence he envisions. But his "emblems of adversity," as he called his
prophetic images, owe nothing to a psychology of identification, and
we would be mistaken to assume that Yeats approved or took a hidden
share in the violence of his time. On the contrary, worldly rage provoked
in Yeats his own defiant frenzy, a fearless agitation enabling him to face,
and name, the terror he beheld.

In Yeats's later visionary poems he confronts the powers of the world with powers of his own, a state of "excited reverie" that depends on a vigorous or even violent act of imagining. Pitched to extremes, the poet's prophetic energies develop an interior intensity in response to the press of the real—precisely a "violence within" pushing back at the "violence without," as Stevens would say; or as Kant put it in his notion of sublime encounter, "a power of resistance of quite another kind." That the source of creative vigor is rage, rather than pleasure, is a measure of the poet's task in dark times. Another measure is the peculiar use Yeats makes of *reverie*. The easeful dreaming of an earlier time (his own early poems, for example) has become a lost luxury. To "repose in the well-being of an image," as Bachelard put it in *The Poetics of Reverie*, is no longer possible.[17] There is no repose, no well-being, but only the embattled excitement that comes of confrontation.

Yeats stood up to terror by naming it; that was his pride and his valor. He knew that when a thing or occasion is named, when its principle is either *found out* or *assigned* by force of acute description, power is gained over (or granted to) that which is named. In bardic practice, moreover, a name can be mimetic or visionary; it can represent appearance or, through the force of metaphor, penetrate to essence. In his prophetic work, Yeats relies on visionary naming, the assignment of images to capture energies not otherwise describable. For any poet, the problem is how to face political violence and reveal its *hysterica passio*, its demonic spirit in times of extremity. From the prophetic section of "Meditations in Time of Civil War," this is how Yeats does it:

'Vengeance upon the murderers,' the cry goes up,
'Vengeance for Jacques Molay.' In cloud-pale rags, or in lace,
The rage-driven, rage-tormented, and rage-hungry troop,
Trooper belabouring trooper, biting at arm or at face,
Plunges towards nothing, arms and fingers spreading wide
For the embrace of nothing; and I, my wits astray
Because of all that senseless tumult, all but cried
For vengeance on the murderers of Jacques Molay.

What Yeats sees in prophetic vision, and knows from neighborhood news, is mutilation of the human image as the means and end of politics in extremity—precisely the madness of Creon's decree. The New Leviathan, as we might call it, is a self-devouring mass impelled by a rage wholly innocent, wholly murderous—and exceedingly contagious. It is the kind of evil that befouls life's sweetness and mocks faith in politics as an art of the possible, an evil so blindly terrible that finally just to stand and face it, to pace the battlements and *see* the undelivered world destroying itself, compels a furious, wildly creative distress. As the poet says in lines introducing the passage above:

> Frenzies bewilder, reveries perturb the mind;
> Monstrous familiar images swim to the mind's eye.

In the same poem Yeats compares his tower, with its winding stair and "chamber arched with stone," to the place of Milton's visionary poet:

> *Il Penseroso's* Platonist toiled on
> In some like chamber, shadowing forth
> How the daemonic rage
> Imagined everything.

When poets like Yeats, or Milton, confront the political sublime, they depend on a "daemonic rage" that is provoked by, and then that pushes back against, the monstrous rage of the world. From this violent meeting comes a nobility of diction equal to the darkness upon us.

"Nineteen Hundred and Nineteen" is the great poem of Yeats's political-prophetic maturity, to which "Prayer for my Daughter" and "Meditations in Time of Civil War" stand as sister poems with "The Second Coming" for a preface. "Nineteen Hundred and Nineteen" takes for granted that politics is given to violent extremes and that against the levelling wind there's nothing that will stand. Rage is palpable and we see, moreover, that the inclination to curse takes its justification from events.

In December 1918 the party of revolt, Sinn Fein, won the vote in Ireland and on January 21, 1919, a republic was declared. The Irish Republican Army attacked police stations and British troop trucks, and the war with England began. Soon the Black and Tans arrived, a freelance soldiery very like the proto-fascist *Freikorp* in Germany (organized at the same time), given to random atrocity and terrorizing the countryside. Elsewhere in 1919, a British unit opened fire on a political rally in the Punjab, killing four hundred and wounding more than one thousand. The Amritsar Massacre, as it came to be known, started a politics of revolt that would finally break the British hold on India. In Paris, meanwhile, the Versailles Treaty humiliated Germany enough to insure another war, and gave the victor nations permission to recarve the colonial map of Africa. Perhaps the most obvious sign of the times, in 1919, was the Russian Revolution, which was just then reaching its peak of madness in the war between Whites and Reds. In Moscow the Communist International was established, and for a few weeks of 1919 Marxist forces took control of cities like Munich and Berlin. It was at this point, with the murder of Rosa Luxemburg for a symbol, that roving bands of German veterans methodized violence and set a model for fascist order in Germany. And now, finally, a small anti-Semitic group calling itself Deutsche Arbeiterpartie, The German Workers Party, arrived on the scene. Hitler was its spokesman and then its leader, and by the end of 1919 he had done two things: hammered out his twenty-five-point platform and found out—in a backroom of the Hofbrauhaus, in the hall on Dachaustrasse—the power of his voice.

All told, 1919 was not as lethal as the years directly preceding, but in Ireland, in Europe, and in the new-born Soviet Union, it was sufficient to inspire dark foreboding. Originally entitled "Thoughts upon the Present State of the World," Yeats's "Nineteen Hundred and Nineteen" announces the new disorder, and designates 1919 as the moment when the downward slide of the West began to feel certain. The poem is therefore "a lamentation," as Yeats said in a letter, "over lost peace and lost hope,"[18] and the first lines of the opening stanza strike that note and toll that bell:

> Many ingenious lovely things are gone
> That seemed sheer miracle to the multitude,
> Protected from the circle of the moon
> That pitches common things about. . . .

That the poem surveys more than the war in Ireland is made clear by beginning not with Irish matters—there is little in the poem that is specific to Ireland alone—but with Periclean Greece, the fountainhead of Western splendor, and just at the moment when Athenian empire was at the peak of its grandeur and about to be sacked. Here again Yeats takes up the heroism of defeat, but gives it a new turn in his reference to "Phidias' famous ivories." He who built the colossal gold and ivory Athena for the Parthenon, he whose Zeus was one of the world's Seven

Wonders, is known in terms of loss. There is great pathos in the fact that no work of his remains, that Phidias is heroic by reputation only. To fame of this kind Yeats pays homage. He sees, however, that reputation comes to nothing; that immortality conferred by fame is doubtful at best. Hellas is gone, and gone as well our older faith in art as the one thing transcending time and politics.

Phidias' heroic works, moreover, are not stressed so much as his ornamental "grasshoppers and bees," suggesting that for an empire in its prime, indulgence and display certify illusions of permanence. But for the British as for the Athenian empire, peace at home was purchased by continuous "little wars" elsewhere. To those well away from frontiers, the claims of progress might seem genuine, and in "Nineteen Hundred and Nineteen" Yeats blames his generation for having accepted power's fraud. Even in Ireland the myth of moral advancement thrived:

> 　　　　　habits that made old wrong
> Melt down, as it were wax in the sun's rays;
> Public opinion ripening for so long
> We thought it would outlive all future days.
> O what fine thought we had because we thought
> That the worst rogues and rascals had died out.

Contempt for "fine thought" now turns, in stanza three, to the way empire promotes itself through spectacle—the irony of power pretending innocence:

> All teeth were drawn, all ancient tricks unlearned,
> And a great army but a showy thing;
> What matter that no cannon had been turned
> Into a ploughshare?

The political charade was, for a time, a promise that Yeats and the friends of his youth had wanted to believe, an illusion that for the Irish began to crack in 1916 and in 1919 collapsed outright. Hence the sudden leap into the violent imagery of stanza four, the only part of the poem in which atrocity is directly depicted. The specific reference is to the killing of Ellen Quinn by the Black and Tans, an incident that happened in Yeats's own neighborhood, and that he takes as *the* sign of political intrusion:

> Now days are dragon-ridden, the nightmare
> Rides upon sleep; a drunken soldiery
> Can leave the mother, murdered at her door,
> To crawl in her own blood, and go scot-free;
> The night can sweat with terror as before
> We pieced out thoughts into philosophy,
> And planned to bring the world under a rule,
> Who are but weasels fighting in a hole.

For the first time, visionary diction (lines one and part of two) announces the theme of demonic possession that will gradually take over the poem. The effect is to magnify local atrocity and the terror that random killing inspires. Visionary and mimetic dictions now proceed in counterpoint, and the metaphorical last line, the "weasels fighting in a hole," increases the sense of nonhuman forces at work. Most important, the stanza as a whole enacts the moment of political intrusion—the way an event breaks in to break up the dreams and abstract designs we use to keep ugliness distant.

Three kinds of disturbance intrude: there are demonic energies on the loose; there is the news of killing; there is the spectacle of high-mindedness reverting to rodent frenzy. These are "the signs" referred to at the start of the next two stanzas, which complete part one of the poem by turning back to the unbelievable but de facto ruin (or ruin in progress) of all things good and beautiful. For those who can see, the lesson is that nothing stands, no monument or masterwork, nor is there comfort to be had:

> He who can read the signs nor sink unmanned
> Into the half-deceit of some intoxicant
> From shallow wits; who knows no work can stand,
> Whether health, wealth or peace of mind were spent
> On master-work of intellect or hand,
> No honor leave its mighty monument,
> Has but one comfort left: all triumph would
> But break upon his ghostly solitude.
>
> But is there any comfort to be found?
> Man is in love and loves what vanishes,
> What more is there to say? That country round

None dared admit, if such a thought were his,
Incendiary or bigot could be found
To burn that stump on the Acropolis,
Or break in bits the famous ivories
Or traffic in the grasshoppers and bees.

Yeats reads the signs and knows no work will stand, his own included.
He would therefore retreat, as he did at the end of "Meditation in Time
of Civil War," into the comfort of a "ghostly solitude." But now the
well-used strategy fails, and at *this* point the caldron of the poem—its
torment of political intrusion—begins to boil. Hemmed in by animal
terror on the one hand, by demonic intimations on the other, is real
escape possible? To say that "man is in love and loves what vanishes"
ought to suffice; it ought to be the last word, but it isn't. There is more
to be said even if "none dare admit." For while comfort is not to be
"found," incendiary and bigot are "found" in every direction. In this
extremity, consoling truths are neither sweet nor consoling.

Despite his ideas of historical necessity, Yeats is unable to accept
neighborhood horrors with visionary calm. At the end of the poem's
first section, he is back where he started, pressed by a knowledge of
political intrusion worse than his own fine thoughts had prepared him
to subdue. A greater effort is called for, and the poem reformulates itself
(section two) in visionary terms that bring the demonic element visibly
to the fore:

When Loie Fuller's Chinese dancers enwound
A shining web, a floating ribbon of cloth,
It seemed that a dragon of air
Had fallen among dancers, had whirled them round
Or hurried them off on its furious path;
So the Platonic Year
Whirls out new right and wrong,
Whirls in the old instead;
All men are dancers and their tread
Goes to the barbarous clangour of a gong.

The earlier vision of "dragon-ridden" days now summons an image
from the art of Yeats's own time, a prophetic emblem that lends familiar
substance to the second half of the stanza. The "new right and wrong"

of the Christian era is driven out by a feral "dragon of air." The forces now at work are demonic and beyond mere human will; but what counts most, in this stanza, is the way visionary and mimetic dictions begin to work together. By the last line Yeats has achieved a harder diction, has called on a "violence within" to equal the "violence without."

The progress of "Nineteen Hundred and Nineteen" begins to be clear if we compare earlier formulations of the poem's theme with the one at the end of part two:

> Many ingenious lovely things are gone
> That seemed sheer miracle to the multitude.

*   *   *

> Man is in love and loves what vanishes,
> What more is there to say?

*   *   *

> All men are dancers and their tread
> Goes to the barbarous clangour of a gong.

The change is from a generalized lilt to the harder music of uncompromising metaphor. This turn suggests the direction the rest of the poem will take and offers an answer to the question Yeats put in a letter to Olivia Shakespear: "I wonder will literature be much changed by that most momentous of events, the return of evil?"[19] The message of "Nineteen Hundred and Nineteen" is that some part of poetry will be changed if the political climate continues to worsen. And in fact the change takes place before our eyes as progressive shifts in rhythm, diction, and stance alter the character of the poem as a whole.

"Nineteen Hundred and Nineteen" announces the return of evil, and its immediate occasion is the experience of political intrusion. This occasion provokes the poet's most bitter curse upon his time, and gives rise, finally, to a vision of the demonic nature of politics in our century. Yeats discovers that when one is caught up and terrorized by violence in one's own backyard, protective strategies that should work don't— not the consolations of philosophy, not the distance gained through myth, not retreat into solitude. In part three of the poem, Yeats tests these options by comparing "the solitary soul to a swan." He aligns the public confession of part one ("we") with a more private confession of his own ("I"), and will be satisfied if for a moment he can see, as in "a troubled mirror," his soul as he hopes it might be—as the image of a swan in free and confident flight:

> The wings half spread for flight,
> The breast thrust out in pride
> Whether to play, or to ride
> Those winds that clamour of approaching night.

Two things discourage a vision so masterful. The soul becomes "lost" in its own defenses; then it finds that having preserved itself through art it cannot, even in death, shake off what its art has engaged. This is a startling admission for Yeats, that he cannot get free of his work. The discontent of poems confronting politics—the outcome of living one's time in one's art—becomes part of his soul's last condition:

> A man in his own secret meditation
> Is lost amid the labryinth that he has made
> In art or politics;
> Some Platonist affirms that in the station
> Where we should cast off body and trade
> The ancient habit sticks,
> And that if our works could
> But vanish with our breath
> That were a lucky death,
> For triumph can but mar our solitude.

Instead of solitude there is only desolation. This sudden insight triggers a burst of self-destructive rage that is reflected in the leap (or is it the fall?) of the swan; and with it a renewal of the experience of political intrusion—from dreaming of goodness to facing evil's return—that Yeats had hoped to escape:

> The swan has leaped into the desolate heaven:
> That image can bring wildness, bring a rage
> To end all things, to end

What my laborious life imagined, even
The half-imagined, the half-written page;
O but we dreamed to mend
Whatever mischief seemed
To afflict mankind, but now
That winds of winter blow
Learn that we were crack-pated when we dreamed.

The recognition that ends part three is final—so final that in a further burst of rage Yeats insists on the spite of naming it again, jamming the entire experience of hope and despair into a single bardic rann that is the whole of section four:

We, who seven years ago
Talked of honour and of truth,
Shriek with pleasure if we show
The weasel's twist, the weasel's tooth.

In this intensely bitter mood Yeats goes on, with part five, to utter the most sustained curse in his poetry. The madness of *hysterica passio* is barely contained, and the curse is directed as much against himself as any of the great, the wise, or the good:

Come let us mock at the great
That had such burdens on the mind
And toiled so hard and late
To leave some monument behind,
Nor thought of the levelling wind.

Come let us mock at the wise;
With all those calendars whereon
They fixed old aching eyes,
They never saw how seasons run,
And now but gape at the sun.

Come let us mock at the good
That fancied goodness might be gay,
And sick of solitude

> Might proclaim a holiday:
> Wind shrieked—and where are they?

> Mock mockers after that
> That would not lift a hand maybe
> To help good, wise or great
> To bar that foul storm out, for we
> Traffic in mockery.

Yeats does not usually blame defeat, but here he seems to side with the levelling wind, as if for once the stirring beast beneath were not held wholly down. Here Swift's savage indignation is complete, provoking the poet to speak *in the voice of* what he hates. Despite precision of the verse, rage is so total in its irony that it become indistinguishable from what it attacks. He calls his tribe to curse its elders, and we are invited—"Come let us mock"—to join in, to make of the curse a choric counterpoint to the tragedy in progress.

The answer to "What more is there to say?" might be to curse the darkness and die. But that kind of defeat Yeats could never abide. No matter the internal depths, he goes on, as Milton did, to body forth the "darkness visible." This he does in the great last section of "Nineteen Hundred and Nineteen." Throughout the poem, images of the wind have gathered force and mass—a dragon of air, a wind of winter and approaching night, the storm's foul shriek. Now these energies regroup into an image arising directly from the violence of the Irish countryside. In language at first mimetic but almost at once visionary, the levelling wind shows forth the horror at the heart the poem:

> Violence upon the roads: violence of horses;
> Some few have handsome riders, are garlanded
> On delicate sensitive ear or tossing mane,
> But wearied running round and round in their courses
> All break and vanish, and evil gathers head:
> Herodias' daughters have returned again,
> A sudden blast of dusty wind and after
> Thunder of feet, tumult of images,
> Their purpose in the labyrinth of the wind;

And should some crazy hand dare touch a daughter
All turn with amorous cries, or angry cries,
According to the wind, for all are blind.

In its grim magnificence, this is one of poetry's great images of politics out of control, power devoid of reason or self-interest, *hysterica passio* with no aim but glee in destruction. None knows what nor why nor whither, but only the blind excitement that comes from desecration. Here Yeats says what "none dared admit"; not just that incendiary and bigot arrive in multitudes, but that the spectacle of ruin fascinates—that delight in destruction is part of power's enchantment.

How might this obscene seductiveness be named? If twenty centuries of stony sleep are vexed to nightmare, what vexing shape comes now to pass? Yeats says in his note to the poem that "these horsemen, now that the times worsen, give way to worse"; and also that the culminating image is "an evil spirit much run after in Kilkenny at the start of the fourteenth century," an incubus whose victims consorted with demons.[20] This, then, is Yeats's emblem of evil returning:

But now wind drops, dust settles; thereupon
There lurches past, his great eyes without thought
Under the shadow of stupid straw-pale locks,
That insolent fiend Robert Artisson
To whom the love-lorn Lady Kyteler brought
Bronzed peacock feathers, red combs of her cocks.

In the end, even Eros is suborned, the sea's innocence again made murderous by the wind. The gloss on these lines comes from "Dove and Swan," the section of *A Vision* in which Yeats surveys the playing out of Western hegemony. He says that "a civilization is a struggle to keep self-control," and that as control is lost and things fall apart there is "first a sinking in upon the moral being, then the last surrender, the irrational cry, revelation—the scream of Juno's peacock."[21] I take it that the scream of the peacock is one with the shriek of the wind, the sound of calamity in a time when brazen undraped power is the welcomed god, and politics is destiny. Other poets have had intimations of monstrosity, but none has been as bold as Yeats with outright prophecy of this kind. If we wonder why poets sometimes write in a manner so appalled and seemingly hopeless, we have an excellent reply in Yeats's example. He wrote this poem to confront the political sublime and not be cowed by what his vision forced him to behold.

There is a small late poem entitled simply "Politics." The poem has been dismissed by critics as a "little lyric," as "happy-thoughted," or as "an old man's gay goodnight,"[22] and readers of Yeats know that in the official *Collected Poems* the closing poem is "Under Ben Bulben," with "Politics" fifth from the end. In Richard Finneran's 1983 edition of Yeats's complete poetry, however, "Politics" rightly stands last, an order we have known since Curtis Bradford established the correct sequence for the last poems in 1966.[23] Throughout his career, Yeats arrayed his poems for publication with meticulous care, and now that we are certain he intended "Politics" as his end-piece, we might ask why. The further question is whether or not Yeats's bardic ambition had any bearing on the final arrangement of his poetry; and if so, what sort of hindsight he himself provided for his work as a whole. Here, then, is "Politics":

> How can I, that girl standing there,
> My attention fix
> On Roman or on Russian
> Or on Spanish politics,
> Yet here's a travelled man that knows
> What he talks about,
> And there's a politician
> That has both read and thought,
> And maybe what they say is true
> Of war and war's alarms,
> But O that I were young again
> And held her in my arms.

The poem was written in late May 1938, less than a year before Yeats died. Much of the quarrel about its meaning—does it dismiss or accept the importance of politics?—hinges on how the poem answers the epigraph that announces it, a remark attributed to Thomas Mann:

In our time the destiny of man presents itself in political terms.

Yeats did not take these words from Mann, but from an essay by
Archibald MacLeish, and his account of the poem's inception is given
in letters to Dorothy Wellesley, dated 24 May and 10 June 1938. The
following remarks are from the first letter:[24]

> There has been an article upon my work in the *Yale Review*,
> which is the only article on the subject which has not bored
> me for years. It commends me above other modern poets be-
> cause my language is 'public'. That word which I had not
> thought of myself is a word I want. Your language in 'Fire' is
> 'public', so is that of every good ballad. (I may send you the
> article because the criticism is important to us all.) It goes on
> to say that, owing to my age and my relation to Ireland, I was
> unable to use this 'public' language on what is evidently con-
> sidered the right public material, politics. The enclosed little
> poem is my reply.

Against the charge that he is "unable" to manage a public style in
cases of political import, Yeats counters with the poem. Then as an
afterthought he says: "No artesian well of the intellect can find the poetic
theme."[25] What theme? Yeats might be arguing that his art can *evade*
politics successfully; that politics is not a worthy theme. Or, he might
be saying that his work does *confront* politics in a suitably public language. What is certain is that he thought a public style essential, and
that the poem is some kind of answer to the notion of politics as destiny.

In "Politics" the scene is a public place in which the speaker goes
about his business. The woman is *there* while the poet, caught up in the
day's news, is *here*. Between them—between the first and last lines—
comes the body of the poem, most of it about politics with special
reference to Mussolini, Stalin, and Franco. The poem is also, of course,
about the despair of desire. An old man admires a young woman's
beauty. That is ordinary enough. What makes it dramatic and of consequence is the way politics intrudes to make the moment unusual—
insofar, that is, as "war's alarms" are out of the ordinary.

But then, it might be that war and war's alarms have become the
normal state of affairs, the expected thing in our time, so that now it's
the moment of erotic longing, seldom unharried, that is rare. And if
politics intervenes from without, it is also integral to the poet's (the

speaker's) position in life. Either way, politics is part of the poem's occasion. We might say that the intense yearning expressed in the last lines has been present from the beginning and that desire undercuts political response. But it's also the case that public issues are frustrating private desire, that erotic reverie is upset by bad news. The romantic theme undermines the political theme, but the political theme disrupts the romantic theme, displacing it for nine of the poem's twelve lines. The two themes twine about each other and cannot be kept separate.

The specific references to Roman, Russian, and Spanish politics are signs of the time, a time from which anyone might wish to withdraw. It's not, therefore, only alarm and consternation that compose this example of political experience, but also the hapless yearning for escape that melds with another yearning, also escapist, for youthful unconcerned delight. The urge to escape is what makes "that girl standing there" so very present to the poet. Were he undisturbed by history, he would lack the sounding board that makes his emotion dramatic. Private desire becomes significant when complicated by public impediment, a situation as elementary as *Antigone*. That is one sense in which destiny finds its meaning in political terms. Moreover, because he is old the poet is only fit for politics and must, against his will, forego erotic dreams; politics is *his* destiny, like it or not. The themes of age, desire, and political intrusion play upon each other; but also, as I've suggested, a poet committed to heroic themes will know that private destiny becomes heroic in terms of—and in conflict with—public forces.

"Politics" supports a political reading of Yeats's poetry. It can be taken, moreover, as a specific genre in bardic tradition—the kind of vision poem called the *aisling*—and viewed this way it makes a fitting conclusion for the poetry of an Irish poet in love with his nation as well as with his art. As a bardic form, the *aisling* arose when the Irish chiefs were driven into exile; it became widespread after James, the last of the Stuarts, was defeated in 1690 by William of Orange at the Battle of the Boyne. From then on, a principal kind of bardic lament framed itself as the fleeting glimpse of a wonderful young woman who represented Ireland's one day being free. The *aisling* became a way of preserving hope against the reality of political defeat. The vision of nationhood still lives, as Hanrahan says in his song, "hidden in our hearts." Did Yeats know this tradition? At the close of *Cathleen ni Houlihan*, after the old woman leaves with the son who will die for Ireland, a returning brother is asked: "Did you see an old woman going down the path?"

He answers in the play's last line: "I did not, but I saw a young girl, and she had the walk of a queen."

In dreams begins responsibility, and so it was with Yeats at the end of his life. Mired in loss and alarm, he stamped his career with a backward look to "all that delirium of the brave," long since betrayed and played out. There is no nationality without great literature, John O'Leary had told the young poet, and no great literature without nationality. Bringing the two together was a lifetime's labor and, as Yeats came finally to feel, a lifetime's defeat. Yet the dream was exceedingly fair. It was like the glimpse of a goddess or, with her queenly unconcern, "that girl standing there," impossible to reach.

·THREE·

ATTACK
&
MALEDICTION

·V·

Bertolt Brecht, Germany

A Brechtian maxim: do not build on the good old days,
but on the bad new ones.
                                    —Walter Benjamin[1]

No poet has done more to advance the prestige of political art than Bertolt Brecht. He is one of the prime figures in European literature and has influenced writers of every kind in many countries. Most of us in America, however, know him better for his plays than for his poems despite the fact that Brecht owes his dramatic excellence directly to his language—to his powers as a poet. The two careers ran broadly parallel, and in view of Brecht's poetry, his later poems especially, the famous cynicism of his plays looks less savage, less brazenly tough. Not that Brecht can be praised for his tenderness; like Yeats, he was chiefly a hater, a poet whose foremost gift was for cursing. His hard-boiled hauteur was part of an unwillingness to be kind when kindness flatters established order. It was his proof against his enemies, the Nazis in particular. As he put it in "To Those Born Later": "Anger, even against injustice / Makes the voice hoarse."

Brecht's theater overrides his poetry because his fame as a playwright came early and lasted; but also because he published a mere fraction of poetry during his lifetime. Events kept upsetting plans for printings, and what did appear came out in a confusion of ways, from poems stuck in the plays to those in the small gray chapbooks, the *Versuche*, that Brecht issued over the years. Of substantial volumes there were only three: the early *Hauspostille* or *Devotions for the Home* of 1927; the *Svend-borg Poems* published in exile in 1938; and finally, five years before his death in 1956, *A Hundred Poems*. Around this last book a situation developed that made its occasion an example of politics and art in collision.

John Heartfield designed the book's cover, which featured the picture of a Chinese tea-root carved in the shape of a lion. Brecht liked it but his East German (Soviet) publishers did not. They argued that the design would brand the poetry as "formalism" and be condemned by party-line critics. The situation was typical for Brecht, and so was the solution. *A Hundred Poems* appeared in an initial edition of ten thousand copies, half with the lion, half in plain cover. To the hacks went the latter, while booksellers preferred (because it sold better) copies with the design. As a final touch Brecht put the following poem on the cover with the lion:

> The bad fear your claws.
> The good enjoy your elegance.
> This
> I would like to hear said
> Of my verse.

The aggressive element in Brecht's work is well known, and the little poem about the lion, so simple and direct, is Brecht at his elegant best. But to value the whole of his poetry for its "elegance" is surely odd. In the German the last word of line two is *Grazie*, denoting "grace" or "charm" or a kind of "suppleness." Graceful and charming Brecht's work isn't. He detested decorum and evident polish, any sort of visible re-finement, preferring instead the vigor of the street and lowbrow forms like ballads, pop songs, tunes of the music hall and the street. Brecht's preference was for a language down to earth, and his turn toward the rude and unmannerly was less "a protest against the smoothness and harmony of conventional poetry," as he says of his early poetry, than "an attempt to show human dealings as contradictory, fiercely fought over, full of violence."[2]

A lion might be supple, but hardly charming, certainly not the bristly creature of Heartfield's design; and this points to one of the problems reading Brecht. His poetry does not charm, invite, or tease out thought. It would be heard, not overheard, and does not bank on its status as Art. Its import is in its occasion and it does not, therefore, claim to be transcendent or self-contained; it insists, rather, on its place in history, its provisional nature as utterance in situ. Poets, Brecht believed, ought to say something; and what they say ought to be worth hearing even in a world where frightful forces attack and erode our self-possession. History is too much with us, and if we would believe Max Frisch, looking upon the ruins of Europe after World War Two, Brecht's poetry is of the kind most worth having: the kind that "can stand up against the world in which it is spoken."[3]

Brecht was born in 1898 and came of age as a poet and playwright during the ugly years after World War One, when Germany was ruled by defeat and the vengeance of Versailles, by upheaval and paramilitary violence, by resentment, poverty, and rampant profiteering. He witnessed the rise of fascism and when Hitler assumed power in 1933, Brecht began a life in exile that lasted sixteen years. From the time of his return, in 1948, until his death in 1956, he lived in East Berlin under a Stalinist regime and amid the hysteria of the Cold War. When Brecht speaks of "dark times" he knows what he is talking about:

> Truly, I live in dark times!
> The guileless word is folly. A smooth forehead
> Suggests insensitivity. The man who laughs
> Has simply not yet had
> The terrible news.

Written in 1938, those are the first lines of "To Those Born Later," a poem sometimes translated as "To Posterity." The phrase "dark times" occurs often in Brecht's poetry. It refers to half a century during which, by conservative estimate, more than one hundred million men, women, and children died in wars, in concentration camps, by bombings and firing squads. Millions more lived out their lives in harrowing dread. To say that civilization collapsed is not to exaggerate, and the great questions—how to stay human, or, as Adorno put it, how to have poetry after Auschwitz—are still with us. In "To Those Born Later" Brecht goes on:

> I would also like to be wise.
> In the old books it says what wisdom is:
> To shun the strife of the world and to live out
> Your brief time without fear
> Also to get along without violence
> To return good for evil
> Not to fulfill your desires but to forget them

Is accounted wise.
All this I cannot do:
Truly, I live in dark times.

In an age of enormity the old wisdom fails, drifts out of reach, becomes a luxury. How, for example, return good for evil when genocide or the threat of nuclear wipeout confronts us? How remain sane amid madness or bring up children without the desire for a decent peace? We are embedded in the world's strife and cannot shun it even if we would. Everything has become political and "dark times" prevail. And this condition affects not only how we view the world morally, but also how we see it in aesthetic terms:

What kind of times are they, when
A talk about trees is almost a crime
Because it implies silence about so many horrors?

That was the question Brecht faced, and it remains a question for poets today. Can poetry keep its innocence? Do any of us have the right to ignore *what we know?* Nature is either a false retreat or is so politicized that images of earth no longer uphold our need for nature's "counterpoise." Poems that celebrate self-sufficient nature hint at a class-bound or elitist poetic not valid for the state of affairs that is in fact the world. Is poetry a universal human gift or is it the exclusive province of those who, by birth, money, and education, can afford to see the earth and world as they please? In one of his "notational poems," as I would call this form, Brecht takes up the problem and has—as usual—his answer, severe though it may be. "Reading Without Innocence" was written in 1944, in response to an entry in Gide's journal of July 3, 1940, immediately after France gave in to the Nazis, while Gide vacationed in the Pyrenees:

In his wartime journals
The writer Gide mentions a gigantic plane tree
He's been admiring—quite a while—for its enormous trunk
Its mighty branching and its equilibrium
Effected by the gravity of its preponderant boughs.

In far-off California
Shaking my head, I read this entry.
The nations are bleeding to death. No natural plan
Provides for a happy equilibrium.

A classic example of casting blame, this poem; its title is meant as a description of Brecht's position, but clearly the idea of "reading without innocence" applies in a multitude of ways, literary, political, plain human, to the texts of our time. At the same time, of course, we need contact with earth's quiet powers, need it the more desperately as the world pushes to cancel nature's solace. Surely none of us would want Gide's wondrous tree expunged from the face of the earth. We behold the tree of life, are uplifted by its strength. We know, however, that even as we seek renewal the spectacle of life in torment goes on. We know, that is, that deep images are loaded with desire, in this case the desire to get away from it all, to think that in the end things balance out.

In Brecht's art there is little care for nature in itself. This is consistent with his later Marxism, a perspective from which nature is the realm of necessity that humankind struggles to transcend, a field of force opposed to freedom until it is humanized. When nature appears in Brecht's poetry, a human element usually intrudes. The abundant cherry tree has a thief in it, the spectacular Finnish countryside is viewed by a refugee, or this:

> Fog envelops
> The road
> The poplars
> The farms and
> The artillery.

Brecht sometimes uses nature symbolically, the purity of the empty godless sky, for example, or water's constant flow. But his preference is for earth in its humanized aspect. By disposition Brecht prefers the imagery of human acts and agencies—tools and utensils, houses, people doing things—and poetry informed by an alertness to politics commits itself to the human sphere in any case. Brecht was appalled by Gide's journal entry because while nations and peoples are being wiped out a famous writer pursues a private consolation. Gide was seeking, maybe, no more than a moment's relief, but for Brecht something further is at stake. By ending with "No natural plan / Provides for a happy equilibrium," he means that no natural design or governing Providence, but solely the concerted efforts of men and women, will bring about a peaceful world. He suggests that Gide's aestheticism, with its mystical tinge, induces blindness to history and allows a feeling of well-being where no well-being is.

When Brecht refers to "dark times" he has in mind the Hitler years in Europe first of all, and then the Stalinist period in Russia, with—in all cases—the afflictions of capital causing disaster in the background. These forces compose the world his art would "stand up against." For the poet in exile, it is a world that feels this way: "When I listen to the news on the radio in the morning, at the same time reading Boswell's *Life of Johnson* and glancing out at the landscape of birch trees in the mist by the river, then the unnatural day begins not on a discordant note but on no note at all."[4] We know what he means, listening to "news on the radio"—the way it enters the mind to grate on the soul. In its ambiance "unnatural" days begin. The press of the real subverts existence and shoves life askew—as in this cottage on an island:

> An oar lies on the roof. A moderate wind
> Will not carry away the thatch.
> In the yard posts are set for
> The children's swing.
> The mail comes twice a day
> Where letters would be welcome.
> Down the Sound come the ferries.
> The house has four doors to escape by.

Entitled "Place of Refuge," the poem might almost be read as a portrait of summer bliss. The place is quaint, the kids are set, the postal service works. If neighbors become bothersome, one can slip out the back and maybe, in a better world, the poem *would* be that. But that kind of innocence, as Brecht put it in another context, is "like having a cloud of dust blow into one's face. Can you imagine that sort of thing ever coming to mean anything again?"[5] The poem describes exile and its range of reference includes a *complex of circumstance* not fully manifest in the poem but that functions as part of the poem nonetheless. Context, in this case, includes knowledge of the historical situation and of the poet's life.

Brecht left Germany in 1933. His name, although he did not know it then, was number five on one of the Nazi death lists. In "Place of Refuge" the time is 1937, the site is a fisherman's cottage outside the Danish city of Svendborg. Hitler would soon invade Denmark, forcing him to use one of the "four doors to escape by." (From there he went to Sweden, then Finland, then on across Russia to the Pacific, and finally to America until the end of the war.) Poetry like Brecht's brings history with it—restores to art, even to a poem so slight, a dignity and amplitude not otherwise obtainable. Brecht's early poetry invents its imagery as it goes; but gradually his images come more and more from historic situations of which the poems are a part. No doubt a paint-peeled oar lay on the picturesque roof. But oar-on-thatch is an image of disorder, of things out of place, and we understand that destructive winds might come. Boats also come, and in the poem's context these images of things approaching take on sinister tones. The children play, but not safely. Mail brings pain more than gladness, and business as usual—ferries crossing the water—is not to be trusted.

Like many of Brecht's poems, "Place of Refuge" is based on personal circumstances, but it is not really personal. Of his work Brecht once said: "maybe the poems in question describe me, but that was not what they were written for. It's not a matter of 'getting acquainted with the poet' but of getting acquainted with the world, and with the people in whose company he is trying to enjoy it and change it."[6] To be acquainted with the world is to discover that no place is safe, no refuge secure. This is the experience of political intrusion, one example among many in Brecht's work. History requires evasions that, like the poet's retreat, cannot be counted on, neither in life nor in art. Brecht takes this sense of intrusion further with a poem in which the old death-and-rebirth theme stands for a very tenuous and shaky hope, hope edged by hostile facts and brute foreboding, which is to say hope in its modern, political form. Here is the first stanza of "Spring 1938":

To-day, Easter Sunday morning
A sudden snowstorm swept over the island.
Between the greening hedges lay snow. My young son
Drew me to a little apricot tree by the house wall
Away from a verse in which I pointed the finger at those

Who were preparing a war which
Could wipe out the continent, this island, my people, my family,
And myself. In silence
We put a sack
Over the freezing tree.

We might consider which of his fingers Brecht was pointing, and how he pointed it.

Brecht's Easter Poem would be a sentimental rerun of the theme of rebirth, were it not for the political references. For now rebirth cannot be counted on; our defenses, our stock of old themes, no longer keep us intact as once they did. Yet there are only the old themes. Brecht gives them new life by allowing politics its place, and in consequence a mythic experience, beset by history, regains its authority. Anyone with children, watching for signs of war, knows how poignant that silence is, when with nothing but a miserable sack, son and father go out to save a dying tree. Slight in itself, the poem is like a stone at the neck.

Political exile is as old as its ancient Greek and Roman examples. In our time it becomes ordinary, a condition bereft of basic trust, home-lessness as a way of life and of knowledge, and with a terror all its own. The fifth section of a poem called "1940" goes this way:

I am now living on the small island of Lidingo.
But one night recently
I had heavy dreams and I dreamed I was in a city
And discovered that its street signs
Were in German. I awoke
Bathed in sweat, saw the fir tree
Black as night before my window, and realized with relief:
I was in a foreign land.

To fear one's home is a mutilating reversal of the normal. So is the tree "black as night," ordinarily frightening but here a comfort. And so, above all, is the poet terrified of his own language. Brecht portrays a situation that is surreal but actual, a plight that goes to the heart of a time during which life uprooted by politics—the century's deportations, displacements, and forced migrations—has been the fate of millions.

· · ·

Brecht declared himself a Marxist in 1929, and critics often speak of his "conversion" as if there are two Brechts, the strident satirist and then the faithful ideologue. Over time, of course, his poetry shows change. Early expansiveness gives way to later concentration; more poems are rooted in fact as time goes on, and Brecht's didacticism moves from ironic depiction to straightforward statement as its central vehicle. What stays unchanged is his basic disposition, his rapport with outcasts and his militant stance toward the world. The early poetry is as hostile to the prevailing order as the later work of his Marxist years; but between early and late came the abyss, the shock of moral and political vacuum in the wake of the First World War. Brecht's work assumes that the defeat suffered by Germany was a defeat for the whole of Western Europe insofar as Christian traditions and humanistic codes had been discredited by violent events. With inflation and unemployment rampant, the walking wounded, meanwhile, the million crippled veterans from the war were seen in their silent parade on any street in any town or city. The upper bourgeoisie, with no thought for the dehumanizing plight of the masses except to keep it, the misery, quiet at any cost, including violent repression, insisted on business as usual, seeing nothing of its own social cost. Brecht later described the world of his early work this way: "The bulk of the poems deal with decline, and the poems follow our crumbling society all the way down. Beauty founded on wrecks, rags becoming a delicacy. Nobility wallows in the dust, meaninglessness is welcomed as a means of liberation. The poet no longer has any sense of solidarity, not even with himself."[7]

The poems in *Devotions* are a sustained attack against Weimar decadence, a round-robin hymn to disorder insofar as the virtues of anarchy—authenticity and vitality, life free and intense and one's own—are preferred to the cant and dreadful pieties in the "carrion land" of postwar Germany. His attack on religion, as well as his attack on middle-class claims, suggests that both are infected with a nihilism that neither would acknowledge. Brecht acknowledged it; he took pride in brute candor and turned his sense of emptiness into a weapon:

> I admit it: I
> Have no hope.
> The blind talk of a way out. I
> See.

His "Hitler Chorales," for example, were to be sung to the melodies of traditional Lutheran hymns, the first of which begins, "Now thank we all our God / For sending Hitler to us," and ends:

> He'll paint the filth and rot
> Until it's spick and span
> So thank we all our God
> For sending us this man.

Parody of liturgical forms is one of Brecht's favorite devices; implemented by the ironies of cliché and doggerel, the result can be clawlike indeed.

His arrogance allowed him his sarcastic cheer, and vitality—the intensity of life in itself—was the only virtue he would recognize. His ballads in praise of life in the gutter, the vigor of his poems about outlaws and lost souls, mock a culture unwilling to face its own decline. Against moral duplicity Brecht pits the appalling innocence of his antiheroes. He speaks up for "sullen souls, fed up with their own crying," and permits all manner of outcasts their say—as if their every word were glorious, "the cursing included." He mocks the anomie of his own situation: "You smoke. You shit. You turn out some verse." And in general he refuses to make judgments: "Off we went then, friend and foe." Or again, preaching against preaching:

> In the house of the hanged man it is not
> Proper to talk about the noose.

The saint shall lie down with the shark and life be what it is—crude and unmediated, to be praised in passing or blessed with gleeful spite toward those who object. In "Ballad of the Secrets of Any Man at All," the spat-upon hero crams bread in his mouth and with a "shark-look" laughs. If he is killed, "it's no great loss." Brecht offers a blessing anyhow, and would have us join in:

> But laugh with him! And wish him luck!
> And let him live! Even help him, too!
> Oh, he isn't good—you can count on that—
> But you don't know yet what will be done to you.

Brecht salutes the debris of society, the outcasts and pariahs whose existence questions the official pretense of well-being. Against a destructive milieu he takes up a destructive position, until what is ironic and what is not is hard to say. Even so, Brecht says it repeatedly, in the following instance with an aggressive nonchalance that is clearly satirical, but also, in a dim time, plain sense:

> One shouldn't be too critical
> Between yes and no
> There's not such a great difference.
> Writing on white paper
> Is a good thing, so are
> Sleeping and having one's evening meal.
> Water fresh on the skin, the wind
> Pleasant clothes
> The ABC
> Opening the bowels.

Brecht had *Devotions for the Home* printed in the format of a prayerbook. He offers his blasphemous poems under the headings of homily and spiritual exercise, and concludes with "Do Not Let Them Fool You!" in which we are asked to see that after death there is nothing, that life is all there is. Brecht is unyielding toward bourgeois notions of exalted selfhood and private destiny. His animus against self-aggrandizement becomes a part of his own stand as a poet, an aspect of self-judgment that Hannah Arendt, herself no stranger to dark times, has valued this way:[8]

> What set him apart was that he realized how deadly ridiculous it would be to measure the flood of events with the yardstick of individual aspirations—to meet, for instance, the international catastrophe of unemployment with a desire to make a career and with reflections on one's own success and failure, or to confront the catastrophe of war with the ideal of a well-rounded personality, or to go into exile, as so many of his colleagues did, with complaints about lost fame or broken-up life. There is not a shred of sentimentality left in Brecht's beautiful and beautifully precise definition of a refugee: *"Ein Bote des Unglücks."*

A bringer of bad news—that was Brecht's position long before he went into exile, and this poetic disposition makes sense of his turn to politics. To be acquainted with the night, as he was, was to have a choice; he could take courage in the candor of nothingness, or he could stem the tide of nihilism in his art by taking a political stand. And once Hitler arrived on the scene, taking a stand was imperative. The wonder is that Brecht made so much of his early art, that he could extract beauty, as he puts it, "founded on wrecks." But certainly he did, and by way of a last example here is "Grand Chorale of Thanksgiving," a poem attacking the ego's claim to a significant private fate by summoning Pascal's terror of infinite spaces. In terms that are very nearly sublime, Brecht parodies a seventeenth-century hymn ("Praise ye the Lord"/"Praise ye the night"), and by sanctifying the void his praise-poem is also a curse. In the rendering of H. R. Hays, here is the whole of "Grand Chorale":

Praise ye the night and the darkness which surround you!
Gather in crowds,
Look into the heavens above you,
Already the day fleeth from you.

Praise ye the grass and the beast which neighbor you, living and dying.

Behold, like to yours
Is the life of the grass and the beast,
Like to yours must be their dying.

Praise ye the tree which groweth exultant from carrion to heaven!

Praise ye carrion,
Praise ye the tree that ate of it
But praise ye the heavens likewise.

Praise ye from your hearts the unmindfulness of heaven!
Since it knoweth not
Either your name or your face,
No one knoweth if you are still here.

Praise ye the cold, the darkness and corruption!
Look beyond:

It heedeth you not one jot.
Unmoved, you may do your dying.

How earnest it sounds, how sternly funny. But perhaps for Brecht it *was* a blessing, an honest encounter with nothingness that became the condition for rebirth. Brecht's early art, I would say, anticipates the existentialism of the generation that would come of age in the Second World War. His turn to politics exhibits a route that was later to be mapped out by others, by Albert Camus in particular, who answered *The Stranger* with *The Plague* and put off estrangement in favor of collective commitment. In dark times, how to be and what to do become ultimate questions. Coming out of the war, Camus had the benefit of hindsight. Going in, Brecht had the risk implicit in the stand he took.

Early and late, what never changed was Brecht's bedrock loyalty to victims—to losers and outcasts, the underclasses doomed to misery from birth. His choice, moreover, can't be laid to sentimentality; no poet is less given to wearing his heart on his sleeve. To honor the wretched of the earth is to be on earth's side and to call upon earth's powers, as Antigone does, against a world brazenly unjust and therefore inhuman. And the virtue of this perspective is simply its honesty, its unwillingness to be fooled by worldly vanities. Many of Brecht's early poems, furthermore, are political in a nascent sense; they take a plural point of view and address collective experience. Images of mass death occur often. And Brecht's dominant early form, the narrative, is handled with the dedication proper to a poet whose concern would always be with the ways men and women determine, or have forced upon them, the basic conditions of their life.

For example, while the war was still on (1918) and he was serving in a military hospital, Brecht wrote his famous "Legend of the Dead Soldier." In the fifth springtime of the war, as the poem begins, the soldier dies a hero's death, but—

Because the war was not quite done
It made the Kaiser blue
To think the soldier lay there dead
Before his time came due.

So the dead man is dug up, revived with schnapps and declared fit for service. Soon the corpse is goose-stepping off to a second death, blessed by churchmen and cheered on by patriotic crowds. The ballad, with its cynical clichés, its jaunty rhythms and grotesque imagery, is typical. Rimbaud, Villon, and Kipling sound in the background, as does other antiwar poetry written in Germany at that time. The poem rides on the nihilism it mimes, and depicts the horror of perpetual war in terms impossible to stomach (the Nazis *hated* this poem). Brecht always preferred satire to invective; evil is best exposed, and its authority deflated, by letting it display its own disfiguration—a process of naming informed by the curse. And repeatedly, by using emphatic rhyme and barroom rhythms, by exaggeration and blunt refrains, Brecht condemns the voice through which the poem seems to speak. This corresponds to his theory of theater, to the way he wanted actors to carry their parts. They were not to identify with, but rather to "quote," the role they played, and in such a way as to show moral judgment.

The following poem, "The Ballad of Paragraph 218," was written in 1930 during the distress of the Great Depression. The number 218 refers to the section of the criminal code outlawing abortion, and the situation of the poem, as the first line indicates, is that of a pregnant woman begging a doctor to help her:

> Please, doctor, I've missed my monthly . . .
> Why, this is simply great.
> If I may put it bluntly
> You're raising our birthrate.

The three dots are part of the poem; they occur each time the woman begins to give her reasons—her husband is out of work, they have no home, no money—but she never gets far before the doctor cuts her off with this refrain:

> You'll make a simply splendid little mummy
> Producing cannon-fodder from your tummy
> That's what your body's for, and you know it, what's more
> And it's laid down by law
> And now get this straight:
> You'll soon be a mother, just wait.

The lines are very cruel, and Brecht intends them to be. Whether a doctor would use such cynical terms is not the point. From the vantage of the state this is the expedient function of motherhood; the poor are there to be used and used up, and their dehumanized plight is expressed in the doctor's brute command. Brecht tears away the mystique surrounding the notion of "motherhood," revealing woman's role as mere producer. And here also he makes a connection still not understood by many of us. Very few people who oppose abortion on principle are also opposed to war on principle. The pro-lifers, one is tempted to suspect, are gearing up for death on a grand scale and won't feel secure until a surplus of manpower is at the state's disposal.

Brecht sets forth the doctor's position in a manner he came to call *gestisch* or "gestic" writing, a technique for exposing the interior logic of a situation in terms of a gesture or action at the level of language. The basic unit in Brecht's poetry is not the image or the musical phrase, as in so much of modern poetry, but rather the line. Like a Bauhaus beam, each line contributes to some larger structure but at the same time declares its own shape and strength. To read Brecht correctly is to halt with subtle emphasis at line breaks. Even enjambment works this way, and in Brecht's management of line, moreover, the end of the German phrase or sentence is usually a substantial word, not the *ab* or *auf* we might expect. The rapid pileup of pointed lines can be very forceful, especially when stressed by rhyme. These techniques, in turn, are compounded still further by Brecht's use of paratactic syntax (*"And* it's laid down by law / *And* now get this straight"), which makes of the poem the inventory of a subjective state revealing, through its specific gesture, the political situation.

Brecht's bald and deliberate application of the gestic principle is remarkably suited for jamming pathos and violence together. Below is a last example from the early poetry, "Of the Infanticide Marie Farrar," written in 1922. Like many of Brecht's poems, this one was inspired by an event, in this case a young woman (a servant) who without assistance gave birth to her child in the servants' outdoor latrine and then, senseless with pain and desperation, killed it. The poem pretends to be an itemized record of the girl's own testimony, a police report rather than the tragedy it is. Praise and blame are intimately tangled, but not so tightly that we can't sort them out. Of the poem's nine stanzas, the following is the eighth:

Between the servants' privy and her bed (she says
That nothing happened until then), the child
Began to cry, which vexed her so, she says
She beat it with her fists, hammering blind and wild
Without a pause until the child was quiet, she says.
She took the baby's body into bed
And held it for the rest of the night, she says
Then in the morning hid it in the laundry shed.
 But you I beg, make not your anger manifest
 For all that lives needs help from all the rest.

Paratactic sequence (one thing after another) plus the jabbing repetition of "she says" suggests a torment verging on hypnosis. The rest
of the poem makes clear that the child's death is the outcome of a life
brutalized beyond endurance, the grim last act of a woman whose existence had been unbearably grim from the start. The irony of "nothing
happened until then" is overwhelming but also instructive. Marie Farrar
truly does not know what brought her to this awful pass, nor does her
ordeal—giving birth alone, in the winter dark of a cesspool—seem to
her unusual in its degradation. The story is horrible, but also matter-
of-fact. Brecht's sympathy is with the servant. But that the poem does
have a political thrust, and is not merely social criticism, depends on
how we read the final couplet.

On the face of it, the last lines address those who judge the crime,
and then anyone who, upon hearing the story, would be appalled by
something so "unnatural" and "inhuman." Part of the irony, therefore,
lies in reversal: Brecht aims for us to see that the child's death follows
"naturally" from a life that start to finish could only be called inhuman
and unnatural. And further, that those to whom the couplet addresses
itself—those whom servants serve—are not as natural and humane as
they themselves like to suppose. By repeating the couplet after each
stanza, it gradually takes on the character of a formula, a plea uttered
by rote, a useless gesture. And so it is. The plea is genuine but empty.
The real message of the last lines is that such an appeal—a Christian
appeal made to a Christian society—falls on deaf ears. Those for whom
the message is meant are victims like Marie Farrar, who suddenly see
their fate in hers and see also that to beg help from the class that keeps
them down will get them nowhere.

The last lines do not ask forgiveness but state a great truth—"all that lives needs help from all the rest"—which is, or ought to be, the guiding principle for any sound political order. That the appeal is made in earnest but also in vain creates the dialectical perception that gives the poem its political character. As always, Brecht speaks *of* the exploiters and *to* those exploited, exposing infamy and instructing the oppressed. What "Marie Farrar" says finally is said again and again in Brecht's poetry, right up to one of the last poems ("And I Always Thought") he wrote:

> That you'll go down if you don't stand up for yourself
> Surely you see that.

When cursing is wholly absent, praise becomes suspect. Almost against its will, poetry promotes acceptance of the world, lyrically through celebration, tragically by leaving us with the feeling that, yes, that's how things *are*. Homer's *Iliad* is great and uplifting, but its subject is horrendous. We admire the grandeur of *King Lear*, but who would wish Lear's wheel of fire upon him? When a poem would neither praise nor blame, it ends up praising; its figural language heightens any subject and gives it, in capable hands, nobility. This is what Nietzsche had in mind when he said that history is bearable only from an aesthetic point of view. Brecht, however, would not put up with that result, which is, after all, the option of a leisured elite. This would be, in his vocabulary, art of the "culinary" kind. But if poetry's capacity to praise becomes suspect, if a purely aesthetic point of view is ruled out, how might art's cosmetic power be used against itself? And at what cost?

One solution, for Brecht, is satire as brutal as history itself. Another is reliance on didactic forms, which draw their strength from the conviction that life can be changed. A third strategy is to avoid metaphor, especially insofar as metaphor creates the illusion of transcendence—of being "above" X by seeing it in terms of Y. Of his *Svendborg Poems* Brecht said: "From the bourgeois point of view there has been a staggering impoverishment. Isn't it all a great deal more one-sided, less 'organic,' cooler, more self-conscious (in a bad sense)?"[9] One-sided like an ax, cool like metal at night, and thus a poetry that is sometimes disrespectful of the reader's sensibilities, at other times insisting on a distance between reader and poem, a sort of thoughtful estrangement. Brecht's notion of *Verfremdungseffekt* or "alienation effect" applies not only to his theory of theater, but to his poetry as well. There is no emotional solace, no catharsis, no tidy resolution. The appeal, in Brecht's poems (the didactic works most especially), is to the mind rather than the heart. We are not to indulge but to *see*, and to see we must not feel too much at home. In bardic terms, Brecht's willful disruption of the reader's expectations is the summoning of a special audience—a warrior tribe, so to say; a group committed to the general war on injustice.

In 1934, in a poem that takes its title from the first line, Brecht set forth his definition of poetry, and not as a theory only, but as the decision any poet trapped in dark times might make:

> Solely because of the increasing disorder
> In our cities of class struggle
> Some of us have now decided
> To speak no more of cities by the sea, snow on roofs, women
> The smell of ripe apples in cellars, the senses of the flesh, all
> That makes a man round and human
> But to speak in future only about the disorder
> And so become one-sided, reduced, enmeshed in the business
> Of politics and the dry, indecorous vocabulary
> Of dialectical economics
> So that this awful cramped coexistence
> Of snowfalls (they're not merely cold, we know)
> Exploitation, the lured flesh, class justice, should not engender
> Approval of a world so many-sided; delight in
> The contradictions of so bloodstained a life
> You understand.

No semicolon occurs in the German original; the poem is one head-long sentence, a "gestic" enactment of the clarity and conviction with which the poet intends to proceed. In line nine the word here translated as "indecorous" is *unwürdige*, which carries the sense of being unworthy, undeserving or, in sum, not respectable. And in the German version of the poem, Brecht slams the issue home by putting *unwürdige* in quotation marks, thereby transforming the word into its opposite. The concluding irony of "You understand" challenges, or perhaps insults, the "decorous" reader. We see, too, why Brecht brings the indecorous diction of politics into his poems; it allows him *not* to approve of the world as it is, to write poetry that does not inadvertently take "delight in / The contradictions of so bloodstained a life."

Outright political vocabulary seldom appears in Brecht's poems. When it does it bears a dignity entirely free of jargon. The following example, "A Bed for the Night," was written in 1931 in the depths of the Great Depression when the streets of Europe and America were thick with jobless men:

I hear that in New York
At the corner of 26th Street and Broadway
A man stands every evening during the winter months
And gets beds for the homeless there
By appealing to passers-by

It won't change the world
It won't improve relations among men
It will not shorten the age of exploitation
But a few men have a bed for the night
For a night the wind is kept from them
The snow meant for them falls on the roadway.

Don't put down the book on reading this, man.

A few people have a bed for the night
For a night the wind is kept from them
The snow meant for them falls on the roadway
But it won't change the world
It won't improve relations among men
It will not shorten the age of exploitation.

The poem is a good instance of Brecht's dialectical vision. Irony is static, a form of despair, at most a form of subversion that comforts the ironist but does not expect to get very far. Dialectic, on the other hand, offers a form of hope. Two conflicting views are not merely juxtaposed and left to mock each other. The older ethic (stanza two) is turned inside out and made to yield its opposite (stanza four), while the latter is seen to emerge from that which it goes beyond through contradiction. Helping people at the local level was sufficient once, in the era of rural and small-town neighborliness, maybe; but in times of great suffering and whole families homeless, the appeal to individual charity—the street-corner approach—cannot hope to meet mass needs. The Christian ethic, based on the good deed, now defeats itself; the behavior it promotes is decent, but inadequate and finally sentimental. Also harmful; for as long as we accept face-to-face help (and the good will of passersby) as the limit of human obligation, we shall not see the magnitude of the problem nor move toward organized solutions. But of course, those who profit from the status quo can hide behind strategic charity; they may even persuade those whom they exploit that real care exists—the self-advertised munificence of corporate kingdoms, for example, promoting token programs.

By using a didactic voice and the dialectical viewpoint within a political framework, Brecht restores in a minimal, no-nonsense way poetry's visionary element, its capacity to reach beyond the actual. This is all the more astonishing in his case, for no poet has had a better grasp of the actual. Yet in just this way poetry reclaims its integrity, its power to *be* in the daytime world of public forces. And the simplicity with which Brecht makes this work is remarkable. Who would think that hope for the future resides in present despair? Who would guess that to repeat, word for word, lines in reverse order could provide the literary means for a historical-political vision that might otherwise require volumes of argument? The poet renames, in this case, not by naming anew but by turning the old name downside up.

The dialectical process, or rather its poetic enactment, is a good example of poetry and politics working together. The poetic aim is to capture a serious part of the world—a social-political complex—in an instant of time. The political aim is to cut through false pieties and reverse accepted attitudes. Here is another example:

> The peasant's concern is with his field
> He looks after his cattle, pays taxes
> Produces children, to save on labourers, and
> Depends on the price of milk.
> The townspeople speak of love for the soil
> Of healthy peasant stock and
> Call peasants the backbone of the nation.
>
> The townspeople speak of love for the soil
> Of healthy peasant stock
> And call peasants the backbone of the nation.
> The peasant's concern is with his field
> He looks after his cattle, pays taxes

Produces children, to save on labourers, and
Depends on the price of milk.

Translated as "concern," the German *Kummer* loses its sense of grief
and constant worry, just as *Knechte*, rendered as "labourers," no longer
hints of slavery. Meanings of this kind slip away in translation, but
Brecht's major meanings are carried by formal gestures sturdy enough
to survive. The poem above depends entirely on gesture, in particular
the collision of romantic generalities with grim facts, as when "healthy
peasant stock" becomes "children, to save on labourers." And the political point is obvious: as in Hegel's master-slave dialectic, the peasants
serve the townspeople while the townspeople depend on the peasants,
and this the laborers should see. The peasants depend on the price of
milk, which is fixed in town, but the town needs the milk. The situation
is dialectical, hence the form of the poem, the way stanza two inverts
stanza one. How the dual act of reversal and repetition contributes to
the poem's success is puzzling. Either stanza contains all the *visible* information, yet either stanza alone would be trite compared to the power
of the two faced off against each other. It's as if the poem's contradiction,
in the instant of enlightenment, arrives at a truth beyond the reach of
irony merely—a fine example of announcing against.

The didactic element is constant in Brecht. He thought of himself as
a teacher, a guide, a keeper of practical wisdom. The point of his work,
as he often said, is to make people see. There have of course been great
didactic poets, Virgil and Lucretius among them, but for formal inventiveness and aesthetic effects as powerful as any "pure" poet might hope
to create, the poetry of Brecht is the outstanding example of successful
didactic art in our time. The didactic mode served as Brecht's most
durable device for bringing poetry and politics into fruitful union, and
if, as Walter Benjamin has argued, the important artist not only uses a
mode but also transforms and extends it, then Brecht's importance is
obvious. Satire of the modern kind is inherently didactic, but the lyric
is not; that Brecht could be didactic *and* lyrical enlarges our idea of
poetry itself. He cleared the way for new options and also used the
didactic stance to solve perhaps his biggest problem; for in sharp contrast
to the Soviet brand of Marxism, which would speak *for* oppressed peoples, Brecht goes no further than speaking *to* them, propounding no
authorities or programs but only insisting that victims everywhere
should see themselves in the full sadness of their plight and see also that

if politics is part of the human condition, a great deal of the human condition is political.

And yet there is something else, subtler, more delicate, about Brecht's use of didactic form. It allows him to remain impersonal, it rules out small talk and self-pity, and where deep emotion arises the didactic stance becomes a technique for restraint, for expression of feeling about world events without splashing the event or its corresonding emotion all over the page. If his role as teacher demands discipline, it also gives Brecht moments of happy freedom. Consider the following poem, quoted complete:

> Refresh yourself, sister
> With the water from the copper bowl with bits of ice in it—
> Open your eyes under water, wash them—
> Dry yourself with the rough towel and cast
> A glance at a book you love.
> In this way begin
> A lovely and useful day.

A love poem, of course; it is addressed to the actress Carola Neher, one of the women Brecht loved. That she later died in a Soviet concentration camp suggests the retrograde impact of future events on Brecht's kind of poetry—or perhaps any art that dares a political content. But in the little love poem, the poet's aim is not politics or advice. He wants to preserve a moment of beauty "so that painters could make pictures of it," as once he said.[10] The tenderness, in this case, is heightened rather than curbed by the rigor of its expression, and this leads to a general observation about Brecht's style: his severity, his militant push, his sometimes savage irony, these are formal strategies through which, in dark times, care and humanness remain active.

When Brecht started out, in the aftermath of World War One, he, along with Rilke and Gottfried Benn, represented the ways open to poetry in dark times. Rilke retreated into an exalted mysticism that glorified death and said, in effect, that the world is not as it seems. Benn, on the other hand, embraced the abyss, the primacy of slime, and took cold comfort in precise delineation of physical decay as the emblem of the human world. On the one side, praise and blessing, on the other a level cursing. Brecht was determined to do both, to blame the world before him and praise its possibilities. He was surely aware of decay, but never seduced by easeful death. Rather, he attacked the nihilism of his age head-on, through satire, and worked toward a political position that would give him the strength, purpose, and also the scope, necessary to confront history without loss of hope or compassion. But to speak in terms of options is misleading. With very little choice, any poet is always committed to his or her vision; or rather, is obliged to honor the relation between self and world that provokes poetic creation. In Brecht's case there is no doubt what this relation was:

> The great boats and the dancing sails on the Sound
> Go unseen. Of it all
> I see only the torn nets of the fishermen.

Those lines are from "Bad Time for Poetry," written in 1939. Brecht's favorite way of cursing Hitler was to name him "the house-painter"; here are the last lines from "Bad Time for Poetry":

> Inside me contend
> Delight at the apple tree in blossom
> And horror at the house-painter's speeches
> But only the second
> Drives me to my desk.

For Brecht the curse would always come first. Praise was a privilege he valued but could seldom afford. Not joy or celebration, but rather the need to take a stand and announce against informs his art. But if poetry arises from the soul's need to sing, how does song survive the world's horror? Brecht offered an answer in a little poem, "Motto," that he used for an epigraph in the *Svendborg Poems*:

> In the dark times
> Will there also be singing?
> Yes, there will also be singing
> About the dark times.

In German the last two lines go this way:

Da wird auch gesungen werden.
Von den finsteren Zeiten.

He does not say yes; that would be too easy, too thoughtless. He restates the question as its own answer, a crucial reversal that is again an example of dialectical form. His placement of a period after the second-to-last line not only makes the line stronger and more final, it also calls for a halt and a silence before going on to the last line, a halt and a silence that, in a cliché I think Brecht would appreciate, speaks volumes. *There will also be singing.* How? What kind? *About and against the dark times.* And the cost will be large. The range of vision will narrow, and worse, will focus on unhappy and often terrible things. This entails an obligation that will not, once accepted, be lightly cast off. And the poetry itself will be of a kind that some among us might dismiss as too spartan, too seldom an occasion for delight and happy grace.

Brecht measured these costs and took them for granted. But two things he did not anticipate. The logic of his politics *and* the logic of his poetry would come to dominate his personal fate, leading him—a German, a Marxist, a man returning to his country—to end up in East Berlin. His early travel back and forth, his Austrian passport, his Swiss bank account, all this confirms, as I see it, Brecht's decision against grave personal doubts to stay in the struggle, despite Stalin, despite the shabby and sometimes grim conditions of life in East Germany. Hannah Arendt missed the main point when she condemned Brecht for his choice; it was the outcome (not the betrayal) of his whole life as a poet. If living in the Soviet sector did damage to his poetic capacity, that too was part of the cost for one who would sing about and against the dark times.

But the worst cost could not be seen coming until too late. Brecht's poetry embraces a political vision, inspiring in its ideals, which did not survive its totalitarian perversion. The historical failure of Marxism has had enormous consequences for all of us, but for people directly involved the outcome was shattering. Recurring anti-Soviet sentiment and outbreaks of bitterness in Brecht's late poetry reveal the suffering of a man coming to see—as a generation of decent men and women came painfully to see—that the great moment had passed, that the magnificent dream of liberty would go unrealized. But if defeat is the likely outcome in actual politics, in poetry the case is strangely otherwise. Brecht's vision was betrayed by history but his poetry does not therefore suffer forfeit or become irrelevant. Defeat, on the contrary, becomes the proof of its power. It gains in retrospective depth, taking on dignity and an import that did not exist when the poems were written but which exists now because of the way things turned out.

After the war Brecht returned from exile in America and arrived in East Berlin on October 22, 1948. He lived there six and a half years before he died in 1956 at the age of fifty-eight. That is a short time for any artist—especially amid political unrest on all sides—to begin a new life, to set up a theater company and see to its success. He had been refused entry to the American sector of Berlin, but he would have gone to the Eastern zone in any case. He was a Marxist and this would be Marxism on German soil, his own tribe's chance to rebuild from the rubble on socialist principles. Germany, we might recall, was not yet two countries and Brecht had enormous hope for a unified nation. With a national theater in mind, and knowing the urgency of gathering the best of German talent before it dispersed across Europe, Brecht urged his friend Picastor to join him: "It is a good moment, one should not put it off much longer, everything is still in a state of flux and the direction things take will be determined by the forces at hand."[12]

Despite gossip to the contrary, it is now certain that Brecht was not bribed, not promised a theater of his own, to settle in East Berlin. His recent German biographer, Klaus Volker, is emphatic on this point. There was no "official invitation." Volker thinks, on the contrary, that in his usual style Brecht "forced his way in."[13] His idea for a theater first met with indifference and then with much difficulty before it was realized officially, more than two years after Brecht's departure from America, and the Berliner Ensemble would not have its own building until March of 1954. Only six productions were staged before, in 1951, a new round of Soviet purges and the vicious atmosphere of the Cold War destroyed, once and for all, Brecht's hopes for a national theater that would contribute to the creation of a united Germany. It was at *this* point that Brecht observed: "Time will show if pessimism is to be rated negatively."[14]

He nonetheless pushed on with his task, building up a first-rate acting company and adapting plays to fit his own ideas of dramatic art. He began new plays, and he was also writing poetry. His last poems are spare and swift and might appear slight on first reading, but many are excellent, the "Buckow Elegies" in particular. What chiefly characterizes his art during these last years is the frequency and bitterness of poems

bearing anti-Soviet sentiment, such as "Still at It," the theme of which—
everything changed but nothing changed—was strong in Brecht's work
at the time:

> The plates are slammed down so hard
> The soup slops over.
> In shrill tones
> Resounds the order: Now eat!
>
> The Prussian eagle
> Jabbing food down
> The gullets of its young.

Some of his late poems are sarcastic in the fiery early style, for example
"The Solution." After the East German regime crushed the workers'
uprising of June 17, 1953, Brecht wrote that perhaps the best course
for government would be to "dissolve the people / And elect another."
Many of the late poems are muted and subtle, as if these were the last,
half-uttered words of a man talking only to himself, a man, say, whose
entire life had taught him that "as always the lovely and sensitive / Are
no longer," and who steps into the ragged shade of an abandoned
greenhouse to see "the remains of the rare flowers."

A final and perhaps stronger criticism is that Brecht's basic disposition—to attack and to curse—was relentless against Hitler, but that he
deployed no similar assault against Stalin, despite the death of dear
friends in the Soviet Union. It's true that Brecht was in Russia only
briefly, but he followed the Soviet scene with keen interest. When Walter
Benjamin asked him, in 1938, if his support for the Russian program
might need changing he answered that "unfortunately or God be praised,
whichever you prefer,"[15] available news had not yet coalesced into certainty. Meanwhile, as a realist, as an especially strong dreamer, he would
take his courage from setbacks and put up with a great deal of adverse
evidence before quitting. As in any long fight, victory would require
sacrifice. That there would be no victory is a point too easily made by
those who make it in hindsight. For Brecht there was only a wall of
urgent wrong against which any decent person might make the choice
to stand and fight. And there was also this: Brecht's tribe at large was
composed of men and women who embraced a Marxist vision and,
anywhere in the world, fought for radical change. But his more intimate

audience was the tribe of his mother tongue, the German nation that he attacked, blessed, defended, and called to like a prophet. He *knew* Hitler, knew him by his language early on, which suggests that his poetry is focused less on international politics than on the political condition of his own disbanded homeland.

It is the fate of all poetry to be overtaken by time, and after death it reads differently—after, that is, the world it addressed and drew life from no longer exists. For art that addresses history directly, in any case, and especially for poetry that fathoms the human interaction with time itself, the outcome is often melancholy, the more so when the poet has been in love with a cause that like all causes fails. About the way poetry has of surviving itself, this much needs keeping in mind. Political art—the kind attached to a cause—possesses a destiny, and when its destiny ends in defeat, the result is not failure but tragedy. When we read it now, Brecht's poetry bears within it a tragic sense of life that the poet himself could not have detected. Or no, in his late years Brecht began to feel it deeply, and in the following poem, one of the last he wrote, the destiny of his art—which is the tragedy of hope in dark times—is fully recognized:

> At the time when their fall was certain—
> On the ramparts the lament for the dead had begun—
> The Trojans adjusted small pieces, small pieces
> In the triple wooden gates, small pieces.
> And began to take courage, to hope.
>
> The Trojans too then.

In 1947, with Europe still flat and the Cold War order already conscripting the world, Max Frisch observed: "Most of what goes by the name of poetry looks like irony of the crassest sort when I compare it for even only a single day with my own life."[16] One knows exactly what he means. One knows the distractions of art that is blind to the world. Poetry that confronts its time, on the contrary, can't claim innocence of any sort. Like Frisch, I find Brecht sustaining, even beautiful, for the way his poems stand up to the world in which they were written. He took the risks and kept his art open, allowing history its maiming intrusions, making the best of bad prospects. In "To Those Born Later," Brecht says of himself:

All roads led into the mire in my time.
My tongue betrayed me to the butchers.
There was little I could do. But those in power
Sat safer without me: that was my hope.
So passed my time
Which had been given to me on earth.

His hope was betrayed, as hope usually is. And no doubt there was little he could do. All honest vision leads into the mire—as Yeats noted—and not just the familiar squalor of selfhood but the bloody, man-created sorrow that darkens the world, from which no one is exempt, about which no one can claim not to know. In a recent poem, half horror, half surreal play, Charles Simic inserts some lines to suggest how politics grips those swept up, but also the rest of us—those who only behold:

The act of torture consists of various strategies
meant to increase
the imagination of the homo sapiens.

Coleridge never thought of that one. Neither did Emerson. For the Romantics and their offspring, imagination was its own sweet proof, a passage to worlds elsewhere. For those born later, imagination faces and defends, and the irony of Simic's lines makes terrible sense. Brecht, at least, would think so.

·VI·

Breyten Breytenbach,
South Africa

But what does one do if you are White, if in fact you
are part of the privileged minority in power? When
you come in revolt against such a system, how do you
oppose it effectively?

—Breyten Breytenbach[1]

In the harrowing light of his prison memoir—*The True Confessions
of an Albino Terrorist*—Breyten Breytenbach's poetry comes at us
differently than when it began to appear (in English translation) during
the 1970's. What started out with extravagant purpose ends up reduced,
doubtful, almost melancholy. Militant high spirits gave way to pessimism, and with Breytenbach's career in view, the prison years especially,
poems that once seemed distinctive for their wildness now appear com-
mendable for their candor and patience. One looks back to the early
surreal work, full of blood and rot, and thinks: "So he meant it after
all." One wonders at the vehemence of his attack on apartheid politics
and then sees—thanks to the news and photojournalism—a world-class
tragedy in progress. South Africa is going down and this poet, with his
Afrikaner rootedness, had known it all along. "I fear," Breytenbach said
in 1983, "that the price to be paid—in the cruel game directed and
enforced by those now in power—will be exorbitant; the suffering will
rip the country asunder and create generations of blindness, bitterness
and hate. Are we not heading for an ungovernable Lebanon-type situation where killing will be the only form of communication?"[2] That is
the view from *Confessions*. It is also the view from most of Breytenbach's
poetry, with its imagery of dismemberment, its bitter twistings of sense,

its brave but cramped attempt to envision life clearly, beyond the veil of *hysterica passio*.

Not that seven years in South African jails was Breytenbach's choice. Still less that it takes extremity to certify one's art; but rather that for poetry confronting politics, context is fate. He bears witness in a very off-beat manner, disdainful and urgent at once, but it's clear that the experience of political intrusion has always been Breytenbach's sounding board. In a poem that would later amaze his Afrikaner prosecutors, a poem called "breyten prays for himself," humor mutes but does not tune out the bitterness. It begins:

> There is no need of Pain Lord
> We could live well without it
> A flower has no teeth [.]

Breytenbach goes on, in his mock-Christian way, to implore that while "we are only fulfilled in death . . . let our flesh stay fresh as cabbage." He calls for "mercy on our mouths our bowels our brains," so that "we" may decay in peace. Then the poem swings around, turning the plea to a grievance:

> And gradually we will decompose like old ships or trees
> But keep Pain far from Me o Lord
> That others may bear it
> Be taken into custody, Shattered
> > Stoned
> > Suspended
> > Lashed
> > Used
> > Tortured
> > Crucified
> > Cross-examined
> > Placed under house arrest
> > Given hard labour
> Banished to obscure islands till the end of their days
> Wasting in damp pits down to slimy green imploring bones
> Worms in their stomachs heads full of nails
> But not *Me*
> But we never give Pain or complain

The list, although it gives way to metaphor toward the end, is a straight catalogue of the misery inflicted on South African blacks by their Afrikaner bosses, including the "damp pits" of the mines and banishment to the notorious obscurity of Robbins Island, where black dissidents, Nelson Mandela among them, were being held in Breytenbach's time. Much of this he would endure or witness in his own person while inside Maximum Security. The poem from which I've quoted was written prior to 1964, when it was published in an early collection. Breytenbach knew, with precision even then, what his country was coming to.

But there is more, of course, than context merely. The poem is a curse made sharper by pretending to bless. But if the poet is "Me," who is "we"? Breytenbach is parodying a well-known poem, "St. Ignatious prays for his order," published in 1956 by H. P. van Wyk Louw, an established Afrikaner poet. One of Breytenbach's constant enemies is Afrikaner piety, the huge hypocrisy of a nation pledged to apartheid in Christian terms. This is the more loathsome in that he has himself absorbed a good deal of the Christian ethic, and in a better world would have been glad to follow Christ's way. As things stand, Breytenbach deploys his heritage against itself, sometimes bitterly, sometimes with delight, as in the following lines from a poem that plays with the Lord's Prayer:

Give us this day the chance to earn our daily bread
and the butter, the jam, the wine, the silence,
The silence of wine,
And lead us into temptation of various kinds
So that love may jump from body to body
Like the flames of being—being from mountain to mountain

Brambles of fire brought to the whitest moon

But let us deliver ourselves from evil
So that we may reckon with the trespass of centuries
Of stored up exploitation, of plunder, of swindling[. . . .]

His attack, here, is against the overbearing presence of the fathers in Afrikaner tradition, and Breytenbach's maledictions are most often levelled directly at patriarchal power. There might be a genuine religious element in his work as well, in which case his liturgical or scriptural references (of which there are many) will be ambivalent to a radical degree, a blessing and a curse together.

In South Africa, religion and politics join forces, a condition that allows Afrikaner political culture, like most political cultures, including your own, to subscribe to the myth of exceptionalism. This rugged tribe with its errand in the wilderness was assigned by God a privileged role in world affairs, a role that might require the suppression or even extermination of alien peoples along the way, but that assures the master race immunity from wrongdoing because the Lord himself is guiding them to glory. And hence, in Afrikaner consciousness, the right to exemption from suffering such as "others may bear," and hence their righteousness: "we never give Pain or complain." Breytenbach would like to defeat these notions or, as he would later declare, to see them destroyed outright. But here, in "breyten prays for himself," and long before he fell into the hands of the state, his duty is to curse the world that Afrikaner piety upholds. This he does by mocking the Afrikaner heritage. He deploys a lively irreverence and uses irony to speak *for* the tribe that in fact he is speaking *against*.

Devices of this kind cut deeper than their technical use might suggest. As a poet whose native tongue is Afrikaans, Breytenbach *must* speak for the tribe he rails against, and the poet's "prayer," in this case, is a curse upon himself as well as the tribe he attacks. His accusation is as much against himself as the Afrikaner poet he mocks, and in consequence his art finds itself at odds with itself. Praising or blaming, Breytenbach must go forward in a language preempted by the state—a situation very like Antigone's. As he says in *Confessions*, "Afrikaans is the language of oppression and of humiliation, of the Boer. Official Afrikaans is the tool of the racist."[3] The jugular rending of language in Breytenbach's poetry is disturbing on any account, and its destructive force derives from this circumstance: here is a man without a nation, and a poet without a language, of his own. Breytenbach says of his condition: "nothing can ever bridge the gap between the authorities of the Afrikaner tribe and myself."[4] And also, as recently as 1983: "I do not consider myself to be an Afrikaner."[5] Like the work of other poets who confront political experience, Breytenbach's art thrives on situations that permit the poem's occasion to bring poet and tribe together. But unlike the other poets studied in this book, he has rejected the audience his language naturally summons. This misfortune defines the character of his art. Quite consciously, he is a bard without a tribe.

· · ·

Breytenbach's poetic reputation is inseparable from his role as exile, as political prisoner, as outspoken enemy of one of the ugliest states on earth. Among South Africans, as André Brink has observed, his renegade fame insures that "every line of poetry he writes—even if it is the purest lyrical verse—acquires *political* implications."[6] Born in 1939, Breytenbach is of solid Afrikaner lineage. Part of his good fortune was to grow up in the southern part of South Africa, within the more relaxed hegemony of Cape Town rather than the narrow rectitude of Pretoria—a difference comparable to the split between Leningrad, with its cosmopolitan spirit, and Moscow's phobic dark. He left home in 1959, wandered Europe for several years, then settled in Paris to paint (first exhibit, 1962) and write poems (first book, 1964). Because his wife is Vietnamese, his marriage to Hoang Lien Yolande was an "immoral" act according to South African statute, and in this way Breytenbach cut himself off from the freedom of homecoming. He has done almost all his work in exile, and the exile's plight is a recurrent theme in his work. In 1973 he and his wife were allowed a ninety-day return to South Africa, out of which came *A Season in Paradise*, a visionary prose work that is part memoir, part political tract, and part exuberant poem. Then in 1975 Breytenbach reentered South Africa illegally, in disguise and bearing a false passport. After three weeks—the police were tracking him the whole time—he was arrested, then convicted of terrorism and sentenced to nine years in prison. He served seven, two in solitary, and was released in 1982. Since then Breytenbach and his wife have lived in Paris.

At the time of his arrest, and for most of his imprisonment, it wasn't possible to get dependable information about Breytenbach's condition or the circumstances that led to the charge of terrorism. But in 1983 *True Confessions of an Albino Terrorist* came out, and Breytenbach acquits himself rather well, I think, not least for the candor with which he admits his shortcomings—in particular the sort of naivete and unpreparedness for action that one might expect of a visionary embracing politics. While living in Paris, Breytenbach helped start a clandestine group called Okhela (the Zulu word for "spark"); then he returned to South Africa with a copy of the group's manifesto in his pocket (with language like "armed struggle" and "offensive direct action"). The aim of Okhela, as I understand it, was to gather disaffected South African whites into a network in order to assist the general struggle under, ultimately, the black leadership of the African National Council (ANC). Okhela also hoped to foster a socialist alternative to the Soviet brand. Breytenbach's mission was to make contacts, to seek out leaders and test the political climate. But he was fingered by someone inside the European group—South African surveillance is *that* well organized—and Okhela's plan of action was dead before it got started.

Breytenbach's art has thrived and now falters in the nightsoil of politics. In his case, moreover, poetry and politics don't just collide; they are violently yoking, historically, culturally, to a condition of language. English and Afrikaans, in South Africa, are both authorized languages, but Afrikaans comes first politically. The British won the Boer War, but that has mattered little in the disposition of power, which since 1948 has been in the hands of the intensely tribal Afrikaners. Apartheid is their rule and likewise their word. It means, in Afrikaans, *apartness*. It means 87 percent of the land given over to whites exclusively, with mass deportation of blacks, mass arrests, and, more recently, mass killings as the conditions for civil war increase. Under provision of the Terrorism Act, apartheid means a state security apparatus that detains whom it pleases, tortures whom it pleases, conducts interrogations in such a way that black men fall to their deaths from high windows. It means a system of domination rooted in a local tongue evolved from Dutch, a language little more than two centuries old, largely empty of tradition, its historical function to keep a small people, the Boers, the Afrikaners, united and on top. Like other colonial languages, Afrikaans isn't innocent, and this is bound to cause trouble for poets, especially a poet like Breytenbach who has stationed himself against his own identity as a native Afrikaner.

In a poem called "(lotus)," the poet enters a world where a "horse of air" comes charging across the sky, the sky "a blue tent," the sun "a banner." We might suppose the horse to be Pegasus in an airy world of poesy. But the voice of the poet, on the contrary, rises out of the muck to curse his poetic destiny:

> the Great Task is
> to turn dog turds
> into stars
> and to trample down the Great Void[.]

To evoke the world's waste, even by way of cursing, is to be on earth's side, and this is Breytenbach's habit. He does not inherit the sun, as he might like, but a solid plate of night that he must somehow face and transform. The problem is words themselves:

> all words are only phantoms
> galloping like horses of breath
> through the emptiness[.]

The poet goes on to identify his "tongue" with his "shadow," and addressing the lotus (a tree of life?) he concedes a defeat:

> for I must shake that shadow
> from the night-mouth
> and with that shadow as a knife
> bareback and astride that tongue
> I must be able to unfold all your leaves
>
> to here where you turn to a pearl,
> to the blind, self-fulfilling pearl
>
> don't you smell the stars now?
> everything comes up out of experience
> and sinks back into it again:
> the horses eat pearls[.]

Breytenbach pits tongue against horse, and the horses, we see, are words—language itself devouring the results of the poet's "Great Task," permitting the Void to prevail. It's not language per se that's the villain, but language politically suborned and in service to an antihuman order. No poet with solid tribal connection would feel as Breytenbach does about words—words that in the volume *Death White as Words* are delimited by "death" and by "white." Among so much else, words are social realities, powers that take their specific substance from the history of the tribe that gives them their life. Surely the relation of language to its political base is not so arcane, or not, at least, in Breytenbach's example. Language is informed by power, and then against by power's lack. The enemy is the state, and the way the state exploits language to uphold its authority. Of course, governmental powers everywhere attempted to control and empty out words. But few poets have had the problem facing Breytenbach and his South African colleagues.

There was, of course, a scattering of poetry already available in Afrikaans, but early stirrings of an Afrikaner voice stayed within the pale and at a time when apartheid was not yet the official order. For the poets of Breytenbach's generation, there has been no counterculture, no alternate or adversary tradition to fall back on, unlike, say, the Russian language with its tradition of revolt against tzarist imposition. When the Soviets appropriated Russian culture there was an earlier legacy—the gift of Pushkin, Gogol, and Chekhov among others—in place to depend on. In English we have the subversive powers of Swift in his savage indignation, of Milton in his darker moods, of mad saints like Blake and Smart, and then the renegade stance of American English in the hands of poets aiming to improve on the "belched words" of Whitman's speech, the "crotch and vine" of his expandable syntax. The situation nearest to Breytenbach's today is in poetry of the women's movement. But even here, as in Adrienne Rich's steady summoning of a feminist past, there *is* a past, a Dickinson to bless the new beginning.

No similar resources are available to the poet who must pursue his or her art in the language of state power, although, as I'll suggest later, Afrikaans is not a lost cause by necessity, if only because those who find themselves officially damned are beginning to use their linguistic inheritance in drastically unofficial ways, much as Breytenbach himself has used it—this "tongue" that shows up everywhere in his poetry as an image of dismemberment, a tongue with no body, no worthy tribe to empower it. But overall, as political conditions deteriorate it would seem that the situation in South Africa weds Afrikaans ever more closely to the violence of the state. This is Breytenbach's view in "The Struggle of the Taal," a poem written in 1976 about the struggle to keep "the Taal" (the official version of Afrikaans) alive and, in Miroslav Holub's phrase, as "clear as the conscience of a gun." The poem was smuggled out of prison, and has appeared in several places. I quote from the translation in *Confessions*, where the poet takes up a righteous wrathful voice against those who have "yet to master the Taal," those for whom the Taal has been so good and done so much:

> From the structures of our conscience
> from the stores of our charity
> we had black constructions built for you, you bastards—
> schools, clinics, post offices, police stations—

and now the plumes of black smoke blow
throbbing and flowing like a heart.

Since then the "plumes of black smoke" have grown longer, thicker,
more numerous, and we behold in the voice of the Taal (which speaks
for the Afrikaner's tribal "we") how language and violence are yoked:

> For we are Christ's executioners.
> We are on the walls around the locations
> gun in one hand
> and machine gun in the other:
> we, the missionaries of Civilization.
>
> We bring you the grammar of violence
> and the syntax of destruction—
> from the tradition of our firearms
> you will hear the verbs of retribution
> stuttering.

Those beneath the lashing of the Taal are given "new mouths for
free," and each mouth is a bullet hole—"where each lead-nosed word
flies / a speech organ will be torn open." And therefore: "you will please
learn to use the Taal." This is Breytenbach's most direct use of the voice
of the oppressor. He turns the enemy's position against itself, as Brecht
often did, but with the added irony that he is satirizing a voice and a
culture inescapably his own. Brecht went back to Luther, among others,
but Breytenbach goes back to none but himself. Were it not for the
restraint his art allows him, his vehemence would be frantic, out of
control. At moments he falls into the kind of "demonic" despair we saw
Yeats enthralled by. This is a dangerous position because it depends on
the tactics of the enemy, and as the level of political violence escalates
the problems of poetry also escalate. At what point does a language
informed by the berserk power of a dying state become too terrible for
native sons and daughters to digest? At what point can the poet only
"vomit," as Breytenbach often puts it?

In 1983, shortly after his release from prison, Breytenbach told Donald Wood that he would write no more in Afrikaans: "I've long felt
there was hope for it only if it were used in resistance to apartheid, but
I think it is now too late."[7] In an after-note to his *Confessions*, Breytenbach

is more detached yet: "To me it is of little importance whether the language dies of shame or is preserved and strengthened by its potentially revolutionary impact."[8] I don't know that Breytenbach has produced any poetry since the poems written or published while he was a political prisoner. If he abandons his native tongue for good, how likely is it that he will go on writing poetry? Novelists have been successful at making the switch to a new language, Conrad and Nabokov for example, but few poets even try. The mother tongue is an absolute source, impossible to replace. Poets like Joseph Brodsky or Czeslaw Milosz will sometimes do their own translating after a poem is alive in its first language. But to take up another tongue—that's as intimate as having one's actual tongue cut out and another stitched over the wound. The only prominent example is that of Paul Celan, whose success is admittedly astonishing. Celan was Romanian and, after the death of his family in the Second World War, wrote in a shattered sort of German. But his language seems alienated even from itself, and in the end, perhaps for many reasons, Celan committed suicide.

Breytenbach, meanwhile, has declared himself still committed to the struggle for liberty in South Africa, and his political position is bound to affect his poetic options in ways that cannot, perhaps, be judged by anyone, not even Breytenbach himself. Two of his collections, *Death White as Words* and *In Africa even the flies are happy*, are available in English translation, enough to convey an art and a spirit. The poetry is characterized by a surrealist tenor that from poem to poem is more or less distraught and ill-tempered, more or less the cry of *hysterica passio*. There is little calm or tenderness, although some of his poems to his wife are wholly gentle and bright with blessing. Everywhere the problem of language shows up, a radical ambivalence magnified by feelings of guilt and self-doubt. There are moments when he is able to identify with the black condition, or when he manages to become one with the land apart from those who defile it. But in the main, Breytenbach's poetry is notable for its surreal dismemberment of biological forms; for a comic spirit that is playful and raucous but that darkens quickly; and for a sense of woundedness, sometimes muted, sometimes grimly festering. These signs of maiming are the cost of close proximity to politics, the faithful record of a nation's political experience. And how else, except by close proximity, could a testament of this kind come into existence?

A nation that keeps its flies happy is a place, as Hamlet would say, far gone with rot. And more than a little, Breytenbach recalls Hamlet, vexed and melancholic, darkly playful and given to antic fits. In "Good-bye, Cape Town," the poet is on his way into exile; this is his leave-taking, addressed to the city.

if someone would grant it me I'd search beyond your walls
for a Jonah tree
if you were a woman I'd elaborate on the smells
of your pocked skin and gurgling glands
lovely arch-whore
slut flirt hell-cat bitch
but you're not even a mother
you're an abortive suicide
gushing wounds of water between the quay and the flanks of this boat
my cape, man's cape, capelove, heart's cape
I wanted to breathe you into a full blown rose
but you stayed just a mouth and a tongue[.]

Mere name-calling, you might say, and offensive as well for its sexism. But the calling of names is any poet's job. And what sex can a city be, a prolific city at one with climate and terrain, but female, as the land itself is female beneath its patriarchal burden? Still, in the lines above the rapid renaming seems frantic or obsessive. While there is no denying Breytenbach's metamorphic vigor, his surge of naming seems stuck, as if for all its steady inventiveness the poem were unable to surmount its occasion. Breytenbach's ambivalence, in this case, is rooted in outright love and hate. We are with a poet for whom peace, if it comes at all, is momentary in the image of an isolated tree; with their small zones of saving shade, trees appear often in his poems. The reference to Jonah suggests further that Breytenbach is unsure of his prophetic appointment. His mission is urgent but its success is in doubt—here the poet's capacity to breathe life into a language that, as he receives it, is no more than a mouth.

Much of Breytenbach's harshness, his fitful intensity, is the result of his fight with Afrikaans. The Taal must be subverted, its authority broken. But in what manner and at what cost? The task is formidable; it provokes distrust toward poetry itself, and there are times when writing in Afrikaans feels like going over to the enemy. But in that case what is poetry? In a poem called "Constipation," Breytenbach offers one of his several answers:

Not that Coleridge doesn't belong to the school of damned poets
        he says
the outcasts capable of ejecting at a given moment
a waxy fart of hideous pain
through the tunnel and turnstile of blood
        and there I agree
for what is a poem
other than a black wind?

Again Breytenbach allies himself with the muck, and seems to agree
with Artaud that "all true poetry is cruel." But cruel to whom? The
poem's epigraph is from Artaud's commentary on van Gogh: "No one
has ever written or painted, sculpted, modelled, built, invented except
to get out of hell."[9] Hell, for Breytenbach, is the moral torment of being
white in South Africa. And hell is language itself. This poet writes, then,
to escape the infernal predicament that his poetry keeps him locked into.
What are his options? There are the Fathers, whom he rejects. And then
there are the Brothers, with whom he knows he is not one. Describing
his first night in Maximum Security, Breytenbach writes: "And in the
background all around me in this weird place, I heard male voices; it
sounded like scores of voices singing in unison very rhythmically, very
strongly, what sounded like tribal music and sometimes like religious
hymns."[10] He would later learn that when a black man walks to the
gallows, the entire population of the prison—the *black* population—
chants its strength to the man about to die. Such intense communion
can be admired, even envied, but tribal rapport of this kind is not,
Breytenbach knows, a poetic resource in his case.

"Reality," he says in one poem, is "just a boundary, a rumour." But
having conferred that sort of potency upon his art, he goes on, elsewhere,
to take it back: "poems are just day trips." Seeking solid ground, Breytenbach's imagery settles at the biological level; and while there is much
stench and rot, there is also life's sweetness, a mothering plenitude that
blesses and protects. In "Fiesta for an eye" he defines his place of reprieve:

>   you know no other fig tree which stands
>   as this one stands cleaved by the butchering sun
>   bleeding over its litter of coolness
>   stuffing its figs full of palates so that later it can
>   taunt the sun

> no tree rivals this mother of coolness
> where wedlock is celebrated
> where the firm root is fitted
> to the red-mouthed orifice in the ground
> flesh rouses flesh
> and the figs are full of milk[.]

That is life under the aspect of the Mother, fruitful, erotic, a good unto itself; and here is a female power, moreover, with male capabilities, as when its "firm root" penetrates the "red-mouthed" earth. But these images of fecundity are countered by another imagery, sterile and cold-blooded. This is the domain of the Father, where life is empty, caged, at best a shabby affair or even a kind of death. The following lines are from a poem called "I will die and go to my father":

> friends, fellow mortals
> don't tremble; life still hangs
> like flesh from our bodies
> but death has no shame—
>   we come and we go
> like water from a tap
> like sounds from the mouth
> like our comings and goings:
> it's our bones which will know freedom
> come with me
>   bound in my death, to my father
> in Wellington where the angels
> use worms to fish fat stars from heaven;
> let us die and decompose and be merry:
> my father has a large boarding-house[.]

As we have seen, blasphemy and biblical parody are constants in Breytenbach's work. His easy reference to both the Old and the New Testaments suggests a rich religious upbringing. He presumes, in any case, that Afrikaners take their Christian National Education seriously, and he attacks state religion as an especially repugnant hypocrisy. The poet's assaults are sometimes dancing, sometimes heavyhanded. His saving grace is humor, humor as an irreverent aside that keeps him safely to the side. It also turns grimness to whimsy, and Breytenbach's zaniness is among his best strengths. Often, however, he lets his sense of urgency hobble what might otherwise impress us as true wit. We are left to guess how much is laughter, how much grimace. In a poem called "icon" he surveys the gory world depicted in a Bosch-like painting, then concludes:

> above all this a spiky jesus stands out on a cross
> with no more hope of decomposing
> than a butcher bird's prey on a barbed wire fence,
> with a sneer along his beard;
>
> further behind for ever out of reach (like marilyn monroe)
> rises an empty cool grave[.]

Too often Breytenbach seems fierce in his focus yet reckless in his connections. But on closer inspection, the passage holds much that is his hallmark. Of the six lines above, each in turn surprises; none could be predicted, yet they add up to a complex image. Who is this sneering Jesus if not the poet himself, a savior who cannot save or remove himself from the horror he beholds? And seen through the barbed wire of apartheid, who is Monroe but the White Goddess promising a bliss not to be had, neither in life nor in death nor in art, certainly not in South Africa. We might wonder at the exact balance of humor and distress, but the passage itself is a convincing emblem of impotence, of anger venting itself in bitter play. The religious reference counts as well. In this land, the poet says, there is no redemption in sight.

There is no denying Breytenbach's hyperbolic tendency, his deliberate unpleasantness, his penchant for insult. But these tactics are applied at various temperatures, with the barometer sometimes dropping toward storm, sometimes rising to a wispy sky. And he does not always write in a black wind of rage and disgust. We might even guess that Breytenbach's poetic disposition favors praise and blessing, but that in his circumstances, his exile and status as a poet without a tribe, there is little he can celebrate. On occasion, however, he reaches altogether beyond these entrapments. The small poem below comes to us quietly, with kindness and unusual lyricism. It is called "First prayer for the hottentotsgod," and we need to know three items of background information: first, that *hottentot*, like *kaffir*, is an Afrikaner term of derision for blacks; next, that *hottentotsgot* means "praying mantis" in Afrikaans;

and then that in Bushman myth, this small insect is thought to be a god. Here is Breytenbach's prayer:

they say, little beast, little creator, the elders say
that the fields of stars, the earth-dwellers and all things
that turn and rise up and sigh and crumble
were brought forth by you, that you planted an ostrich feather
in the darkness and behold!   the moon!
o most ancient one,
                          you who fired by love
consume your lover, what led you to forsake
the children of those—the human stuff—
remember?   summoned by you
from the mud?
there are fires in the sky, mother, and the moon
cold as a shoe, and a black cry like smoke
mixed with dust—for your black people, people maker, work
like the dust of knives in the earth that the money
might pile up elsewhere
for others—
grassyyellow lady of prayer,
                          hear our smoke and our dust—
chastise those who debased your people to slavery[.]

Empowered by prayer and a myth not his own, Breytenbach transforms an Afrikaner saying ("plant a feather and a chicken will sprout up"), goes on with humor to make serious use of rhetorical stuttering, then moves from myth into history, from the high sorrow of the Human Condition to a particular plight, in the course of which a second diction intrudes, to end where a poem of this kind must end, not with the consolations of *lacrimae rerum*, but with the black cry rising from its definite pain. Breytenbach's surrealist tilt, in this instance, rests lightly in his appeal for an insect's intervention in human affairs, a joke not altogether joke when we consider the likely efficacy of any black appeal to any South African deity, be it God or god or little beast. In this poem Breytenbach identifies successfully with the voice of the victims. When he does, the interdictions of the white fathers give way to the wisdom of the black elders. And as befits a creation myth in Breytenbach's erotic cosmology, we are again within the governance of the Mother, she who in her ardor devours the Father. In every way but one—the prayer won't be answered—the poem works to appease and absolve the poet's political torment. He does not expect peace, but guilt dissolves and rage no longer consumes him.

Especially effective is Breytenbach's use of repetition. Midway the poem starts renaming itself. The first half culminates in the stammer of its big question, and then the poem goes on in a way that demystifies myth and allows history to show through—a Fall, in this case from eternity into the specific anguish of time. The little creator becomes a people-maker, the starry fields turn to fire. The moon, now a cold shoe, loses its consoling splendor. Life rising, sighing, falling, becomes a particular people being worked, as we might say, to death, ground down like the blade of a knife. Humankind's muddy genesis thus ends up concretely with blacks enslaved. Here a second diction intrudes upon the first, clashes, takes over. The result is a minor infraction of poetic statute, not unlike the marriage of white and "non-white," which, in some places, isn't lawful.

My analogy may seem out of place, but I use it to suggest the way this poem, by permitting the language of politics to intervene, becomes an allegory of political intrusion—life debased by injustice politically imposed. The poem's subject is not only the spectacle of Creation and the Fall, but also the reality *behind* the myth, in this case the plight of millions of human beings enslaved and brutalized, working *in* the diamond mines, the asbestos mines, working *for* the more than one thousand international corporations that, until their profit line began to quiver, used these people and used them up. And plainly, through labor of this kind money does pile up elsewhere, for example in the endowments of American universities. Nothing is gained, I realize, by citing our government's support for the regime in South Africa; but we might at least recognize our connection to Breytenbach's world. More than a little, my remarks are like the poem's last lines—these do not, it might be argued, belong to poetry or proper criticism. But the test of the poem's last lines is not received taste or purity of diction. The test is how false and trivial the poem would be without these lines. If the political references were absent, or veiled in metaphor, the poem might be more pleasant, but it would also be inconsequent, an assurance got by habitual retreat into myth. History would then appear as we prefer it to appear, under the aspect of eternity—in other words *necessary*, as if slavery were in the nature of things, which it isn't.

. . .

Breytenbach's debt to surrealism is fundamental. It defines his art as much as his problematic relation to Afrikaans. The psychic rending his language forced upon him may have predisposed him to surrealist solutions, but timing is also an important factor. The young poet-painter arrived in Paris in 1961, just as the upsurge of the sixties was getting under way—a time of zany politics and tactics quite bizarre. Surrealism itself, as the brainchild of Breton and his friends, was still much in evidence, in fact established and respectable, even a tradition. Exhibitions and journals devoted to surrealist art had become part of the cultural environment, and the movement's basic techniques—summed up by Picasso as "a horde of destructions"—had become a resource for poets anywhere. The principle of radical freedom in the arts is now commonplace and any poet might use surrealist techniques on occasion, if not centrally then as one resource among many.

But for Breytenbach surrealism meant more than taking easy liberties. The movement's originating impulse—insurrectionary and bent on cultural demolition—is very much alive in Breytenbach's need to dismantle official versions of reality. No doubt the weapons of ridicule and dark humor appealed to a poet whose job was to curse. Humor is essential to the surrealist spirit; but surrealism's lighthearted delight in havoc should not obscure its more ferocious intent. To *fire a pistol randomly into a crowd* was the movement's emblem. The surrealist game of chaotic sentence construction, in its first and most famous session, came up with *le cadavre exquis boira le vin nouveau*—new wine to be sipped by an exquisite corpse. And the image of the slashed eye in *Un chien andalou* suggests more now than it did in 1928 when Buñuel haphazardly made the film. In retrospect the surrealist assault on the human image seems clear, and in his memoirs Buñuel says of himself and the band of exterminating angels to which he belonged: "we all felt a certain destructive impulse, a feeling that for me has been even stronger than the creative urge."[11] Much of this can be written off as *épater les bourgeois*, but not all. And the logic of assault, once let loose, can't be recalled. The distance between the pen and the gun is less than once it seemed. This doesn't mean that artists should be timid, but that context generates consequence and no poet, today, can pretend to innocence. In our time, as Camus put it, to create is to create dangerously.

It may be that all art harbors delight in destruction; that the motive for metaphor is as much transgression as transformation; or that visionary faith in a new world is fuelled by a fury of disgust for what is. The patron saint of surrealist assault is Rimbaud, from whom, along with Lautréamont, the surrealists in France took their lead. They were the first poets and painters of our century to proceed as a group, with manifestos and programs and tribal rites, eager to tap the soul's darker energies. These they hoped to put at art's disposal—and in some cases, notably for Éluard and Aragon, at the disposal of the Communist Party. Breytenbach himself has not been a doctrinaire Marxist. But the revolutionary spirit of surreal attack must surely have spoken to the youthful poet's need.

That Breytenbach has seen his own identity in this fracturing light is apparent from his private myth of Rimbaud. *A Season in Paradise* is his re-envisionment of Rimbaud's *Season in Hell*, and in it Breytenbach locates Rimbaud as his special precursor. The French poet, in this telling, dies several deaths and then, after the loss of his leg, returns again to Africa. "What is clear," Breytenbach says, "is that the track of his single foot was later noticed in the desert. He vanished without trace, gloriously, like a white line on a sheet of white paper. Africa is reality. And in Africa you cannot die."[12] The renovated Rimbaud begins "to migrate southward." He turns up in Namibia, in the mines of Kimberley, is a hunter, a bartender, a mercenary. In one of these appearances Rimbaud causes the death of Eugène Marais, the poet often called the father of serious poetry in Afrikaans. And if, as Breytenbach concludes, "there's arms smuggling again these days off the Skeleton Coast,"[13] that too is Rimbaud's doing. The point of this sketch of Rimbaud, as I read it, is that the history of the surrealist spirit began in France and then passed to the African continent, where now, with Breytenbach in the vanguard, it continues in the land of the Boers.

Every writer constructs his or her own prehistory, but for an Afrikaner the task is especially difficult. With no illustrious tradition to take in and cast out, the bearers of Afrikaans must go elsewhere to escape from parochial constraint. Breytenbach went to Paris, received the confirmation of Rimbaud, created a voice never heard before. This has been his strength, and also the cause, maybe, of his downfall. For like the mythical Rimbaud, Breytenbach returned from France to Africa with revolutionary objectives. "Everyone," he wrote in *Season*, "should be an arms-smuggler at least once in his life."[14] So it was that in 1975 Breytenbach came back. He arrived, made some contacts, and the Bureau of State Security—known as the BOSS—swept him up like a fly.

· · ·

A conceit became grimly real, and paradise passed into hell. Breyten-bach's example provides a glimpse of the *literary* secret agent. I do not mean the writer who puts forth revolutionary ideas in his work only, but one who like Byron begins to take his literary identity seriously and comes to believe that what he is in his poems he must also be in the world. From the *Confessions* it would appear that some of Breytenbach's European friends were more eager than he was to view the poet and the revolutionary as one. In any case his misreading of Rimbaud's life—the abandonment of poetry for African gun-running—suggests the logic of what came next. Except that whereas the French surrealists had been satisfied to barge into halls and theaters to cause scandal and break up cultural events, Breytenbach aimed to crack the BOSS, one of the world's most efficient organs of terror. At best, we can say that he took poetry seriously. But then, we might say as well that he did not take it seriously enough.

The situation suggests that Breytenbach had grown dissatisfied with the kind of power to be had from words alone. He was sick of his impotence as *mere* writer, and wanted literary commitment to be more, or different, than it can be. During his 1973 return he joined a sym-posium at the University of Cape Town and there delivered what can only be called a diatribe, aimed point-blank at himself and his South African colleagues. His remarks, and even more the tone of his address, throw light on his poetry and reveal the state of mind that would shortly land him in prison. He began by saying that "all talk in this bitter motley-funeral-land is politics—whether it is whispered talk, talking shit, spitting into the wind or speaking in his master's voice."[15] Breytenbach's cate-gories are revealing, especially the agony implicit in "speaking in his master's voice." Presumably, his own category would be "spitting into the wind." He went on to ask: "Are we nothing, then, as writers, but the shock-absorbers of this white establishment, its watchdogs?" He attacked not only *apartheid* but also American policy in Vietnam, and advocated "taking a stand." In conclusion he put the problem of his art this way: "I want to come as close as I can in my work to the temporal—not the infinite; that has always been around. And infinity says nothing. What hurts is the ephemeral, the local."

Breytenbach's Cape Town manifesto is not without point, but it brims with *hysterica passio* and what it tells us, finally, is that his burden had become more than he could bear. Art and life crossed, and the larger truth of his predicament is that politics drags eternity down into time. The temporal *is* what hurts—conditions that do not have to exist but that do, to the detriment of many and the benefit of some few, so long as men and women support or do not seek to change the status quo. Breytenbach's response also suggests that apartheid devastates not only bodies but the soul as well. For those who think that poetry's proper realm is the human condition minus its political torment, Breytenbach's run-in with politics might seem to prove their point. But for those in search of a poetry that would confront rather than evade, Breytenbach deserves honor for the chances he took and the mistakes he made.

Impossible to say what might come next. Almost by accident Breytenbach has created, in his native tongue, the precedent he needed but could not find when he began. In his *Confessions*, moreover, he notes a hopeful development: "already," he says, "the language which is spoken in township and prison and in the army, on fishing-boats and in factories, has escaped entirely from the control of the Afrikaners. In that shape it is a virile medium, ever being renewed, which so far finds but little reflection in the writing."[16] Perhaps, then, despair is premature. There may be, surely there will be, young poets for whom Breytenbach opened a way. He was the first, he was there, his example stands.

CODA: Afrikaans is a small language made smaller by its almost total lack, at present, of moral appeal. To volunteer as students of the Taal is not a likely choice for most of us. At the same time, however, few are avid to know—as perhaps we *need* to know—the spiritual temper and moral quality of events now taking place in South Africa. Because of censorship and the news blackout, we get only the poorest sense of things from the usual media sources. In this respect our situation recalls conditions during the First World War, when propaganda and tight censorship cut off the reality of the trenches from the rest of the world so that the awful truth, when it came, was carried entirely by poets. Still today, we know the spiritual climate of Flanders and the Marne through the poetry of Owen, Sassoon, Graves, and their peers. And even when other information is available, the life of poetry cuts deeper, reaches further, is more accessible to imagination.

The Dutch set foot on the Cape of Good Hope in 1652. During the next two centuries the interaction of native Africans with Dutch colonialists generated a new tongue, a historical process described by André Brink: "the Afrikaans language emerged from the efforts of non-Dutch speakers to speak Dutch in an African environment. Hence the very development of the language implied a dimension of the exploration of the African experience, a process intrinsic to the language itself."[17] While patriotic Afrikaners sometimes still insist on its Teutonic pedigree, discerning scholars are convinced that it is a creole language, a local patois that by chance and circumstance arrived at its present incarnation. Moreover, after 1806 the British attempt to impose English meant that Afrikaans was under siege, and something of a siege mentality informs the posture of Afrikaans even now. After the Boer War the Afrikaners were de facto rulers in local affairs, and in 1948 the whole of this embattled history came to a head with the emergence of the South African state on an apartheid base, with Afrikaans the language of power. That Afrikaans is also the first language of many blacks has always been overlooked; today, in South Africa, more blacks than whites speak Afrikaans. Hein Willemse describes (in 1987) the situation for black writers in these terms:[18]

> Given the generally high level of bilingualism in South Africa, some black Afrikaans writers may expediently opt out and write in English, in the process avoiding the suspicion of being less committed and literarily in cahoots with Afrikaner rule. Personally, however, this would have meant the premature death of my creative endeavors, and the beginning of an unbearable language schizophrenia. The task now is to continue writing in Afrikaans and to be constantly aware of this dichotomy: the oppressed writing in the language of the oppressor.

It's not unlikely, therefore, that Afrikaans as Breytenbach has used it, along with the politicization of black usage, will play its part in big changes, changes that will reverberate throughout the African continent, and that Americans, with their government's long-time loyalty to Afrikaner tyranny, shall want to understand. But we do not, of course, have Afrikaans at our disposal; and if we attend to political experience in that crucial part of the world, getting the feel of history as its victims and dissidents know it, we shall have to turn to translation. That's clear enough, and it seems possible that what goes for South Africa goes finally for political experience in all the earth's reaches. The moral drama of our time is most distinctly played out in totalitarian states and third-world nations; we shall have little sense of our own being-in-the-world without imagining the torment of others through, first of all, their poets.

Traditionally, the American commitment to other languages has been limited to French and German, perhaps Spanish and Italian also. But few among us know any second language finely enough to penetrate its poetry, and even fewer of us know a third or fourth language—in which case, what becomes of the rest? The multitude of urgent tongues around us? What, for example, of the great Russians, Akhmatova and Mandelshtam, Pasternak and Tsvetayeva? Or of Polish poets like Milosz and Herbert? Of Seferis and Ritsos in Greek? Or, without Spanish, of our great neighbors Neruda, Vallejo, and Para to the south? What, in other words, can be the fate of global consciousness deprived of the means to consciousness that languages provide? Are we at the mercy of official pronouncements and partial news reports? Is the soul, the sharing of resistance to indignity, to be both blind and nine-tenths mute?

Translation's new authority is abundantly visible. The poets cited above are available to us in many renderings, and the recent surge in translation corresponds to awareness of the world at large, an alertness heightened by multiple catastrophes and nuclear threat, a consciousness whose blooming has been specific to this century. When higher education crystalized in the nineteenth century it took its inspiration from the German model with an emphasis on philology; in practice this meant that any educated person—almost always white, male, and upper class—would master Greek and Latin as well as languages endorsed by European powers. Hence the equation of "civilization as we know it" with proficiency in languages that constitute "Western culture." And hence the duplicity of a privilege that was quick to condemn anyone who did not, say, read Dante in Italian, but that had no such reservations when, early in the century, the astonishments of Russian fiction burst—in translation, of course—on Western sensibility.

The world is bigger than we are, larger than the superpowers that battle for control. Earth juts back, and its affirming undervoice arises in tongues and traditions not a part of elite education. Perhaps we were never meant, by the logic of cultural hegemony, to know the power of voices beyond our own self-interest. But with the planet itself in view, imagination either loses contact with the travail and resilience of our time, or it pays tribute to poets from linguistic tribes not our own. Translation is no longer an exotic indulgence; it is an act of solidarity, a political choice.

·FOUR·

WITNESS
&
BLESSING

·VII·

Thomas McGrath, North America West

"America is too terrible a subject for an American."

"Then we can forget the West."

"No, no. We cannot forget the West. There is no American outside the West, and there never will be. It is the dream, and that dream is the only hope. No, we cannot forget the West. Where all the races meet in a place of beauty, not in a place of blood. The land cannot grant amnesty."

—from *McGrath on McGrath*[1]

Sweetened with a harvest song, the work goes well.
—Christopher Caudwell[2]

Thomas McGrath has been writing remarkable poems of every size and form for nearly fifty years. In American poetry he is as close to Whitman as anyone since Whitman himself. McGrath is master of the long wide line (wide in diction, long in meter), the inclusive six-beat measure of America at large. The scene of his work is the whole of the continent east to west, with its midpoint in the high-plains rim of the heartland. His diction, with its vast word stock and multitude of language layers, is demotic to the core yet spiced with learned terms in Whitman's manner, a voice as richly American as any in our literature. But for all that, McGrath is little known. He has been championed by one no less worldly than E. P. Thompson, as well as other poets, Kenneth Rexroth and Donald Hall among them, devoted to his work. In the main, though, McGrath hasn't had the attention that a whole flotilla of our lesser poets enjoy, a situation out of joint with the facts of the matter and a scandal to those who know McGrath's four-part epic, *Letter to an Imaginary Friend*, a poem of witness to the radical spirit—"the generous wish," as McGrath calls it—of American populist tradition.[3]

If McGrath remains an outsider, his humor might be part of the reason. Apart from Stevens' wispy playfulness and some of Auden's wit, we don't expect an important poet to be broadly comic, especially when the same voice rails in earnest against the time's worst abuses. McGrath holds high expectations for poetry—he wants to see it change the world by calling us to recovery of our finest dreams—yet he delights in excess and in punning and is, seemingly, hyperbolic by conviction. Humor of this kind supports irreverent freedom and a desire to pull things back "down to earth." In his will to dislodge prevailing pieties, McGrath aligns himself as Twain did in *Huckleberry Finn*, with oddity and outcasts:

>   —I'm here to bring you
> Into the light of speech, the insurrectionary powwow
> Of the dynamite men and the doomsday spielers, to sing you
> Home from the night

McGrath's diction is more expansive than the sort now in fashion. Some of us will probably be shaken by his vigorous vocabulary, and jolted still further by a bawdy argot of physical frankness informing the whole. McGrath's language is an amalgam of field-hand grit and Oxbridge nicety seasoned by working-class dialect from the 1930's and 40's. These choices give him an almost fabulous voice, at least on occasion, and a range of lyrical textures uniquely his own. Finally, there is the singular way he manages materialism (Marxist) and sacramentalism (Roman Catholic) side by side as if they composed a doctrinal continuum that surely they don't—except in McGrath's special usage.

McGrath identifies himself mainly with the western side of the country and sets much of his best work in the place and rural spirit of the Dakotas, a region by definition graceless and provincial to the dominant urban-eastern sensibility, a place and spirit that to many among us is noplace and thus a sort of utopian badlands politely forgot. On top of that comes McGrath's politics—an insurrectionary stance that in its Marxist emphasis might have been international but which, nourished by the grain-land countryside west of Fargo, is decidedly homegrown, a radicalism that McGrath calls "unaffiliated far Left."

When McGrath says in *Letter* that "North Dakota is everywhere," one can fairly hear the strain upon an urbane sensibility that isn't easily able, and may in fact be unwilling, to imagine that the West (outside of California) exists. McGrath says that his own family had to deal with "Indian scare[s]"; that "the past out here was bloody, and full of injustice, though hopeful and heroic."[4] What, after all, is *American* about America if not the frontier experience and how the fate of the Indians questions ours:

From Indians we learned a toughness and a strength; and we gained
A freedom: by taking theirs: but a real freedom; born
From the wild and open land our grandfathers heroically stole.
But we took a wound at Indian hands: a part of our soul scabbed
                                                        over[.]

As a boy McGrath saw "the Indian graves / Alive and flickering with the gopher light." In his art the landscape is weighted with the human world. Even when abandoned, the land is not empty. Nature is peopled, strife-ridden and—"where the Dakotas bell and nuzzle at the north coast"—of surpassing beauty. For most of us, however, these early defeats and distant splendors are of little consequence. Most of us pretend freedom from history and would go weightless into tomorrow like leaves in a wind, whereas McGrath summons the past of his own time and place, the essential history of personal, and then of national, experience insofar as each—the private and the public testaments—bears witness to the other. Like any bard, he preserves the memory of events in danger of being repressed or forgotten. This is not an easy job, given that much worth recalling is gone for good. It is important to remember that McGrath's grandparents homesteaded the farmland his family worked and his own generation was forced to leave; here (from *Echoes Inside the Labyrinth*) is "The Old McGrath Place":[5]

The tractor crossed the lawn and disappeared
Into the last century—
An old well filled up with forgotten faces.
So many gone down (bucketsful) to the living, dark
Water . . .

> I would like to plant a willow
> There—waterborne tree to discountenance earth . . .
>
> But then I remember my grandmother:
> Reeling her morning face out of that rainy night.

McGrath plants the poem instead, and his attention turns from cursing to blessing. The outcome is a praise-poem in the manner of elegy, its nostalgia nipped in the bud by "bucketsful." The scene is the dead site of a family farm—of which, in America, there are still sights countless. The aim of the poem is to regenerate the past through memory's witness; or rather, to claim that task as the poet's mission. The "faces" won't be forgotten. The farmyard well is still there, still alive, and becomes an entrance to ancestral sources, a complex emblem of death and rebirth. In its dark water abide the mothering powers of farm and family that McGrath grew up with and from which, as a poet, he draws his strength.

Thomas McGrath was born in 1916 on a farm near Sheldon, North Dakota, of Irish Catholic parents. Every aspect of this heritage—the place, the hard times, the religious and political culture—informs his art. His religious upbringing figures centrally in Part Three—"the Christ mas section"—of *Letter*, and in his poetry at large there is a steady preference for the ritualistic forms and sacramental language of the Church. Being Irish also worked in his favor when, in 1941, he entered the maritime world of seamen and longshoremen—the Irish community that worked Manhattan's West Side docks—where the fight for reform went forward on the piers and in the bars and walk-ups of Chelsea. There McGrath worked as a labor organizer and, briefly, as a shipyard welder. His politics led him into a world of experience that, in turn, backed up his political beliefs in concrete ways. To be a Red on the waterfront was to be the natural prey of goon squads patrolling the docks for the bosses and the racketeers. It was also to see the world of industrial work at first hand. In Part Two of *Letter* McGrath recalls his job as a welder at Federal Drydock & Shipyard:

> "After the war we'll get them," Packy says.
>   He dives
> Into the iron bosque to bring me another knickknack.
> The other helpers swarm into it. Pipes are swinging

As the chain-falls move on their rails in.
                                  Moment of peace.

The welders stand and stretch, their masks lifted, palefaced.
Then the iron comes onto the stands; the helpers turn to the wheels;
The welders, like horses in flytime, jerk their heads and the masks
Drop. Now demon-dark they sit at the wheeled turntables,
Striking their arcs and light spurts out of their hands.

                                           "After
The war we'll shake the bosses' tree till the money rains
Like crab-apples. Faith, we'll put them under the ground."
After the war.
              Faith.
                    Left wing of the IRA
That one.
          Still dreaming of dynamite.
                                    I nod my head,
The mask falls.
              Our little smokes rise into roaring heaven.

These lines are alive of commotion and wordplay, for example the
double meanings of "faith" and "war" and the "nod" at the end. The
scene itself suggests McGrath's larger figure of the "round-dance," his
emblem of communal action wherein his double vision—materialist and
sacramentalist at once—is reconciled with itself. In the passage above,
the rites of work become an act of prayer, a moment of *working together*
beneath the hegemony of a "faith" now defeated. After the war the
bosses had won and it was Packy O'Sullivan gone, him with his curse
on capital. McGrath returned to Chelsea to find everything changed,
his friends dead or departed, the vigorous radicalism of the National
Maritime Union bought off and a new breed of "labor-fakers" running
the show:

And the talking walls had forgotten our names, down at the Front,
Where the seamen fought and the longshoremen struck the great ships
In the War of the Poor.
                        And the NMU had moved to the deep south
(Below Fourteenth) and built them a kind of Moorish whorehouse

For a union hall. And the lads who built that union are gone.
Dead. Deep sixed. Read out of the books. Expelled.

McGrath's family emigrated from Ireland, and the Sheas (his mother's
side) were Gaelic-speaking. Some arrived by way of Ellis Island, others
through Canada. Both grandfathers worked their way west as immigrant
laborers on the railroad. They got as far as the Dakota frontier and
settled as homesteaders, living at first in the ubiquitous dirt-built "sod-
dies." For young McGrath, the specific gifts of family and place included
the liturgical richness of Catholicism to fill up frontier emptiness, but
also the political richness of farming in a part of the country and at a
time when the broad-based Farmers Alliance was strong enough (during
the 1880's and early 90's) to pursue the first and only nationwide attempt
at a national third party, the People's Party, thereby awakening radical
consciousness and endorsing a spirit of grass-roots insurgency. From
Texas up through Kansas and into the great Northwest, the Farmers
Alliance gave rural populations their first taste of dignity. For the first
time power was more than a courthouse coterie. Decent life for a while
looked possible. And from early on, this unique addition to American
political culture, now called Populism, was strong in the Dakotas.[6]
Neighborhood, for McGrath growing up, was part of an adversary
culture, an order against the mainstream economy, with collective traditions of self-help and sharing. This state-within-a-state gave countless
small farmers a defense against the unchecked plundering of grain com-
panies, banks, and the baronial railroads. When McGrath curses wealth
and the money system, we should keep in mind that his family was
working to get a foothold in America during the depths of the Gilded
Age, our most ruthless era of capital accumulation. Boom and bust were
the signs of the time, when economic depression and political helpless-
ness ruined "plain folks" by hundreds of thousands and, an important
point, made every year's harvest—each autumn's race with nature and
the money supply—a time of national crisis.

The glory days of the Farmers Alliance were over by McGrath's time,
but the political imagination of the populist tradition was ingrained and
open to new forms of expression each time economic disaster shredded
the nation. Until the First World War, members of the Industrial Workers of the World—the Wobblies—were a strong and often strong-armed
force in key sectors of labor (lumber and mining most firmly), carrying
forward the tradition of agrarian revolt. After the war the Non-Partisan

League (started in 1916, the year of McGrath's birth) organized the vote and worked toward the public ownership of vital facilities. In North Dakota the League came to control the state legislature and established a public granary system. The populist spirit thrived on these successes; it also counted on a tradition of communal work that rural peoples have known since the dawn, maybe, of independent yeomanry. This broader background, as McGrath suggests in an interview, underwrites his own kind of visionary populism:[7]

> The primary experience out in these states, originally, anyway, was an experience of loneliness, because the people were so far away from everything. They had come out here and left behind whatever was familiar, and you find this again and again in letters that women wrote out here. The other side of that loneliness was a sense of community, which was much more developed—even as late as thirty or forty years ago—than it is now. The community of swapped labor. This was a standard thing on the frontier; everybody got together and helped put up a house or put up a soddy when a new family came along. You helped with this, that or the other, and you swapped labor back and forth all the time and that community was never defined. It wasn't a geographical thing; it was a sort of commune of people who got along well together, and right in the same actual neighborhood there might be two or three of these. . . . This sense of solidarity . . . is one of the richest experiences that people can have. It's the only true shield against alienation and deracination and it was much more developed in the past than it is now.

In McGrath's poetry this "community of swapped labor," and the populist sentiment rising from it, cannot be overestimated. This was the political milieu, or simply the spirit of place, that he inherited. Parts One and Two of *Letter to an Imaginary Friend*, in which McGrath evokes his roots, are devoted to moments of compact drama recalling the populist legacy as it spun itself out and into his soul. The Great Depression was the definitive learning experience for McGrath's generation, the testing ground for political belief of any kind and, as it seemed to McGrath from his own encounters, the historical proof of populism's capacity to endure as a force. Drifters of every sort filled the land, men from different backgrounds, some of them schooled, others not, all of them angry and talking politics nonstop. Companionship with laborers like these provided the forum for McGrath's education—working, for example, with a logging team:

All that winter in the black cold, the buzz-saw screamed and whistled,
And the rhyming hills complained. In the noontime stillness,
Thawing our frozen beans at the raw face of a fire,
We heard the frost-bound tree-boles booming like cannon,
A wooden thunder, snapping the chains of the frost.

Those were the last years of the Agrarian City
City of swapped labor
Communitas
Circle of warmth and work
Frontier's end and last wood-chopping bee
The last collectivity stamping its feet in the cold. [. . .]

The weedy sons of midnight enterprise:
Stump-jumpers and hog-callers from the downwind counties
The noonday mopus and the coffee guzzling Swedes
Prairie mules
Moonfaced Irish from up-country farms
Sand-hill cranes
And lonesome deadbeats from a buck brush parish.

So, worked together.

Diction shoves and bristles within a theme of solidarity, affording McGrath's figuration of harmony-in-conflict another lively example. The object of praise is again a community united through work, and again the world it comes from is gone. Some hundred lines later McGrath's mood turns elegiac as he remembers the collective rapport of a time when people of all sorts came together in common need to help out; and then how they lost and disappeared:

The talk flickered like fires.
The gist of it was, it was a bad world and we were the boys to
                                                    change it.

And it *was* a bad world; and we might have.

In that round song, Marx lifted his ruddy
Flag; and Bakunin danced (And the Technocrats
Were hatching their ergs . . .)
                                        A mile east, in the dark,
The hunger marchers slept in the court house lobby
After its capture: where Webster and Boudreaux

Bricklayer, watchmaker, Communists, hoped they were building
The new society, inside the shell of the old—
Where the cops came in in the dark and we fought down the
                                                    stairs.

That was the talk of the states those years, that winter.
Conversations of east and west, palaver
Borne coast-to-coast on the midnight freights where Cal was
                                                    riding
The icy red-balls.
                    Music under the dogged-down
Dead lights of the beached caboose.
Wild talk, and easy enough now to laugh.
That's not the point and never was the point.
What was real was the generosity, expectant hope,
The open and true desire to create the good.

   Passages of this kind epitomize McGrath's poetic enterprise, and I
quote at length to mark the tonal shifts, the conjunction of blessing and
cursing, and then the reach of language establishing historical complexity. No mere catalogue, this is a kind of lyrical documentation at which
McGrath excels, and through which he preserves his firsthand sense of
the nation at odds with itself. He bears witness to "the generous wish,"
and curses the McCarthy years ("the hunting" conducted by HUAC)
for ending that hope:

Now, in another autumn, in our new dispensation
Of an ancient, man-chilling dark, the frost drops over
My garden's starry wreckage.
                  Over my hope:
                             Over
The generous dead of my years.
                       Now, in the chill streets
I hear the hunting, the long thunder of money.
A queer parade goes past: Informers, shit-eaters, fetishists,
Punkin-faced cretins, and the little deformed traders
In lunar nutmegs and submarine bibles.
And the parlor anarchist comes by, to hang in my ear
His tiny diseased pearls like the guano of meat-eating birds.
But *then* was a different country, though the children of light,
                            gone out
To the dark people in the villages, did not come back . . .
But what was real, in all that unreal talk
Of ergs and of middle peasants (perhaps someone born
Between the Mississippi and the Rocky Mountains, the unmapped
                            country)
Was the generous wish.
                    To talk of the People
Is to be a fool. But they were the *sign* of the People,
Those talkers.

The parts of *Letter* I've been quoting mark episodes of personal importance to McGrath's political development. They are also—the em-
passioned talk of the Depression years, the welders on night shift during
the war—representative moments in the life of the nation. McGrath has
deliberately stationed himself to document the populist spirit *in action*
from the 1930's on through the 40's and 50's, and then beyond into
our own time. He is on the lookout for evidence of political promise,
and a witness to communal possibilities. His care is for people working
and living together—the productive spirit of *Communitas*. Without question, this is McGrath's grand theme, based on his poetry's recollection
of his own experience as a boy, as a young man, and then active poet.
His art is motivated by a visionary care for the future, but also by "grief

for a lost world: that round song and commune / When work was a handclasp."[8]

When McGrath began publishing in the early 1940's, his work was shaped by the strain and agitation of the 30's. For political visionaries it had been a painful but exciting time to come of age. On the disheartening evidence of events, the future was bound to be a glory. After the lament, the exaltation. This doubling—first the bad news, then the good—is the form of the American jeremiad, a type of political-visionary stance that thrives on unfulfillment.[9] Each failure to fulfill our destiny as a people becomes a period of probation and then revival along the way to triumphant conclusion. This view of the country's course and prospects owes everything to our nation's founding fathers and nothing to Marx, but it yields an enlarged notion of consensus when recast in Marxist terms. For McGrath, in any case, the jeremiad is a natural vehicle for enduring failure and keeping faith in "the generous wish"; it allows him to rail and reconfirm, to deplore the backsliding and lean years of his tribe, without flagging or abandoning hope.

In the poems of the 1940's, McGrath announces and proclaims. His language is abstract and mythical, a style distinct from the kind of line and language in *Letter*. Repeatedly, in these early poems, the poet calls to his tribe and predicts redemptive apocalypse. In "Blues for Warren," a poem of 197 lines with the inscription "killed spring 1942, north sea," the dead man is praised as one "who descended into hell for our sakes; awakener / Of the hanging man, the Man of the Third Millennium."[10] A radical prophecy is informed by traditional archetypes; Marx and the Church are made to join in common cause, while the hero, a "Scapegoat and Savior," is united—in spirit and in body—with the dispossessed multitudes his death will help redeem:

> Those summers he rode the freights between Boston and Frisco
> With the cargo of derelicts, garlands of misery,
> The human surplus, the interest on dishonor,
> And the raw recruits of a new century.

Much of McGrath's work in his early style—collected in *The Movie at the End of the World*—declares belief, addresses action and actors in the political arena, blesses and blames. Many of these poems are informed by a sense of humor that is tough and playful at once, a manner that reaches a comic highpoint and takes on a broad, easygoing confidence with a little volume of poems printed by International Publishers in 1949. Entitled *Longshot O'Leary's Garland of Practical Poesie*, the book is dedicated to the friends of McGrath's waterfront days in New York. Most of these poems express the spirit enacted by the title. The centerpiece is a ballad of nineteen stanzas, "He's a Real Gone Guy: A Short Requiem for Percival Angleman,"[11] celebrating the death of a local gangster. Like Brecht, from whom he learned a great deal, McGrath often praises renegades and losers, figures that rebuke the prevailing order as part of capital's bad conscience. "Short Requiem" is an exercise, so to say, in jocular realism, a satire that goes to the tune of "As I walked out in the streets of Laredo." The violence of the West comes east and this is stanza one:

> As I walked out in the streets of Chicago,
> As I stopped in a bar in Manhattan one day,
> I saw a poor weedhead dressed up like a sharpie,
> Dressed up like a sharpie all muggled and fey.

The poem portrays a man who was a worker getting nowhere and who turned, therefore, to the profits of crime. Here is the core of dialogue between the poet and the crook:

> "Oh I once was a worker and had to keep scuffling;
> I fought for my scoff with the wolf at the door.
> But I made the connection and got in the racket,
> Stopped being a business man's charity whore.
>
> "You'll never get yours if you work for a living,
> But you may make a million for somebody else.
> You buy him his women, his trips to Miami,
> And all he expects is the loan of yourself."
>
> "I'm with you," I said, "but here's what you've forgotten:
> A working stiff's helpless to fight on his own,
> But united with others he's stronger than numbers.
> We can win when we learn that we can't win alone."

In the uproar and aftermath of the Depression, a poem like this would find its grateful audience. But by the time it appeared in 1949, labor was damping down and in the schools the New Criticism was setting narrower, more cautious standards of literary judgment. McGrath, with his Brechtian huff, was out in the cold, although any reader nursed on Eliot might still appreciate the poem's hollow-man ending:

> He turned and went out to the darkness inside him
> To the Hollywood world where believers die rich,
> Where free enterprise and the lies of his childhood
> Were preparing his kingdom in some midnight ditch.

The poem surpasses its Marxist scene (the world as classes in conflict) with a vision of community (the workers of the world united), and translates a political predicament into spiritual terms. In *Longshot O'Leary*, McGrath's style is at once streetwise and jubilant. Slang and local patois invigorate his diction, and a distinctly "Irish" note (nearly always at play in the later poetry) is struck in namings, allusions, and parody. Humor becomes a leavening element, and the comedy of word-play keeps the spirit agile in hard situations. And now McGrath can imagine his audience, lost though it might be. His model derives from the men and women he worked with in New York before the war, tough-minded socialists devoted day by day to the cause, a working commune worthy of tribal regard. To call this tribe back into action, to witness its past and praise its future, becomes McGrath's poetic task.

In 1954 McGrath took a job at Los Angeles State College, a teaching position that did not last long. The spirit of McCarthy was closing down "the generous wish," and McGrath, after declaring to a HUAC sub-committee that he would "prefer to take [his] stand with Marvell, Blake, Shelley and Garcia Lorca,"[12] found himself jobless and without recourse. Being blacklisted was an honor of sorts, but money and prospects were in short supply. So was the hope for a better world. It was then that McGrath began his thirty-years' work on *Letter*. It was then, too, that the earlier, more formal style gave way to the lyrical expansiveness that marks McGrath's best poetry. As a friendly critic puts it, "We can at least make an honest guess that McGrath's direct experience of repression in the early fifties threw him back into touch with his earlier experiences."[13] Counting his losses, it must have seemed that praise and blame were not enough; that the defense of his art would require enlargement of resources as a witness—some way, that is, of speaking for the nation as well as for himself, a song of self made valid for all.

What McGrath discovered is that each of us lives twice: not only that we are first in the world and then make of it what we can through the word; but also that each of us bears a representative (political) as well as an individual (private) life. The representative parts occur when history and the path of personal life intersect, and to make this distinction is to suggest one way that politics and poetry converge. By the time he came to write *Letter*, McGrath saw that "In the beginning was the *world!*"[14] and that he would have to locate himself exactly at the crossroads where self and world meet:[15]

> All of us live twice at the same time—once uniquely and once representatively. I am interested in those moments when my unique personal life intersects with something bigger, when my small brief moment has a part in "fabricating the legend."

By way of "fabricating the legend," *Letter* begins: "—From here it is necessary to ship all bodies east." McGrath has said the line was given to him by poet and friend Don Gordon during the blacklisting 1950's when, out of work and uncertain in spirit, McGrath was living "in Los Angeles at 2714 Marsh Street, / Writing, rolling east with the earth." The opening sequence of *Letter* continues with a shift in voice: "They came through the passes, / they crossed the dark mountains in a month of snow, [. . .] Hunters of the hornless deer in the high plateaus of that country." Then the two voices join as McGrath goes on to declare his relation to the grandest of our native themes—America's heroical westering:

Aye, long ago. A long journey ago,
Most of it lost in the dark, in a ruck of tourists,
In the night of the compass, companioned by tame wolves, plagued
By theories, flies, visions, by the anthropophagi . . .

I do not know what end that journey was toward.
—But I am its end. I am where I have been and where
I am going. The journeying destination—at least that. . . [.]

At the onset of *Letter*, the poet stations himself at land's end, but he does not yearn in the way of Whitman or Jeffers for further passage, some intenser rapport of solitary Self with the Universe at large. Rather he turns, faces back to consider where he's been and what he's learned and how, in some added stretch of time, this northern continent might become the great thing it has always symbolized. America, having ful-filled its claim to manifest destiny, having defined itself through west-ward migration, finds itself in some way finished. This terminus is either a dead end or a new beginning, and simply put it comes to this: the vision of ourselves that Whitman strained to realize, McGrath aims to recover. *Letter* is a poem of remembrance and what it celebrates is the American Dream in its first freshness, countless times exploited, count-less times betrayed, but still alive in memory and actual terrain; the covenant and the promise, not of a city on a hill like a fortress, but of a loose-knit neighborhood upon a spacious plain. He will approach this mighty task by summoning—out of a farmyard well, maybe—the voices of family, companions, co-workers; the chorus, in short, of what he calls his "generous dead."

McGrath's distinction between "personal" and "representative" kinds of experience suggests that the voices in *Letter* address events larger than the person or persons speaking, events in which private and political destinies intersect or collide. These points of conjunction are generally shared by more than one voice, and from them comes an enlarged view—an "expanded consciousness," in McGrath's terms—of the nation's gains, losses, and wrong turns, together with the seeds of possible redress and renewal. In Part Two, for example, McGrath confronts the historical irony of "the Dakota experience": how, that is, a land of pioneer farms was bled and broken to make way for the ranges of missile sites (the ICBM's) that now infest the landscape. The poet looks out upon "the abandoned farmhouses, like burnt-out suns, and around them / The planetary out-buildings dead for the lack of warmth," and asks: "where / Have *they* gone? Those ghosts that warmed these buildings once?" The missiles hum in their silos, but "the people?" In answer comes this voice:

"First they broke land that should not ha' been broke
                                                                                     and they *died*
Broke. Most of 'em. And after the tractor ate the horse—
It ate *them*. And now, a few lean years,

And the banks will have it again. Most of it. Why, hellfar,
Once a family could live on a quarter and now a hull section won't do!"

Disastrous economic policy has cleared the land for a weaponry of
global destruction. As E. P. Thompson has put it: "if Dakota were to
secede from the United States it would be, with its battery of Minute-
men, the third most powerful nuclear state in the world."[16] He isn't
joking. As recently as 1985, the nuclear count in McGrath's part of the
country stood this way:[17]

> North Dakota ranks 3d with 1510 nuclear warheads deployed
> and 10th with 19 facilities in the nuclear infrastructure. It
> houses two main SAC bases, Grand Forks AFB and Minot AFB,
> both housing a B-52 bomber wing as well as a Minuteman
> missile wing, two of only three such bases in the world.

That North Dakota, one of the first and firmest of our populist states,
one of the few places in America where democracy has been tried in
earnest—that North Dakota should now bear the brunt of our nuclear
arsenal is an irony replete with American consequence. McGrath's sense
of Indian genocide as the nation's first "wound" suggests that our trium-
phalist culture pushes us to reenact the country's primal scenes; that the
killing of native Americans now stands as an Original Sin of the Republic
permitting more recent evils like Hiroshima or death-squad governance
in our Latin vassal states. The battle of Wounded Knee, which elimi-
nated the Sioux nation and ended our "Indian Wars," was replayed in
whiteface with the defeat of rural populism, and then replayed again,
this time in the noface of nuclear weaponry taking control of the land.
These are events of national magnitude, but *in the same place?* Three
stages of destiny inflicted one on top of another in McGrath's own
neighborhood? Searching throughout *Letter* for examples of "the
wrong turn," moments when the American Dream went bad, McGrath
has good reasons for saying "Dakota is everywhere."

But he is even more concerned with moments when the nation's dream
was decently realized. At the heart of *Letter to an Imaginary Friend* beats
the rhythm of work in the rural countryside of McGrath's youth, reminding us how narrow our habitual poetics has been. The theme of
work has been indispensable to the nation's sense of itself, but in our
poetry it has seldom appeared. One can go back to Whitman, in a vague

sort of way, and Gary Snyder's celebration of work has been exemplary. Some of Frost's New England pieces, and Philip Levine's vision of Detroit, have taken work seriously. More recently our feminist poets, Adrienne Rich among them, have insisted on the theme of work, in particular the thankless labors necessary to the life of the body. Apart from these, however, McGrath is alone in his insistence on the primacy of work to American experience.

He is most concerned with the community-creating aspect of work— the "erotics of labor," if I might put it so, having in mind the notion of Eros as the binding energy shaping social units into larger and larger productive wholes. There were, for example, the work teams that assembled haphazard every fall for harvest, matter on the face of it unpromising, but from which McGrath takes moments of real and mythical beauty. In Part Two, Section IV, there are a number of episodes from the earth-bound world of that time, starting with a barnyard version of *in principio*. Note the active character of McGrath's wordplay, and then the multiple destinies within a common fate:

Morning stirring in the haymow must: sour blankets,
Worn bindles and half-pitched soogans of working bundle-stiffs
Stir:
     Morning in the swamp!
               I kick myself awake
And dress while around me the men curse for the end of the world.

And it *is* ending (half-past-'29) but we don't know it
And wake without light.
            Twenty-odd of us—and very odd,
Some.
     One of the last of the migrant worker crews
On one of the last steam threshing rigs.
               Antediluvian
Monsters, all.
     Rouse to the new day in the fragrant
Barnloft soft hay-beds: wise heads, grey;
And gay cheechakos from Chicago town; and cranky Wobblies;
Scissorbills and homeguards and grassgreen wizards from the
                              playing fields
Of the Big Ten: and decompressed bankclerks and bounty jumpers

Jew and Gentile; and the odd Communist now and then
To season the host.
                        Stick your head through the haymow door—
Ah!
        A soft and backing wind: the Orient red
East. And a dull sky for the first faint light and no sun yet.

4:30. Time to be moving.

The scene is the last of America's unfallen moments, before the Flood,
as McGrath suggests, but with the Crash of '29 on its way. The men
don't see what's arriving and yet they do not seem lost; "without light"
they may be, but with the wind for "backing" and the "new day" coming
at them out of the "red / East." And it's no accident that the Crash comes
now, at *this* time of the year. When McGrath says Dakota is everywhere
let us not forget that the Great Depression allowed Hitler to come to
power and World War Two to transpire and the nuclear order to rise
from those ashes. And let us recall how every autumn, during the early
years of the century, the economy fell into financial crisis as western
banks put too much strain on eastern banks for loans to process the
buying, shipping, selling, and profit taking for the year's harvest.

But here the Fall has not yet occurred, and McGrath goes on to depict
his boyhood's descent into a "green" world of purely animal existence,
a prelapsarian realm recalling Whitman's praise for dumb and placid
beasts. Here is the still unfallen earth—world of animals as McGrath
recalls it from his youth:

                        Into the barnfloor dark
I drop down the dusty Jacob's ladder, feeling by foot,
The fathomless fusty deep and the sleepy animal night
Where the horses fart, doze, stomp: teams of the early
Crewmen: strawmonkey, watermonkey (myself) and the grain haulers
They snort and shift, asleep on their feet.
                        I go, carefully,
Down the dung-steamy ammonia-sharp eye-smarting aisle
Deadcenter: wary of kickers, light sleepers and vengeful wakers.

A sleep of animals!
                    Almost I can enter:
                            where all is green[. . . .]

The barn with its "aisle" becomes a holy place. But to enter the green world's hush, and then to sense its otherness, is directly to recoil at humankind's intrusion, as the imperatives of work tie man to beast and beast to man. And thus the moment of the green world's fall:

                            But, in the world
Of work and need that sacred image fails.
                                    Here,
Fallen, they feed and fast and harrow the man-marred small acres
Dull; and dulled.
                    Alas, wild hearts, we have you now:
—Old plugs
            hayburners
                    crowbait
                            bonesack
                                    —Hail!

At once slangy, sacral, traditional, and nonce, McGrath's diction welds the universality of ancient pastoral images with grass-roots patois that only a namer could know—having grown up, as McGrath did, on the strength in names like *crowbait*, *bonesack*, *hayburner*, ambivalent terms that curse and bless at once, thick with echoes of pathos and fate.

There are many passages in *Letter* devoted to scenes of physical labor and to the theme of communal order that work inspires. The finest of these occurs early in the poem—the whole of Section III in Part One. Section III opens out of childhood's sleep, with the call of the steam-driven thresher usurping the mother's call—no soothing voices of nurse and stream, as in Wordsworth, but the blast and clamor of a vast machine. On this day, during the harvest season of McGrath's ninth year, the bitter knowledge of work and politics begins:

Out of the whirring lamp-hung dusk my mother calls.
From the lank pastures of my sleep I turn and climb,
From the leathery dark where the bats work, from the coasting
High all-winter all-weather christmas hills of my sleep.

And there is my grandfather chewing his goatee,
Prancing about like a horse. And the drone and whir from
        the fields
Where the thresher mourns and showers on the morning stillness
A bright fistful of whistles.

The field teams are short a man and the boy must take his place. There is, moreover, greater urgency in this moment than might at first appear. Harvest is each year's season of crisis, the time of time running out with all life governed by the twin gods of machinery and the sky:

The machine is whistling its brass-tongued rage and the jack-booted
                      weathers of autumn
Hiss and sing in the North.
The rains are coming, the end of the world
Is coming.

If the rains come, if the harvest fails, the end of *this* world is certain; the banks will foreclose and the farm will be lost. Thus a child steps into a man's job "too soon, too young," with no allowance for playful rites of passage.

                    Aloft on the shaking deck,
Half blind and deafened in the roaring dust,
On the heaving back of the thresher,
My neck blistered by sun and the flying chaff, my clothes
Shot full of thistles and beards, a gospel itch,
Like a small St. Steven, I turned the wheel of the blower
Loading the straw-rack.
The whistle snapped at my heels: in a keening blizzard
Of sand-burrs, barley-beards and beggars-lice, in a red thunder
Where the wheat rust bellowed up in a stormy cloud
From the knife-flashing feeder,
I turned the wheel.

This is the harvest of savage work and ruthless circumstance described by Christopher Caudwell, a thoughtful Marxist critic during the 1930's whose book *Illusion and Reality* McGrath has praised and often cites. Harvest is Caudwell's primary example of our collective struggle with nature, the historical contest that defines reality and social relations. Poetry was born of this struggle, or so Caudwell believes. Around actions essential to survival—chiefly war and harvest—the tribe builds festivals of dance and song to generate the energy, enthusiasm, and communal focus necessary to the hard days ahead. Caudwell puts it this way:[18]

> In the collective festival, where poetry is born, the phantastic world of poetry anticipates the harvest and, by doing so, makes possible the real harvest. But the illusion of this collective phantasy is not a mere drab copy of the harvest yet to be: it is a reflection of the emotional complex involved in the fact that man must stand in a certain relation to others and to the harvest, that his instincts must be adapted in a certain way to Nature and other men, to make the harvest possible.

Caudwell argues that ancient harvest was poetry's first occasion; that art mediates, collectively, the ceaseless struggle between need and reality. His stress is on *need*, not on *desire* merely. And no need is stronger or more often in jeopardy than feeding the tribe—true even now, as famine sweeps the sub-Sahara or, during the Reagan Era, as the American family farm goes down the drain, some 3,000 lost per month in the last year. Caudwell claims that poetry in a festival setting gives—or did once give—humankind the heart and communal will to work in common and accomplish urgent tasks.

McGrath's boyhood experience of harvest was both traumatic and exalting. From that past he summons a superlative image, festive in mood and gritty in detail, with the threshing rig at its center:

> Feathered in steam like a great tormented beast
> The engine roared and laughed, dreamed and complained,
> And the pet-cocks dripped and sizzled; and under its fiery gut
> Stalactites formed from the hand-hold's rheumy slobbers.
> —Mane of sparks, metallic spike of its voice,
> The mile-long bacony crackle of burning grease!
> There the engineer sat, on the high drivers,
> Aloof as a God. Filthy. A hunk of waste
> Clutched in one gauntleted hand, in the other the oil can
> Beaked and long-necked as some exotic bird;
> Wreathed in smoke, in the clatter of loose eccentrics.

And the water-monkey, back from the green quiet of the river
With a full tank, was rolling a brown quirrly
(A high school boy) hunkered in the dripping shade
Of the water-tender, in the tall talk and acrid sweat
Of the circle of spitting stiffs whose cloud-topped bundle-racks
Waited their turns at the feeder.
And the fireman: goggled, shirtless, a flashing three-tined fork,
Its handle charred, stuck through the shiny metallic
Lip of the engine, into the flaming, smoky
Fire-box of its heart.
Myself: straw-monkey. Jester at court.

The threshing machine with its steam engine is at the heart of the
scene, or rather *is* the scene. And what a vast thing it is. In the 1950's,
when McGrath began *Letter*, there were still threshing machines to be
seen, belt-driven by combustion engines. Even these were mammoth,
but the earlier steam-driven threshers were by all accounts awesome—
and dangerous too, as Willa Cather reminds us in *My Ántonia*. In
McGrath's rendering, however, the dread machine possesses festive fea-
tures, it laughs and dreams and complains. It slobbers like a monstrous
animal with sparks for a mane. Its voice is a steam whistle, always
described in metallic images, signalings a boy might take to heart. Clearly
McGrath *likes* machines, the threshing rig first of all. Machines are the
primary site for the world of work, and this one stands in union with
the land like a blessed and blessing monster—"its whistling brass com-
mandments" amid "the barb-tongued golden barley and the tents of the
biblical wheat."

Those who work the rig take from it even identity—names like water-
monkey, straw-monkey, spike-pitcher—festival figures ranged from
mock-God to mock-devil, in this case a dirty engineer and a fireman
armed with a pitchfork. Using the harvest machine as his anchor,
McGrath goes on to create a monstrosity of a world, brimming with
abundance and unruly beauty, full of ambivalent names and exaggerated
figures, set forth in language that brings "down to earth" all that would
otherwise be fearful or official, a communal world seething with energy.
And over all of it, the straw-monkey poet as "Jester at court."

Once the boy begins his job in the fields, even dreaming is occupied
by the threshing rig: "the whistle biting my ears, / The night vibrating, /

In the fog of the red rust, steam, the rattle of concaves"—all a permanent part of McGrath's imaginative world:

> So, dawn to dusk, dark to dark, hurried
> From the booming furious brume of the thresher's back
> To the antipodean panting engine. Caught in the first
> Circle.

Hell's first circle, of course, one of *Letter's* many echoes of Dante. But also the circle to be transformed into commune and round-dance. The boy's overriding desire is to work his way into manhood, to go as an equal in the circle of men who run the rig and move the grain. Impossible, of course, for a child of nine years; he can be a "man to the engine's hunger, to the lash of the whistle," but not to the young toughs, the old-timers, or to his uncle, who is "boss of the rig." His luck is to have a mentor: "Cal, one of the bundle teamsters, / My sun-blackened Virgil," who would teach him to take his time, not grow too fast, a field hand whom McGrath calls a "good teacher, a brother." The figure of Cal becomes one of the tutelary spirits of *Letter*, a quiet man aged about thirty, with a "brick-topped mulish face," who reads *The Industrial Worker* and is one of "the last of the real Wobs." Initiation into the world of work will thus be compounded by a bitter first taste of politics. When Cal leads the men against McGrath's uncle, any notion of rural romanticism—the spacious skies and amber grain of our collective pastoral fantasy—is dispelled from McGrath's view of the heartland:

We were threshing flax I remember, toward the end of the run—
After quarter-time I think—the slant light falling
Into the blackened stubble that shut like a fan toward the headland—
The strike started then.

Cal speaks for the men, is cursed by McGrath's uncle; a fight starts between them and the boy is appalled:

>   I heard their gruntings and strainings
> Like love at night or men working hard together,
> And heard the meaty thumpings, like beating a grain sack
> As my uncle punched his body—I remember the dust
> Jumped from his shirt.

This is Eden invaded by real-world conflict, a forceful instance of political intrusion. What happens next is remarkable and signals the coming together of two voices, McGrath's and the metallic blast of the rig. Shaken by the violence, the boy runs in anger to the idling machine and tries to throw it into gear:

> And the fireman came on a run and grabbed me and held me
> Sobbing and screaming and fighting, my hand clenched
> On the whistle rope while it screamed down all our noises—
> Stampeding a couple of empties into the field—
> A long, long blast, hoarse, with the falling, brazen
> Melancholy of engines when the pressure's falling.

Here, it seems to me, McGrath allies himself *with* the voice of the machine. Then directly after the drama of the fight comes a long lyrical expanse of the poem (nearly three pages) in which the boy goes off toward the river, alone in the gathering dusk:

Green permission . . .

                              Dusk of the brass whistle . . .
Gooseberry dark.
Green moonlight of willow.
Ironwood, basswood and the horny elm.
June berry; box-elder; thick in the thorny brake
The black choke cherry, the high broken ash and the slick
White bark of poplar.
                     I called the king of the woods,
The wind-sprung oak.
                     I called the queen of ivy,
Maharani to his rut-barked duchies;
Summoned the foxgrape, the lank woodbine,
And the small flowers; the woodviolets, the cold
Spears of the iris, the spikes of the ghostflower—
It was before the alphabet of trees
Or later.
                     Runeless I stood in the green rain
Of the leaves.
          Waiting.

He enters the "green world," hoping for contact with a peace at life's heart. Instead, "under the hush and whisper of the wood, / I heard the echoes of the little war" as hawk and mink go about their separate hunts. Later he goes for a swim and "under the river the silence was humming, singing." Finally his grief breaks into weeping and he encounters for the first time the burden of the mystery, the gore amid grandeur of life's rapacious innocence. He hears "the night hawk circling," but also the "comfort of crickets and a thrum of frogs." For the first time, the horror and the glory exist together:

> The crickets sang.   The frogs
> Were weaving their tweeds in the river shallows.
>
> Hawk swoop.
>
>   Silence.
>
>   Singing.
> The formal calls of a round-dance.
> This riddling of the river-mystery I could not read.

This is, I think, the primal figuration in McGrath's poetry, this coming together of violence and harmony in ways that serve to keep his knowledge of class conflict and his vision of communal oneness united. American pastoral is ersatz without its historical disruptions; at the same time, political violence cannot be redeemed—or perhaps even borne—without the festive dream of pastoral solidarity. When, finally, the boy returns to the farmyard his father is kneeling in the dust, fixing a harness by lantern light outside the barn—his gesture of atonement to Cal lying hurt inside:

> "Hard lines, Tom," he said. "Hard lines, Old Timer."
> I sat in the lantern's circle, the world of men,
> And heard Cal breathe in his stall.
>   An army of crickets
> Rasped in my ear.
>
>   "Don't hate anybody."
> My father said.

All unexpected, this has been the boy's passage into manhood; that same night the men leave in "a rattle of Fords." The harvest is ended, far from the spirit of festival that for a moment emerged. Referring to the strike in the fields, McGrath concludes by letting the momentum of his narrative carry him forward in time, in jumps of quick transition that anchor other of the poem's episodes and voices in this one strong incident—as if what had just happened were opening remembrance into the future:

> They had left Cal there
> In the bloody dust that day but they wouldn't work after that.
> "The folded arms of the workers" I heard Warren saying,
> Sometime in the future where Mister Peets lies dreaming
> Of a universal voting-machine.
>   And Showboat
> Quinn goes by (New York, later) "The fuckin' proletariat
> Is in love with its fuckin' chains. How do you put this fuckin'
> Strike on a cost-plus basis?"

The condition of the workers—their will to join ranks, their fear and hesitation—is seen both in the episode of the strike and again in the voices at the end of Section III, a raucous outburst cut short by a tone growing somber and quieting out. What happens, in these last fading lines, links the pioneer dream (populist) to the newer vision of justice (socialist). Both are tangled in violence, both rooted in the meaning of the West and with the lofty, meat-eating hawk for an emblem:

> "The folded arms of the workers."
> I see Sodaberg
> Organizing the tow boats.
>   I see him on Brooklyn Bridge,
> The fizzing dynamite fuse as it drops on the barges.
> Then Mac with his mournful face comes round the corner
> (New York) up from the blazing waterfront, preaching
> His strikes.
>   And my neighbors are striking on Marsh Street.
> (L.A., and later)
>   And the hawk falls.

A dream-borne singing troubles my still boy's sleep
In the high night where Cal had gone:
>   *They came through*
> *The high passes, they crossed the dark mountains*
> *In a month of snow.*
> *Finding the plain, the bitter water, the iron*
> *Rivers of the black north . . .*

Hunters

>   in the high plateaus of that country . . .
Climbing toward sleep . . .

But far

>   from the laughter.

And there, no doubt, McGrath stood: far from the laughter but in
sight of the mystery—a burden to be shouldered and, somehow, made
light of. And finally that is what happens: McGrath goes on to make
light of the sorrowing world by a laughter that brings it down to earth.
This notion of making-light-of, moreover, is not an easy pun but the
key to McGrath's remarkable combination of contrary states, Marxist
materialism and Catholic sacramentalism on the one hand, historical
necessity and frontier freedom on the other, and then his serious recovery
of the American Dream to be carried out, more and more as works
progress, by comic means.

Into his art McGrath introduces, gradually, a jocular spirit composed
of praises and curses together. He envisions the human predicament as
an extended Feast of Fools and himself as the "Jester at court." Drawing
on Old World traditions, he turns to the rites of festival and feast day,
and takes up a carnival style. And always his choices have political as
well as poetic implications. Here is a humor no hierarchy can digest or
tolerate. Nor can any imposition stamp it out. When this sort of laughing
takes effect, "the great night and its canting monsters turn[s] holy around
[us]. / Laughably holy." McGrath possesses a comic charity that pre-
cludes *hysterica passio*, but also a grotesque, expansive laughter that pushes
back (like the "violence within," in Stevens' notion) against the intrusive
world. This is the comic spirit in its most rampant, freely ruthless mood,
a humor that is raucous, earth-bound, carnivalesque.[19]

In *Letter*, the first sign of carnival comes early, in Section I of Part One, where McGrath turns to the matter of his family. At age five he ran away from home, as children will. He says he has never been back; but says also he "never left." Running from family, he took them along and "had the pleasure of their company":

> Took them? They came—
> Past the Horn, Cape Wrath, Oxford and Fifth and Main
> Laughing and mourning, snug in the two seater buggy,
> Jouncing and bouncing on the gumbo roads
> Or slogging loblolly in the bottom lands—
> My seven tongued family.[. . .]
> Conched in cowcatchers, they rambled at my side.
> The seat of the buggy was wider than Texas
> And slung to the axles were my rowdy cousins;
> Riding the whippletrees: aunts, uncles, brothers,
> Second cousins, great aunts, friends and neighbors
> All holus-bolus, piss-proud, all sugar-and-shit
> A goddamned gallimaufry of ancestors.
> The high passes?
> Hunter of the hornless deer?

Excess and exaggeration are primary signs of carnival style. As a diction the lines above might be called the magnified colloquial, a colorful popular idiom found almost anywhere (at one time) in rural America, certainly in the middle south and heartland plains, where people slog over the gumbo roads even now. Some of McGrath's diction appears literary, like "gallimaufry," and some, like "loblolly," might be archaic; but who's to say these very words didn't come off the boat with McGrath's grandparents. The point about obscurity is that most *spoken* language, the local speech of a place and its spirit, goes unrecorded. When found in literature it tends to be discounted as regionalism and remains "unofficial." For McGrath, however, the unofficial forces in language are best suited for utopian attack against the press of the established world. Terms for bodily functions—the primary four-letter words—remain off the record despite the fact that they have been the argot of all times and places, the core of nonconsensus (but universal) speech. These are the anchor-words of carnival style, and one or more of them will be operative, setting the earthward pitch in McGrath's later poetry. Often, as in the example above, an entire batch comes at us holus-bolus, at once in a lump. Language like this is in league with the tall tale (the buggy "wider than Texas") and is decidedly *of the people*, even of the *folk* in the American sense of "just plain folks."

The primary "curse words," as they are often called, can be relied on to upset prevailing taste and established decorum, while at the same time they can *also* convey covert alliance and express goodwill or solidarity. This is an idiom that can be used both to curse and to bless, to reduce and magnify, to pull down and elevate. It is, furthermore, a language independent of scene, wording in no way tied to a specific place or time or class or subject matter, language as available and packed with loamy energies as earth itself. When McGrath calls his family "sugar-and-shit" and "piss-proud," he casts blame while expansively showering praise. This part of McGrath's idiom is, so to say, the spittin' image of Mark Twain, the first master of American vernacular. Whitman had this goal as well, but only as a goal; and Twain, of course, had to contend with censorship. With McGrath an American vulgate comes into its own, a *basso continuo* of the populace at large.

To judge from the likes of Whitman, Twain, and McGrath, to be an American poet is to speak the language of the hard-pressed but irrepressibly optimistic masses. It's at this linguistic gut level that the "violence within" pushes back at the "violence without." To *speak American* is to combine one's regional idiom with the vernacular at large. It's also to appropriate any other language that seems apt, be it learned, technical, foreign, or just the day's jargon. And to speak American is to exaggerate routinely, to talk in a larger-than-life voice megaphoned by the continent itself. In an interview McGrath has said that "one of the modes of this poem is exaggeration." He is referring to *Letter*, and goes on to say: "exaggeration in terms of language, the exaggeration of certain kinds of actions to the point where they become surreal, fantastic—yes."[20] The surreal element in his earlier style becomes, in the later poetry, the distortive aspect of carnival excess—as in McGrath's bardic image of himself:

And now, out of the fog, comes our genealogizer
And keeper of begats. A little wizened-up wisp of a man:
Hair like an out-of-style bird's nest and eyes as wild as a wolf's!
Gorbellied, bent out of shape, short and scant of breath—
A walking chronicle: the very image of the modern poet!

McGrath's combination of excess and vulgarity might puzzle or offend some readers, and we see the excuse it affords to deny him his seriousness. But then we see as well that McGrath's language has earnest, even valiant, purposes. *In the beginning is the word, the curse word; the new world starts by get down to earth.* That is the logic of carnival. Certainly it's the order that governs McGrath's epic poem, a logic writ large in the following example. Out of the depth of the Second World War (McGrath was in the air force, stationed on a snow-blind island in the Aleutians) he extracts "a hero" who is destroyer and builder, who gets rid of and creates, a figure most lowly and therefore most high. I quote at length because the following lines (from Book X of Part One) make a typical unit in the rhythm and expanse of *Letter*:

> —From those days it's Cassidy I remember:
> Who worked on the high steel in blue Manhattan
> And built the top-most towers.
>   Now on our island [Amchitka],
> He was the shit-burner. He closed the slit-trench latrines
> With a fiery oath.
> When they had built permanent structures
> And underlaid them with the halves of gasoline drums,
> He took the drums out on the tundra in the full sight of God
> And burned them clean.
>   Stinking, blackened, smelling
> Like Ajax Ajakes, he brought home every night
> (Into the swamped prymidal, where, over two feet of water,
> Drifting like Noah on the shifting Apocalypse
> Of the speech of Preacher Noone, I read by the ginko light)
> Brought home mortality, its small quotidian smell.
>
> There was a hero come home! (The bombers swinging
> Around his neck, the gunners blessing his craft
> From dropping their load in comfort!) Him who on the high and windy
> Sky of Manhattan had written his name in steel, sing now,
> Oh poets!
>
> But that's a hard man to get a line on.
> Simple as a knife, with no more pretension than bread,
> He worked his war like a bad job in hard times

When you couldn't afford to quit. He'd had bad jobs before
And had outwon them.

        Now in a howl of sleet,
Or under the constant rain and the stinking flag of his guild,
He stood in his fire and burned the iron pots clean.

 Meanwhile: "Into the gun-colored urine-smelling day, heroic / The
bombers go," and when the crews returned in their shot-up planes "we
ran like rabbits down the dead flat road of their light / To snatch them
home to the cold from the fiery cities of air." The war, for McGrath,
was just such a city of air, a sky in need of clearing and renovation.
Between the dead and unborn worlds comes Cassidy, construction-
worker, shit-burner, time's hero—except that he too is gone. Hit by an
off-track aircraft, he never came back:

        Nowhere, now, on the high
 Steel will he mark on the sky that umber scratch
 Where the arcing rivet ends.

 An "umber scratch," the color of rust, feces, and fertilization, scrapes
the sky and maps the next reach of creation. It is the hero's signature
blazing the heavens—an image not without its grotesque majesty. This
is, moreover, a primary case of earth asserting its claims against the
worldly cities of air; life and the sources of life must be free and kept
uncowed, particularly in bad times like war, when the official world
demands complete submission. Then especially the earth pushes back.
And as we saw in *Antigone*, there can be no overestimating the degree
to which the human body is the foremost location of the earth-world
antagonism. The body is earth's domain in creatural terms but equally
the world's insofar as social-political order inscribes itself in bodily functions through sexual mores, eating habits, and excretory rites of the kind
over which McGrath's Cassidy presides.

 The point of carnival—its symbolic action—is to turn the world upside
down; to pull down ranks, privileges, pretensions; to suspend official
hierarchy in favor of a radical equality, wherein everything is laughed
at and anything can be said. No power setting itself above the community
can escape ridicule, and the lower forms of humor prevail—jokes, puns,
parody, slapstick, and clowning. In this festive manner contact with
earth is renewed at the gross level all men and women share. Con-

sciousness is anchored in the physical foundation of life, most often in the belly and the genitals. If this is "obscene" it is also the key to festive, and communal, affirmation.[21]

In America, affirmation of community is mandatory in public but not, in private, an article of serious faith. We are, most of us, torn between our genuine populist impulse and an economically rewarding self-interest that cannot serve itself and protect its privileges while at the same time taking in earnest the dream of a country held in common. To point to "the people," moreover, is to summon something that hardly exists apart from the rhetoric of its summoning, especially if what's meant is some kind of inclusive, like-minded group organized to act on its own behalf toward emancipation and enlarged consensus. Even so, "the people" is a valuable and very American idea. The early successes of populism in the West suggest that those who are exploited and powerless will eventually reach a collective sense of themselves. As they do, they discover a courage not available in isolation, a resilience reflected in festive forms. The interesting point is that victory over fear, and the purging of self-pity, are registered in speech officially proscribed. Not only *what* but also *how* we praise and blame positions us in the world. What this comes down to, finally, is enlistment of the powers of earth against whatever world is pressing to extradite its earthly foundation.

McGrath's language makes no sense apart from the double-edged freedom of unsanctioned speech. The essence of any creatural idiom is its deep ambivalence. The case with carnival language is not praise *or* blame but *both together*. Cassidy, in *Letter*, flies "the stinking flag of his guild" and works "in the full sight of God." When earth pushes back against world, the forces of riddance and creation set in motion the utopian thrust of McGrath's poetics. In addition to "curse words," his fusion of praise and blame magnifies the contrary thrust of other key words—"stiff," for example, which is McGrath's routine name for nameless field hands and laborers. The working man is a "stiff," a "bundle-stiff," part of "the circle of spitting stiffs." At first it sounds demeaning, slang for "corpse"; "to stiff" or "be stiffed," moreover, suggests victimization, in particular the plight of workers under capital. But the plain "working stiff" can be reborn, can rise again, in the manner of the male sexual member; in which case "stiff" also signifies erection and generative power. The word is multivalent and perfectly suited to a Marxist perspective. Through work the matter of earth is transformed into shapes of world. At the heart of this miracle is the worker, the lowly "stiff," and one day the last shall rise up and be first.

The extraordinary energy of "curse words" in familiar talk, their explosive power in formal situations, their vigor (and valor) in poetic usage—all this is obvious from daily observation. In McGrath's case this multivalent energy is the key to his diction. In *Letter* there are *no neutral words*. That must be true for poetry in general, but in McGrath's work especially. He is always praising or blaming, often both together. Benediction is his final goal, but first comes the need for descent, the poet blazing a path into song with a curse:

>   Listen:
> Under the skin of dark, do I hear the singing of water?
> The trees tick and talk in the almost windless calm
> And the stream is spinning a skein of an old and lonesome song
> In the cold heart of the winter
>   constant still.
>   One crow
> Slowly goes over me
>   —a hoarse coarse curse
>   —a shrill
> Jeer: last of the past year or first of the new,
> He stones me in appalling tongues and tones, in his tried
> And two black lingoes.
>   A dirty word in the shine,
> A flying tombstone and fleering smudge on the winter-white page
> Of the sky, my heart lightens and leaps high: to hear
> Him.
>   And the silence.
>   That sings now: out of the hills
> And cold trees.
>   Song I remember.

The entirety of *Letter to an Imaginary Friend*, in two volumes, adds up to a total of 329 pages, a very large work. The first two parts, published in 1970, are under the sign of Easter, inside the carnival time of Shrovetide festival. The third and fourth parts of *Letter*, published together in 1985, are under the sign of Christmas, within the time of feasting and glad tidings. In the Middle Ages, moreover, Eastertide and Christmas differed from other modes of carnival; during these two seasons sacred dogma and liturgical forms could be openly mocked, and there was a definite name for this license: *risus paschalis* or "paschal laughter." Formal unity of *Letter*, therefore, encompasses as points of departure the popular-festive form of carnival, the occasion of paschal laughter in particular; then the underlying rites of death and resurrection; and last the spectacle of earth in endless becoming with, always, a new world verging into view.

The change, in tone and style, the first to the second half of *Letter*, is decisive. In all ways extravagant, this latter part is the collective belly laugh of high feasting on ancestral holy days, a comic mode from which nothing is spared. In remarks on the poem, McGrath has said that the two halves share a common content, but that in the second half "the method will be wilder."[22] Certainly it is. Language in *Letter*'s first half is mimetic in principle, intent upon the work of witnessing. Parts Three and Four, on the contrary, are joyously antithetical or antimimetic; here language is destructively excessive, hostile to any image of the status quo, determined to push into a further world. I have, however, concentrated mainly on the poetry of Parts One and Two. *Letter*'s first half, I think, reveals McGrath at his finest in terms of witnessing and his art of lyrical documentation. However, the language of One and Two cannot be wholly appreciated without a sense of its final purpose (its symbolic action in broadest terms), which comes to view only in Parts Three and Four, where McGrath subsumes and *goes beyond* the historical world, arriving at the edge of apocalypse.

For an epigraph to *Letter*'s last part, McGrath cites Caudwell and includes this remark:[23]

> . . . the instincts must be harnessed to the needs of the harvest by a social mechanism. An important part of this mechanism is the group festival, the matrix of poetry, which frees the stores of emotion and canalises them in a collective channel. The real object, the tangible aim—a harvest—becomes in the festival a fantastic object. The real object is not here now. The fantastic object is here now—in fantasy. . . . That world [of fantasy] becomes more real, and even when the music dies away the ungrown harvest has a greater reality for him, spurring him on to the labours necessary for its accomplishment.

Poetry creates images of renovation so real and compelling to the mind that we are spurred onward "to the labours necessary." This kind of incitement is, I take it, the political justification for carnival poetry in a visionary mode. It also reminds us of the main point in *Letter*: that at the back of McGrath's epic we find the harvest festival. And at the ritual's center stands a godlike machine that together with the weather determined the pace and shape of life in rural Dakota when McGrath was coming of age. The powerful earth image of the threshing rig holds the poem in place and gives readers an anchor for a text that is otherwise wildly informal. And who shall receive this "letter"? McGrath's "generous dead" to begin with, the ancestral part of his tribe; and then any of us called by the poem as McGrath was called by the blast of a monstrous machine in the remembered fields of his youth.

The "imaginary friend" is you, me, the whole of the disbelieving world. McGrath calls us "friend" and I take him at his word. For all his cursing and "hard lines," his public stance is genial, outgoing, utopian by nature as well as conviction. In a "Note" on *Letter* McGrath says: "Work, for example, is not something which most poets write about. Also communality and solidarity—feelings which perhaps are more important to us than romantic love—never appear in our poetry."[24] When McGrath speaks of "communality and solidarity," he is talking about Eros in its political, all-embracing form. Love of this kind—call it charity, *caritas*, communal husbandry—is at the heart of his poetic enterprise. Generosity and hopefulness go together in his work, fields of blessing empowered by laughter. With these ideas in mind I conclude by citing "The End of the World," published in 1982 in *Passages Toward the Dark*:[25]

The end of the world: it was given to me to see it.
Came in the black dark, a bulge in the starless sky,
A trembling at the heart of the night, a twitching of the webby flesh of
                                                    the earth.
And out of the bowels of the street one beastly, ungovernable cry.

Came and I recognized it: the end of the world.
And waited for the lightless plunge, the fury splitting the rock.
And waited: a kissing of leaves; a whisper of man-killing ancestral
                                                    night—

Then a tinkle of music, laughter from the next block.

Yet waited still: for the awful traditional fire,
Hearing mute thunder, the long collapse of sky.
It falls forever. But no one noticed. The end of the world provoked
Out of the dark a single and melancholy sigh

From my neighbor who sat on his porch drinking beer in the dark.
No: I was not God's prophet. Armageddon was never
And always: this night in a poor street where a careless irreverent
                                                              laughter
Postpones the end of the world; in which we live forever.

The poem might be read in a number of ways, but in one way principally if McGrath's homage to Eros is as steady as I think. The onset
of "traditional fire" would be the final Biblical Wrath that even today
(or especially today) the Fundamentalists among us forecast. But while
men of God call for brimstone, McGrath does not. The only end of the
world is the one we all feel daily, life's senseless silent wasting, its sad
predictable blundering that seems, often, too beastly to go on. But on
it goes, and while much is dying much else is coming to birth. The
world feels open and closed, final and full of possibility. That, as I take
it, is the point of the poem: that once we admit the perpetual burden
upon us, we might then begin to reach out, make an effort, work on
ways of making light of it and sharing it about. Meanwhile what keeps
this life-in-death from death itself is "a tinkle of music, laughter from
the next block." Against the old ultimatum, not thunder and the fall of
sky, but the street's careless laughter and the sigh of a neighbor next
door.

·VIII·

Adrienne Rich,
North America East

We write for ourselves and each other—an
ever-expanding sense of whom is part of our
imagining.
                                    —Adrienne Rich[1]

The poetry of Adrienne Rich presents the clear-eyed instance of a poet whose work began in a formal self-regarding mode devoid of politics; but a poet who has gone on, by virtue of attention to experience, to establish a major voice in forms overtly political. Nor is there any uncertainty about the meaning of politics in Rich's view. When the "way of grief / is shared, unnecessary," we can discern forces—forces as unnecessary as Creon's decree—preempting the fate of private being. That *the personal is political* has been a feminist notion much challenged; but for the experience of women in a patriarchal order I do not see that it can be denied or even declared a special case. Women are Antigone's sisters by virtue of their status as women. In this light the play by Sophocles takes on added relevance, suggesting that the conflict of the individual with the state finds its broadest example in the struggle of women for self-determination.

Rich's poetry is political from the moment she confronts her own condition as a woman, with variations on the primal theme of intrusion that accrue from her roles as wife and mother and daughter-in-law. It is the law, the legalization of power relations, that keeps the daughter a daughter, indentured first to the father and then to the husband's family. There is no moment of day or night, in Rich's view, when women are fully at liberty to define and live their own destiny. Intrusion is public and private together, often extremely intimate, and in ways that the

history of accommodation has not been able to transcend. As with
Antigone, a woman's fate is hers but not her own.

As Alicia Ostriker has pointed out, Whitman could "celebrate
myself" and take for granted "What I assume you shall assume," while
Emily Dickinson had to fight her more difficult battle alone, without
models or encouragement, on the bleak assumption that "I'm nobody."[2]
Together these two compose the fountainhead of our poetry. Both poets
start with evidence of self. But thereafter they go separate ways. Dickinson admits, as Whitman does not, that there are powers beyond the
self, impersonal arrangements curtailing the healthy expansion of self in
the world. Whitman cast his lot with the national experience; he could
enjoy the bonhomie of the open road and grow up with the country.
He could afford to loaf. Dickinson, meanwhile, had to give birth to
herself with no help outside her own willfulness and the natural midwifery of her art—a predicament that Rich knows well:

> your mother dead and you unborn
> your two hands grasping your head
> drawing it down against the blade of life
> your nerves the nerves of a midwife
> learning her trade [.]

That is an image of terrible will and terrible birth, but at least it *is*
birth and not the paralysis implied by Arnold's nineteenth-century use
of the two-world image. He might complain that the old world was
dead with a new one "powerless" to be born, but that kind of flagging
comes from writing at the center of empire, a malady now widespread
in American letters but not, significantly, among poets who are women.

The politicial intrusion that is integral to Antigone's political experience also defines Adrienne Rich's home ground, "the light / that soaks
in from the world of pain / even when I sleep." The primary metaphor—
and concrete case—of political intrusion is rape, and actual or feared
rape is also a primary experience of women. When Rich imagines it in
her poetry she sees its agent as an upholder of prevailing order, a po-
liceman for example. When she theorizes, on the other hand, she equates
rape with military violence; rape as the prerogative of invaders in all
times and places, "the great unpunished war crime in every culture."[3]
Those who thrive in the shadow of the fathers will prefer to ignore the
severity of Rich's claims. But her critique of patriarchy—male reliance

on force relations, male pride in not feeling, male disregard for pain in others—isn't meant to console. The personal-historical symmetry of her feminist vision aligns political experience generally with women's condition in particular, and compels this central point: "woman's body is the terrain on which patriarchy is erected."[4] In *Antigone*, Creon controls the state by controlling the rights of the body; and if we allow for Rich's association of female with earth and male with world, her position incorporates the earth-world antagonism as well.

For Rich and women like her, the first outcome of political alertness is anger—anger as a generator of the will to change, as a prerequisite to the revival of hope. Anger endorses the primacy of the curse, and the examples of Yeats and Brecht or Breytenbach suggest that rage toward public situations can be, and often has been, turned to creative account. To be in a fury at the order of things is to be possessed of oneself through the last emotion still one's own. For poets, indignation is a further "violence within" to be directed against the "violence without." Anger, with its sustaining fearless energy, becomes the dark unspoken side of joy. But for a creative flame to ignite, it has to reach beyond mere sweetness of destruction:

> Each day during the heat-wave
> they took the temperature of the haymow.
> I huddled fugitive
> in the warm sweet simmer of the hay
>
> muttering: *Come.*

Those lines are from "The Phenomenology of Anger." The American ravagement of Vietnam is equated with male domination at home, a compound of experience and insight that, having become conscious, becomes combustible. Like fire, anger is destructive when left to itself; but contained in the service of creation it becomes a source of power.

In one of her recent "tracking poems" (1983–86), Rich says of her work: there is "no art to this but anger."[5] No doubt this element—the pressure of combat—is what readers are offended by in much of Rich. And yes, her art is often *offensive*, in the several meanings of that word, with as much cursing as blessing (although Rich's regular use of lament and consoling intimacy is a mode of muted praise). Her poems, moreover, seldom flatter the reader; they do not seduce or cajole but rather challenge. One feels that agreed-upon laws of decorum are being ignored, the ad hominem rule in particular. Not that Rich attacks people by name; she does, however, often attack the patriarchal goings-on of males-in-power, a violation of etiquette that makes her poetry harsh on occasion but that exposes the ad hominem rule for what it is—an agreement among club members not to criticize colleagues, the better to defend the privileges of the club.

In her critical prose, Rich returns repeatedly to the value of anger as a political/poetical resource. In "When We Dead Awaken," an essay written in 1971 with the subtitle "Writing as Re-Vision," Rich offers these remarks:[6]

> In re-reading Virginia Woolf's *A Room of One's Own* . . . I was astonished at . . . the tone of that essay. It is the tone of a woman almost in touch with her anger, who is determined not to appear angry, who is *willing* herself to be calm, detached, and even charming in a roomful of men where things have been said which are attacks on her very integrity.

> Both the victimization and the anger experienced by women are real, and have real sources, everywhere in the environment, built into society. They must go on being tapped and explored by poets, among others. We can neither deny them, nor can we rest there. They are our birth-pains, and we are bearing ourselves.

There is a direct link between anger and creation, and in "Three Conversations" Rich makes the connection explicit:[7]

> . . . for women to dissemble anger has been a means of survival, and therefore we turn our anger inward. . . . I almost think that we have a history of centuries of women in depression: really angry women, who could have been using their anger creatively, as men have used their anger creatively.

She concludes that "an enormous amount of male art is anger converted into creation," and while anger isn't art's sole source, it plays a cardinal role. Rich connects anger to victimization on the one hand, to creative transformation on the other. Women reach political *and* poetic maturity when they resolve not to be victims merely. The value of anger in poetry is its push for survival. Useful rage turns outward into the world; turned inward, it becomes a tide of destruction and in severe cases contributes to tragedies like those of Virginia Woolf and Sylvia Plath. Anger's value to survival, on the other hand, is apparent in the careers of poets like Rich or Margaret Atwood or, first of all, Emily Dickinson:

> you, woman, masculine
> in single-mindedness,
> for whom the word was more
> than a symptom—
>
> a condition of being.
> Till the air buzzing with spoiled language
> sang in your ears
> of Perjury
>
> and in your half-cracked way you chose
> silence for entertainment,
> chose to have it out at last
> on your own premises.

By repeating the word "chose," Rich isolates the act of will in poetic achievement. That Dickinson was willful in creative ways is plain from her refusal to accept the domestic, religious, or social slots held out to women of her time. Her alternative was poetry, and through it she took a place in the world. In "Vesuvius at Home" Rich says of Dickinson:[8]

> It was a life deliberately organized on her terms. The terms she had been handed by society—Calvinist Protestantism, Romanticism, the nineteenth-century corseting of women's bodies, choices, and sexuality—could spell insanity to a woman of genius. What this one had to do was retranslate her own unorthodox, subversive, sometimes volcanic propensities into a dialect called metaphor: her native language "Tell all the truth—but tell it Slant—." It is always what is under pressure in us, especially under pressure of concealment—that explodes in poetry.

Dickinson is no longer patronized as a "fragile poetess in white," but has become, as Rich says, "a source and a foremother." She confronted the world on her own terms and allowed her art to be her defense. Through language "nobody" became "somebody," though not without social cost. Thomas Higginson could still belittle Dickinson by calling her "my partially cracked poetess at Amherst." But she would answer back, and put her case this way: "You think my gait 'spasmodic'—I am in danger—Sir—You think me 'uncontrolled'—I have no Tribunal."[9]

From that exchange Rich takes the title for her praise-poem: "I am in danger—Sir." The danger, I take it, is anger with no outlet. The danger is not to realize one's gift, to live with "spoilt language." The danger is also, as Rich puts it, that the woman-as-poet will be "split between a publicly acceptable persona, and a part of yourself that you perceive as the essential, the creative and powerful self, yet also as possibly unacceptable, perhaps even monstrous."[10] Dickinson created her own ground and took her place in the world regardless of her image—uncontrolled, spasmodic, cracked—in the eyes of the fathers.

To those upholding the status quo, any person in revolt appears "revolting." A woman not in a woman's place will be a freak, a witch, a monster. Official order demonizes the powers it suppresses; and when, for example, a woman refuses her social role as mother merely, she may expect to seem monstrous—even to herself. In "Night-Pieces: For a Child," the poet-mother beholds herself this way:

> You blurt a cry. Your eyes
> spring open, still filmed in dream.
> Wider, they fix me—
> —death's head, sphinx, medusa? [. . .]
> Mother I no more am,
> but woman, and nightmare.

The image of woman as monster is central to Rich's work. The lines just quoted are fretted with guilt, here the poet is inside the patriarchal point of view, and the image of woman as monster is wholly negative. Women with aspirations that deny or contradict motherhood will be seen as "unnatural." At the core of this curse swirls a dark cloud of misogyny, the male fear of women who don't stay put in places men assign. If archetypes exist, this is surely one, the composite image of loathing and terror that governs male paranoia toward self-possessed women:

> A man is asleep in the next room
>   We are his dreams
>   We have the heads and breasts of women
>   the bodies of birds of prey
>   Sometimes we turn into silver serpents
> While we sit up smoking and talking of how to live
> he turns on the bed and murmurs [.]

On the one hand, a man dreaming; on the other, two women "talking of how to live." That is the great divide in Rich's poetry. Men often think of women as unnatural and distorted if they stray from expected roles. Just as often, women accept such mutilating definitions. In the passage above, monstrous dreaming is countered by talk of "how to live." What these women are working out is how to live with—and then beyond—the obsessional images imposed upon them.

Caroline Herschel, "sister of William," is one among the heroic women Rich praises for not keeping her assigned place. She was an astronomer like her brother, a woman who discovered eight comets, "she whom the moon rules / like us." When she looked up into the night she saw what we see:

> A woman in the shape of a monster
> a monster in the shape of a woman
> the skies are full of them [.]

Those are the opening lines of "Planetarium," and as the poem goes on it becomes clear that the image of woman as monster is no longer negative. The "galaxies of women" are a grand and awesome spectacle. Caroline Herschel is the match of Tycho Brahe and shares with him this wish: "Let me not seem to have lived in vain." In the poem's last part, the images of woman as constellation and as astronomer are called upon to bless the poet who, empowered by Caroline Herschel's example, can claim her self-assigned task:

> I am an instrument in the shape
> of a woman trying to translate pulsations

into images for the relief of the body
and the reconstruction of the mind.

The image of woman as monster might be a vehicle of censure, but not necessarily. It can, in fact, be the badge of heroism. Rich's usage suggests that myths imposed on women can be revised and made to function in ways nourishing to the woman who feels that she, too, is out of place and susceptible to attack as unnatural. This strategy is central to Rich's own mythology. But the image of woman as monster isn't Rich's alone; as a number of feminist critics have pointed out, it is common to a wide spectrum of poets who are women, sometimes used with ambivalence, as much a curse as a blessing, but often too with straight praise. The image of the monster-woman, in Western mythology, goes back as far as mythic memory reaches, to Lilith and the Sphinx, to the Medusa and sometimes, as Yeats reminds us, to Helen. The figure is always powerful, often dangerous, and when viewed from male perspective, rudely unbecoming.

In "Necessities of Life," one of Rich's early manifestos celebrating her identity as a poet who is specifically a woman, Rich constructs an extended image of her poetic self that is grotesque in a modest but resolute way. From out the mouths of monsters, other monsters come.

> Jonah! I was Wittgenstein,
> Mary Wollstonecraft, the soul
>
> of Louis Jouvet, dead
> in a blown-up photograph.
>
> Till, wolfed almost to shreds,
> I learned to make myself
>
> unappetizing. Scaly as a dry bulb
> thrown into a cellar
>
> I used myself, let nothing use me.
> Like being on a private dole,
>
> sometimes more like kneading bricks in Egypt.
> What life was there, was mine,

now and again to lay
one hand on a warm brick

and touch the sun's ghost
with economical joy,

now and against to name
over the bare necessities.

Rich describes herself as an ugly outcast, but she ties herself to earth
by distinctly female images of the bulb and warm bricks. The program
that goes with the description—to be "unappetizing," to "let nothing
use me"—is the kind of behavior that men call unnatural when they find
it in women. The role of monster is embraced, used as a fulcrum of
strength. And among the multitude "kneading bricks in Egypt," might
not a prophet appear? A female Moses with a bardic voice? Armed with
this identify, Rich "dare[s] to inhabit the world / trenchant in motion
as an eel, solid / as a cabbage-head." The poem ends with a blessing
from "old women knitting, breathless / to tell their tales," tales the poet
will absorb, and praise, and transmit.

Adrienne Rich didn't start a leader. Her early work, praised by Auden
and Randall Jarrell among others, shows her the dutiful daughter of
the fathers, Auden and Jarrell among them. Not until *Snapshots of a
Daughter-in-Law*, published in 1963, twelve years after her first book,
does Rich begin to speak *as a woman* and allow that kind of content to
underwrite her vision. Of this turning point Rich says: "Over two years
I wrote a ten-part poem called 'Snapshots of a Daughter-in-Law'
[1958–1960] in a longer looser mode than I'd trusted myself with
before. It was an extraordinary relief to write that poem."[11] A relief and
also, I want to suggest, a breakthrough.
   Part one begins with an older woman as mother, her mind "moldering
like a wedding cake." Part two depicts the sullen daughter who bangs
the coffee pot into the sink as she hears "the angels chiding." They tell
her to have no patience, to be insatiable, to save herself; but stuck in
her anger, she "let[s] the tapstream scald her arm." Part three presents
the dangers of taking anger seriously; when women turn it upon themselves they become "like Furies," distorted and possessed:

> A thinking woman sleeps with monsters.
> The beak that grips her, she becomes.

Part four summons Emily Dickinson, "iron-eyed and beaked and pur-posed as a bird," her life a loaded gun. Part five recalls woman in her standard role as ornament, she who pleases men *dulce*, sweetly, grooming her legs to gleam "like petrified mammoth-tusk." Parts six through nine explore the consequences of enforced shallowness, including the judg-ments of Diderot ("You all die at fifteen") and Dr. Johnson ("that it is done at all") upon "time's precious chronic invalid." Here too, Mary Wollstonecraft is named with praise and thereby defended against the curse—"labeled harpy, shrew and whore"—of men who took her for a monster. At the end of part nine Rich confronts the consequence of following precursors like Dickinson and Wollstonecraft; for women who "cast too bold a shadow / or smash the mold straight off," the curse to be borne will be as painful as "tear gas, attrition shelling." Then, as if in result and repudiation at once, part ten concludes by casting a shadow fierce enough to smash all the molds listed in the poem. Here, in imagery she has not used before, Rich summons the new woman:

>   Well,
> she's long about her coming, who must be
> more merciless to herself than history.
> Her mind full to the wind, I see her plunge
> breasted and glancing through the currents,
> taking the light upon her
> at least as beautiful as any boy
> or helicopter,
>   poised, still coming,
> her fine blades making the air wince
>
> but her cargo
> no promise then:
> delivered
> palpable
> ours.

The meaning of the poem is governed by this composite image of woman-as-deliverer, a ship plunging through the currents with her cargo. As she cuts "breasted and glancing" through the wind, she is also the foremost part of the ship, and I do not see that the image of the *figurehead* (the carved bust on a ship's prow) can be avoided here. She who arrives "more merciless to herself than history" is a monster to the imaginative eye—a ship and its prow, but also a beautiful boy, and then, too, a purposeful airborne machine, the helicopter, cutting the air with sharp pounding blades. To see these images together is to behold a monstrosity that is, nonetheless, the bearer of a cargo long-promised and now at last delivered.

Through the first nine parts of the poem, Rich speaks *to* and *about* ("you bird," "the beak that grips her," "handsome women, gripped") the women who compose the group portrait. In the tenth part a new relation between poet and audience emerges, active rather than passive, in motion rather than stuck. The poet concludes with "ours," a word not used before, suggesting that the isolated earlier parts of the poem have been transformed and regathered into a union decidedly tribal. The tribe, in this case, is made of those who in the poem represent the daughter-in-law in multiple aspect, the many kinds of women confined by patriarchal law. The main point is that Rich begins, in "Snapshots," to speak to and for a definite group. The poem is prophetic, announcing the coming of the tribe's new figurehead and leader. That tribe and leader are consubstantial is marked throughout the poem by a consistent use of imagery associated with monstrosity, climaxing with the "coming"—repeated twice—of this poised and merciless woman, who arrives in an act of maternal/erotic/political delivery. The composite figure of the last stanzas is midwife, lover, and potent monster, vastly female but with male aspects as well. A new totem emerges to "smash straight off" the old taboos. The result is a liberation for the poet and her tribe.

"Snapshots of a Daughter-in-Law" is a curse upon the condition of women, a malediction that turns at the end into a poem of praise and atonement. What is celebrated is the image of a new woman, but also the community of women that the poet is able at last—and with "extraordinary relief"—to feel one with. For the first time Rich assumes, when she speaks, a tribal intimacy. Where once she wrote polite poems for her father to approve while "unspeakable fairy tales ebb[ed] like blood through [her] head," now she writes with a monster's outlaw freedom, addressing the many women to whom the ubiquitous "you" of her work refers in poem after poem. Communal pronouns—"we," "us," "our"—provide the frame for exchanges between "I" and "you."

And now the poet's identity takes its feminist form as midwife, com-
bining creative and procreative powers:

> like a midwife who at dawn
> has all in order; bloodstains
> washed up, teapot on the stove,
> and starts her five miles home
> walking, the birthyell still
> exploding.

How women give birth and who helps them, Rich says in *Of Woman
Born*, "are political questions." Charting the history of midwifery, Rich
points to "the centuries of witchcraft trials, during which midwives were
a particular target."[12] In America, the first person executed for witchcraft
was Margaret Jones, a midwife. Ann Hutchinson was also a midwife.
The practical wisdom of midwifery (seen by men as magical and demonic) is ancient; but by reviving a tradition of healing that men have
condemned as monstrous, Rich is able to combine in one image the
notions of woman as monster and woman as poet with long practice of
female power—specifically, women helping women.

In "When We Dead Awaken," her account of development from a
poet as dutiful daughter to the poet as monster and midwife, Rich
observes that "to be a female human being trying to fulfill traditional
female functions in a traditional way *is* in direct conflict with the subversive function of the imagination."[13] For a woman to claim male
powers goes against the grain of patriarchal order. More, to take up the
role of the bard is to violate a wholly male tradition. Women might be
permitted to speak of private themes and in a quiet voice, *dulce ridens,
dulce loquens;* but to speak out and take place and assume a public voice
has been, until recently, unheard of. Lest we forget, men who cast blame
are honored as prophets, while sharp-tongued women are in league with
the devil and at one time paid with their lives.

In the poem "Orion," written five years after "Snapshots," Rich reclaims a part of herself that in traditional terms is thought to be masculine
only. The poem's imagery of kinship and blood suggests the completeness with which Rich possesses the powers of her male double:

> my fierce half-brother, staring
> down from that simplified west

your breast open, your belt dragged down
by an oldfashioned thing, a sword
the last bravado you won't give over
though it weighs you down as you stride

and the stars in it are dim
and maybe have stopped burning.
But you burn, and I know it;
as I throw back my head to take you in
an old transfusion happens again:
divine astronomy is nothing to it.

As Rich says in her essay, Orion possesses "the active principle, the energetic imagination,"[14] a strength she reclaims for herself while careful to distinguish it from phallic power merely; male posturing has devolved into a "last bravado," and even now the sign of the sword is burning out. We might also recall that Orion was a hunter slain by Diana, goddess of chastity. In this poem, moreover, poetic power is defined as "cold and egotistical," as if loss of love and empathy were the cost of creative assertion. Rich sees that the division of human potential into male and female zones is a mutilation of our humanness made worse by traditional claims that such division is natural and the way things should remain. She is also aware that one definition of monstrosity, in traditional terms, is the merging of gender differences within a single self. She is not, however, going to assume male prerogatives at the expense of female resources. What she does instead is "put on" a suit of "body-armor" such as a merman "in his armored body" wears, and go down into the wreck.

"Diving into the Wreck" takes the theme of woman-as-monster as far as it goes, all the way to "the thing itself and not the myth," an androgynous condition of being that is "she" and "he" together but impossible to visualize. By reading "the book of myths" (in which "our names do not appear") she is able to locate the site of the wreck. And going down, she learns power of a wholly different kind: "I have to learn alone / to turn my body without force / in the deep element." And once at the wreck she finds herself "among so many who have always / lived here." The remarkable thing about this poem is how solid it seems with its paraphernalia of diving, its wrecked ship and quest for treasure; yet at no point does it yield a comprehensible image of that which the poet encounters. As with the composite image at the close of "Snapshots," here too the thing being praised cannot be seen except as a quilting of images. Nevertheless, it's here that the "I" becomes "we," here that the poet arrives at the goal of her quest:

> This is the place.
> And I am here, the mermaid whose dark hair
> streams black, the merman in his armored body
> We circle silently
> about the wreck
> we dive into the hold.
> I am she: I am he
>
> whose drowned face sleeps with open eyes
> whose breasts still bear the stress
> whose silver, copper, vermeil cargo lies
> obscurely inside barrels
> half-wedged and left to rot[. . . .]

The principle of form evident above is characteristic of Rich's mature poetry and, with "Diving" for proof, depends on a kind of wovenness or netting of images held in loose communion—an overlapping of disparate elements from many directions together. What unifies this kind of poem is its *threshold image*, if I may call it that, a larger composite of imagery that almost but not quite reveals its oneness in diversity, as if it were on the point of crossing into visibility, an emerging image in and through the poem's parts, but nowhere dominant in itself. Images of this kind carry Rich's sense of female possibility, her vision of the new woman in the moment of "her coming." This holds for poems like "Snapshots" and "Orion," and for much of the later poetry as well. Rich's important images possess threshold presence and have, as well, the character of a matrix. They are matrices out of which, and back into which, the disparate imagery of the poetry moves—as if the actual poem were a door, or rather a door frame where, in its crossing, the image resides.

With "Diving into the Wreck," Rich completes her re-vision of woman as monster. It becomes a source of poetic/political identity extracted from the wreckage of self and society under patriarchal rule. The old dispensation is displaced and a new "book of myths" can be written.

But as a matrix or threshold image, woman as monster remains useful. In "Turning the Wheel," written in 1981, Rich travels to "the female core" of the American continent, where she calls back from our native past "the desert witch, the shamaness." She aims to recover from history's normalized mythology the abnormality of a pueblo sorceress, a woman "slightly wall-eyed or with a streak / of topaz lightning in the blackness / of one eye." The figure of the shamaness is then recognized in Mary Colter, our earliest architect to use native American principles of design. Rich suggests that "history" has been largely a male province and that the powers of women have been apart from history, man/ world/clock-time on the one hand, woman/earth/tidal-time on the other.

The summoning of strong women is a constant occasion in Rich's poetry. Thereby she celebrates a feminist genealogy of heroes and martyrs from whom to take courage and direction. Among those who give the tribe its identity are Willa Cather, Marie Curie, Emily Dickinson, Elizabeth Barrett, Diane Fossey, Jane Addams, Susan B. Anthony, Mary Wollstonecraft, Caroline Herschel, Paula Becker, and Clara Westhoff, as well as personal friends of the poet (Audre Lorde, for example), and then finally the eponymous "deviant" woman of "Heroines" and, with no remembered names, the frontier women in "From an Old House in America." The first step toward political union of any sort, as Rich knows, is the establishment of collective identity by naming and praising. This revisionist stance toward history has been a principal aim of the feminist movement, and the fact that the cause of women *is* a movement, a self-conscious effort to acquire power and take place in the world, gives Rich the urgency of her voice, a voice that assumes, as most recent poetry does not, vital relation to widespread real-world needs.

In the feminist movement there are many voices—poets, scholars, critics—addressing the community of women. No one of them can speak for women as a whole, but a striking feature of Rich's work is the intensity with which it is received by its audience, an audience that feels itself embattled and in need of a voice that each of its members can recognize, share, and take to heart. The fact that Rich has championed a separatist movement among feminists, or that she often praises erotic love exclusively female, has not narrowed her appeal nor reduced her authority. Of her work Rich says: "As long as I wrote in the hope of 'reaching' men, I was setting bounds on my own mind, holding back;

trying to make the subversive sound unthreatening, the unthinkable reassuring." And of feminist writing in general, she goes on: "when we write for women we imagine an audience which *wants* our words—which desires our courage, our anger, our verve, our active powers, instead of fearing or loathing them. We write for ourselves and each other—an ever-expanding sense of whom is part of our imagining—passionately listening and reading as we write because other women's words are vital to our own."[15] To be "part of our imagining" is the great condition for political coherence; here it signals a shared excitement in poetry's keeping.

As the voice of her tribe, Rich incites revolt and calls to battle; she combats the curse set upon her as a poet, and upon women in general, at the hands of patriarchal censure. We've seen that one way to do this is to take a principal curse, the woman-as-monster, and transform it into praise and blessing. This kind of transformation is constant in Rich's work, and can be seen as part of the "re-naming" and "re-vision" essential to the feminist program in its literary aspect. Of this revisionary struggle Rich says that "the act of looking back, of seeing with fresh eyes, of entering an old text from a new critical direction—is for women more than a chapter in cultural history: it is an act of survival."[16] She postulates a "dynamic between a political vision and the demand for a fresh vision of literature," and concludes in poetry's favor:[17]

> For a poem to coalesce, for a character or an action to take shape, there has to be an imaginative transformation of reality which is in no way passive. . . . If the imagination is to transcend and transform experience it has to question, to challenge, to conceive of alternatives, perhaps to the very life you are living at that moment. You have to be free to play around with the notion that day might be night, love might be hate; nothing can be too sacred for the imagination to turn into its opposite or to call experimentally by another name. For writing is re-naming.

What happens, say, if the common word *mother* is turned into its opposite or called by another name? How about the word *wife*? or the traditional meaning of *maternal*? What happens is that mystifications collapse and truths emerge that guardians of patriarchal order find appalling and outrageous. Reaction is swift, sometimes violent, and the contest between Antigone and Creon replays itself yet again.

The path of poetic fate in our century suggests that repressive regimes do not tolerate, are in fact afraid of, the subversive powers of language, most especially poetry in the hands of those whom the political order aims to keep powerless. To an important degree, the very different careers of Brecht and Breytenbach reveal the same predicament that Rich and her feminist colleagues find themselves in, a fate and a predicament for which Osip Mandelshtam is perhaps the saintly patron. Viewed from a feminist perspective, established order is not on any poet's side. The hostile impact of Creon's decree, moreover, is for women extremely intimate. When men in the seats of power manipulate women by inscribing laws on the wall of the womb, when self-determination is withheld and women do not have control of their own bodies, we are back to the situation in *Antigone*, where carnal desecration is the sign of spiritual rape. For reasons of this kind, Rich is adamant about the moral centrality of physical existence. In her view, mind and body are one agency; poetic knowledge is a "thinking through the body," and the truths of the flesh are never trivial. Rich might even say, as I would, that physical recoil is our first response to evil, the initial (and initiating) stage of revolt that makes us human:

> The will to change begins in the body not in the mind
> My politics is in my body, accruing and expanding with every
>   act of resistance and each of my failures
> Locked in the closet at 4 years old I beat the wall with my body
> that act is in me still[.]

Maturity of vision arrived, for Rich, when she began to feel "that politics was not something 'out there' but something 'in here' and of the essence of my condition."[18] Thinking through the body is the bedrock of moral intelligence for much of feminist writing, a way of judging the world in direct relation to physical need and physical vulnerability, including the vulnerability of childbirth and nurturing generally. To recognize this simple concrete condition, furthermore, is to revise some very old and honored principles. The male obsession with high versus low, with spirit versus the flesh, with the cultural versus the natural, gives way in the feminist view to a mutuality of categories, a network of values that are complementary rather than opposed, and a care for earth as strong as allegiance to any world. We must, says Rich to her tribe, "view our physicality as a resource, rather than a destiny."[19] In one of her "tracking poems" she praises the body as our connection to earth, as the raft that saves us from abstract foundering:

> The best world is the body's world
> filled with creatures   filled with dread
> misshapen so   yet the best we have
> our raft among the abstract worlds
> and how I longed to live on this earth
> walking her boundaries   never counting the cost[.]

A gynocentric order would affirm "our bond with the natural order, [and] the corporeal ground of our intelligence."[20] In the contest between earth and world, Rich allies her hope for the future with the odds of the earth.

For women, self-determination begins with "repossession" of the body, including the processes of birth. The male demand for control of female destiny is spelled out in medical and legal constraints, and quite apart from the genuine problems surrounding abortion as a moral issue, nothing reveals the hypocrisy of the prevailing system so readily as proclamations of "reverence for life" or "the sacredness of life" by an order that thrives on war and prides itself on the destructive prowess of its machines. Without question we live in a world that celebrates the power of technology. Without question the glory of patriarchy is conquest. Like Simone de Beauvoir before her, Rich thinks that the masculine disregard for life and pain (the male preference for armored states of body and mind) is the product of interaction between men and their technologies. As she suggests in "The Knight," men wear armor even when the destructive momentum of machines is plain to see. Against such potent seductions, how shall the frail claims of bodily life be respected? Perhaps it *is* the spectacle of destruction that excites us most. Perhaps, as Mary Daly speculates, violence against women is the stem and prototype of all violence—against other bodies, against the earth itself. Meanwhile, abstract desires compel us. Contempt for life, contempt for pain, contempt for all that's powerless and open; that is the content of Creon's decree. It is the logic of power in a world where might is right, the product of patriarchal order like a levelling wind or rabid god of air against which, in Rich's urging, women must take a place of their own. And thus this manifesto:[21]

> One of the devastating effects of technological capitalism has been its numbing of the powers of the imagination—specifically, the power to envision new human and communal relationships. I am a feminist because I feel endangered, psychically and physically, by this society, and because I believe that the women's movement is saying we have come to an edge of history where men—insofar as they are embodiments of the patriarchal idea—have becomes dangerous to children and other living things, themselves included; and that we can no longer afford to keep the female principle enclosed within the confines of the tight, little post-industrial family, or within any male-induced notion of where the female principle is valid and where it is not.

By the time she wrote *Diving into the Wreck*, Rich had become the woman "merciless to herself" that she had envisioned the coming of in "Snapshots of a Daughter-in-Law." And she had answered her greatest question—"With whom will your lot be cast?"—in a way that settled her politics and her poetry together. She casts her lot with women, and then with the internal colonies at the mercy of superpower empires, and finally with third-world peoples in general. Rich is consistently critical of an earlier feminist position that spoke mainly to women who were white and educated, a middle-class feminism of the campus and suburbs. She has always been critical of "exceptional" women, those who abandon the cause of women to excel professionally and enjoy a male-approved margin of freedom. Feminism, as Rich sees it, does not mean that women are turning their backs to the world or to men; women are simply, and at last, turning to face each other. And power, in Rich's definition, is "not power of domination, but just access to sources."[22] Among the sources of power denied to women have been their own history of struggle and endurance, their own tradition of heroes and role models, and perhaps most of all in Rich's view, the access of women to each other.

Speaking of how "Snapshots" came to be written, and of the change in direction that the poem represents, Rich says that she "had been taught that poetry should be 'universal,' which meant, of course, nonfemale."[23] Language seems open to everyone, of course, and insofar as inclusive experiences (oppression, endurance, revolt) can happen to any group or class, poems about particular experience will speak to anyone in general. But poets do not speak with a "universal" or disembodied voice. Particular voices arise from particular occasions; the poem becomes valid generally when its values are shared. Significant form is shared form. Language is timeless but also of the moment; or rather, because language is timeless it is available to the moment, and the moment's impact can't be discounted. Poetry begins where we begin, in a concrete time and place, in the body of a man or woman alert to concrete problems, the difficulties of power and gender especially. General wisdom might be offered, but always to a definite tribe, in relation to which the voice of the poet is always in situ. In "North American Time," Rich says it this way:

> Try sitting at a typewriter
> one calm summer evening
> at a table by a window
> in the country, try pretending
> your time does not exist
> that you are simply you
> that the imagination simply strays
> like a great moth, unintentional
> try telling yourself
> you are not accountable
> to the life of your tribe
> the breath of your planet.

"Poetry," as Rich says in the same poem, "never stood a chance / of standing outside history." One of the more successful illusions of high culture has been the usage of the humanistic "we" in reference, supposedly, to all of us or "man" in general. But this "we" has always been the property of an educated elite, male, white, and eurocentric. Rich escapes this illusion by relying on the forms of "you." If "you" refers to a man the rhetorical slant of the poem might be to blame or curse. If "you" refers to a women the poem will be informed, most of the time, by praise and blessing. But at all times, in her mature poetry, Rich speaks in her own voice. She has no liking for the ploys of persona. Her voice is responsible to its time and place, and accepts what humanists would rather escape: that even poetry (or especially poetry) is positioned for and against, that the political problem of us-and-them is the poet's limit as well. The poetry of utopia might someday transcend these divisions; here and today, meanwhile, divisions continue in force, and Rich will not be fooled by "humanity" or "the human condition" when such terms are used to mask discord. She stands against an order that is male-governed and that keeps women alien to themselves and each other. She distrusts "revolution" in the old style because after much violence the old patriarchy is replaced by a new patriarchy and women are no better off than they were. Rich sums up this position in an interview:[24]

> I do see saving the lives of women as a priority. The "humanity" trip—not women's liberation, but human liberation—tends to feel too easy to me. Women have always supported every "human" liberation movement, every movement for social change; there have always been women womaning the barricades, but it's never been for us, or about us. I think that women ought to be putting women first now. Which is not to say that we're against the other half of humanity, but just to say that if we don't put ourselves first, we're never going to make it to full humanity.

The political identity that does not limit itself, the movement that goes forward in the name of everyone, can expect to be at odds with itself and exploited by covert interests. Simply to use the term *woman* or *women* is perilously wide, and in fact Rich usually has in mind a more specific tribe, one overtly feminist and antipatriarchal. One might expect, then, that a majority of Rich's readers will be offended to some degree when, in fact, some are and some are not. One doesn't have to be a woman to see the decency of feminist concerns. Men enjoying a measure of male privilege can see the damage done by patriarchal claims. Being female is not in itself the criterion for valuing Rich's poems against males, like "Trying to Talk with a Man," for example, which integrates nuclear and patriarchal orders, or the merciless "Ghost of a Chance," with men like beached fish, or—to my mind one of the best—the pained and somber "August," in which the poet's curse is pitted against what might be called the primal curse of the fathers. The poem develops mythical time, beginning with the collapse of Eden in the first four stanzas:

> Two horses in yellow light
> eating windfall apples under a tree
>
> as summer tears apart   milkweeds stagger
> and grasses grow more ragged
>
> They say there are ions in the sun
> neutralizing magnetic fields on earth
>
> Some way to explain
> what this week has been, and the one before it!

To "explain" the sullen days of late summer, we can point to electro-magnetic goings-on in the heavens. And if it were only the "yellow light" of dog-day afternoons, the scientists might be right. But for Rich the seasons correspond to spiritual conditions, with oppressive heat sig-nalling the pain of political intrusion. In "Burning Oneself In," written along with "August" in 1972, the summer "heat-wave" lifts at last but awful news from the war in Vietnam "has settled in" and "a dull heat permeates the ground / of the mind." In "August," something similar is tearing things apart and "neutralizing" the earth's "magnetic" powers, a force that throws eros (the binding power of life itself) into ragged confusion. And "it," whatever it is, goes on and on; this week was bad, but "the one before it!"—the one before was worse. As we enter the rest of the poem we see the poet torn by, and struggling to confront, her own recognitions:

> If I am flesh sunning on rock
> if I am brain burning in fluorescent light
>
> if I am dream like a wire with fire
> throbbing along it
>
> if I am death to a man
> I have to know it

His mind is too simple, I cannot go on
sharing his nightmares

My own are becoming clearer, they open
into prehistory

which looks like a village lit with blood
where all the fathers are crying: *My son is mine!*

A merciless poem, hard-edged and honed to its purpose—which is
to confront the curse of the fathers—and a poem that cuts to the quick
of its painful occasion. As the summer devolves toward its ruin, so the
poet begins to see how men imagine women, a recognition that forces
a further terrible knowledge, impossible now to avoid or rationalize
further. She beholds, that is, the curse of the fathers in its blood-lit
origin, while off in the background Mister Kurtz is whispering "the
horror, the horror."

"August" and "Diving into the Wreck" were written at about the same
time. Both are poems of confrontation. Having seen through the book
of myths, the poet is face to face with the thing itself. What to *do* has
become a question of what to *be*. The "I am" of the middle stanzas
asserts self-possession by confronting the monster in male nightmare,
which is to say that the poem makes little sense until we grasp its
threshold image, in this case a reptilian thing that suns itself on a rock
and that, like the Medusa, is believed by men to be death to him who
beholds it. We are back to the sleeping man of "Incipience," dreaming
of female monsters while women talk of "how to live." In "August,"
the mind of the dreaming man is "too simple" because as victor and
beneficiary he can be satisfied with myths. He does not *need* to contem-
plate complexity, nor does he *wish* to acknowledge the ancient cry of
the fathers. Meanwhile, the patriarchal curse resounds through the
poem, and once heard it opens on awful truth: the male child is separated
from the life-serving body-world of women and inducted into the warrior cult of men, the moment when mother-right is defeated. That is
the horror implicit in "My son is mine!" The fathers claim the son for
themselves. They raise him to scorn life and women. They ready him—
Pro patria!—for the wars they will declare. Women are "given" in marriage, men in battle.

But how is it that someone like myself, or any man, reads Rich's work with care and benefit? The question isn't only how men enter into and enjoy poems by women who are feminists, but how any of us, male or female, enter into the world of any poet who is actively for and against; how we come to value Brecht blasting the Nazis, or Breytenbach cursing his native tongue while blessing the cause of blacks in South Africa. I am not of the tribe to whom these poets speak, yet I join in and feel involved. In the presence of the poet's voice I willingly suspend disbelief in my own exclusion. How is that?

The problem of belonging is extended by recalling the age-old obligation of poetry to give, with so much else, pleasure; and then to consider what pleasure can be found in poems as filed and tuned to pain, or as merciless, as those by Rich when she is least lyrical, least reconciled. If the politics of her work can be off-putting, so can the splintlike diction and edgy imagery that give her art its feel, and then the unrelieved attention to torment that keeps this poet from solace and joy. If, for example, we have been trained to take delight in language, its music and its elegance, what are we to make of Rich's poem called "A Woman Dead in Her Forties," which begins with this stanza:

> —Your breasts/ sliced off The scars
> dimmed as they would have to be
> years later[.]

No lyricism or lifting rhythm sustains that language; phrasing is bland or even banal except for the startling intimacy of its occasion. Yet the poem with its ungainly lines and fractured stanzas turns out to be an elegy intense with female travail, a declaration of love complete with the scars and wounds that, in Rich's art generally, attend her praises of women's selves. The lines above, moreover, help suggest why Rich is not like other poets cited in this study. Working with her art does not yield the same enjoyment got from working with Yeats or Brecht or McGrath. Only with Breytenbach has the case been similar. He, like Rich, is wild with the burden of injustice, is often angry and feels besides that his art must go forward, *if* it goes forward, against a language that is grossly patriarchal. But he is not as resolute as Rich, not as starkly willful, nor does he pass up small consolations, humor among them. Rich stands alone. And her poetry takes its tribe into poetic-political terrain so unknown and newly entered that we might speak, as Rich does, of "a whole new poetry beginning here."[25]

Rich stands up to the world. She takes place as a poet and a woman, with poetic conduct and the conduct of life informing each other. Language is held accountable to history, to women's collective experience first of all. And insofar as her poetry and her politics share a common vision, her example has about it a "nobility" such as Stevens might point to, a moral symmetry that is cause in itself for delight. In the following section from "Natural Resources," poetry becomes a *vita activa* and the way itself a communal continuum:

> There are words I cannot choose again:
> *humanism   androgyny*
>
> Such words have no shame in them, no diffidence
> before the raging stoic grandmothers:
>
> their glint is too shallow, like a dye
> that does not permeate
>
> the fibers of actual life
> as we live it, now;
>
> this fraying blanket with its ancient stains
> we pull across the sick child's shoulder
>
> or wrap around the senseless legs
> of the hero trained to kill
>
> this weaving, ragged because incomplete
> we turn our hands to, interrupted
>
> over and over, handed down
> unfinished, found in the drawer
>
> of an old dresser in the barn,
> her vanished pride and care
>
> still urging us, urging on
> our works, to close the gap

in the Great Nebula,
to help the earth deliver.

Rich's art arises immediately out of history, out of life's embattled
moments day by day, and with the added sense that where "I" am there
also "we" are. This tribal construct has a firm grip on the actual, but it
also extends the poem's occasion to include readers outside the tribal
exclusivity at issue, and allows any one of us, finally, to join in and "help
the earth deliver." That something like this occurs I cannot doubt, given
my own attention to, and pleasure in, the poetry of a feminist like Rich.
Her work offers an alternative vision, one that curses the sins of patriarchal order and goes on to praise strengths and virtues basic to everyone,
precisely the life-reclaiming strengths and virtues of women through the
ages.

For all the radicalness of Rich's feminism, her work has about it a
radicalism that goes even deeper, a way of life that men can no longer
scorn or despise, a *vita activa* that anyone might find worth having in
this, the twilight era of nuclear politics. The poet, therefore, summons
a tribe, and we—men and women—respond to the call. The situation
is startling, perhaps, but only at first. For if poets in times of political
upheaval tend to revive bardic practices, might not the case be likewise
that we, as readers in a time of political strain, tend to fall back on the
older relation to poetry and take up our role in the bardic situation? In
adversity the bard emerges. So, it would seem, does the tribe.

The feminist poetics that Rich has worked to realize depends on ca-
pacities essential to women, including alertness to the pain of others, a
fierce attention to relationships of all kinds and, along with these, a sense
of self with boundaries less rigid and guarded, more flexible and embracing, than most men's. Women do not wear armor, do not go pan-
oplied with weapons, do not automatically see people as challengers and,
in consequence, do not reify the world of selves into a wall of otherness.
This, in part, is Rich's sense of female powers, a view she praises in the
following lines:

And I think of those lives we tried to live
in our globed helmets, self-enclosed

bodies self-illumined gliding
safe from the turbulence

and how, miraculously, we failed[.]

The failure of the self to shut down and close off, the refusal of poetry
to turn in contempt from the earth—these "failings" are part of women's
strength in Rich's view, and they provide her feminist poetics with a
crucial element. For her the virtues of reception and response are primary. She wants to mobilize empathy, compassion, the imaginative
capacity for suffering with—a seeing *beyond* the self *into* the world; or,
a seeing *through* the self, an entrance into the experience of others via
one's own self-knowledge. In "Hunger," Rich responds to the spectacle
of African famine in terms that are more actual than metaphoric:

> I know I'm partly somewhere else—
> huts strung across a drought-stretched land
> not mine, dried breasts, mine and not mine, a mother
> watching my children shrink with hunger.
> I live in my Western skin,
> my Western vision, torn
> and flung to what I can't control or even fathom.

To reduce these lines to a poetics of guilt is to forget the power of
anger to override indulgence. It would also be to ignore Rich's consistent
melding of self and world, private grief and public pain, insisting that
between the two no demarcation exists except, of course, the false division of experience into separate categories as a stratagem of evasion.
The following lines are often quoted, but not always with sufficient care
for the actualization of metaphor that takes place:

> In the bed the pieces fly together
> and the rifts fill   or else
> my body is a list of   wounds
> symmetrically placed
> a village
> blown open by planes
> that did not finish   the job[.]

The reference is to Vietnam, and the poem in which these lines occur is "Nightbreak," written in 1968 at the peak of the war when the horror has reached such a pitch that the poet, so to say, is cracking up. The poem goes on to encircle napalm with anger, then devolves into the following characteristic (for Rich) stanza:

> Time is quiet   doesn't break things
> or even wound   Things are in danger
> from people   The frail clay lamps
> of Mesopotamia
> row on row under glass
> in the ethnological section
> little hollows of dried-
> up oil   The refugees
> with their identical
> tales of escape   I don't
> collect what I can't use   I need
> what can be broken.

The "dried- / up oil" of the ancient lamps, which once afforded sacred light, is played against the "oildrum" of napalm that balls into fire over an Asian village. The clay lamps, now useless, are preserved with great care when, meanwhile, the breaking of vessels elsewhere goes without notice. In the last stanza of "Nightbreak," the night itself seems to shatter, and the pieces, which are also the bits of the shattered self, at dawn "move / dumbly back / toward each other." The theme of this poem is the shattering impact of political intrusion on a self that feels shockingly continuous with the suffering of children in a distant place. The poem's threshold image is the earthen vessel (signalled by the clay lamps) that Rich links to the creative powers of women. Rich argues, in *Of Woman Born*, that "the woman potter molded, not simply vessels, but images of herself, the vessel of life, the transformer of blood into life and milk." She goes on to say that "the pot, vessel, urn, pitcher, was not an ornament or a casual container; it made possible the long-term storage of oils and grains, the transforming of raw food into cooked; it was also sometimes used to store the bones or ashes of the dead." The earthen vessel, then, "is anything but a 'passive' receptacle; it is *transformative*—active, powerful."[26]

"Nightbreak" is an angry probe into the experience of political intrusion. The poet's openness to the world makes her vulnerable to the world's horror, especially the violence her own nation visits upon helpless children elsewhere, a violence Rich apprehends as a citizen and as a woman acquainted with the pain of motherhood. The outcome is devastating. Even sleep is "cracked and flaking," and the dawn feels like a "white / scar splitting / over the east." If we follow "the woman/vessel association," as Rich calls it, we see that the poem is about the breakup of self, including the self's poetic capacity, under the ruinous press of the real. This sounds extreme, but the crisis portrayed in "Nightbreak" is not, I think, overdone. To an open imagination the Vietnam war was everywhere. Its atrocities and ravaged faces—chiefly of women and children—filled the news and haunted the places of sleep. We in America were always safe, unless of an age and a class to be drafted, but not, after a certain point of horror's surfeit, immune.

What happens in the world happens over in the heart, not in an exact equivalent way, of course, but as suffering transformed by imagination; pain is pain however we know it, and can be called the ground (and cost) of alertness to life. Speaking of feminism and the "connection between inner and outer," Rich says:[27]

> We are attempting, in fact, to break down that fragmentation
> of inner and outer in every possible realm. The psyche and the
> world out there are being acted on and interacting intensely
> all the time. There is no such thing as the private psyche,
> whether you're a woman—or a man, for that matter.

Rich praises acts of extended awareness. Unfortunately, this opening outward of self, and the vulnerability that must follow, are often criticized as a fault which men avoid and women fall prey to. Rich thinks of it as a "source of power" and therefore a hopeful gift. She says: "the so-called 'weak ego boundaries' of women . . . might be a negative way of describing the fact that women have tremendous powers of intuitive identification and sympathy with other people."[28] That is the point, of course; and if it should be considered a fault—if empathetic imagination is thought unmanly, or if care for life beyond one's own is discounted as "feminine" and therefore weak—then masculine preference for detachment and "objectivity" is more vicious than we usually admit. In patriarchal culture, transcendence has meant "rising above it all"; in Rich's feminist ethos, on the other hand, transcendence means reaching beyond oneself in sympathy with the plight of others. Male transcendence negates and masters; female transcendence moves to acknowledge and interact. There are easy formulations, of course, but even so one sees the benefit to a poetics incorporating female *virtu* of this kind. A truly *political* imagination moves beyond the self and into the world. The kind of political experience I've called political intrusion becomes, in Rich's poetry, more than historical torment. It becomes her art's occasion.

Adrienne Rich bears witness to pain that is shared and unnecessary. She curses those who ignore the suffering they create and sustain. She praises those who absorb the impact and survive. In "Hunger," the closing image stares back at us indelibly:

> Swathed in exhaustion, on the trampled newsprint,
> a woman shields a dead child from the camera.
> The passion to be inscribes her body.

An image of African famine got from a photograph, its import resides in its political dimension. "The decision to feed the world," Rich says earlier in the poem, "is the real decision. No revolution / has chosen it." That, I take it, is the plain shocking truth of the matter. And at its heart is the victim's lack of public existence—a "passion to be" that fails to be acknowledged. Those who suffer have neither a name nor a voice, a condition that makes their lives easy to ignore and dispose of, and reminds us that worldly power controls people by controlling names. If she could, Rich would praise the mothers and children in "Hunger" by lamenting their lives and cruel lot. She would, that is, restore them to their name. To create a public existence, however, requires a revelation of private being. In extremity private being is often inaccessible to anyone outside the circle of suffering. It's here, too often, that "political" poetry gives way to propaganda and falls back on ideology.

In "Hunger" Rich returns repeatedly to the image of mothers and children; as a woman and a mother, she trusts maternal anger to guide her art. In "Integrity" she praises "anger and tenderness: my selves," and in "From an Old House in America" rage and compassion are united with the will to bear witness:

. . .

Who is here. The Erinyes.
One to sit in judgment.

One to speak tenderness.
One to inscribe the verdict on the canyon wall.

These lines announce a feminist poetics. Rich's defense of poetry rests on the moral and imaginative power of maternal anger and female care. Not everyone, however, can or would wish to invoke the Furies. There are several ways to stand *in relation* to suffering not directly our own—the kind of disturbance that photojournalism is capable of causing, for example. In representations of suffering it's the experience of relation—the submerged connectedness of self to other selves—that poets like Rich explore. We might even define poetic imagination, in this case, as willing suspension of disbelief in other people's pain. Rich has spelled out the relation of poetry to political distress this way:[29]

> No true political poetry can be written with propaganda as an aim to persuade others "out there" of some atrocity or injustice (hence the failure, as poetry, of so much anti-Vietnam poetry of the sixties). *As poetry*, it can come only from the poet's need to identify her relationship to atrocities and injustice, the sources of her pain, fear, and anger, the meaning of her resistance.

In "Hunger," Rich explores her relationship to disaster. She faces the experience of political intrusion, in this case the impact of catastrophe abroad upon moral awareness at home. But here also she envisions the solidarity of all women whose pain is shared and unnecessary:

> Is death by famine worse than death by suicide,
> than a life of famine and suicide, if a black lesbian dies,
> if a white prostitute dies, if a woman of genius
> starves herself to feed others,
> self-hatred battening on her body?
> Something that kills us or leaves us half-alive
> is raging under the name of an "act of god"
> in Chad, in Niger, in the Upper Volta—
> yes, that male god that acts on us and on our children,

that male State that acts on us and on our children
till our brains are blunted by malnutrition,
yet sharpened by the passion for survival,
our powers expended daily on the struggle
to hand a kind of life on to our children,
to change reality for our lovers
even in a single trembling drop of water.

Rich offers a global summary of suffering anchored in famine, then curses its political cause, and then with small praises goes on to the ordeal of women surviving. What this poem blesses, grim though it may be, is a state of mind generous enough to grasp the underlying oneness of victims. What it curses is the claim that some kinds of suffering are less (or more) terrible than others. Rich abhors the notion that "pain belongs to some order." She would bless all cases with equal urgency, as if victimization were the basis of tribal union. But if the solidarity of political victims exists de facto it remains to be recognized and acted upon. Hence the poem's end: "Until we find each other, we are alone."

The "true nature of poetry," Rich says elsewhere, is "the drive to connect." The chief means in Rich's possession is her own experience of erotic rapport. In this regard, "Twenty-One Love Poems" is one of her finest works so far, a poem of steadfast blessing, in which a lesbian relationship is praised and offered as a testament. This is also Rich's longest poem, too lengthy to examine in detail, but with salient points that can't be overlooked. And finally, "Twenty-One Love Poems" names and honors—allows to take place with dignity—an experience that is profoundly challenging to patriarchal norms. The poem was composed through 1974–76. It is set in Manhattan, and section one maps the hard terrain through which "two lovers of one gender" make their way:

Wherever in this city, screens flicker
with pornography, with science-fiction vampires,
victimized hirelings bending to the lash,
we also have to walk . . . if simply as we walk
through the rainsoaked garbage, the tabloid cruelties
of our own neighborhood.
We need to grasp our lives inseparable
from those rancid dreams, that blurt of metal, those disgraces,
and the red begonia perilously flashing

from a tenement sill six stories high,
or the long-legged young girls playing ball
in the junior highschool playground.
No one has imagined us. We want to live like trees,
sycamores blazing through sulfuric air,
dappled with scars, still exuberantly budding,
our animal passion rooted in the city.

From the ugly dreams surrounding them they need to take back their lives, grasp them in a way that makes the two inseparably one, and then go on to comprehend the broader fact that life together is embedded in the reality of the streets through which they must walk. Public and private realms intersect from the start, and the poem's *raison d'être* is announced by saying simply: "No one has imagined us." Many names have and will be given them, including those on the street's obscene marquees. Against these the poet creates a different name that is, in sum, the poem. But none of it, neither the poem nor the relationship from which it springs, will be easy or encouraged. Beauty, whether the red begonia or the young girls at play, shows itself "perilously." Every sort of life is "dappled with scars," yet still, like the trees, things persist:

> *Tristan and Isolde* is scarcely the story,
> women at least should know the difference
> between love and death.

And in the end, "the story of our lives becomes our lives." This one won't have a happy ending, but it's not a tragedy either, no *Liebestod* to distract from survival. The main thing is not "to make a career of pain," and on this point Rich is resolute: "The woman who cherished her / suffering is dead. I am her descendant."

"Twenty-One Love Poems" includes an unnumbered "floating" poem replete with erotic detail. This poem serves as threshold image for the whole, an emblem of physical love to uphold—as earth upholds the airy world—the more meditative poems. Modern love poetry speaks in a small voice, nowadays, off somewhere to the side amid the passions of our century, recalling lines from Shakespeare's sonnet: "How with this rage shall beauty hold a plea / Whose action is no stronger than a flower." Rich answers by making politics love's occasion, not only as love's embattled backdrop but also the fight to extend love's meaning in feminist terms. In this way very personal poetry takes on dignity and historical weight.

Rich is firmly of the belief that love alone, love apart from the world (like poetry lost in the isolated self) can never be an answer to life, contrary to its representations in Western art. In "Splittings" Rich announces against "abnegating power for love," announces against "splitting / between love and action." Even when love's fulfillment is real and privately wondrous, as it is at the end of "The Origin and History of Consciousness," it does not suffice:

> Trusting, untrusting,
> we lowered ourselves into this, let ourselves
> downward hand over hand as on a rope that quivered
> over the unsearched. . . . We did this. Conceived
> of each other, conceived each other in a darkness
> which I remember as drenched in light.
>   I want to call this life.

> But I can't call it life until we start to move
> beyond this secret circle of fire
> where our bodies are giant shadows flung on a wall
> where the night becomes our inner darkness, and sleeps
> like a dumb beast, head on her paws, in the corner.

Plato's cave, perhaps—or any beneficent place where life is but a shadow and night appears the image of one's own unwakeful self. Within this circle, restful and apart, comfort is real but (for the poet) a danger to courage:

> When my dreams showed signs
> of becoming
> politically correct
> no unruly images
> escaping beyond borders
> when walking in the street I found my
> themes cut out for me
> knew what I would not report
> for fear of enemies' usage
> then I began to wonder[.]

Most of us would back off from such hard demands, even seeing their need politically—or poetically, for that matter. Rich does not back off. She confronts, and then again confronts. If there is a line where battle is joined, she scouts that line without respite. In her example we see great bravery, and understand the urgency that gives her art its willfulness. We can also appreciate her puritan strain, disconsolate and sometimes grimly dogged, despite her care for earth and bodily life. These are some of the costs a woman who is a poet will assume in the kingdom of the fathers.

Adrienne Rich is nothing if not a survivor, and so long as she keeps faith with earth against the world's oppressiveness, she draws on strengths that run very deep. Every peak a crater, she says; "no height without depth, without a burning core." Now and again, in "Transcendental Etude" most securely, height and depth connect; then the earth is sound beyond doubt. Willfulness abates and the "immense fragility" of life seems, briefly, enough:

> Still, it persists. Turning off onto a dirt road
> from the raw cuts bulldozed through a quiet village
> for the tourist run to Canada,
> I've sat on a stone fence above a great, soft, sloping field
> of musing heifers, a farmstead
> slanting its planes calmly in the calm light,
> a dead elm raising bleached arms
> above a green so dense with life,
> minute, momentary life—slugs, moles, pheasants, gnats,
> spiders, moths, hummingbirds, groundhogs, butterflies—
> a lifetime is too narrow
> to understand it all, beginning with the huge
> rockshelves that underlie all that life.

A rare poetic confidence has kept Rich sane and creative through a lifetime of combat. At the end of "Transcendental Etude," she presents us with an emblem of womanly art as she discovers it—the woman "turning in her lap" the scraps and rags of her life—then goes on to close the poem with a poetics that reaches beyond will or anger merely, to a clemency or gentleness without which "the passion to be" could not take place:

Such a composition has nothing to do with eternity,
the striving for greatness, brilliance—
only with the musing of a mind
one with her body, experienced fingers quietly pushing
dark against bright, silk against roughness,
pulling the tenets of a life together
with no mere will to mastery,
only care for the many-lived, unending
forms in which she finds herself,
becoming now the sherd of broken glass
slicing light in a corner, dangerous
to flesh, now the plentiful, soft leaf
that wrapped round the throbbing finger, soothes the wound:
and now the stone foundation, rockshelf further
forming underneath everything that grows.

"Transcendental Etude" is the closing poem in *The Dream of a Common Language*, and the book's last section, in turn, is called "Not Somewhere Else, But Here." Exactly what "dream of a common language" means has provoked much critical debate. Usually the several meanings of "common" are stressed—plain and ordinary on the one hand, accessible and shared on the other—but the sense of "dream" is also important, suggesting a goal, the visionary state of poetic thinking, maybe also a *second* language, preconscious and unbroken, like a rockshelf of linguistic resource underlying poetry in general. For a feminist poet, in any case, the condition of language as she finds it will be a vexing problem, "a knot of lies / eating at itself to get undone." How shall the integrity of female experience be kept intact once "rendered into the oppressor's language"?

Rich's solution is implicit in her sense that "Only where there is language is there world." This notion has been formulated most succinctly by Wittgenstein in his *Philosophical Investigations*, where he says, for example, that "to imagine a language means to imagine a form of life."[30] To imagine a language befitting a feminist form of life is, I take it, Rich's "dream." Wittgenstein also says that "the *speaking* of language is part of an activity," a specific way of taking place in the world. He adds that "only those hope who can talk." That the basic scene in a Rich poem is two women talking—the poet speaking to and with a woman like herself—suggests the kind of language, and the form of life, Rich works to imagine. Language and world together make up "the weave of our life," as Wittgenstein puts it. And when, finally, he observes that the totality of our linguistic milieu consists "of language and the actions into which it is woven," he endorses Rich's fundamental belief as an activist-poet: "Poetry never stood a chance / of standing outside history."

This, finally, is where Rich stands: inside her own body's sorrow and deeply settled into time—"not somewhere else, but here." Her language is time's stark vernacular, the idiom of being-in-the-world where "being" is female and "the world," as ever, is still a kingdom of the fathers. Against the patriarchal order she sets her art and her life because, as things now stand, it's an order given to conquest and illusions of mastery, hostile to earth and the flesh. In the tradition of bardic practice, her poetry announces communal identity, calls for courage and fortitude in battle, keeps a language (and a lore) by which members of the tribe can stand up, take place, and together realize their collective "passion to be." In Rich's case, moreover, it's not difficult to say when she took up her political station. It began when she "was finished with the idea of a poem as a single, encapsulated event, a work of art complete in itself."[31] It began, that is, when she started appending dates to her poems, beginning with those that make up *Snapshots of a Daughter-in-Law*, her volume of 1963 in which she breaks free to imagine herself as "long about her coming, who must be / more merciless to herself than history." To herself she has been merciless, and often to her enemies as well, but with tenderness to temper her anger, and always with "care for the many-lived, unending / forms in which she finds herself."

Conclusion:
Toward a Changed Poetics

Living in the Age of the Bomb, it's not hard to see that between them the superpowers have recolonized the globe; that they have carved the planet into spheres of influence, forcing smaller nations to toe the new alignment, and that now they proceed with the standoff they've locked themselves into. This means that most of the fighting gets done by proxy, by pitting groups or nations against each other to no end, of course, except *this* end—the demise of cities and countrysides as, over and over, populations get caught in the cross fire. About these cross-fire situations, furthermore, there is a redundant pathos, a familiar sorrow, reminding me that life for all of us, today, depends on two empires not unlike Athens and Sparta, dividing their version of the world between them, preparing for war and surmising it must come because one seems to be gaining an edge on the other. As Thucydides puts it, "Finally the point was reached when Athenian strength attained a peak plain for all to see." And thus the Spartan vote for war; because—as Thucydides says—"because they were afraid." It's an old story, except for the nuclear angle. For Thucydides it was Hellas going down. Now it's life on earth. None of this is news, of course; but being caught in the cross fire provokes interesting questions, in particular what we might still expect from fiction and poetry—enlightened feeling? finer sensibilities?—amid the *hysterico passio* of nuclear Cold War politics.

I've always thought of literature as a fierce vote for the future, but now that's not so certain. Recently Günter Grass has reminded us how much good writing depends on a hearing at some point forward in time. Sometimes a new style or vision will not find its audience for decades; and often, too, writers must outlive, through their work, the censorship and silence that governments have a habit of imposing. Literature's "superior staying power" is what Grass has in mind when he says: "Sure of its aftereffect, it could count on time even if the echo to word and sentence, poem and thesis might take decades or even centuries to make itself heard. This advance payment, this provision of time, made the poorest writers rich." But now the promise of delayed reception can't be counted on, nor the hope of immortality through fame. Thinking on his own career, Grass concludes: "I know that the book I am planning to write can no longer pretend to certainty of the future. It will have to include a farewell to the damaged world, to wounded creatures, to us and our minds, which have thought of everything and of the end as well."

Writers must, it seems to me, vote to see the world keep going. Creating an idea or image is like planting a tree: its fullest foliage will be well beyond one's time. But if history has often shown us the long-term victory of truth, it also reveals the catastrophic outcome, both short-term and long, of power-politics. I mean to say that while notions of fate and historical necessity don't convince me, the sameness in political behavior, especially the way powers contend and empires fall, is hard to ignore. The past, in any case, seems most real to me as parable, the way Cavafy used Hellenic anecdote, or the way Zbigniew Herbert does now, to get a handle on chaos and better comprehend the odd way personal experience has begun to feel collective. Recasting big events as old tales restores, at least, a sense of scale. I can even suppose that in a post-nuclear era the pretensions of a civilization built from debris will include, among its inheritance of hearsay and junk, legends of the Bomb.

I'm trying not to fool myself, although lately I find myself thinking a good deal about the hereafter—not some thirty-minute shoot-out that brings on nuclear winter, but beyond that, in quick flashes forward, the shapes the maiming will finally settle into. For the first time, always having loathed science fiction, I discover substance in imaginings of the future. Maybe that's dangerous, implying as it does that the world I love is lost already. I am encouraged, however, by what Elaine Scarry says in *The Body in Pain*, especially her idea of personal language as counterforce to political injury, and also by this remark: "Beyond the expansive ground of ordinary, naturally occurring objects is the narrow extra ground of imagined objects, and beyond this ground, there is no other. Imagining is, in effect, the ground of last resort."

Why does that way of saying it seem so accurate? The ground of ordinary, naturally occurring objects now includes the Bomb, "Star

Wars," feelings of doom. Beyond that lies whatever imagination can construct. And beyond that there's nothing. Between ourselves and nothing, then, nothing intervenes except the small creations we ourselves put forth for use, among them images of the world going on in some post-nuclear way, or, harder and more urgent, images of ourselves surviving intact despite current forecasts. Elaine Scarry can speak of imagination as a *last resort* and Czeslaw Milosz speaks of poetry as a *last rampart*. Scarry came to part of her conclusion from studying Amnesty International's reports on torture. Milosz came to his after surviving the German and then the Russian savaging of Poland. Are we ready to receive such notions and take them at face value? If we profess the value of creative language, are we ready to grant that poetry can be important? And if so, can't we go on from our limited experience to say when poems are most *wanted?*

I think we can, and by calling on nothing that I have not myself felt or witnessed, I recommend (quietly, always amazed) this example—the intense degree to which men and women live by and sometimes die for words, sheer words upheld by nothing but the strength in saying, wording that seems weightless until uttered in the force of deep feeling. Robert Hass, for example, writes of himself as a young man desperate to engage his destiny, walking the streets repeating Lowell's lines:

> And blue-lung'd combers lumbered to the kill.
> The Lord survives the rainbow of His will.

Or in Warsaw during the Nazi occupation, as Milosz tells us, "an entire community is struck by misfortune" and "poetry becomes as essential as bread." Or this, Akhmatova's image of Mandelshtam as she saw him in Voronezh near the end:

> But in the room of the banished poet
> Fear and the Muse stand watch by turn,
> and the night comes on,
> which has no hope of dawn.

At times like these, perhaps because there's nothing else, poetry becomes the one thing needful. Or maybe it's because in moments that seem ultimate, nothing else is *good* enough, shared enough, of a precision equal to our joy or suffering. What's wanted to celebrate a marriage or a birth, what we ask to get us through pain, what we need by the side of the grave isn't solemn claims nor silence either, but rather the simple saying of right words. Literature, as Kenneth Burke puts it, is "equipment for living." I take Burke seriously when he talks this way, and his ideas about "symbolic action" and "disburdening" are worth remembering. When through language we confront the worst, or discover ourselves in ways that convince us we matter, we partake of available blessings. "As essential as bread" is what Milosz says, and I think yes, the gain in strength and nourishment is real.

Between the self and the terrible world comes poetry with its minute redemptions, its lyrical insurgencies, its willing suspension of disbelief in tomorrow. These ministrations, I take it, compose our chances. I don't mean that poems can have a say in nuclear matters, or that through poetry we may expect a general change of heart. Power listens to none but itself; and the myth of progress through enlightenment, in my view, died in 1914. What I mean to say is that right language can help us, as it always helps in hard moments, with our private struggles to keep whole, can be a stay against confusion, can start the healing fountains. And whatever helps us repossess our humanity, able again to take place and speak forth, frees us for work in the world. This is imagination's special task, as Wallace Stevens would say, because this contrary force, by pitching itself against external pressures, pushes back and makes space for liberty of spirit. Confronted by negation, imagination automatically starts asserting itself. We cannot *not* imagine, in which case the question becomes a matter of strategy. Shall imagination confront, or shall it evade? I think that it must confront—that poetry can no longer turn away from political torment, and for the following reason. Nuclear threat touches everyone everywhere, but unlike private kinds of death, collective wipeout has no mystery, no myth to temper its terror except the crudities of cold-war propaganda. The Bomb is a reality so pressing and so naked that it cannot be ignored. One day we *see* the enormity of it, and then also we see that between the self and the cold-war world there is no interceding champion, no worldly power on our side, but only, as Elaine Scarry puts it, imagination as last resort.

I've been speaking of imagination as the great good thing, but those who control our external fate, the handful of men in Washington and Moscow, are deep into war-games and nuclear scenarios, so it's clear that imaginative energies also serve destruction and are not always, by definition, on the side of care. This duality of function is summed up in a single hard remark by Octavio Paz: "Facing death the spirit is life, and facing the latter, death." Imagination, Paz is suggesting, pushes back *that* fiercely against the urgencies that threaten it. Politics, having always to face unruly life, in crisis ends up serving death. And if, finally, we wish to identify the kind of demonic imagination now on the loose in high places, it has been rendered with jolly grit by Thomas Pynchon in *Gravity's Rainbow*, a Zone, as he calls it, under the rule of rampant paranoia, automatic systems, and idolatry of global weapons.

Imagination can be dangerous, no doubt about that; and even to be firmly on the side of life is no guarantee. The problem with facing death in order to defend life is that death begins to cast its shadow everywhere. A sort of vertigo sets in, as if the hysteria of the world were infectious, which it is. Sometimes, in my own experience, the nuclear issue becomes so pressing—this is one of the Bomb's worst consequences, simply as threat—that it turns me from life, makes me blind to the needs of my neighbors. But living in the age of atrocity is no excuse for dismissing lesser claims because they are local or private. By way of correcting myself, I think of a woman I recently met, writing a book about sexual abuse as a child, about years of rape by Dad and brothers, the whole town knowing but crusted with silence, a Christian community deep in the heartland, letting some of its children be ruined. For this woman, the act of writing becomes a settlement of memory, a recovery of self by dreaming back through nightmare. These are very personal matters, but no, not altogether; for this awful story is precisely of the kind that, so long as it goes untold, sealed in silence, supports the larger cover-up of violences (for example, the way the superpowers keep the international arms market, on which small wars depend, stocked to overflowing). Power isn't only hierarchical, as Foucault reminded us. It accumulates in multitudes of small enactments, forcings of any sort, including those within the closed-up family. So yes, the world hangs by a thread, but no case counts less than another.

What makes our experience valuable to others is of course the way we word it. This is always a lonely task, and well might we wonder, inside the solitude of writing, where empowerment comes from. That all language assumes relation to power is visible in the fact that simply to verbalize, to use words at all, is instantly to be *with* or *against*. To the extent that this is so, writers choose their base, and not all powers are alike. Some pay off in dollars and nonsense, or in safety, more handsomely than others. The structure of political-institutional powers is vast, a kingdom with many mansions. Some writers, however, will seek a different potency, poets especially; but if so, what power can there be besides the big ones that run the warring world? What power was it, exactly, that tribal bards possessed when they went about their office of blessing and cursing, of praising and casting blame? Or the Irish rat-rhymers, what did they think they had that allowed them to clear infested places with chants? Wallace Stevens spoke of a "pressure within" that pushes back against the "pressures without." By external pressure he meant the political horror of World War Two, and by the inward kind he meant imagination, which he identified with "the sounds of words."

The self that cannot speak, as the man or woman being tortured cannot, or the self that cannot find words to make its own, has not the means to join or withdraw from the world. As poets and politicians know, *right words count that much*. And language is right when its fictive status makes no claims, serves no program or outside power, but only when, by taking place, it inspires us likewise to behold and take our place. The power base of poetry is poetry itself, the one kind of discourse that stands on its own, empowered by ceaseless imaginative motion and the vigor of its own interior music. Other discourse gains authority by indenturing itself to political orders of one stripe or another. Only poetical language, I'd like to repeat, is capable of authorizing its own generation.

This freedom is poetry's special strength, and, today more than ever, chief among its benefits. For now that we are cornered by the force of cold-war politics, we must consider in the plainest ways our access to reality, our confidence in fact, our capacity to cut through information overload. Here, from an article by John Newhouse (the *New Yorker*, July 22, 1985) is the problem we get when knowledge bends to power:

> Reality in the nuclear age tends to become what people whose voices carry say it is. Competent technicians are available to shore up any side of any argument. A given point of view may be vulnerable to ridicule but not to being disproved by facts; these are obscured by unknowns and abstractions arising from the nature, the role, the destructive potential, and the reliability of nuclear weapons.

Is that how it is? I think most certainly yes, and not with nuclear issues only, for how we respond to matters of ultimate import circumscribes our thinking in general. It's worth noting, furthermore, that what Newhouse says is written by a journalist. The experts disagree with each other, but they won't be discrediting themselves (and their institutions, and their careers) by stating the larger predicament. So there it is: when it comes to the hard questions, smart people with impeccable credentials can certify any side of any issue. Where does that leave the rest of us? Is sensible knowledge now beyond us? Does reality depend on power's endorsement? Will wars be fought, as Lyotard suggests, over information?

Truth too near to power is very like light enduring the gravity of large bodies—both, in their passage, get bent from their course. Our situation in the Nuclear Age isn't so different from Winston Smith's in *1984;* he agrees, finally, that reality is what O'Brien and the Inner Party say it is. The distinction between ourselves and Smith is small, but in one particular, at least, we have a tool, and therefore a weapon, not available in Orwell's nightmare world. We still have poetry and fiction, the language of concrete perception, and the office of art isn't located in a government bunker but in the obligation to behold and witness, praise, denounce. Just here, it seems to me, the importance of poetry has never been greater. As the age of information spills over us, as ships of state drift and list in the nuclear night, the old anchor holds. A solidly imagined story, a fiercely felt poem, still tells us where and who we are, discovers the world and us in it, gives us a sanity the "competent technicians" don't lay claim to.

Poetry won't change the nuclear order. But I want to stress that a poem can make something happen. It allows me to know what I fear, to understand (by standing under) the burden of my humanness. It also makes possible the essential decency of compassion, of suffering with— a symbolic action, to be sure, but one without which the spirit withers, the self shuts down.

Notes

Prolog

1. Kenneth Burke, "Literature As Equipment for Living," *The Philosophy of Literary Form* (Berkeley: University of California Press, 1973), pp. 293–304. First edition, 1941.
2. Czeslaw Milosz, "The Poor Poet," tr. by author, *Selected Poems* (New York: Seabury Press, 1973), p. 53.
3. *Ibid.*, "Elegy for N.N.," tr. Lawrence Davis, p. 96.
4. André Brink, *Writing in a State of Siege* (New York: Summit Books, 1983), p. 48.
5. Henry James, "Preface to Portrait of a Lady," *The Portrait of a Lady* (New York: Penguin Books, 1986).
6. Charles Simic, "Notes on Poetry and History," *The Uncertain Certainty* (Ann Arbor: University of Michigan Press, 1985), p. 124–125.
7. Edmund Spenser, *Spenser's Prose Works*, Variorum Edition, ed. Rudolf Gottfried (Baltimore: Johns Hopkins Press, 1949), p. 124.
8. Kenneth Burke, *Attitudes Toward History* (Boston: Beacon Press, 1959), p. 57. First edition, 1937.

I. Creon's Decree

1. James Joyce, *A Portrait of the Artist as a Young Man* (New York: Viking Press, 1982), p. 204.
2. Sophocles, *The Three Theban Plays*, tr. Robert Fagles (New York: Viking Press, 1982), p. 50.
3. Giambattista Vico, *The New Science*, tr. Thomas Goddard Bergin & Max Harold Fisch (Ithaca & London: Cornell University Press, 1975), p. 53.
4. *Ibid.*, p. 55.
5. G. W. F. Hegel, *The Phenomenology of Mind*, tr. J. B. Baillie (New

York: Harper & Row, 1967), p. 472. For Hegel's discussion of *Antigone*, see pages 466–482.

6. *Ibid.*, p. 472.
7. *Ibid.*, p. 472.
8. *Ibid.*, p. 470.
9. George Steiner, *Antigones* (New York: Oxford University Press, 1984), p. 11.
10. Erich Auerbach, *Mimesis: The Representation of Reality in Western Literature*, tr. Ralph Manheim (Princeton: Princeton University Press, 1974). p. 457.
11. *Ibid.*, p. 459.
12. Milan Kundera, "Conversation with Milan Kundera on the Art of The Novel," with Christian Salmon, *Salmagundi*, No. 73, Winter 1987, p. 123.
13. Martin Heidegger, "The Origin of the Work of Art," *Poetry, Language, Thought*, tr. Albert Hofstadter (New York: Harper & Row, 1975), pp. 48–49.
14. *Ibid.*, p. 49.
15. A more familiar description of "world" and "earth" is given by Jonathan Schell in *The Fate of the Earth* (New York: Knopf, 1982): "The destruction of human civilization, even without the biological destruction of the human species, may perhaps be called the end of the world, since it would be the end of that sum of cultural achievements and human relationships which constitutes what many people mean when they speak of 'the world.' The biological destruction of mankind would, of course, be the end of the world in a stricter sense. As for the destruction of all life on the planet, it would be not merely a human but a planetary end—the death of the earth. . . . We not only live on the earth but also are of the earth, and the thought of its death, or even of its mutilation, touches a deep chord in our nature" (p. 7). From a nuclear standpoint, "the world" is informed by, and responsive to, the nuclear cold-war order. The superpowers coerce a single world; and should a nuclear exchange occur, it would be the ultimate act of power on behalf of a world destroying itself in the moment when its apocalyptic logic is fulfilled.

II. The Press of the Real

1. Wallace Stevens, "Credences of Summer," *The Collected Poems* (New York: Vintage Books, 1982), p. 376.
2. Wallace Stevens, "The Noble Rider and the Sound of Words," *The Necessary Angel: Essays on Reality and the Imagination* (London: Faber

and Faber, 1951), pp. 3–36. All prose citations are from this essay in this edition.

3. C. P. Cavafy, "Dareios," *Collected Poems*, tr. Edmund Keely & Philip Sherrard, ed. George Savidis (London: Chatto & Windus, 1978), pp. 78–79.

4. John Pilling, *Fifty Modern European Poets* (London & Sydney: Pan Books, 1982), p. 57.

5. Stevens, "An Ordinary Evening in New Haven," *Collected Poems*, p. 473.

III. Yeats and the Rat-Rhymers

1. Edmund Spenser, "A vewe of the present state of Irelande," *Spenser's Prose Works*, Variorum Edition, ed. Rudolf Gottfried (Baltimore: Johns Hopkins Press, 1949), p. 124.

2. Yeats, "Easter 1916."

3. T. S. Eliot, "Yeats," *On Poetry and Poets* (New York: Farrar, Straus & Company, 1961), p. 308.

4. Yeats, *The Oxford Book of Modern Verse* (New York: Oxford University Press, 1937), p. xxxiv.

5. A. Norman Jeffares, *A Commentary on the Collected Poems of W. B. Yeats* (Stanford: Stanford University Press, 1968), p. 399.

6. Ulick O'Connor, *A Terrible Beauty Is Born* (London: Granada Publishing Limited, 1981), p. 17.

7. Yeats, "Modern Ireland: An Address to American Audiences, 1932–33," *The Massachusetts Review* (Winter, 1964), p. 258.

8. On the primacy of voice in Yeats's poetic, see Yeats, "Literature and the Living Voice," *Explorations* (New York: Collier Books, 1962); and Walter J. Ong, *Orality and Literacy* (New York: Methuen & Co., 1982), pp. 44–70.

9. Yeats, *The Letters of W. B. Yeats*, ed. Allan Wade (London: Rupert Hart-Davis, 1954), p. 811–812.

10. Yeats, *Letters*, p. 851.

11. Yeats, *Letters*, p. 691.

12. T. F. Thiselton Dyer, *Folk-lore of Shakespeare* (New York: Harper & Brothers, 1884), p. 197.

13. Robert C. Elliott, *The Power of Satire* (Princeton, Princeton University Press, 1960), p. 36.

14. Osborn Bergin, *Irish Bardic Poetry*, ed. David Greene & Fergus Kelly (Dublin, The Dublin Institute for Advanced Studies, 1970), p. 4.

15. Daniel Corkery, *The Hidden Ireland* (London: Gill and Macmillan, 1967), p. 96.

16. Oliver Goldsmith, *Collected Works*, Volume III, ed. Arthur Friedman (Oxford: The Clarendon Press, 1966), p. 118.
17. T. R. Henn, *Poets and Dreamers: Studies and Translations From the Irish By Lady Gregory* (New York: Oxford University Press, 1974), p. 5.
18. Fred Norris Robinson, "Satirists and Enchanters in Early Irish Literature," *Studies in the History of Religions*, ed. David Gordon Lyon and George Foot Moore (New York: Macmillan, 1912), pp. 98–99.
19. Robinson, *Ibid.*, pp. 105–106.
20. Douglas Hyde, *A Literary History of Ireland* (London & Leipzig: T. Fisher Unwin, 1910), pp. 518–519.
21. Fynes Moryson, "An Itinerary," *Elizabethan Ireland*, ed. James P. Myers, Jr. (Hamden: Archon Books, 1983), pp. 199–202.
22. Elliott, *The Power of Satire*, pp. 3–48, 285–292.
23. James P. Myers, *Elizabethan Ireland*, Davies p. 179, Campion, p. 24.
24. Edmund Spenser, *Spenser's Prose Works*, p. 125.
25. Yeats, *The Collected Letters of W. B. Yeats*, Volume I, ed. John Kelly and Eric Domville (Oxford: The Clarendon Press, 1986), p. 133.
26. Yeats, *Uncollected Prose of W. B. Yeats*, Volume I, ed. John P. Frayne (New York: Columbia University Press, 1970), pp. 163–164.
27. Yeats, *Memoirs*, ed. Denis Donoghue (New York: Macmillan Publishing Company, 1972), p. 59.
28. Douglas Hyde, "Bards (Irish)," *Encyclopaedia of Religion and Ethics*, Volume II, ed. James Hastings (New York: Charles Scribner's Sons, 1913), pp. 414–416.
29. Yeats, *Memoirs*, p. 54.
30. Yeats, *The Autobiography of W. B. Yeats* (New York, Macmillan Company, 1964), p. 266.
31. Yeats, *Mythologies* (New York: Collier Books, 1969), pp. 213–261.
32. David Lynch, *Yeats: The Poetics of the Self* (Chicago: University of Chicago Press, 1979), pp. 17–28.
33. Elizabeth Cullingford, *Yeats, Ireland and Fascism* (New York: New York University Press, 1981), p. 95.
34. Cullingford, *Ibid.*, p. 100.
35. Cullingford, *Ibid.*, p. 94.
36. Yeats, *Letters*, p. 613.
37. Yeats, *Uncollected Prose*, Volume II, ed. John P. Frayne and Colton Johnson (New York: Columbia University Press, 1975), p. 196.
38. Yeats, *Ibid.*, 319.
39. Edmund Burke, *A Philosophical Enquiry into the Origin of our Ideas of the Sublime and the Beautiful*, ed. James T. Boulton (Notre Dame: University of Notre Dame Press, 1968), p. 64.

40. Immanuel Kant, *The Critique of Judgment*, tr. James Creed Meredith (Oxford: The Clarendon Press, 1969), p. 111.
41. Kant, *Ibid.*, p. 111.

IV. Yeats and *Hysterica Passio*

1. Yeats, *The Letters of W. B. Yeats*, ed. Allan Wade (London: Rupert Hart-Davis, 1954), p. 690.
2. Yeats, *Essays and Introductions* (New York: Macmillan, 1961), pp. 249–250.
3. Yeats, *Ibid.*, p. 519.
4. Yeats, *The Oxford Book of Modern Verse* (New York: Oxford University Press, 1937), p. xxxiv.
5. Conor Cruise O'Brien, "Passion and Cunning: The Politics of W. B. Yeats," *In Excited Reverie*, ed. A. N. Jeffares, (New York: Macmillan, 1965).
6. Yeats, *The Autobiography of William Butler Yeats* (New York: Macmillan, 1953), p. 118.
7. Yeats, *Essays and Introductions*, p. 526.
8. O'Brien, "Passion and Cunning."
9. Richard Ellmann, *Yeats: The Man and the Masks*, rev. ed. (New York: Norton, 1978).
10. Elizabeth Cullingford, *Yeats, Ireland and Fascism* (New York: New York University Press, 1981), p. 79.
11. Yeats, *Memoirs*, ed. Denis Donoghue (New York: Macmillan, 1972), p. 157.
12. Yeats, *Ibid.*, p. 157.
13. Yeats, *Letters on Poetry from W. B. Yeats to Dorothy Wellesley* (London: Oxford University Press, 1964), p. 86.
14. Yeats, *Letters*, p. 742.
15. A. Norman Jeffares, *A Commentary on the Collected Poems of W. B. Yeats* (Stanford: Stanford University Press, 1968), p. 86.
16. Yeats, *The Collected Poems* (New York: Macmillan, 1956), p. 524.
17. Gaston Bachelard, *The Poetics of Reverie*, tr. Daniel Russell (Boston: Beacon Press, 1971), p. 193.
18. Yeats, *Letters*, p. 668.
19. Yeats, *Ibid.*, p. 680.
20. Yeats, *The Collected Poems*, p. 455.
21. Yeats, *A Vision* (London: Macmillan, 1981), p. 268.
22. Respectively: John Unterecker, *A Reader's Guide to W. B. Yeats* (New York: Farrar, Straus & Giroux, 1977), p. 289; Joseph Hone, *W. B.*

Yeats (New York: Macmillan, 1943), p. 502; Curtis Bradford, "Yeats's *Last Poems* Again," *The Dolman Press Yeats Centenary Papers MCMLXV*, ed. Liam Miller (Dublin: The Dolman Press, 1968), p. 275.

23. Bradford, *op. cit.*; Richard J. Finneran, *The Poems of W. B. Yeats, A New Edition* (New York: Macmillan, 1983).
24. Yeats, *Letters on Poetry*, pp. 179–181.
25. Yeats, *Ibid.*, p. 180.

V. Bertolt Brecht, Germany

1. Walter Benjamin, "Conversations with Brecht," *Reflections*, tr. Edmund Jephcott (New York: Harcourt Brace Jovanovich, 1978), p. 219.
2. Bertolt Brecht, *Poems 1913–1956*, ed. John Willett and Ralph Manheim (New York & London: Methuen, 1976), p. 465.
3. Max Frisch, *Sketchbook 1946–1949*, tr. Geoffrey Skelton (New York & London: Harcourt Brace Jovanovich, 1977), p. 151.
4. Brecht, *Poems 1913–1956*, p. 460.
5. *Ibid.*, p. 460.
6. *Ibid.*, p. 463.
7. *Ibid.*, p. 458.
8. Hannah Arendt, "Bertolt Brecht," *Men in Dark Times* (New York: Harcourt, Brace & World, Inc., 1968), p. 225–226.
9. Brecht, *Poems 1913–1956*, p. 458.
10. Klaus Volker, *Brecht: A Biography*, tr. John Nowell (New York: Seabury Press, 1978), p. 129.
11. Bertolt Brecht, *Gedichte* (Frankfurt am Main: Surkamp Verlag, 1960), Vol. 4, p. 19.
12. Klaus Volker, *Brecht*, pp. 333–334.
13. *Ibid.*, p. 333.
14. *Ibid.*, p. 338.
15. Walter Benjamin, *Reflections*, p. 215.
16. Max Frisch, *Sketchbook 1946–49*, p. 152.

VI. Breyten Breytenbach, South Africa

1. Breyten Breytenbach, *The True Confessions of an Albino Terrorist* (New York: Farrar Straus & Giroux, 1985), p. 73.
2. *Ibid.*, p. 359.
3. *Ibid.*, p. 354.
4. *Ibid.*, p. 280.
5. *Ibid.*, p. 280.

6. André Brink, *Writing in a State of Siege* (New York: Summit Books, 1983), p. 86.
7. Donald Woods, "A South African Poet on His Imprisonment," *The New York Times Book Review*, May 1, 1983.
8. Breytenbach, *Confessions*, p. 354.
9. *Ibid.*, p. 31.
10. Breytenbach, *Confessions*, p. 31.
11. Luis Buñuel, *My Last Sigh*, tr. Abigail Israel (New York: Knopf, 1984), p. 107.
12. Breytenbach, *A Season in Paradise*, tr. Rike Vaughan (New York: Persea Books, 1980), p. 144.
13. *Ibid.*, p. 145.
14. *Ibid.*, p. 142.
15. *Ibid.*, p. 152.
16. Breytenbach, *Confessions*, p. 354.
17. Brink, *Writing in a State of Siege*, p. 106.
18. Hein Willemse, "The Black Afrikaans Writer: A Continuing Dichotomy," *Triquarterly 69*, Spring/Summer 1987, p. 238.

VII. Thomas McGrath, North America West

1. "McGrath on McGrath," *North Dakota Quarterly*, Fall 1982 (Volume 50, Number 4), p. 22. McGrath attributes these remarks to William Eastlake, "from Arizona."
2. Christopher Caudwell, *Illusion and Reality: A Study of the Sources of Poetry* (London: Lawrence & Wishart, 1977), p. 38. First published 1937.
3. McGrath, *Letter to an Imaginary Friend*, Parts I & II (Chicago: The Swallow Press, 1970); Parts Three & Four (Port Townsend: Copper Canyon Press, 1985). Unless otherwise noted, all citations are from Parts I & II.
4. McGrath, *North Dakota Quarterly*, p. 23.
5. McGrath, *Echoes Inside the Labyrinth*, (New York & Chicago: Thunder's Mouth Press, 1983), p. 33
6. For a history of the populist movement in relation to our political culture more generally, see Lawrence Goodwyn, *Democratic Promise: The Populist Moment in America*. (New York: Oxford University Press, 1976).
7. Mark Vinz, "Poetry and Place: An Interview with Thomas McGrath" (July 25, 1972), *Voyages to the Inland Sea, 3*, ed. John Judson (Center for Contemporary Poetry, Murphy Library, University of Wisconsin–LaCrosse, LaCrosse, 1973), pp. 39, 41.

8. McGrath, "Trinc: Praises II," in *Echoes*, p. 14.
9. See especially Sacvan Bercovitch, *The American Jeremiad* (Madison: The University of Wisconsin Press, 1978).
10. McGrath, *The Movie at the End of the World: Collected Poems* (Chicago: The Swallow Press, 1972), p. 47.
11. McGrath, *Longshot O'Leary's Garland of Practical Poesie* (New York: International Publishers, 1949), p. 14.
12. McGrath, "Statement to the House Committee on Un-American Activities," *North Dakota Quarterly*, p. 9.
13. Rory Holscher, "Receiving Thomas McGrath's *Letter*," *North Dakota Quarterly*, p. 116.
14. "McGrath on McGrath," *North Dakota Quarterly*, p. 19.
15. "McGrath on McGrath," *North Dakota Quarterly*, p. 25.
16. E. P. Thompson, "Homage to Thomas McGrath," *The Heavy Dancers* (London: Merlin Press, 1985), p. 324. Reprinted in *Triquarterly*, No. 70 (Fall 1987), p. 106.
17. William M. Arkin & Richard M. Fieldhouse, *Nuclear Battlefields: Global Links in the Arms Race* (Cambridge, Mass.: Ballinger Publishing Company, 1985), p. 203. The scale of comparison is global.
18. Caudwell, *Illusion and Reality*, p. 81.
19. Mikhail Bakhtin, *Rabelais and His World*, tr. by Helene Iswolsky (Bloomington: Indiana University Press, 1984). This book was written in the late 1930's, but not published in the Soviet Union until 1965. First published in English 1968.
20. Mark Vinz, *Voyages to the Inland Sea*, p. 47.
21. Bakhtin, *Ibid.*, p. 19.
22. McGrath, *Passages Toward the Dark* (Port Townsend: Copper Canyon Press, 1982), p. 94.
23. Caudwell, *Illusion and Reality*, p. 34.
24. McGrath, *Passages*, p. 93.
25. McGrath, *Passages*, p 22.

VIII. Adrienne Rich, North America East

1. Adrienne Rich, *On Lies, Secrets, and Silence: Selected Prose 1966–1978* (New York: W. W. Norton, 1979), p. 108.
2. Alicia Ostriker, *Writing Like a Woman* (Ann Arbor: University of Michigan Press, 1983), p. 1.
3. Adrienne Rich, *Of Woman Born* (New York: W. W. Norton, 1986), p. 74.
4. *Ibid.*, p. 55.

5. Adrienne Rich, *Your Native Land, Your Life* (New York: W. W. Norton, 1986), p. 98.
6. Adrienne Rich, "When We Dead Awaken: Writing as Re-Vision," *On Lies, Secrets, and Silence*, pp. 37, 49. The last sentence does not occur in this edition, but is retained in Gelpi & Gelpi, p. 98, cited below.
7. Barbara Charlesworth Gelpi & Albert Gelpi, *Adrienne Rich's Poetry*, Norton Critical Edition (New York: W. W. Norton, 1975), p. 111.
8. Rich, *On Lies, Secrets, and Silence*, pp. 161–162.
9. Gelpi & Gelpi, *Adrienne Rich's Poetry*, p. 30.
10. Rich, *On Lies, Secrets, and Silence*, p. 175.
11. *Ibid.*, pp. 44–45.
12. Rich, *Of Woman Born*, pp. 128, 149.
13. Rich, *On Lies, Secrets, and Silence*, p. 43.
14. *Ibid.*, p. 45.
15. *Ibid.*, p. 108.
16. *Ibid.*, p. 35.
17. *Ibid.*, p. 34, 43.
18. *Ibid.*, p. 44.
19. Rich, *Of Woman Born*, p. 40.
20. *Ibid.*, p. 40.
21. Gelpi & Gelpi, *Adrienne Rich's Poetry*, p. 104.
22. *Ibid.*, p. 119.
23. Rich, *On Lies, Secrets, and Silence*, p. 44.
24. Gelpi & Gelpi, *Adrienne Rich's Poetry*, pp. 120–121.
25. Rich, "Transcendental Etude," *The Dream of a Common Language* (New York: W. W. Norton, 1978), p. 76.
26. Rich, *Of Woman Born*, pp. 97–98.
27. Gelpi & Gelpi, *Adrienne Rich's Poetry*, p. 114.
28. *Ibid.*, p. 115.
29. Rich, *On Lies, Secrets, and Silence*, p. 251.
30. Ludwig Wittgenstein, *Philosophical Investigations*, tr. G. E. M. Anscombe (New York: The Macmillan Company, 1969), pp. 8^e, 11^e, 174^e.
31. Adrienne Rich, *Blood, Bread, and Poetry: Selected Prose 1979–1985* (New York: W. W. Norton, 1986), p. 180.

Select Bibliography

Brecht, Bertolt. *Bertolt Brecht: Poems 1913–1956*, eds. John Willet and Ralph Manheim (New York & London: Methuen, 1976).

Breytenbach, Breyten. *And Death White as Words*, ed. A. J. Coetzee (London: Rex Collings Ltd., 1978).

——————— . *In Africa Even the Flies Are Happy: Selected Poems and Prose, 1964–1977*. (London: John Calder Ltd., 1978).

——————— . *A Season in Paradise*, trans. Rike Vaughan (New York: Persea Books, Inc., 1980).

——————— . *The True Confessions of an Albino Terrorist* (New York: Farrar Straus & Giroux, 1985).

McGrath, Thomas. *Echoes Inside the Labyrinth* (New York: Thunder's Mouth Press, 1983).

——————— . *Letter to an Imaginary Friend, Parts 1 & 2* (Chicago: The Swallow Press, 1970).

——————— . *Letter to an Imaginary Friend, Parts 3 & 4* (Port Townsend, WA: Copper Canyon Press, 1985).

——————— . *Longshot O'Leary's Garland of Practical Poesie* (New York: International Publishers, 1949).

——————— . *The Movie at the End of the World: Collected Poems* (Chicago: The Swallow Press, 1972).

————————— . *Selected Poems 1938–1988*, ed. Sam Hamill (Port Townsend, WA: Copper Canyon Press, 1988).

Rich, Adrienne. *Adrienne Rich's Poetry*, eds. Barbara Gelpi and Albert Gelpi (New York: W. W. Norton & Company, 1975).

————————— . *Blood, Bread and Poetry: Selected Prose 1979–1985* (New York: W. W. Norton & Company, 1986).

————————— . *Diving into the Wreck: Poems 1971–1972* (New York: W. W. Norton & Company, 1973).

————————— . *The Dream of a Common Language: Poems 1974–1977* (New York: W. W. Norton & Company, 1978).

————————— . *Of Woman Born* (New York: W. W. Norton & Company, 1986).

————————— . *On Lies, Secrets, and Silence: Selected Prose 1966–1978* (New York: W. W. Norton & Company, 1979).

————————— , *Your Native Land, Your Life: Poems* (New York: W. W. Norton & Company, 1986).

Yeats, William Butler. *The Autobiography of William Butler Yeats* (New York: Macmillan, 1964).

————————— . *The Letters of W. B. Yeats*, ed. Allan Wade (London: Rupert Hart-Davis, 1954).

————————— . *The Collected Poems* (New York: Macmillan, 1956).

————————— . *Memoirs*, ed. Denis Donoghue (New York: Macmillan, 1972).

————————— . *A Vision* (New York: Macmillan, 1961).

Acknowledgments

Chapters I and II of *Praises & Dispraises* first appeared in *The American Poetry Review*, July-August 1988; Chapter VII in *TriQuarterly 70*; and "Toward A Changed Poetics" as "Equipment for Living" in *TriQuarterly 65*.

Grateful acknowledgment is made for permission to reprint the following copyrighted works:

Excerpt from "From the Canton of Expectation" from *The Haw Lantern* by Seamus Heaney. Copyright © 1987 by Seamus Heaney. Reprinted by permission of Farrar, Straus & Giroux, Inc.

Excerpts from "The Poor Poet" and "Elegy for N. N." from *The Collected Poems 1931–1987* by Czeslaw Milosz. Copyright © 1988 by Czeslaw Milosz Royalties Inc. Published by The Ecco Press in 1988. Reprinted by permission.

Excerpt from *A Portrait of the Artist as a Young Man* by James Joyce. Copyright 1916 by B.W. Huebsch. Copyright renewed 1944 by Nora Joyce. Copyright © 1964 by the Estate of James Joyce. By permission of Viking Penguin Inc. and The Society of Authors as the literary representative of the Estate of James Joyce.

Excerpts from "Credences of Summer" and "An Ordinary Evening in New Haven" from *The Collected Poems of Wallace Stevens*. Copyright 1947, 1950 by Wallace Stevens. By permission of Alfred A. Knopf, Inc.

"Dareios" from *Collected Poems* by C.P. Cavafy. Copyright © 1978 by C.P. Cavafy. Published by Chatto & Windus. Used by permission.

Selections from *The Poems: A New Edition* by W.B. Yeats, edited by Richard J. Finneran. Copyright 1916, 1919, 1924, 1928, 1933, 1934 by Macmillan Publishing Company, renewed 1944, 1947, 1952, 1956, 1961, 1962 by Bertha Georgie Yeats. Copyright 1940 by Georgie Yeats, renewed 1968 by Bertha Georgie Yeats, Michael Butler Yeats and Anne Yeats. Reprinted with permission of Macmillan Publishing Company. Published in Great Britain as *The Collected Poems of W.B. Yeats*. By permission of A.P. Watt Ltd. on behalf of Michael B. Yeats and Macmillan London Ltd.

Excerpt from "Conversations with Brecht" from *Reflections* by Walter Benjamin. By permission of Harcourt Brace Jovanovich, Inc.

Selections from *Bertolt Brecht: Poems 1913–1956*, edited by John Willett and Ralph Manheim. By permission of the publisher Routledge, Chapman and Hall by arrangement with Suhrkamp Verlag and Methuen London. All rights reserved.

Excerpts from "The Struggle for the TAAL" and other material from *The True Confessions of an Albino Terrorist* by Breyten Breytenbach. Copyright © 1983 by Breyten Breytenbach. Reprinted by permission of Farrar, Straus & Giroux, Inc.

Selections from *And Death White as Words: An Anthology of the Poetry of Breyten Breytenbach*, selected, edited and introduced by A.J. Coetzee. Published by Rex Collings Ltd., 1978.

Selections from *In Africa Even the Flies are Happy* by Breyten Breytenbach, translated by Denis Hirson. Published by John Calder (Publishers) Ltd., London and Riverrun Press Inc., New York. Copyright © 1976, 1977 by Yolande Breytenbach and Meulenhoff Nederland, Amsterdam. English translation copyright © 1978 by John Calder (Publishers) Limited, London.

Excerpt from *Illusion and Reality: A Study of the Sources of Poetry* by Christopher Caudwell. By permission of Lawrence & Wishart Ltd.

Excerpts from "Blues for Warren" from *The Movie at the End of the World: Collected Poems* and excerpts from *Letter to an Imaginary Friend, Parts I and II* by Thomas McGrath, Swallow Press, 1970. Reprinted with the permission of Ohio University Press/Swallow Press.

Excerpts from "He's a Real Gone Guy" from *Longshot O'Leary's Garland of Practical Poesie* by Thomas McGrath. By permission of the author.

Excerpt from "The End of the World" from *Passages Toward the Dark* by Thomas McGrath. By permission of Copper Canyon Press.

Selections from *Snapshots of a Daughter-in-Law*; *Diving into the Wreck: Poems 1971–1972*; *The Dream of a Common Language: Poems 1974–1977*; *On Lies, Secrets and Silences: Selected Prose 1966–1978*; *Of Woman Born: Motherhood as Experience and Institution*; and *Blood, Bread and Poetry: Selected Prose 1979–1985* by Adrienne Rich. Reprinted by permission of the author and W. W. Norton and Company.

About the Author

Terrence Des Pres is the author of *The Survivor: An Anatomy of Life in the Death Camps*. He taught at Colgate University in Hamilton, New York. He died on November 16, 1987.